Praise for Forever ___

In the spirit of Brave New World, Mark Lavine has written a compelling science fiction tale with a strong message delivered in a pristine narrative style. The book is hard-hitting in the way it delves into authoritarianism, liberation, and experimentation. We want to believe that we have freedom of choice, and this must-read work will remind you why. **Readers' Favorite (five stars)**

Vividly wrought imagery, steady pacing, and an intriguing cast mark Lavine's engrossing dystopian tale. Questions of oppression, government corruption, individualism, freedom, and autonomy are skillfully raised, examined against an inventive futuristic backdrop in which genetic alteration is the norm and value of human life without the genetic interference is zero. A must-read. **The Prairies Book Review**

Mark Lavine has created a fast paced story that is well thought-out and well told. His vision of the future is fascinating, and definitely an original idea. It is actually quite thought-provoking in many ways, showing aspects of our present world and its values from a whole new perspective...All in all, an excellent, well-written story that had me hooked from the very first page. **SFF World**

ForeverChild

Mark Lavine

The characters and events of this novel are purely the result of the writer's imagination. Any resemblance to actual persons or events is coincidental.

For Galen and Daniel and Saturday mornings

Part One

The Great Earthquake of 2315

1

I t called mysteriously from beyond his dreams, a sound of unaccountable familiarity which drew Kianno into the coolness of that soft summer evening. A sound from deep within him, from before his time yet concealed inside his memory like a hidden package placed there by generations of ancestors: the sound of running water. It sliced and tripped rhythmically through the night and into the partially dismantled back room of this ancient wooden structure his parents had claimed for a full thirty days now.

Kianno sat up on the bug-eaten and unraveling carpet, pulled off his blanket, and looked through the open beams to the sky above and the oak trees overhanging the old house. Listening keenly, intent on finding the source of this mystery, he relaxed now, satisfied of no intrusion, no sudden violence setting upon them, yet uncertain of the dangers from this new visitor to their home. He stood up and steadied the grogginess of the night with a balancing step forward, then set off through the house toward the oak shrouded yard where the soft interruption continued unabated. Stepping carefully so as not to wake his parents sleeping in the front room, the boy threaded a path through the abandoned home cluttered with dismembered pieces of itself- rotting planks, chunks of misplaced concrete, bricks fallen from broken mantles which had long since let fall forgotten photographs of wedding days and the repressed smirks of posed relatives.

When he stepped into the yard he was suddenly aware of small voices surrounding the persistent but undeniable murmur of flowing water, and as he moved closer over the hard packed dirt he could see the silhouettes of his parents raised up against a starry horizon of silent oaks. He held back in the shadows so as to secret himself into their muted whispers.

"Well, whatever the reason, we can't stay now," his father was saying. "You know that, don't you?"

His mother did not respond but only continued gazing at the water flowing freely from a rocky slope which rose at the far end of the yard. The water ran between the rocks and explored a channel which formed the bottom of the slope. At length, she replied.

"A few more days, then. No one can see." She nodded to the great trees overhead. "We're hidden. You said so yourself when we first arrived."

"Hidden?" His father scoffed, sliding circles in the dirt with his shoes. "This can't stay hidden. Not for a few days, not for a day even."

"It's a gift," his mother protested. "A sign that's meant for us."

"Maybe a sign, but a sign to leave at once. This will draw them to us, and with Kianno still..." he trailed off, deep in thought, then began again. "We'll go back to Lexington. It may be safe now, at least until we can figure out where to go next. But we leave tonight. They'll be here in the morning. They'll follow it here."

"Then I'll wake him." His mother turned toward the house to rouse her small son, but instead found him standing before her in the clearing of hard dirt and yellowed weeds. Filtered moonlight played over his delicate face and his steady, persevering brown eyes.

"No!" he blurted, much too loud and knowing full well. "No we don't have to go!"

"Quiet." His father rushed to his side. "You'll do what we tell you, what will protect you, and us all."

"No," the boy insisted once more, but quieter this time. "This is where we're staying." He turned to his mother. "You said so. You said this was the place."

His mother remained silent, but took his hand and led him to the side of the streaming water, running fast and clear. For several minutes all three stood over it, entranced by its abundance, wondering silently at the forces which had brought it into their own private world. Like a poisoned apple shining before them, its frightening allure convinced them all, including the boy. It was a gift too glorious and magnificent to safely accept. So they left, stole away to the sound of coyotes howling madness into the hills of old Los Gatos, and made their way under cover of darkness along trails leading toward Lexington. And as they ascended the tangled, broken roads, the coyotes raised their voices even higher, and the lions sniffed only a passing interest at the ragged troupe, too absorbed in chasing the restlessness of the night to bother a small boy and his family.

***

Farther down the slopes, in the Valley of Santa Clara, past the monolithic Hives of Los Gatos, Campbell, and Cambria, the Great Hive of San Jose slept peacefully through the night, unseen moonlight reflecting from its soliglas panels. It was an imposing sight for the outsiders who scavenged the hills above and would never see the world inside: a single structure twenty miles long and ten miles wide, rising fifteen hundred feet into the summer evening. Enormous soliglas panels covered the entire city, brazed onto t-steel girders locked together in endless rows, panels which served perfectly their primary purpose of reflecting each world from the vision of the other, leaving the goings-on inside the gigantic edifice to stories and imaginings. Earlier in the day, seven hundred thousand residents of this Great Hive coursed through its one hundred and fifty levels, but now, at the late hour of ten o'clock, all families were sound asleep, the entire city closed and slumbering peacefully en masse beneath a starry sky that few of them would ever see in their long lifetimes.

In family unit GGG-2354, tucked innocently away on level 87, in a small bedroom three slots over from the unit room, slept a young boy. Like Kianno, he was about ten years old, and, also like Kianno, his sleep was disturbed tonight by visions of threatening water. Dreams of ocean waves rising ominously before him and crashing down, swirling him in their froth and confusion, tossed Seelin through the night until one crashed with such ferocity that it shook the boy from his sleep and threw him running through the halls to his mother's room.

"I'm scared," he uttered quietly, somewhat ashamed of his fear. "Mother wake up. I'm scared."

"What is it?" His mother was instantly awake from her own shallow sleep. "What's the matter Seelin?"

"The ocean, tomorrow...I'm afraid. The waves are so big."

"But I'll be with you, and all your classmates. And the viewing platform is perfectly safe. Do you remember the visuals?"

"Yes..." He sat on the bed and kicked his legs a little, feeling immediately relieved.

"And do you remember how the viewing platform is high above the waves, so they can't touch you, they can't even come close?"

"But what if a really big one hits the platform, what then?" Seelin persisted, more to justify his intrusion than for reassurance.

"The platform is made of the same material as this unit, the same material as this entire Great Hive. Just because you can see the ocean doesn't mean you won't be entirely enclosed and safe from it. I promise."

"What about the snatchers? Will they get us if something happens?"

"Nothing can happen, Seelin. You've heard stories, that's all. The outsiders can't touch us, they can't even see us, even when we'll be watching from the platform."

"But what if we see them?" he asked curiously. "What will they do if we see them?"

"I told you, even if we see them they won't know it, because they won't be able to see us." She paused, then added, "This is a very special occasion, Seelin. I told you before you don't have to go, but you'll probably never get another chance. You may see the sky, if we're lucky." She remembered when she had visited only twenty years earlier. A mist had pressed down upon the water, hiding the sky. Another chance now, with a little luck.

She reached out tenderly to smooth the damp hair across the child's brow. "Go to sleep now, dearest," she urged him. "It's late, and tomorrow will soon be here. You'll see for yourself then."

With her words, Seelin obediently left her bedside, walked slowly through the halls past his father's room, and retook his own sleep much quicker than his mother, who still held the quizzical face of her only son in her mind's eye (Yes he was her son; to herself she would never deny it). Seelin had grown almost to her own height now, with just a hint of seriousness shading his even features. Soon it would be time to begin the regulators, she thought; already the family had begun to question the timing. For a fleeting moment she glimpsed an imagination of her son grown beyond the threshold, but she did not allow herself more than a moment's vision. Such ideas could be dangerous and painful. So she turned her thoughts to the excitement of the coming day, thoughts tinged with a certain unrevealed fear of her own. The snatchers were there, it was true, ready to take advantage of any slip up, even creating their own, she had heard. But what could go wrong? A mechanical failure? They had sealed the tunnels with another layer of t-steel; even the primest of synthars would take more than an hour to cut through, plenty of time to return via another spotter. And yet there was always risk, she knew that, and to see the true sky she was prepared to take this very small chance of leaving the hive behind and flying the transpotters south to the ocean side.

2

The next day, after a morning send off from their family, Seelin and his mother, Sofia, stepped into the slider with excitement and a little trepidation. It was the first time the boy had ever flown the transpotters, and for Sofia only the third time in her twenty-four years. She had taken this same journey fourteen years ago with her first schooler classmates, a practice which had started out on her own GGG Level but which had since developed and spread throughout the hive into something of a ritual for all ten-year-olds. The other two transpotter trips had been to neighboring hives for meetings which neither Seelin, nor anyone else in the family, knew anything about. The secrecy of those trips only accentuated the excitement of this one, giving her an opportunity to relax and enjoy the prospect of momentarily escaping this great hive without looking over her shoulder for anyone who might recognize her.

When the door lifted and the soft whir of a chime signaled readiness, they entered the eastbound slider, a small room about thirty feet square, and looked around them as the doors closed and the room picked up speed toward the next stop. About fifteen other residents sat on pillowed high-backed benches spaced in a series of concentric circles about the room. Most were accompanied by their visual companions, and several carried on quiet conversations with these carefully programmed, individually assigned holographic projections available for any kind of entertainment or companionship. Consequently, the sound of conversation filled the slider, although none of it was actually being exchanged between the citizens lounging inside. The fully informed and electronically responsive dialogue was much more satisfying and amusing than anything these strangers could generate amongst themselves in the short time they would spend slipping away to other quadrants. Seelin wished he could also share the visuals, but his mother was old fashioned and would periodically disable the sender at certain special times when she believed he would be better off paying attention to the 'real world', and today was one of those times. So the two sat quietly until they reached quadrant GGG576, where they exited directly into a switching chamber and immediately boarded a vertical slider to the sublevel.

"In front of Port fourteen, that was it, wasn't it?" Sofia asked her son after they had stepped off the slider and entered the confusion of the Depot.

"Yes Sofia, Port fourteen," he replied, and took her hand to lead her through the bustle of hurried citizens, feeling more at home here than his mother, even though he knew the Depot only through his school learning.

"Sofia? Who's Sofia? I don't think I know anyone of that name, do you?" she chided him in a mocking voice.

"OK Mother..." He pulled her along even faster now.

"You'll realize some day how fortunate you are to have a mother, and yet you call me Sofia, like the other boys." Her words chased after him, hurrying to catch up. "Listen to me, Seelin!"

At this he stopped and looked back at her, sensing that same anxious worry in his mother that kept resurfacing and which instilled in him a vague fear he could express only as irritation.

"Mom," he started, looking across at her, the two of them standing still now with the flow of traffic coursing around them. "Mom, it's OK. I know you're my mother, and it's all right. You know I love you and all." He spoke quickly, rushing past the awkwardness. "But everyone else doesn't have to always know, do they? All the other kids..."

"All the other kids aren't bothered with mothers and fathers," she finished his sentence.

"Yea, but only when we're with them, you know, that's the only time I call you Sofia." He gripped her hands and leaned over to kiss her forehead, in the way of one family member greeting another, but his mother responded by reaching her arms around Seelin and pressing him close to her, in the way she had been taught and intended to teach her son. As if sensing the need in his mother, the young boy pulled from his pocket a small gold ring with the letter M formed in gold leaf against a background square of black jade. He slipped the ring quickly over his too small right index finger and held it, cupped and out of sight, for only his mother to see. It was a gift she had given him two years ago, a gift passed down from her own father, who had in turn received it from his father- the one for whom the ring had originally been sized. It was a sign of a family beyond those assigned as keepers, a sign of something deeper that Sofia had tried to instill in the boy. And now, hidden from all but the two of them, Seelin held the ring in place around his child's finger, a ring his mother had presumed to be lost among the boy's other trinkets and gifts, but which had secretly earned a place in the boy's pocket as a remembrance of what his mother had told him, a remembrance of who Sofia really was. At the sight of the keepsake, Sofia uttered a short exclamation and started to say something but abruptly caught herself. Instead she looked into his eyes to tell him that everything was all right now, and with that the boy replaced the ring in his pocket and again took her hand to resume their dash in the direction of gate fourteen.

They found the rest of the group assembling and readying themselves in front of the gate entrance. The band was comprised of about twenty of Seelin's classmates, boys and girls running and laughing excitedly within the confines of the invisible boundary their instructor had set, as well as four adults, the current keepers of their respective children, who had been permitted to accompany the group to help keep order. Since the keepers were all still relatively young, they were for the most part distinguishable from the children only by their relative calm and composure, as well as by red armbands which facilitated identification. As the two new arrivals approached, they were noticed by the instructor and a couple of keepers who were engaged in conversation.

"It appears as if Seelin and his keeper have arrived. I think that completes the assembly," said the instructor, whose relative height and frazzle of red hair stood her out from the rest of the crowd.

"Yes. Sofia's her name," replied another, in a somewhat skeptical tone. "She's the boy's mother, is what I've heard."   "His mother? That would be an interesting affair, now wouldn't it?" laughed another. "I've heard of the immaculate conception, but her being the mother of that boy would be an even greater miracle." When the laughter subsided she added, in a much more serious voice, "She carries the old way, is what I've heard. She refuses others their turn."

"And they go along? How can that be?"

"She has another with her. They're together and claim Seelin as their son. It's as if they refuse to accept reality, living as if it were still the year two-thousand."

The instructor had been trying to remain silent, but now let the curiosity get the better of her. "But surely they aren't Naturalists? I've heard nothing of their involvement."

"Oh no, not Naturalists!" scoffed the other sarcastically. "That would mean refusing the regulators. Believing is so much easier when your own life isn't at stake. I'd like to see her with the courage of her convictions!"

"I bet you would," joked another who had eased up on their conversation. When the expected appreciation of his humor failed to materialize, he added "They want to live as mothers and fathers but stay within and live on the regulators. I've heard they're organizing for easement of the Outsider laws. It's only a matter of time before all of them end up as outsiders as well, if you ask me."

As Sofia and Seelin melted into the group, the boy broke off to run with his classmates and Sofia greeted the instructor and her small entourage with an unsuspecting warmth.

"Are we late?" she asked the instructor. "It took us awhile to find our way." At this the others remained silent, cut off from their prior train of conversation, so Sofia continued. "This is his first trip, and me, well I haven't been here in quite some time. I've heard the transpotters are twice the speed now."

"Sofia, it's so good to see you," the instructor now replied, looking past her to the children playing beyond. "No, you're not late, but I believe they're ready for us now. Can you help round them up. I'd hate for us to miss our spot on this rotation." At this the group broke up and began gathering the excited children into an orderly line before a tall, narrow door, where a transpotter official counted them before waving his hand to open the door and allow them entrance into the gateway tunnel.

As Seelin stretched himself up on tiptoes to try and see above his classmates into the dimly lit passageway, a girl behind him pinched his arm.

"Hey Seelin," she whispered conspiratorially, "I've heard the snatchers hide in the tunnel and grab you away so quickly no one even notices you're gone."

"Ha Ha, very funny Nata. I'm not afraid of any monsters in here."

"They turn you into monsters, you know. They turn you into one of them. Then you won't be scared, cause you'll be a monster yourself. Seelo the monster!"

"Shut up," the boy answered, clearly irritated by the distraction. "Look, we're headed down now."

They followed the tunnel, in single file, as it led them around a semi-circle and down at a significant incline. The class quieted considerably in anticipation, and only a few pokes and titters could be heard when the winding descent finally emptied them into a long, narrow chamber with a platform on one end and a single rail raised above the metal floor, bisecting the length of the chamber for as far as the eye could see. Sitting atop the rail, adjacent to the platform, was a tram consisting of a series of small carts linked together, looking almost like an old roller coaster carriage. Each cart held two passengers in a seating chamber which was nested into the main body of the cart, attached to the body by only two thin steel rods, one at each end, such that the chamber seemed to float within the cart, suspended by the merest of pins which permitted it to swing freely.

As the first children paired off and loaded themselves into carts at the head of the series, Sofia looked forward into the group for her son, wanting to share this excitement with him, but the boy had taken great care to place himself toward the front, at a safe distance from his mother. She knew better than to call out, and so resigned herself to sharing an awkward anticipatory silence alongside another keeper as the entire group claimed their seats and awaited the famous rush. After the last pair had been loaded, the official surveyed the train briefly, then exited the same tunnel they had entered, leaving behind an unexpected quiet which further stilled the antics of the children and caused the edgiest of them to look back over their shoulders for the reassurance of an official announcement of some kind, but all that could be heard were the diminishing steps of the lone official as he retraced his way back to the depot level.

Finally, a low rumble seeped into the room, felt first as vibrations, then heard clearly as it ascended in both pitch and volume. Almost immediately, the seating chambers simultaneously froze their mild rocking in a vertical position and the tram began to smoothly accelerate forward.

"Here we go. This is it, hold on!" said Seelin's seating partner, who squirmed and made a play at squeezing him up against the side of the chamber, but thoughts of entering this game were quickly overcome by the rapid approach of what had now become a roar, chasing them down from behind as their own tram continued to accelerate in an effort to stay out in front. Soon the thunder beneath them seemed to merge into their own unrelenting acceleration as the speed raced upward, wind now blasting their awestruck faces, until a certain equilibrium between the two forces could be felt. Then the acceleration eased off and the tram began a series of adjustments in speed, tailoring itself to the huge transpotter flying only two thin layers of t-steel beneath them.

Meanwhile, one hundred feet above, hidden away in a cramped control room, twenty anxious spot-controllers monitored not only the take-off on port fourteen, but also twelve other simultaneous take-offs occurring up and down the length of the huge transpotter, now flying directly beneath the depot at a reduced station-speed of eighty miles an hour. Ordinarily, the controllers had a pretty routine time of it, as sensors in all take off strings communicated automatically with similar sensors on the transpotter, bringing all strings racing along in perfect alignment in preparation for the drop. But all day long the control room had been plagued with non-alignment warnings, and now, as decision time rapidly approached, controllers at three of the gates, including port fourteen, furiously made manual adjustments in an attempt to avoid aborting the take-offs.

"I can't seem to bring them in. They're still off!" explained one controller to his supervisor, who had come over to help out.

"How's the speed?"

"Speed's not the problem. It's the alignment I can't bring in."

"Shit. What the hell's the matter today? Alignment's never been a problem. Now all of the sudden it's like the whole damn level got moved over a few inches. Bring it in as far as you can."

"Still red," answered the controller breathlessly. "This one's gone. I'm slipping it."

"No wait. Let's see..." They both watched the line-up on the screen, the controller's hand poised over a small lever. As they watched, the lower half of the screen changed to a bright purple, while the upper half remained red.

"We're there! We're in the drop zone!" exclaimed the controller, and his hand jerked toward the lever, but just at that moment the upper half of the screen flashed green.

"There, drop now!" ordered his supervisor. "Now!" The controller's hand instantly pounced on a large triangular button directly beneath the screen.

"Shit, this one's going to be close," he breathed, then sat back in his chair to sweat it out.

Two levels below, racing along now at eighty miles an hour, wind whipping around the screen in front of him, Seelin peered over the side of his small seat and watched as the floor of the cart slid away beneath him. And as he watched, frozen in the deafening roar all around him, he could see the great transpotter revealed, seemingly motionless beneath, shadowing the cart perfectly as huge panels over the top of the spotter also retracted, unveiling the inner compartment which would carry them over the mountains to the ocean side. As the boy whooped with excitement, their seating chamber lowered gracefully down to the transpotter, the floor of the loading room flying by them as the only indicator of the tremendous speed at which they were going. Just as they had crossed into the transpotter but before they had settled safely onto the floor, a sudden grinding of metal could be heard from behind them, a harsh sound not belonging to the loud but consistent thundering which had surrounded them the last thirty seconds. Both Seelin and his partner quickly turned to see a huge shower of sparks spitting from a car further back, as the side of the seating chamber grazed the t-steel loading room floor.

"Nata! Look!" Seelin screamed, grinning with the thrill of a fireworks display, but then suddenly realized that this could be, probably was, unplanned.

"The tram is scraping. Something's wrong!" Nata voiced the same thoughts now running through his own mind. Sofia was back there somewhere, and if the scraping kept the chamber from dropping...

"Who is it? Who's in the cart?" he yelled at Nata, struggling to be heard over the pounding noise.

"I can't see. Look at all the fire sparks!"

"Sofia!!" yelled the boy, "Sofia where are you?" But as soon as the words had tripped from his mouth the grinding noise evaporated to an echo and the sparks disappeared into the darkness. Seelin turned forward once again, and in another three seconds the two children found themselves safe inside the transpotter compartment, a spacious room fitted with silks draped over the walls and luxuriously soft red silk couches lining each side. Immediately after unstrapping himself, the boy ran backwards through the spotter, followed closely by Nata, who was more excited than worried by the possibility of disaster.

When they reached the next car, they found the instructor and all the keepers, including Sofia, huddled around two children- the two occupants of the ill-fated cart. Both children had stripped off their shirts, and as Seelin pushed forward he could see each had terrible red welts across their backs where the heat of their seats, caused by the friction of the cart against the metal floor, had burned into their skin. Although upset by this unexpected danger, Seelin was primarily relieved that Sofia was still safe. When he found her, he looked up with eyes that said maybe his fears the night before weren't so unreasonable after all.

"They'll be OK," reassured his mother in a tentative voice. "They'll be removed and treated at Cambria. You'll be running around with them again in no time." Unless there is the infection, in which case you may never see them again, she thought to herself.

"I know," the boy lied.

"Where are you sitting? Can I come and see?"

"Sofia..." he whimpered.

"All right. I'll let you be. But promise me when we get there you'll at least let me share the view with you."

"O.K. When we get there," he conceded, relieved that she allowed him no option. Then he turned and ran back to the forward room with his ever present playmate once again trailing behind, as the transpotter continued it's acceleration through the zero-friction fluid filled tube, headed south toward Cambria, then over the mountains to the sea.

***

By the time the earliest southbound slider had exited the perimeter of the Great Hive, a welcome morning coolness had already dissipated into the summer heat bearing down on the outsiders inhabiting the buildings of old Lexington. Originally built as one of the last ultra-secure, fully fenced and gated communities for the very wealthy, it had been one of the last towns to have been abandoned when the inevitable decision was made in the late twenty-second century to give up on failing attempts to confine the massive prison population. Instead, the improvement in construction technology allowed for consolidation of the Valley's population into the four hives, with the prisoners released to the outside to fend for themselves. It proved much easier confining the citizens than the prisoners, and so the great division began. Lexington, like other abandoned city centers, was now populated by a mixture of a few thieves and dangerous criminals, along with a great many more who were either innocent descendants of criminals, or guilty only of contrived or petty crimes but banished nonetheless as a result of not 'belonging' inside. These outsiders were separated from legal residents as much by their size and appearance as by their location.

The city itself was situated on the banks of what had once been a sizable lake, but which had long since been drained and cultivated into fields of strawberry, avocado, lettuce, corn, and other highly valued delicacies. The fields spread southward from the base of a crumbling but still impressive former dam which had been spot-reinforced and topped with several towers used for monitoring the laborers as they worked in the fields. Punishment for true-food theft by an outsider was immediate and entirely at the discretion of the guards; disintegration of one hand by foil was not at all excessive, and so such theft was exceedingly rare. Workers spending long days picking strawberries for the wealthiest residents on the topmost levels of the hives would never dream of lifting even one berry to their mouth for a taste. Even wild berries scavenged from the surrounding woods fetched a high price on the outside market, and so synthetic food remained the only staple for outsiders, as well as most citizens.

Kianno and his family had arrived before sunrise and had spent several hours going from house to house trying to locate the whereabouts of friends who might be able to hide the boy for a few days while his parents recharged their accounts and gathered supplies before retreating once again to the isolation of the decaying outskirts of old Los Gatos. Finally, after a tip from an elderly man they found wandering the streets, they arrived at a sprawling , Spanish style estate now occupied by fifteen separate families. In the back, inhabiting a pool house overlooking a concrete crater half filled with dirt and weeds, was an old friend who answered their knock only after Seelin's father called through the door.

"Geryl, Sylvi! You're back," uttered the tall, balding man of about fifty, squinting his eyes at the morning sunlight. "Come in, please."

"Sooner than expected, I'm afraid," replied his father as the three of them were ushered into the dark room.

"Thieves? Are you O.K.?" He looked at Kianno, then back at his father.

"No, no thieves, thank God. The house..." his father groped for words, "we could no longer stay." Even with his best friends he felt an unreasonable need for restraint. Anything which did not have a specific reason for being revealed must always remain a secret, was a rule which had served their family's survival well. "Can you keep him here? Just for four days, a week at the most?"

"Of course. You know I will." The man looked down at Kianno. "But you'll have to amuse yourself while we're gone. No sneaking out to go exploring this time. We don't want you accidentally running into any watchers. Please have some water; you must be thirsty from your trip."

As they drank from a large bladder kept on a table nearest the back window, Jorge explained that they should have no trouble at all registering for work later on that morning. Apparently, just yesterday there had been some unexplained pooling of water in the strawberry fields directly below the old dam. While this had at first prompted True-Food Corp. to assign an extra contingent of guards to protect against expected looting of the water, before long they realized that unless it was bailed out quickly the current crop would be lost to fungus. So they had been recruiting, and ordering into service, just about anyone they could find; registering for a week of work would be especially easy right now.

"Pooling in the fields?" Seelin's father questioned. "That whole area used to be under water, you know. I've seen pictures. You would have loved it Kianno, the meadows and forests falling right down to a clear blue lake. Lexington Reservoir, they called it. Some day, if we get our freedom, we may get together to patch and restore the dam- restore what they've taken away: our own water."

"We'll be free of them. Maybe not in my lifetime, but we'll be free." Jorge paused, then looked down at the boy and added "Perhaps in yours, Kianno, perhaps in yours." He replaced his drinking tube. "But now we must work. We should arrive early to assure both of you time to register." He then closed the window shutters, and locked and bolted a back door while Kianno's mother and father quickly unpacked their bag. When all three were ready, his father addressed him one last time before leaving.

"Don't stray, son. I know you're tempted, but it isn't a safe time for you. Soon you'll be beyond the threshold and then you can explore to your heart's content. But for now, promise me you'll not venture out."

"I promise, Dad, I promise," replied the boy. He would remember, much later and with great pain, how he had broken the last promise ever made to his father.

***

It entered Kianno's consciousness first as sound: a huge, booming shudder overhead, and the boy looked over his shoulder for what cataclysm was surely descending from the sky, but the sky revealed nothing beyond its innocuous blue heat. Then he felt it. A rippling along the trail beneath his feet, a trail winding through this upper meadow high above the valley and fields below, a ripple growing into great waves he could see rolling over the meadow like waves over an ocean, and Kianno struggled to keep his footing before giving himself up to the tall grasses. Gripping the earth, he looked up to see the trees along the meadow fringes shaking violently as if in a gale, snapping and throwing their limbs in the wild dance. And still the sound from nowhere thundered overhead. Waves of panic and dread now washed over him, the full power of the quake finally reaching the boy as he sat silently watching the distant scene playing itself out far below. It was a full half hour that the boy sat there, afraid to face his suspicions, thinking that if only he waited just a little bit longer the world would shift back to how it had been. But it would never shift back, not in an hour, not in ten hours, not in ten years. The earth had rolled over in its sleep, and in the process had turned Kianno's life in a direction he could never have imagined.

Instinct lifted the boy from the ground and set him running down the path, as if escaping a wild animal, but the shifting ground only threw him down even more furiously this time, so he rode it out, pressed against the warm dirt and grasses, hugging the writhing earth through that eternal minute and a half. Laid flat, and beyond the initial shock of fear, the boy rolled and pitched with growing amusement and wonder. Away from any structures, the magnitude of the earthquake did not reveal itself; there was no shaking, no obvious damage or threat, save the snapping of tree limbs, and even that abated as the quake progressed. A full ninety seconds it lasted, and when it was over the meadow appeared no worse off, and the trail as well was intact, except for a small web of tiny cracks which now frosted the hard packed dirt. An adventure it had been, even more than he could have hoped for, and as he pulled himself up and started back down the trail, Kianno had only the mildest hint of worry in the back of his mind that perhaps this might be more than something to talk about later on.

In his morning expedition he had climbed a good thousand feet above the city, through dense oak forests spaced with open meadows. Except for the disappearance of the redwoods, which until the last hundred years had pocketed the deepest canyons but which had not survived the increasingly dry winters, the natural topography of the undeveloped land had changed very little in the last thousand years. As the trail steered the boy into a grove of oaks and madrones, he now noticed much larger cracks scarring the forest floor- some as wide as several feet, with loose dirt still crumbling from their sides. At one point, a small fissure crossed the trail, and he was forced to make a running jump of the chasm, from which he continued in a jog, anxious now to confirm that this really was no more than a diversion, but growing ever more concerned as he continued through the woods. He climbed over a small ridge, the last before the trail dipped into a creek bed which it followed into the valley, and as he neared the ridge top, now breathing heavily and sweating in the afternoon sun, he left the trail and climbed to a spot which afforded a good view of the surrounding area.

What he saw beneath him was a vision he would always remember, even to the last days of his life. A huge brown cloud hung over the fields, casting a shadow over the entire lower end of the basin. But there was nothing rising to form the cloud; no smoke, no steam, no apparent origin whatsoever. Massive fissures divided the valley floor, one of which cut right across the raised concrete transpotter tube which skirted the hills on the opposite side. His eyes followed the severed tube northward, then he saw it. The great wall no longer guarded the entrance to the lower canyon. Where it had stood for centuries was now only a collapsed shallow mound of cement and dirt. At the base of this mound hundreds of people dug frantically with their hands, throwing rocks and cement fragments behind them in a desperate attempt to uncover those buried in the rubble. But they were like ants against a mountain, Kianno could see this from his high vantage point.

Waves of panic and dread now washed over him, the full power of the quake finally reaching the boy as he sat silently watching the distant scene playing itself out far below. It was a full half hour that the boy sat there, afraid to face his suspicions, thinking that if only he waited just a little bit longer the world would shift back to how it had been. But it would never shift back, not in an hour, not in ten hours, not in ten years. The earth had rolled over in its sleep, and in the process had turned Kianno's life in a direction he could never have imagined.

***

"Seelin!" screamed Sofia, choking from the smoke which had filled the car. "Seelin!" But there was no response, only the slight creaking of metal which had followed the agonizing sounds of a few moments earlier.

After recovering from the initial quake, she, along with the instructor and several of the keepers, had struggled up to the edge of the frontmost accessible car. Daylight streamed in through the transparent panels and they could see the forward car tilted away, still connected to the main section of the transpotter but with one side sunk into a huge chasm, supported tenuously by a ledge in the opposite side of the fissure. Sofia could see that the zero resistance fluid at this end had poured into the chasm, and for a second she stared upward at the true sky, but she quickly turned her attention to the car holding her son and eleven of his classmates.

"Careful! Move slowly, we don't yet know if this car is stable. Everyone to the back of the spotter, now!" commanded one of the keepers who had taken charge, and the other keepers began to shepherd the frightened children away from the horrifying sight, but Sofia remained unable to move, transfixed by the sunshine glaring off the disabled spotter car carrying her only son.

"Stand back, I'm going to open the release," instructed the keeper, then he pressed a red button and the end of the room slid open. This permitted a full view of the crippled spotter car. It was sloped downward, into the chasm, and also tilted to the left slightly. The far end was jammed into the side of the crevice so tightly that a full three feet of the car were buried into the dirt and mud.

"It's still connected, that's a good sign," said the keeper, gesturing to two thin rods which joined the cars. "We might be able to pull her out if we reverse the wave."

"Where are the spotter officials?" asked Sofia. "Isn't there anyone who can help us?"

"No one on board. They don't require that anymore. I'm sure they're working on it at the Depot, though. They have full control, as long as power is still up." He began to search the inside of the car. "There should be an emergency escape foil that will have been released by the interruption. There..."

The keeper reached behind a silk curtain and pulled out a small, cone shaped object looking much like an ordinary flashlight except it was flared significantly on one end. He eyed the distance to the front end of the car carefully, then entered in a code on the top panel of the foil. Pointing the flared end at the spotter car, he rotated the foil one full circle, then placed it on the floor, still pointing in the same direction. Immediately a very low rumbling could be heard, and the front end of the spotter car appeared to be covered with an even, gray coating of foam, not sprayed from the foil, but rather emanating from the surface of the car itself. As Sofia watched (she had seen this before in the visuals but never in person), the gray coating slowly turned to a deep black color, then slid from the surface with a hissing sound. As it dripped into the chasm, the entire panel dripped away as well, revealing the inside of the spotter car.

It could not have been a more horrible sight. The force of the crash had opened a gash in the top of the compartment and zero-friction fluid had leaked into the car, burning away half the flesh of most of the children who had been trapped inside. The few who were still alive were screaming and moaning with their intense burns; the fluid literally dissolved flesh instantaneously, and several of the children had open, gaping wounds where their hands or feet used to be. Sofia gripped the sides of the car desperately and began to try and jump across to the other side, but the lead keeper stopped her and forced her to safety. Once again she brought herself to look into the terror-chamber, and when she did she sighted Seelin, still in his seat but on high ground, away from where the fluid had formed its deadly stream. Semi-conscious from the impact, he lifted his head and squinted into the light.

"Seelin!" screamed Sofia, choking from the smoke which had filled the car. "Seelin!" But there was no response, only the slight creaking of metal which had followed the agonizing sounds of a few moments earlier.

"Mother," he called weakly upon seeing Sofia's now hopeful face. "Mother help me..."

***

For the spot-controllers underneath the Great Hive, the earthquake had been the culmination of a day of uneasiness and narrow misses. Now everything had broken loose and the controllers were desperately trying to assess the status of the three spotters out in the tubes at the time of the quake. Power had been lost for four full minutes before the reserves kicked in, and when they did, the controllers were already in position over their instruments, scanning for information.

"Spotter number two's in trouble," yelled one as he maneuvered the control panel. "There's been a break in the tube, segment 4785, a full separation!"

"Loss of fluid?"

"Loss of fluid in 4784 and 4785. But the seal at 4783 held, and we have full containment from that point back."

"O.K. how many cars have progressed past 4783. We may be able to bring the rest back." By now five or six other controllers had gathered around.

"Only the lead car and part of number two."

"Good, we may be able to release the lead and reverse the wave. Just maybe it'll be enough to pull number two back in. If not we'll have to release them both." The supervisor had taken charge at this point, leaning closely over the panels as the rest backed off slightly. "Are we entirely up yet?"

"No. We have full sensor action, but no activation power."

"Well, damn it, we can't do anything without activation power! How much longer?"

"Any time now; power is spreading down the intact portions of all levels. We've heard it's already reached level BB."

"All right. Program the sequence for disengagement of number one, with wave reversal at minimum acceleration for the rest. All we can do now is wait for that power."

***

The keeper in charge now positioned the reverse side of the foil and targeted it at the railing midway up the side of spotter car number one. Squeezing the foil tightly, a beam of light, light visible even in the brightness of the day, shot across the gap between the two cars. An intensely agitated Sofia watched as the beam remained fixed for three seconds, then appeared to take on a different color, a different texture. Within a few more seconds the beam of light had materialized into a thin but extremely strong cord.

"I'm going across," the keeper informed the instructor, who had since returned from car number three, satisfied that the children were secure. "There're two of them who still have a chance, I think." He stepped out onto one of the narrow rods connecting the two cars. Sofia could see that the rods were stretched and distorted by the impact and the weight of the unbalanced connection. The keeper gripped the cable in his right hand and started out across the tenuous bridge, nothing but the blackness of the chasm far below.

Quickly he slid his feet in sharp, short steps, and reached the other side in a very short time. His additional weight caused the car to tilt even further to the right, in an awful groaning of metal against rock. Fortunately, the toxic zero-friction fluid had found an outlet through the vent openings in the bottom of the compartment, so he could negotiate a path through the car filled with corpses and children in the last throes of death, to the highest part of the car where Seelin and Nata sat, still strapped into their seats. Seelin mumbled semiconsciously, while Nata was entirely blacked out. The keeper reached to undo the boy's straps, thinking he would be the most likely to survive, but then thought again. Nata was younger and smaller, easier for the keeper to carry across the bridge. Seelin, on the other hand, was his size entirely, and he would need help to bring him over. He would have to come back for the boy, but there was no reason he as well could not be safely removed from the car; after all, it did appear to have stabilized somewhat. Struggling to pull Nata from her seat, he dragged her through the tangle of bodies toward safety.

Meanwhile, in the control room twenty miles to the north, one controller was having second thoughts about the plan introduced by their superior.

"Shouldn't we alert them?" he asked. "What if there are any survivors in number one?"

"At full transpotter speed, and with loss of fluid containment, that would be nearly impossible. Plus we have no idea when communications will be re-established."

"Why not wait, though? What can we lose?" the other controller argued.

"An aftershock, and you know there will be aftershocks, and the whole spotter slides away. You want that on your hands?"

This was greeted by silent acceptance. A few behind him mumbled, but no one could argue the logic. Then the one seated before the panel raised his hands.

"I think we're coming back on line," he announced. "Prepare to run it!"

"I'll need someone else to help out with the boy. He's too big for just one of us." He turned to the instructor. "Can you help out?"

The instructor returned the invitation with a wary glance. At once Sofia stepped up. "He's my boy, I'll help."

"You saw what we have to do. It'll be even more difficult with him."

"I don't care. Let's go, now," she replied, but at that instant the entire car shook violently, a horrible crunching sound once again asserting itself over their voices.

"Aftershock!" someone yelled, taking off for the back end of the spotter, and the two other keepers followed him, running unsteadily through the car. Only the heroic keeper and Sofia remained behind.

"We'll have to wait it out. Hold on to something," he advised her, then felt a different sort of vibration underneath, a mechanical, motorlike humming. "They've got power back now, it looks like."

Then, as Sofia watched in horror, the thin rods connecting the two cars retracted smoothly, and number one car slumped away, not falling entirely, but wedging itself even more securely into the chasm.

The keeper saw the look on Sofia's face, and tried to comfort her. "We can still reach him, it'll just take some more time." But at that moment the car shook violently and began pulling away from the chasm, leaving behind the stricken spotter car in an awful scraping of t-steel against bare tube.

"No, No!!" screamed Sofia, watching with terror as her son slowly fell away from her.

The keeper realized what was happening, and quickly pressed the release button once again to seal the car, and as the door slid shut the young mother strained for one last glimpse of her boy, but it was too late. He was gone, left behind in a spotter car full of death as they picked up speed and re-entered the safety of the sealed tube.

3

It was the fourth such home for lost children that Sofia and Jaslo had visited in the past two agonizing days, and each one appeared more full of grief and misery than the previous one, leaving them with less and less hope of ever finding Seelin, or of even finding any kind of resolution to their uncertainty. Now they scanned the hopeless faces of lost children packed into the squalor of this small former residence near the center of old Los Gatos. Dirt covered the walls and the stench of urine and feces assaulted their senses, forcing them into hurried, expectant glances over the thirty grimy faces peering back at them. A few naked younger kids played with a flower pot in the corner of the room, and two small girls nearly ran them over in a chase to the hallway, but most of the children sat quietly on the hardwood floor, conserving their energy against the meager rations they had been allotted the last week. They sat thinking of food, cool breezes, misplaced brothers and sisters, just about anything other than where they knew their parents to be, still holding out some hope they might be found, but growing ever more skeptical and discouraged as waves of well fed forever children looked them over as if they were souvenirs for sale.

As Sofia and Jaslo walked through the crowded rooms, they were escorted by both the home's temporary caretaker as well as their own private guard, who was required to accompany them at all times when outside the hive.

"These children were mostly found in the Valley area. Where did you say your boy was lost?" the caretaker asked Sofia.

"Lexington," she answered wearily.

"And you already checked the two centers in that area?"

"Yes. He might have walked down from the hills, perhaps..."

"Yes. perhaps." They had come into another, smaller room, and now the caretaker stopped to allow the entourage some time to scan for their child. Set apart from the rest, a boy sat in a corner with his back to them, playing with a rusted hinge he had found buried in the yard. Instantly Sofia knew; she had washed those ears, had combed that hair so many times before.

"Seelin!" she called out in a rising voice. "Seelin!" she called a second time even though the boy did not respond. "He's confused; he can't hear me," she insisted to Jaslo's shake of the head, and immediately took off toward the boy.

"Sofia, No..." Jaslo called after her, but she had by now reached the child and placed a hand upon his shoulder, turning him toward her as if readying an embrace, readying a long overdue kiss. But the boy revealed only a sullen, unrecognizable stare and a mumbling of profanities. Shocked, she tried to kiss him nonetheless, and was met with a quick shove to her neck which caught her off balance and knocked her to the ground.

The guard at once pushed his way roughly through the scattering of child refugees to get to Sofia, drawing his synthar and pointing it at the boy threateningly.

"No, please, there's no need!" she screamed, getting up shakily. "I'm fine. Don't hurt him, please!" But the guard continued to hold his stance, retreating only when Jaslo ordered him to leave the boy alone.

"We'd better go now. He isn't here." advised Jaslo. Then, turning to the caretaker, he added "You'll take care of him for us, won't you?"

"Yes, we'll see he doesn't bother others the same way, you can be sure of that."

"Thank you," he replied. Then together they steered Sofia away as she continued to look over her shoulder at the boy who could have been her only son.

As they exited, masks replaced firmly over their mouths to protect from the infection, they were once again confronted by the angry crowds which had met them at each of the 'homes' they had visited. Makeshift fences had been constructed to keep the crowd at bay, and additional guards had been placed with synthars always activated and in hand.

"Child stealers!" someone shouted. "Go back where you belong!"

"Leave our children alone!" yelled another, as the crowd reacted now to their re-emergence and pressed upon the fences. "They're our children! Let us in to see them! Child stealers!" The crowd then took up this chant in a frenzy driven by desperation, hunger, and the delirium of dehydration. "Child stealers, child stealers, child stealers..."

Suddenly, a strong young man of about thirty rushed from the crowd and began to climb the fences, darting quickly almost to the top before any of the guards could react.

"Stop," one of them yelled, but at the same time another had already aimed his synthar and fired, missing and burning a hole in the metal fencing. The crowd now ran from the fence in fear, yet some remained to watch the lone attacker reach the top and start down the other side, only seconds from Sofia and Jaslo.

The second, third, and fourth beams, fired instantaneously by all three guards, hit their mark, converging at once on the young man and completely disintegrating his upper body. His arms, head, and lower body fell in separate awful thumps to the ground. Sofia watched in horror as the head rolled toward her and came to a stop, the young man's mouth still slowly forming silent words before all life drained from his features. She recoiled in terror and started to scream, but no sound would come, and soon her husband and their personal guard had ushered her quickly down the path.

"I told you this was foolish; we're in danger coming this far at such a time as this," admonished Jaslo. "We could easily have searched the visuals, then have had him brought to us." He put his arm around his wife's small shoulders and turned to her, slowing their pace now as the crowd's yelling and protests receded behind them. "You'll need to accept that he's gone."

Still shocked, the forever girl could not bring any words to her companion's challenge, could not avert her gaze to meet his eyes, so they continued along toward the depot lodge in silence.

At length, Jaslo spoke again, once the guard had fallen a few steps back. "I told you before I have good connections at the Laboratory. It wouldn't take longer than a few weeks. We need to rebuild our own lives, and it would help, once you've accepted..."

Sofia shrugged from his arm. "I can't believe you've accepted this. What does he mean to you, anyway? How can you just turn away?"

"He's dead Sofia. I'm sorry, and you know I miss him as much as you do. But he's dead and we aren't. Like it or not we need to accept that and move forward. It hurts, but it will hurt less if you accept it."

"Not until we've finished our search. Not until we're sure."

"My dearest, we risk infection every day we're out here. Killing ourselves won't bring Seelin back. When will you understand that?" He took her arm gently, and this time she returned his gaze, too tired to defy him.

"All right," she conceded. "All right, but after we finish the last three centers in this southern zone. That won't take but a day more. Then we'll return for good." She looked back over her shoulder, tired and still full of tears, in case he might be following, in case they might have missed him hiding alongside the trail.

***

For three days Kianno wandered the mountains, deathly afraid of all the dangers his parents had always protected him from so carefully, afraid of diving all alone into the chaos and anarchy of a devastated, lawless world. Three days he hiked trails he had walked before with his mother and father, scrounging water where the earthquake had opened cracks in the covers kept tightly over all year-round streams. But there was no food of any kind in the woods, and the water he was able to find came from shallow, summer-still pools covered over with algae and muck.. Desperate for food and water, he slowly made his way back toward the family's last homestead, traveling by night and hiding out by day. He knew not only of the magical fountain in the yard, but also of a secret stash of food his father had placed in the closet of the main bedroom. It had been standard practice for the family to leave enough supplies at each house so they could use it again as a stopover if they needed one. So the boy carefully backtracked down the mountains to the edge of the old neighborhood. There he spent one more miserable day trying to sleep in a thicket of bush which kept him well hidden, but did little to protect him from the midday sun. When the cover of darkness finally spread across the sky, he emerged to sneak his way back to where he knew food was waiting.

It took only a few minutes to reach the house, and once he had gained the familiar oak canopied residence he could see at once that another group had already claimed it. A fire burning in the yard behind the structure shone through the empty front windows into the street, and Kianno now stopped and looked cautiously in all directions before proceeding slowly ahead. Depending on who the group was, he might still have a chance at some water, and perhaps even some welcome assistance, so he stole around to the side of an adjacent structure to get a better view. As he closed to within earshot of the fire, however, it became quite apparent that no help would be forthcoming. Standing around the blaze were four youths of about twenty, loud and obviously drunk with sabilla. They took turns ripping planks from the house and feeding the fire while the other three passed around the bottle and interrupted each other's boisterous stories with noisy and aggressive laughter. Better judgment told him to leave immediately, but he was ruled by his hunger now, and so curled up in the bushes, vainly trying to cup some warmth inside that curl, until he fell fast asleep.

He awoke to familiar silence, reassuring silence which had been his only companion of late, and immediately turned his attention to the house next door. If they had not already found it, and chances were they hadn't since it had been very well hidden, less than one hundred yards from where he now stood shivering were three proto-food packets and one sinta-food packet. He slowly began walking toward a downed fence separating the yards. Stepping gingerly over the rotting boards, he surveyed the situation. Two of the youths were asleep near a still smoking fire; that meant two were unaccounted for and probably inside somewhere. He was counting on the sabilla to keep them deeply beyond his light crunchings underfoot, and indeed neither one of them stirred as he tiptoed, in full view, past the fire and into the house. As he crept by, the boy saw once again the bubbling spring, still streaming but not nearly as full as before.

He planned to stop for a drink after he had secured the packets; that way if they found him he would already have the food and could dart away into the night.

Once inside, he became disoriented very quickly. He remembered the layout well, but there was no moon tonight and finding his way in the complete blackness was more difficult than he had imagined. He had groped his way through the old kitchen and into the main hallway, counting doors along the way, when he stumbled awkwardly onto something which caught his foot and caused him to land heavily and noisily on the ground. Trying desperately to quiet his heavy breathing, he lay motionless for three full minutes, listening intently. At first he thought he had heard a nearby rustling, but as the seconds ticked off he heard nothing more, so he slowly pushed himself off the cold floor and rose once again. Immediately a large hand descended from above and gripped his shoulder.

"Well, look what we got here," a voice broke the stillness and sent Kianno's only companion scampering into the corners. "A bug, I think. A little bug crawling around inside our house." Now another hand reached down and grabbed the other shoulder, lifting the boy slightly into the air then setting him down again. "Hey Josho, wake up! I found us a little bug, maybe make a nice stew or something."

From the blackness of a nearby room came the sound of heavy footsteps, then a match lit up the hallway and Kianno could see two teenagers staring down at him. One was shorter and heavy set with dark eyes and a full beard; the other was taller and of lighter complexion and eyes, but with a beard and scraggly head of hair equally unkempt. It was the shorter youth who had found him and who now laughed most deviously.

"What do you think, Josho?" He turned away from Kianno now. "Looks like we may have found ourselves a gold mine. What's the going price for little boys these days?"

"Enough to keep us happy for a year or two, that's for sure," answered the other in a more cautious tone.

"Just what I was thinking." He lit another match and turned back to Kianno, examining his face carefully in the flickering light, then walked around him in a circle to take full measure of the boy. "Why, a perfect specimen, don't you think?

No question at all he hasn't even started crossing yet. We'll definitely be the ones calling the shots."

"Yea. We'll need papers though."

At this the shorter youth spit. "Shit, you think they're looking for papers? They didn't even care before this thing, now you think anyone gives the slightest shit about papers?"

"Maybe not," trailed the other. "Wake the others We need to talk."

Now the shorter youth went off to rouse the rest of the gang, and as soon as he was gone Kianno made a play at getting around the side of the other, but he was quickly cornered and gave up any immediate hope of escaping.

"What you come in here for? That's a really stupid thing to do, you know," admonished the youth. "You didn't know we were here or something? There's places all around here for you to hide and you have to choose this one..."

When the other two teenagers arrived, the examination was repeated and the group discussed what to do with their new prisoner.

"I know where we can sell him; no papers, nothing," volunteered one.

"Yea, but what we gonna get for him there? I tell you, we should hold out for top dollar."

"What do you think, maybe have some fun with him in the meantime?" snickered another, tousling the boy's hair. "Maybe have some fun with the cute little boy before we sell him, eh?"

"Shut up Zekil. It's too late to figure this out right now. Let's tie him up and we'll deal with him in the morning." There seemed to be general consensus on this, and with that the two who had been sleeping outside left once again, while the other two tied him to the house frame and bent nails to secure the cord tightly to the boards. Kianno's fear of what lay in store for him the next morning soon gave way to his exhaustion and strange relief at having been found by anybody at all, and after they finally left him alone he soon regained the sleep which by now served as his only means of recouping any energy or spirit whatsoever.

Much later, he was awakened by an animal at his feet. He sat up quickly, then realized that the taller of the youths was silently untying the cord which bound him. Kianno started to say something, but the youth quickly covered his mouth.

"Shh... Shut up. You're one very lucky little kid, at least for now," he said, finishing with the leg cords and starting on the wrists. "You make a sound before you're clear of this place and believe me, I'll be the first one make you pay." He worked slowly in the darkness while Kianno gradually woke fully to the realization that he was being liberated from his short captivity.

"You're gonna end up in the same place anyway," the youth continued as he worked the knots. "And believe me it's probably a whole lot better than here, that's for sure. But Zekil wasn't kidding about having fun with you, and that's something I can't see. So get lost now, will ya?"

His wrists now also free, Kianno stood slowly, blood rushing from his head and swirling before his eyes. Then, having regained himself, he stepped slowly down the hallway toward the open night, a night showing the first signs of morning along the horizon. Giving up all hope of securing the hidden food, he stopped only briefly at the spring before setting off into the broken streets, willing now to settle for any capture which might provide some food, some warmth.

***

It turned out to be the easiest thing in the world. After all the years of avoidance, all the years of wandering the fringes, of moving from camp to camp, hiding desperately from government officials and others who might question and inevitably challenge the boy's ownership, all of that was so easily forsaken for the comfort of a few hundred calories. It took only a short visit to one of the many checkpoints which had gone up since the earthquake and the system sucked him in without any resistance on his part whatsoever. He had remained true for as long as he could, and when he gave in he gave in fully, resigned to whatever destiny they had planned for him.

He found himself thrown together with about a hundred other children who had suffered similar fates, lodged in the remains of an old church where they huddled together, sat silently, or ran wild with play, depending upon the child's current degree of hopelessness and resignation. All colors of the spectrum were present, although the rainbow shaded darker and darker with each passing day. No one knew exactly what was in store for them; still starving but given just enough food and water to keep them wanting for more, rumors ran rampant through the social circles of the older boys and girls.

"Our parents are still in the hospital. When they're better they'll come for us," was the most optimistic of explanations for the unsettling fact that none of the visitors who searched among them appeared fully grown or parent-like in any way. Eight or nine times a day, small groups of serious looking children toured the church, occasionally pointing to a child who was then whisked off, kicking and screaming, to an unknown future.

"They eat children, you know. That's why they all look like children," ventured a young girl who had sided up next to Kianno as he sat staring aimlessly into the morning of his third day in the center. When he didn't respond, she continued. "They kill us, then mash us up into food that makes them look like children; then they never get old."

"I don't care," the boy replied at length. "Let them."

The girl coughed abruptly, then glanced around with apprehension. "They're looking for the youngest and healthiest. They make the best food," she went on with her tale, but was interrupted a second time with a coughing fit which persisted for a full minute. Kianno noticed now that one of the uniformed guards broke off from an entourage he was escorting and approached where they were seated. The little girl as well noticed and tried in vain to suppress her cough, but was still wheezing noticeably by the time the guard arrived.

"You." He pointed at the girl. "Come with me."

"No," she protested, then yelled out for everyone to hear "No. Don't eat me!"

At that, the girl was wrestled away by the guard (the guards were all fully grown), delivered not to the participants of the small tour still in progress, but rather out a back door where the children were not ordinarily allowed. The room hushed slightly at the incident, but then resumed it's hum of activity. Everyone by now had gotten quite used to the idea of children being led away for no apparent reason whatsoever.

It was late afternoon of that third day when he first saw her, when they first entered into that silent, lifelong conspiracy. She was searching their faces like all the rest, for whom the boy did not know and would never ask, even years later. But when her eyes fell onto Kianno they remained fixed, and there was something about those eyes which drew the boy from his silence into the understanding of her gaze. He looked up to a face which appeared at first glance to be no older than his own, but there was something else around the edges, a sense of knowing, a sense that she could feel his inmost soul, could give him what he most needed. Only the tiniest of wrinkles, the smallest hint of experience reflected from within those eyes revealed her age, but it was enough for Kianno to recognize, enough to reassure him and make him understand that she was his final resignation, his final capture.

She walked slowly to his side, by herself, and stood quietly, mirroring his own silence, waiting for him to look up once again to confirm their unspoken agreement of only a minute before.

"Seelin?" She spoke softly the beginnings of a language they would fabricate between them over the following years. "Seelin, that is you, isn't it?"

"Yes, it's me," the boy replied, casting away his given name with everything else he had lost, signing in blood the terms of a conspiracy from which there was no retreat. "Yes, it's me, mother."

4

No one could recall when the gathering room had been so elaborately and impressively decorated. The entire inner chamber was draped in purple silk, and red and purple streamers flew from each of the three rectangular balconies which framed the chamber and upon which nearly two hundred guests milled about waiting for the ceremony to begin. It had been nearly ten years since the last child of the Forshas family had passed through the rite of eternal bestowment, and it would be another five full years before the next such rite of passage. This was a time of great celebration, the greatest, in fact, of all ceremonies, and the twenty-three current members of the Forshas had invited as many friends and as many dignitaries as could fit onto the chamber floor and the balconies above. All were draped in their finest cottons and silks, with ornately decorated gold headbands which proclaimed their ages in bands of bright colors. As they chatted in anticipation of the event, only a very few even casually mentioned the strange fact that indeed the boy seated in the center of this most blessed of sacraments bore very little resemblance to the one they had always known as Seelin. It was as if everyone knew better than to question appearances. Everyone simply accepted without hesitation the concept that this boy was the real Seelin, and that perhaps the one they had known before was the impostor.

For the boy, seated in the great throne centered for all to behold and adorned with regal purple robes, it was the continuation of a dream which had melted from the remains of his former life and flowed like a river he had no choice but to keep riding. Two weeks spent together in the quarantine area waiting for the infection, which thankfully never came, had solidified a certain tentative trust between the three of them, had allowed time to impress the situation with a semblance of normality, of expectedness. So it was with only a little apprehension that the boy Seelin awaited his first taste of the regulators.

This ceremony, anyway, was at least a little more understandable than the secret one his mother had taken him to earlier in the day. Sneaking out under pretext of treating the boy to a true-food breakfast, the two of them had ridden the slider quite a ways to the extreme northeast quadrant, then had met one of the few naturalists who still chose, and were still permitted, to live within the hive. An elderly man with a shock of white hair, he had greeted the two of them and quickly escorted them into his own private room, where he removed vestments and a small metal container. Opening the lid, he dipped his hand in the water and crossed the boy's forehead.

"Do you believe in God Almighty, maker of heaven and earth, of all things visible and invisible?"

"I do," the boy echoed his mother obediently.

"And do you believe in Jesus Christ, his only son..."

To all, Seelin answered with his mother, although the questions were puzzling. Afterward, when he asked his mother for some explanation, she said only that she would teach him in good time, but that for now it was enough for him to know that the private ceremony must precede the public one later on, and that no one, not even Jaslo, was ever to know of it.

Now, six hours later, the boy listened as a deep chime sounded five times, drawing silence from the crowd as they all leaned over the railings to peer down at the invocation of the ritual. After the last chiming, from the far end of the chamber a small, hooded figure approached, accompanied on each side by beautiful small girls with golden hair flowing almost to the floor. As they drew near, the girls removed the hood and unveiled the figure. It was a creature unlike any the boy had ever seen. Up until now, Seelin had come across primarily residents who were relatively young, less than one hundred years of age. Consequently, their appearance was very much like that of any ordinary child, especially if one didn't look too carefully at the fine lines surrounding the eyes. However, standing before him now was a true ancient, one of the very first who had been suspended back when the regulators were first accepted legally, some two hundred years ago. Seelin stared in wonder at the face, still childlike but with eyes deeply clouded and mysterious, and skin covered entirely with small, fine wrinkles which gave the elder a mystical quality. As the boy gazed quizzically at that china white but somehow vacant visage, a chair was brought from the side and the elder was seated. Throughout the ceremony he would do nothing more than gaze off into space, seemingly unseeing and unknowing of what was happening all around him.

As soon as the elder had been seated, one of the young girls came forward. "I speak for Zadar, for he has given me his voice, and I proclaim myself to you all. Do you hear me?"

In unison, the crowd answered. "We hear. Zadar speaks."

"And who have you brought to the threshold of eternal youth, eternal life?"

"We have brought the boy Seelin, of the Forshas."

"And who are his keepers?" At this Sofia, Jaslo, and four others stepped forward. Now the girl-priestess turned to address them. "Is this boy deserving of our life, deserving of entrance into the kingdom?"

"He is deserving. We testify."

"Then bring forth the cup."

Now the other priestess drew forth a gold cup and presented it to the first, who opened the ornate lid and held it high into the air. The crowd surged with cries of anticipation and praise. When she had shown the cup to all ends of the gallery, the priestess reached in and withdrew one tiny green capsule. Inside the capsule was the most potent and reliable regulator formula yet achieved in over two hundred years of analysis, experimentation, and reformulation. If taken daily, the chemical could be relied upon to block production of over 99.9% of all human growth hormone, and suppress sex hormone production to pre-pubescent levels. It had overcome previous side effects and would reliably maintain the body in a fully static state for over two hundred years. Only accidents, infection, rare cancers, or congenital defects posed any threat during those years, as long as the regulator was not withdrawn.

Swinging her flowing hair toward Sofia, the priestess placed the capsule directly onto her tongue, then repeated the ritual for all of the keepers. Finally, she turned to Seelin.

"Do you accept the life we give you, and do you pledge to return this gift forevermore?" She spoke slowly, as if giving the boy time to consider, but he needed no time at all, having been well coached for several days now.

"Yes," the boy replied, and the priestess bowed slightly to place the last of the capsules onto his pale tongue.

Part Two

2035: Renewal

5

"Your highest eminence," Dr. Jaslo of Forshas said, ushering his guest through an open doorway which led from the laboratory offices into the secure inner complex of the medical lab. "We are so pleased that you have agreed to consider our petition for full legalization. Our current status of limited emergency dispensation does not assure that we can carry our work to its full completion, although of course we are very grateful for the government's understanding, considering the, uh, nature, of the experiments."

"It is precisely that which concerns me," replied Public Senator Atascin looking a bit uncomfortable in his lab suit. "Remember that I am here to also consider termination of the project. Frankly I am appalled at the reports I've been reading."

"Of course I also regret that our research must be with human subjects, but there is simply no other way; the brain and nervous system of human beings is unique, as I'm sure you're aware..." Jaslo let out a small chuckle, but then quickly reassumed a serious posture, facing his visitor now and looking him in the eyes. "Let me be frank. Some of the things you'll see are going to be shocking and disturbing, there's no question about that. But isn't it also shocking and disturbing to think that hundreds of people will die this year in this city alone. And thousands more waste away in the stupor of terminal disease, the regulators unable to help their deteriorating mental condition. Please keep in mind, your eminence, that it is the horror of hundreds of needless deaths, including your own some day, which must be balanced against the purposeful suffering of these few outsiders.

Now the doctor took his guest's hand and led him into a large viewing room, where several other doctors awaited them. After greetings were exchanged, Jaslo waved his hand to begin the show, a series of holographic, sound impressed projections filling the center of the room.

"Until fifty years ago, brain transplantation had always been the one goal it always appeared that medical science would be unable to achieve. The delicacy of the tissues involved, the risk of extreme damage, and, most importantly, the resistance of nerve cells in general, and spinal cord cells in particular, to all of our attempts at cultivating regeneration, has made it seem for the longest time as if this dream would never be realized. Until a solution could be found to this obstacle, the re-growth needed to fuse the organ and the host was impossible, and so for the longest time a small group of dedicated researchers focused on how these cells could be stimulated into spontaneous growth."

Now the projection of a human brain was replaced by a crying baby lying alone on a feeding pad. The doctor continued. "It had been known for some time that, at certain stages of a human's development, brain and spinal cord cells divide and grow rapidly and without inhibition. It was natural, then, to look to those early stages in an attempt to understand why and how growth is stimulated. If there were biochemical triggers which turned on and off this growth, simulating such triggers would go a long way toward controlling this growth ourselves." Jaslo cleared his throat as the image changed from crying baby to a silent fetus suspended in amniotic fluid, giving the viewers the peculiar sensation of sharing the womb with this floating human embryo.

"Perhaps you're familiar with the history of research in this field, your eminence? I certainly don't want to bore you with ancient history."

"No, no. Please continue. I find it quite fascinating, and am really only vaguely aware of what has transpired in this field."

"Very good. I do believe a thorough understanding of the background of our research will help you to appreciate what's at stake here." He turned back toward the image of the fetus and continued. "Medical science had always known that brain and spinal cord cells do not regenerate after birth, but do experience a period of rapid growth between the twenty-eighth and thirty-second week of gestation. For quite awhile, then, research attempted to locate a biochemical marker which perhaps was released into the fetal bloodstream and which served as a catalyst for this growth. It was, perhaps, wishful thinking to postulate the existence of such a marker, and years of attempts to identify it failed. We now know, of course, that no such catalyst exists, that the pattern of growth is programmed into the DNA code itself, a situation which discouraged further full scale research efforts along these lines for quite some time thereafter.

Now the image changed once more to a huge DNA helix spiraling through the open room. "However, a small group of dedicated scientists continued, focusing now on identifying the specific gene or gene group which programmed this growth. As you no doubt must be aware, progress was slowed dramatically by ethical issues surrounding the experimentation on live fetuses. The only method of locating and confirming the function of these genes was to remove the DNA from a clone host cell, alter the genes suspected of containing the brain growth code, and then use this altered DNA as the base of a cloned fetus who would be monitored for changes in expected cell growth during that critical gestation period. It was at this time, your eminence, that the most dedicated of researchers were forced to take their work underground, where it has remained ever since. Several times we had been on the verge of identifying the key sequences when progress was needlessly set back many years by the arrest of the researchers themselves. It is only in the past fifty years that the government has seen the necessity of experimentation with live humans and human fetuses, and has condoned our work.

"Perhaps you've forgotten, doctor, that the government does not officially condone or approve of this activity," Atascin interjected abruptly. "Such statements are dangerous and inflammatory."

"Oh yes, of course. I didn't mean to imply the government's approval." Dr. Forshas reminded himself that his eminence was unlike the other government visitors; he was publicly visible, was required to answer to all groups, including outsiders and naturalists, and would undoubtedly stay firm to the official version no matter how warped that version became. "What I meant to say is that the government has become less persecutorial of our efforts, and has seen the wisdom of appreciating the possible benefits of this research."

"I understand," replied the official. "I didn't mean to interrupt. Of course, you are correct that we have eased our position somewhat. Please continue."

"Thank you. As I was saying, eventually we were successful at locating and marking the specific gene pairs responsible for turning on and turning off brain and spinal cord cell division. Of course, many significant obstacles remained. Although we could now create brain cells which had been genetically altered to divide and grow continuously, it was still uncertain how these might be used to fuse an organ to a host. It was hoped that somehow these cells could be used to bridge the organ with the recipient, however, attempts at growing these cells directly from living tissue were a complete failure. A bridge was indeed the answer, but introducing such a bridge proved impossible, and new research began to look at ways in which both the donor and the host organ could reach out toward that bridge, that is, prepare each to be receptive to the newly introduced cells, even before transplantation. When the organs were brought together, then, the layers would grow together seamlessly, thus rebuilding the neural and electrical pathways on the cellular level. Once the technology for selective cell mutation had progressed to the point where we were able to mutate the topmost layer within the short time frames needed even with the most modern surgical techniques, we were then in a position to infuse that layer with the genetically altered cells.

As the doctor spoke, highly technical diagrams of cellular interactions and DNA gene pairs had been presented, but now he drew a deep breath as he touched his fingers together to introduce the image of a smiling girl laying still on her back, her body invisible beneath the bedcovers. "Your eminence, may I introduce Sarah, the first successful brain transplant recipient. And it may surprise you to know that her operation was performed over twenty years ago."

"Twenty years ago? But I thought you were only just now..."

"Yes," the doctor interrupted. "Perhaps I used the word 'successful' a bit too freely. Sarah was the first to survive the operation, and to survive it in a conscious and coherent state. However, the neural shock of the operation left her body essentially useless to her, although vital functions were left intact."

"Is she still alive, then?"

"No. I'm afraid we were unable to counteract the one side effect which had been anticipated but which we felt would be easily controlled- the unchecked growth of the altered cells. All efforts to stop their growth without killing them outright proved futile, and Sarah died of what you might term a form of neural cancer, four months after the operation." The doctor paused, then continued in a slower, more cautious cadence. "We were forced, then, to retreat to using fetal cells exclusively for our work."

"I thought you had been using them all along," answered the politician. "Perhaps I'm getting a touch confused."

"No, no, it's perfectly understandable. Of course we had been using human fetuses in the experiments. However, the intent of the studies into genetically altered cells was that, once the research phase was finished and such transplants took place routinely, artificially created and mutated cells would be used on an ongoing basis. However, timing was the one factor we could not, or at least haven't yet, solved. Cells remember how old they are, and not just how old they are but how old their entire host being is as well, and unfortunately we are still a long ways off from figuring out how they do that. We needed cells which were still reproducing but which also still contained the signal to stop reproducing, and only cells from fetuses within a very narrow age range satisfy this equation."

"Are you saying, doctor, that, supposing your newest techniques to be successful, you still would need a continual supply of human fetuses to perform them?"

"I'm afraid so, your eminence. In fact, we have found two are needed for each transplant." The doctor got up from his chair now and paced across the room, continuing to address the Senator as well as his fellow researchers. "But I assure you, we have made arrangements strictly through legal channels, and full price has always been paid. Indeed, these transactions have assured the continued survival of the outsiders who have chosen to participate."

"There is talk of kidnappings, of raids in the night. Terrorist acts by the outsiders are increasing in response to these reports," responded Senator Atascin.

"Such reports are new? Even if we were guilty of these atrocities it would only be a drop in the bucket, with all due respect, your eminence."

"That only points up the difficulties in your proposition. With the demand already so great just to maintain the population, how can we possibly afford transplantation at the rate you suggest?" He looked now at the other doctors, addressing his question to all present.

"There are ways, ways which some of us have proposed but which the government has not yet seen fit to implement. They may have seemed extreme a few decades ago, but with the possibilities that exist now, I believe others will stop bending to the naturalist sympathizers and do what should have been done long ago."

"Doctor, you're talking to the wrong man," Atascin replied quickly, clearly upset at the direction the discussion had taken. "I am a tolerant man and have come here in the spirit of understanding what you have to offer us. But I will not be given a lecture on the state's politics."

The doctor turned and walked toward the official, who was now standing as if to leave. "My deepest apologies, your eminence. I am not a politician, and it is not for me to decide how and by whom this medical gift will be used. I am only a doctor and a scientist, who is here to demonstrate our findings. I will try to remember this as we continue." He had now reached the Senator, and touched his elbow to invite him to follow. "Come, let me show you how close we are now."

Although indignant at the doctor's remarks, Atascin was too curious to refuse the tour which was to follow. Besides, he knew better than to believe he really had any choice; once news of this was confirmed, the public would not allow him the luxury of standing on his morals. So he followed silently as the tour progressed from the viewing chamber into a long hallway. Halfway down the hall, Dr. Forshas opened a door and waited while the rest of the group paraded into the room and ventured tentatively up to the bedside of a small boy who sat up and smiled at them as they approached.

Now the doctor closed the door behind them and addressed the boy. "Juberi, how are you feeling today?"

"Much better. Thank you so much for the levelers. They do help, you know."

"Certainly. Juberi, I'd like to introduce his highest eminence Senator Atascin. He's here to review our progress. I thought you might want to tell him a little about your experiences over the past few months."

"Well..." the boy answered shyly, "I wouldn't know where to begin. So much has happened."

"Why don't you start by showing him who you were only a few months ago."

At this the boy grasped his wrist and began manipulating the visual controls. Immediately, in the space behind the bed, the figure of a tall man of about forty natural years appeared. His thinning hair turned gray at the temples and cascaded into a ragged, unkempt beard. Seated in a chair, the figure spoke angrily to an unseen respondent.

"You'll not get away with this," he shouted too loudly, and the doctor gestured the boy to reduce the volume. "Oh you may kill me, you may kill many more before we burn your hives to the ground. But burn you will, if not in this life then in the next." At this the man struggled fiercely to rise against the invisible restraints, but gave in and collapsed once more into the chair, sweating and mumbling a rage by then already turning to exasperation. The doctor gestured once more and the boy dissolved the visuals.

"Yes, that was me, in my former life," he replied in his soft, child's voice. Then he yawned and released a long sigh. "I didn't understand what they had to offer me. I could never have realized..."

The Senator now examined the boy's smooth face, inspecting the eyes closely for the smallest sign of fine wrinkles. Even with the most expert resurfacing one could usually tell if one looked closely enough, but not a single line could be found. "You mean, you are really the same man..."

"Yes, I am him."

"And you remember everything?"

"More than I wish to sometimes, sir. But with the levelers..."

"You can see," interrupted the doctor, "how far we've come. We have now perfected the fusing technique and have almost eliminated the brain shock side effects."

"Almost?"

"Yes. I'm afraid we've had to disable Juberi's legs; they get quite out of control when the disablers start to wear off. No, there are still too many side effects." He turned to the boy now. "Juberi, who is this gentleman and why are we here?"

The boy only looked stupidly at Dr. Forshas, then answered. "Have we been introduced? My name is Juberi. What can I do for you?"

"And what have you just finished telling us, Juberi?"

"Stop this!" exclaimed the boy. "Stop this! You know I can't remember so why keep tormenting me. Renew the levelers, doctor, now!"

"No short term memory, I'm afraid. He remembers his former life well enough, and whatever he can put into long term will stay. But nothing sticks from moment to moment."

"But still, this is amazing! He now has his whole life ahead of him, an entire lifetime to relive!"

"I tell you, your eminence, this is the greatest breakthrough since the regulators. We are this close to eliminating all brain shock. Then the world will need to be ready. That is why you must prepare things. You must prepare for the inevitable."

As Jaslo spoke, he fixed his expressionless blue eyes coldly onto the Senator, and as he did so a terrible unease welled up inside Atascin and silenced any response, any protest. Jaslo was right about the inevitable. Once word got out, any hope of reconciliation with the outsiders would be gone. And yet, they would not go quietly, all his years of negotiations told him that quite plainly.

"So this is your most successful, I take it," Atascin finally replied.

"Yes. Others have had more, uh, significant problems. You may visit with them as well if you so wish, although it would serve no purpose. Those failures are in the past, and most have died in any event. A few we keep alive because we have not yet fully solved what went wrong. They will not be forgotten, nor will those who have yet to undergo the operation. They are martyrs, all of them, and while they live we reward them with happiness they've never known before."

As they walked away, Senator Atascin peered back one more time at the small child pleading now more vehemently for renewal.

"Don't be concerned with him," the doctor answered his glance. "They can never seem to get enough, but he won't go long without. Come, let me show you the equipment which makes this all possible."

"But the boy in whose body he now lives..." wondered the Senator out loud.

The doctor stared once again deeply into Atascin's eyes. "It is their lives or our own. Life is never given, your eminence. Life is always taken, in one way or another."

6

Their home was hidden so deeply into the folds of a eucalyptus shaded ravine that only those who truly loved them would ever find Seelin Arear and his nine year old daughter Mistissa. He had built it himself over twenty years ago when his wife had become pregnant with their only child, as a shelter, a protection, a refuge. Now, with the nearest gathering four wilderness miles away, his few remaining friends saw it more as a hiding place. And it had been more than a few years since they stopped finding him. Even his daughter now spent more nights away, in Lexington gathering, with her friends and their families, unafraid of the dangers he knew awaited any child who exposed themselves to the watchers. Until two years ago he had forbidden it entirely, allowing only nighttime visits to the city and requiring any visitors to their home to follow the same circuitous route he devised to throw any watchers off the track. But he could no longer deny his daughter the nourishment of peer companionship, and had gradually come to realize that in depriving her of the very necessities of a fulfilled life, he was giving in to them just as surely as if he had handed her over for the price they were always willing to pay.

It was almost dark when they arrived, signaling their approach with the loud snapping of twigs and crunching of leaves dried by the summer sun. Mistissa out in front, still running with enthusiasm after the four mile hike, followed by her friend Nicoli, and, trailing a good hundred yards back, Nicoli's father and one of Seelin's few remaining friends, Jask Orillo. Seelin caught sight of them as he himself closed in on the old homestead, carrying a large bladder of water he had just finished siphoning from a tube he had inserted into a hole in the surface of the creek which emerged a few hundred yards down the canyon. He greeted the three visitors somewhat warily, searching the hillside beyond for any trailers.

"Seelin, my friend!" Jask reached out with his big arms to hug his old friend. "Why do I never see you? Must I follow my own daughter through these woods to the middle of nowhere just to say hello?"

"Jask." Seelin returned his hug with less strength. "I'm glad you came. You're right that it's been too long." He surveyed the ridge line once more. "You weren't followed, were you? They're very good if you're not careful..."

"Seelin, you've been out here too long. Gone completely paranoid. What would they want with you, anyway?"

"You know full well..." But before he could finish the girls had converged on them from the wide running circle they had been making around them.

"Papa, papa!" Mistissa looked up at her father. "Papa, swing me!"

At this, Seelin grabbed onto her hands and made a play at swinging her in a circle, but she had grown too large and he was not feeling so strong today. "You're too big for swinging, Mista. You've been too big for some time now."

"No, swing me Papa!" Now she pulled at his hands and made her body limp in an effort to conjure a ride. But he would have none of it, and released her to fall into the carpet of pale green leaves.

Now Nicoli had picked up on the game. "Me too! Swing me!" she implored her own father, but Jask only laughed and smiled down at her.

"You two swing each other if you're so fond of it. Poor Seelin and I are not strong enough for you two. Why look at you, you're nearly grown ups!" Indeed, they had grown taller over the past year, although they still had most of their growth spurt, as well as their development, ahead of them. They were only a couple of years away now from safety, and looking down at his growing daughter Jask felt a sense of relief that soon they would no longer be burdened with constantly avoiding the many dangers which faced outsider children.

"Go run and play. I want to talk with Seelin," he instructed the girls, and Mistissa immediately picked herself up off the ground and dashed into the woods. When she had reached a safe distance from her father, she pulled a small metal cylinder from her pocket and placed it on the ground.

"C'mon. It has one more play," she whispered to Nicoli, then pressed a button on the top of the cylinder. Giggling as they watched, a small plume of orange smoke rose in a straight line from the container, then expanded and assumed itself into the figure of a gnome.

"Who has called me here to play?" spoke the sound-impressed figure.

"You play," whispered Nicoli. "It's your turn."

Now Mista spoke to the figure. "I'll play. Over here!" And at that she took off like a dart toward a huge madrone tree down the side of the canyon, spilling over the forest floor with gales of laughter, followed closely by the gnome, who chased her step for step and shadowed her every zig and zag. When she reached the tree she scampered quickly up to a low limb and rested, out of breath, while the gnome hopped up and down in exasperation at the tree's base. Nicoli now caught up with the pair and watched as the gnome transformed itself into a snake which began slithering in circles up the scaly orange bark of the madrone.

"Ahhhh!" both girls screamed in unison. "Jump, Mista, Jump and see what happens!" But the ground was just a tad too far away to jump safely, and besides, the snake was quite entrancing to look at, glowing with a swirling purple and crimson skin, its head raised and bobbing straight toward Mistissa.

"Jump!" Nicoli cried again. "It'll change to a bird!" But at that instant the snake disappeared into thin air.

"Hey, it's not done with," protested Mista, then looked back to where she had placed the cylinder. Coming down the slope from the same direction was her father, and she could see clenched tightly in his hand the small canister which produced the chase game.

"Where did you get this?" he asked his daughter sternly, tossing the cylinder from hand to hand. "Come down out of that tree and explain yourself."

"I didn't steal it," answered Mista defiantly. "Another girl gave it to me."

"Was it a real girl, or a forever girl?"

"I don't know. How am I supposed to know? She was really nice. Her name is Camille."

"Where did you meet her?" he continued, but when he got only a sullen look, he turned to Nicoli. "Who is this Camille? Do you know her?"

"She's new," ventured the girl. "I think she's not really a girl. She talks funny."

"Mistissa, get down right now. I've told you not to accept gifts from forever boys and girls. I've told you never to talk to them, haven't I?"

The girl had been sliding slowly down the branch on which she was perched, and having reached the main trunk she now jumped the remainder of the way, landing loudly right next to her father. By now, Jask had joined up with the rest of them, and, instead of addressing her own father, she turned instead to Jask.

"We have no games at all! Why shouldn't I play with them. They haven't done anything to us!"

"Mistissa." He grasped his daughters shoulders and held her straight. "I'm very serious when I tell you never to play or accept anything from a forever child. Be courteous, but leave them as soon as you can. They're more dangerous than you could imagine. You're never to play with them again, do you hear?"

Mista nodded slowly, then grabbed onto her playmate's hand and trudged off toward the house, kicking at small branches along the way. After they had slammed the door shut behind them, Seelin hurled the small canister far into the woods.

"Did you know about this?" he asked Jask, then caught his accusatory tone and followed up in a softer voice. "I can't believe they can get so close without our knowing."

"There are more arrests every day, kidnappings too. It's not just an occasional story anymore. Everyone seems to know someone..." Jask paused, unable to speak the words. He looked up into the tangle of tree limbs filtering the last rays of the sun. "We'll need to head back soon. I'd rather get started at least while there's still some light."

"How can you do it, I don't understand." Seelin took his friend's cue and began walking slowly toward the home. "How can you live right in the middle of it, with Nicoli so close? Can you even sleep at night?"

"There's no choice. Until we can..."

"But there is a choice," interrupted Seelin. "Bring Paula and Nicoli and come live with us. There's room for you here. I've told you that before."

"That's not a choice for us, my friend. You should know that."

"What do you mean, not a choice?" Seelin ran his hand through his dark hair and turned to his old companion. "Of course it's a choice. It's the only choice if you care about your daughter."

Now Jask for the first time raised his voice in response. "It's no choice to leave your people. If not Nicoli then surely someone else's daughter. I can't abandon the fight to save all of them."

"Like me? Is that what you're saying? Well if you're accusing me of doing everything I can to protect my daughter, then I do plead guilty." Seelin felt the eyes of his friend focused in his direction, but stared straight ahead as he walked nonetheless, refusing to acknowledge them.

"And what of her friends, her playmates? Her entire generation for that matter? What of them? Seelin, we've known each other for many years, and I used to think I understood you. But now I wonder how *you* can sleep at night, knowing you and her may be safe but you're doing nothing. Especially when you've already shown how valuable you are to the movement."

"It's futile," Seelin replied in exasperation. "I know better than anyone how futile it is."

"We need you back, Seelin Arear. You know how our projects have failed, and your hiding out from us is as much to blame as anything. There's a war to be fought, in case you've forgotten."

Now Seelin did return his friend's gaze, returned it with piercing brown eyes gone cold over the years but tinged now with an anger that couldn't restrain itself. "I've lost that war, Jask, I've fought it already and lost it! Who else would you have me lose for this cause?"

His friend did not answer. Indeed, nothing more was spoken between them that evening but the routine pleasantries associated with the good-byes of nine year old girls. And after Jask and Nicoli had departed, the still young father did not join his daughter on the porch to watch their friends march silently up the ravine into an ever darkening forest.

***

Later that evening, as the summer fog crept up the canyon and chilled the air with hints of a coming fall, Seelin and Mistissa sat quietly by the fire working on her learning. The inside of the home was divided into three rooms: a gathering room where the two of them spent most of their time, as well as two sleeping rooms tucked away toward the back, furthest from the entryway. There was no need for any kitchen, although a portion of the front room had been fitted with shelves for a water bladder, cups, and tubes of manufactured food, as well as a table for writing and studying. Constructed entirely of Oak and Bay Laurel logs, the inside of the cabin was almost always cold and damp; only in the height of the summer season did the sun ever reach strongly enough into the ravine to warm the structure, and so for most of the year the two of them could be found bundled up in layers of flocks, sitting close to the fireside. Now, fully two hours after their visitors had left, the flaming logs had surrendered their liveliness to an unassuming warmth of glowing embers.

"So, thirty years after the old city was abandoned, they emerged from their hives," Seelin was telling his daughter.

"Why, papa?"

"Two reasons, Mista. One, the lure of true-food had returned, and the forever children had lived without threat for so long they had forgotten the reasons for sacrificing it in the first place. And two, although their numbers continued to multiply, as more of them began to give their children the regulators, they realized that they couldn't live forever inside the hives without any contact with us. So, of course, they re-established contact by pretending to welcome us as equals into their society."

"You mean, they let us into the hives?"

"No, but they offered to share their food with us, for which we were very grateful. Remember, Mista, that at that time there were very few of us left, since food and clean water were so scarce. Those who did survive were ever at the mercy of the gangs who ruled unchecked. The idea that we might actually be able to earn food rights by means other than stealing or slavery gave some of us hope that order might be restored."

"Then what happened?" Mista bent forward to remove her stockings and position her feet closer to the fire.

"They did share their food with us, but we bought it at much too high a price: either backbreaking work in the fields or selling our very children. We were still slaves, but now we had become organized slaves serving them, instead of the most ruthless among ourselves."

Mistissa sat up and paused for a second before asking her next question.

"Papa, Camille says we're going to die. Is she right?"

"Yes Mista. Everyone dies, you know that. But we probably won't have to start worrying about that for a very long time."

"Camille says that the forever children never die. Is that true?"

"No. Everyone dies, even forever children. It just takes them a little longer, that's all."

"She says I can become a forever child, if I want to. Papa, can they make you live forever, too?"

Now Seelin got up from the hearth and began pacing slowly, struggling to keep his tone of voice from betraying the anger building inside.

"Honey, please tell me you won't listen to the forever children. They're very dangerous. How many times do I have to tell you that?"

"I'm sorry, papa. I just never want you to die, too. I thought maybe..."

Now Seelin sat next to his daughter and ran his fingers through her long blonde hair, to comfort her as they both fought back painful memories.

"Mista," he replied softly, still stroking her hair, "I'm very proud of you for having been so strong. It's been difficult for both of us, but especially for you, having to lose..." Even after five years he still couldn't say her name. "...her, and having to live way out here, away from your friends. But you have to trust me, trust in what I'm asking you to do. Believe me, I have many years yet to live, and to live strongly, both of us together."

The girl didn't answer right away, but only snuggled her head against her father's side while the two of them sat quietly. When one of the embers snapped, shifting the fire, Mistissa jumped up and turned to her father.

"We saw a lion today, on the hike." she said brightly, with the resilience of youth.

"A lion? Did it follow you?"

"No. It was down in McGrave's gully and it just looked at us as we walked by. Nicoli was scared cause she's never seen one before, but I wasn't."

"Good girl." He hugged her and held her close for a moment before she squirmed away, old enough now to be embarrassed. "And there's nothing to be scared of either, as long as you're not alone. And I promise you, you're not ever going to be alone."

That night, as the coyotes howled in the distance and the moon spotted leafy shadows outside his window, Seelin kept hearing his own voice again and again: many years to live, and to live strongly; many years to live and to live strongly...

***

Seven nights later, police officials burst open the doors with a silent blast which woke only the lightest of sleepers on an obscure street in the southeast corner of Lexington. They came at night, as was their usual practice, and their arrival was as surprising and unexpected as death when it finally does show its face. Most of those who did hear the charge remained quiet in their corner bed-burrows, knowing better than to interfere. A few heroic souls, however, swung open their doors to holler warnings to the many other families sharing the old mansion, and all but two of them were able to duck into the safety of darkness before the police synthars found them. The two who couldn't retreat fast enough died in vain, as it turned out, since the invaders, efficiently and with full knowledge of the building's layout, located Jask, Paula, and Nicoli Orilla just moments after they had heard the warnings, still stumbling through the confused shock of a midnight awakening.

"Are you Jask Orilla?" an official uttered matter of factly as he illuminated the room with the harsh light of a magna lamp. He was accompanied by one other official and two hired outsider guards.

"Who are you, and what right do you have bursting in like this?" demanded Jask defiantly, even as the whole of his soul was sinking like a skipped stone at the end of its ride.

"We are official representatives of the Court of the Great Hive of San Jose, as you well know. Now answer the question. Are you Jask and Paula Orilla, and is this Nicoli Orilla?"

Paula grabbed her daughter now and held her close, whispering small consolations against their growing anxiety.   "We are," Jask finally answered, crossing the room to join the rest of his family.

"Then we have orders for a hearing to be held, on grounds of your endangering the welfare of the child Nicoli."

"No! That's stupid! Nobody's endangering my welfare! Get out of here now, you hear. You're the ones endangering my welfare. Now get out!" shouted Nicoli while her parents looked on, too stunned to contribute to her protestations.

"Quiet! Or I will need to immobilize you for the hearing." Now the official turned and commented to no one in particular "It's not at all unusual, your honor, for the child to defend the very ones who are putting her life at risk." Behind him a holographic figure appeared suspended in mid-air: a forever child with blond hair, mild blue eyes, and a pug nose, appearing to Paula somewhat like a defiant boy who didn't get his way often enough. He was dressed in flowing navy robes and seated on a throne three times his size. Looking the scene over nonchalantly, he began to speak.

"Be quiet, all of you. I am Shibretey, Judge of Level KK, outer segments. I have authorized this hearing and I order all to answer only to my questions from this time forward. Otherwise I may instruct the guards to take action."

"The hearing is to be held today, this very moment?" Jask asked incredulously. "How can this be? Even the previous kidnappings…" But before he could continue one of the guards fired an immobilizing agent directly at his midsection, freezing him instantaneously and causing him to collapse onto the ground. His wife bent to help him, but was drawn up by the commanding voice of the child judge.

"Stand up now and listen to this hearing or you'll be next. Do you hear me?"

"Yes," responded Paula, now in a trance of disbelief.

"I am going to ask a series of questions. You must answer the truth, and if you do not we will immediately know it through our biosensor which is operating as we speak. Answer only the questions which I ask." For the first time, silence followed his instructions, so he continued. "How many tubes of nourishment does Nicoli receive each day?"

"More than we do." Paula hesitated, then added "Enough for a child her age."

"How many exactly?"

"Almost always two, sometimes three."

"And sometimes none at all?"

"Sometimes, of course, but we can't always find the work to recharge our food accounts."

"Yes," replied the judge. "I understand you may not be in the position to properly care for a growing child."

"That's not what I said." Paula scuffed her foot across the floor. "This isn't a hearing; it's a pretense for state kidnapping, and we all know it!"

The judge now looked over his shoulder to the second official. "Scan the child; let me know if she is of proper weight and has been bathed recently."

At this, the official removed a small, square metallic object and pointed it in Nicoli's direction. Nicoli immediately ran to hide behind her mother.

"Why do you find it necessary to hide from us?" asked the official of his own accord. "If you've been taken care of then you have nothing to hide."

Now one of the guards stepped forward to pull the girl into the center of the room, fighting off Paula's screams and swinging arms.

"I won't warn you again," admonished the judge, but Paula could not help herself at this point, entirely overcome with anguish. She broke free from the one guard who held her and rushed at her daughter, in a futile effort at freeing them both. The second guard waited till she was midway to Nicoli's side before firing the immobilizer.

Now the hearing continued in relative calm, both parents unable to move or talk, although still able to hear and witness the awful unfolding of events.

"This is not how I would have preferred to have done this," the judge continued, his words choppy from transmission interference. "Believe me, I don't enjoy doing this. But the welfare of the child must come first."

As he spoke, the official scanned the now dazed and resigned young girl, calling out readings which were noted for the official record. "Weight- seventy pounds, ten below acceptable average for height and age; hair- unwashed, matted; skin- unwashed, multiple animal bites, primarily flea and mosquito; nails-overgrown, unwashed..."

As these readings were being called out, the judge released small sighs of sympathy for the pain the young girl must have experienced prior to this intervention. When the guard finished, he spoke once again. "Young Nicoli, I have determined that we must temporarily remove you to a safe shelter where you may recover your strength."

"No, no..." cried the girl, but the judge only continued in a monotone.

"I know that right now this seems unfair. Ironically, more often than not victims of abuse and neglect show incredible allegiance and attachment to their abusers. However, do not worry that you will never see Jask and Paula again, for they may petition the Great Hive for custody, once they have placed themselves in a better position to properly care for you; that is, should they decide to file the petition. We find in a majority of cases the keepers realize they are unfit and never even make an attempt at reclamation. In any event, you have my solemn promise that while in our care you will be given a safe and healthy environment, as well as every opportunity to live the kind of long and full life you would not have otherwise."

Now the judge turned from Nicoli, who had collapsed on the floor near her parents, toward the two officials who were in the process of packing their scanner and preparing their synthars for the trip home. "Thank you, loyal servants. It is to you she owes her safety, and we owe our survival. May you return unharmed and in peace." With those words he disappeared into blackness.

The officials did return unharmed that night; no outsider would dare challenge synthars in the hands of guards returning with a captured child. It would be more foolhardy than approaching a lion dragging a fresh kill to its den. And less than one hour after the explosion first broke the stillness of night, silence and calm returned to this forgotten corner of Lexington. It wouldn't be till daybreak that Jask and Paula would regain the power to weep.

***

News of Nicoli's kidnapping, carried by her closest friend, made its way quickly to the isolated cabin four miles from the outskirts of Lexington gathering. Even still, it was ten long days before Seelin showed up at the door of Jask and Paula, accompanied by his daughter and carrying a first load of clothes and belongings. After opening the door slowly and reluctantly, unenthusiastic about greeting any visitors regardless of how well intentioned, Jask Orillo was taken aback by the sight of his friend having returned to the city from his exile. Staring intently at the face across from him, he thought he saw something familiar but long absent from those eyes, something returned to his friend's expression he had not seen for many years. As the two men stood silently in the doorway, Paula came from behind to join her husband. It was she who finally broke the silence.

"You've come to stay, then." she said, gesturing to the packs.

"Yes," answered Seelin. "We've both come to stay. It's time."

"Please," interjected Jask, "Not on our account. I couldn't..."

"No. Not on your account. Not on anybody's account. It's time, that's all. It's time for us to return, and for me to do what needs to be done."

Paula then opened the door a touch wider and ushered them into the too quiet house.

7

"First order of business," called a tall, rail thin man who appeared ten years beyond his actual age of forty-three, "is to welcome a new member." He spoke to a still shuffling and talkative assembly of about thirty others, mostly men but a few women mixed into this rough looking group which had crowded itself into a dark room lit only with a few lumi-candles scattered about the perimeter. The speaker paused briefly, waiting for attention to focus, but then continued even as small conversations hurried to finish. "Some of you may remember Seelin Arear, Charge of the cause in this district many years ago." Now a new kind of murmur went through the crowd, as a few of the older members uttered quiet exclamations and the rest looked to see what the excitement was all about.

"Seelin, why have you come back? Are you going to lead us once more?" shouted one man over the growing noise, but Seelin only remained quiet, staring ahead at the speaker as if awaiting the next item on the agenda.

"You could've done more had you stuck around," yelled another. "Why do you bother coming around now? Thing's have changed, you know."

When the speaker did not retake the floor as he had hoped, the oldest and newest member stood up and looked around him. It was a more aggressive bunch than he remembered, more aggressive and impatient it seemed to him, and he wondered while surveying the room whether he had done the right thing in returning. The crowd now grew silent for the first time that night, and Seelin addressed them slowly and cautiously.

"I haven't come back to lead you or anybody," he began in a mottled voice, then cleared his throat and continued. "I've only returned to do whatever I can to help gain our freedom, that's all."

"We've heard you have inside knowledge of the Hives, that you used to be one of them," a younger voice yelled out.

"Yes, that's true. But my knowledge is old and useless now. You know more than I do about them at this point." He paused, then added "I'm not sorry I left, but I know some of you may resent me for that. If I were stronger I might have stayed on and fought, but I wasn't. Nothing can change what's already done, but I'm here to help out as much as possible now." He retook his seat, and this time the current charge spoke to return the meeting to more important issues.

"I'm afraid I have some bad news," he said loudly and purposefully. "The prisoner who was captured only last week did not survive the first phase of withdrawal." This news was greeted with sighs of exasperation from those few present who had not already been informed. "I'm afraid we chose badly once again."

"How old was this one, do we know?" asked Jask.

"Said he was forty-eight, but might have been lying to throw us off. Frankly, I don't think it matters much as long as they're below a hundred and fifty or so."

"This is the third failure we've had in the last two months," complained a woman from the back of the room. "We need to choose more carefully; we need to review all previous data and figure out what the risk factors are."

"We've gone over the data endlessly," answered the Charge. "But even though there may be biological risk factors, there aren't any that we can pre-determine and select. At least nothing that has shown up yet."

"How are the other three doing?"

"They appear to be safely into the third month, and their development is almost complete, but Jospin doesn't believe we've reconditioned them fully yet. He's having doubts that any of the conversions will stick."

"Then we need more, as many more as possible." It was the woman again. "A certain percentage will always live, and a certain percentage of those will convert. They're still our best hope for getting someone on the inside."

Seelin had vowed before the meeting to simply watch and learn, but he couldn't hold his tongue any longer. "There are other methods, you know. Are we absolutely sure that these kidnappings, or 'capturings' as you call them, are getting us anywhere closer to our goal?"

"Seelin, it's been a long time since raiding the fields and burning True-Food's transports stopped getting their attention. The stakes are a lot higher now."

"And do we keep raising them higher still? Do we respond to their kidnappings with our own? It's no wonder the few Naturalists left in the hives have lost any political clout they may have once had."

What would you have us do?" the woman retorted. "Make demands and wait for them to charitably leave us alone? This is a war and we've a right to use whatever means.."

"That's just it," another interrupted her. "We haven't even made it a war yet."

"And why should we? If we're no better than they, we may as well send our children off to the hives." Seelin searched the audience but found very few sympathetic faces.

"We'd all love to have the luxury of being self-righteous," argued the Charge to a wave of affirmation, "but this is not a time for pacifism. They're stealing our children, and if that's not enough to go to war over, then nothing is."

Seelin sat wordless, unsure of how to respond, unsure even of what he really believed. He knew the arguments, knew that they were right, but something in him also kept searching for another way.

"I agree with Maricia," the Charge now continued. "We need more prisoners. It's vital for us to get at least a few more on the inside to even consider the next step. Gerrod, you have a target and a plan already worked out, don't you?"

A short man, balding but with a jet-black beard, stood up. "I've been ready to go for some time now . But I need one other to make it work."

"Why not the pacifist, then?" came a suggestion from the front, and this was greeted by a few enthusiastic confirmations but also with some objections.

"Not unless he agrees," said the Charge. "I won't have anyone risk their lives for us unless they know full well what they're doing."

"What do you say, then, Seelin? How far are you willing to come with us?"

As the crowd quieted to hear his response, he could think only of Mistissa running through the woods, hiding in trees and jumping mischievously into his path, then laughing and running to hide once again. Only days before, he had abandoned the safe nest he had tended for them both over the last five years; now he was purposefully stepping into a fringe world of terrorists and kidnappers. The police needed no justification for firing their synthars; they would do so at the slightest provocation or mildest suspicion.

Jask now leaned over to his friend and whispered. "It's all right; they'll understand. You've only just rejoined and it's too early..."

"Gerrod," Seelin stood and spoke directly to his new accomplice, as if the rest of the group was not even there. "Let us meet tonight to discuss these plans of yours."

***

Gerrod turned out to be one of the more devoted members who had stuck with the group for many years, so he remembered Seelin well and smiled broadly when he and Jask came to visit him later on that evening.

"Seelin, my friend," he began, pulling up chairs for his visitors, "We're proud to have you return. You know, most everyone at the meeting today didn't know of you or knew only that you left us. Few of them have even heard of the things you did back then."

"I understand, and believe me they have every right to be upset," replied Seelin, rocking his chair back slightly.

"No, they don't," Jask now interjected. "No one has repeated things you were able to accomplish. Do you know that your rescue of Kylinter from the Great Hive remains the only successful rescue ever. Those who remember still tell stories of that."

Seelin laughed. "Those who remember? You make it seem as if I've been gone forever. It's only been five years, you know."

"Five years is a full generation for us," Gerrod added deliberately. "Most of the new volunteers don't realize how short their life expectancies have suddenly become."

Seelin sat forward and reached for his water tube stretched from the large bladder in the center of the table. For the first time he began to realize the anger of those at the meeting earlier on. His departure may very well have meant the deaths of several taking his place. The three of them sat in thought for a minute, then Seelin pushed the conversation forward. "What are these plans of yours, Gerrod? What's state of the art for kidnapping forever children these days anyway?"

Gerrod pulled at his beard and looked at Seelin. "We've been able to pick off some maintenance workers at Cambria Hive by hitting the transmission lines with synthars..."

"We have synthars of our own?" Seelin interrupted incredulously.

"Yes. Only three, and one of those is low, but we do have them."

Seelin looked at Jask and shook his head, but said nothing, so Gerrod continued. "Once they come out to repair the lines we've been able to nab one of them, but they're wise to us by now, and I think that approach needs a rest for awhile."

"So what else have we come up with?"

"The mines. Amazing what a kik-lift will do to the transpotter feeder tubes, and there's always a couple of poor souls trying to hang onto one of the lower levels who volunteer for assignment out there. They don't do a whole lot to protect them."

"Yea, except we've done that recently too," added Jask. "We need to keep mixing things up, throw something at them they haven't seen before."

"I know, and that's where my plan fits in nicely," said Gerrod. "Plus I think we have a better shot at a conversion." He paused momentarily, waiting for their silence to tell him to begin, then continued. "The plan is basically very simple. Next week it'll be time for the Minongin's yearly Naturalist ritual. Interrupting that and nabbing one or two of them shouldn't be too difficult." Gerrod smiled with the deviousness of his scheme and with the heated argument he knew was coming.

"Are you kidding?" Jask asked in a rising voice. "You're talking about capturing Naturalists; they're about the only friends we've got on the inside!"

"Just a fanatical sect of Naturalists, though. You know most of the Naturalists themselves think it's crazy for them to purposely leave the Hives on this yearly ritual of theirs."

"It's called Intella, and it's not crazy Gerrod. What's crazy is you're wanting to alienate our few friends. You're losing track of whose side you're on."

"Oh, we lose the momentum of all that progress that's been made recently," he replied sarcastically. "Don't tell me you're seriously expecting any real concessions from all that talk. It's pretty clear that the only way to get freedom from them is to make them so afraid of us they'll leave us alone, like they did when they first built those ridiculous hives. So what if we alienate them? What's so beautiful about this plan is not only are they relatively easy marks out there in the middle of the woods, juiced up on hormones and ZPD, but each one of them is already somewhat sympathetic to our cause. Conversion will be that much easier."

Jask was silent, angry with the thought of taking any action against Naturalists, but unable to argue the logic of it. As he pondered the idea, Seelin grabbed his food container and squeezed of a short ration into his mouth. When he had swallowed the paste, he turned to Gerrod. "Is that the thinking nowadays, that no political settlement is worth pursuing? I don't believe that. Personally I think we should be acting with an agreement in mind as the end goal. But I realize things have changed and I may not fully realize the nature of those changes. Right now, I'm willing to go along with the current direction the movement has chosen. And if we really have given up on a settlement, then this plan doesn't sound like such a bad idea."

"So you see, now. Maybe you can convince your friend."

"You do what you want," added Jask. "I'm not a party to this anyway. I'm only along for the ride. It's up to you two to decide."

Gerrod now looked at Seelin. "What do you think, friend?"

Seelin thought for a moment, then answered. "Let's run with it."

His accomplice now jumped from the table and laughed with delight. "This will be most fun, if we survive, of course. You know, I think we'll be giving some lucky Minongin what he or she secretly desires anyway, don't you think?"

***

It had not been easy for Seelin to spy on the strange going-ons of the Minongins all day from a hidden cover of olaliberry bushes a hundred yards uphill from a crude camp the naturalists had set up. Especially toward afternoon, when the morning ceremonies had finished and the small troupe of forty radicals first ingested their doses of hormones and broke off into amorous couples, Seelin had to keep reminding himself that these were indeed adults chasing each other naked through the woods. Toward evening, as things had started to quiet down and the two terrorists readied themselves for their night time raid, a forever boy and girl came splashing through the leaves directly toward them, causing Gerrod to animate the synthar in case they would be forced into a change of plan. But the forever girl stopped short about twenty yards away and stood on a mossy slope, looking back enticingly at her companion who followed closely behind. When he reached her, he took both her hands, then bent forward to kiss her lightly on the lips. She then stroked his back with her hands as the two of them became more and more excited. Seelin turned away, acutely embarrassed, as the two forever children passionately embraced and then fell to the forest floor to make furious physical love, several times in fact before they finally went off to rejoin the gathering down the hillside.

When they had finally left, Gerrod laughed quietly at his friend's embarrassment. "For someone who's been on the inside, you seem to have a hard time remembering they're older than we are," he chided his friend.

"That was a long time ago. I don't think I could ever get used to that. It's unnatural, is what it is. Two children doing that..."

"Not children, remember."

"OK, maybe not children, but child's bodies doing that together. It just doesn't seem right."

"I'll agree with you there, Seelin. But this is their one big day. They don't do it with that much passion the rest of the year, that's for sure."

"I thought the hormones were illegal."

"For just about everyone else. Banned because of the obvious danger in taking too much of them too often. The doses the Minongins use only give them the feeling of true maturity for a single day, with no lasting effects. They're considered such an extreme religious sect that use of the drugs has been permitted for them alone, and then only for this occasion. Of course, illegal use of the drugs continues inside the hives among a certain group."

"So what's next on their agenda? When do we make our move?"

"After dark, when most of them are stoned on ZPD. Are you sure you feel comfortable with me taking the synthar? We can still switch roles if you'd like."

"No. Better in the hands of someone who can use it." Seelin felt almost relieved that the movement would allow them use of only one of the weapons, unwilling to risk any more to a single mission.

"Remember," Gerrod cautioned him, "If I'm in danger but you have a shot at a clean capture, then leave me be. I won't come back for you either in the same situation. One of them for one of us is a good exchange right now." Seelin looked the other way, saying nothing, so Gerrod added "Don't worry. It won't come to that. We've a high chance of success with this one; the element of surprise is ours."

So they waited, as the lovelorn couples strayed slowly back to the gathering, and as the Minongins lit a huge bonfire and cooked the precious true food they had carried all the way from the hive. After the meal, the ZPD was administered through drinks passed between them, purposefully defying the usual precautions against transmission of germs. The raucous nature of the events earlier on now turned quiet and meditative. Conversations continued but among smaller and smaller groups, until most of the participants, although still quite alert and perceptive, sat looking into the bonfire, which was fed by one of the three guards who were also armed with synthars and who had not ingested any of the drugs.

Now that total darkness had fallen, Gerrod roused Seelin from his own stupor induced by the long hours spent waiting, and they carefully emerged from their thicket.

As planned, Seelin crept as quietly as possible to a small clearing visible from the camp below. On the way, he pointed out to himself the hiding spot they had scouted earlier: a clump of Bay trees growing together from a common trunk. When he had arrived at the clearing he waited a few minutes for Gerrod to situate himself, then removed a holographic projection mechanism from his pack. A quite small device, it's sender was naturally detached from the central commands of any of the hives, however it did have a limited memory of its own and the liberationists had been able to program about five minutes of visual and auditory display. Setting the device in the clearing, he looked one last time at the small figures below sitting contemplatively around a dim fire, then turned it full circle twice and replaced it on the ground. Immediately he ran quickly down the hillside toward the hiding spot, as a great sitting Buddha lifted into the cool night air and began to speak.

Meanwhile, Gerrod had positioned himself dangerously close to the encampment, hiding in the trees where he might be discovered at the slightest whim of a forever child to stray from the immediate circle they had formed. He located the guards as soon as he had settled in: three of them, all accounted for, standing at intervals outside the circle. The guards occasionally looked around as if watching for lions, but for the most part they seemed almost as lost in thought as those sitting around the bonfire, and Gerrod wondered hopefully whether they may have also indulged in a little ZPD. He was counting on the drug to impart a certain awe and mystery even to the most simple and obvious of holograms, and indeed as the first Minongins noticed the apparition they stood, pointed, and began wandering off in its direction.

The three guards now shouted quick orders to everyone to stay put, but the forever children remained entranced by a vision now drifting though the color spectrum as it called upon them to return to their homeland. Soon, one of the Minongins, apparently a leader, instructed the lead sentry, after which the three of them consulted amongst themselves, reluctantly agreeing to their orders. As

Gerrod had hoped, only one stayed behind as the other two accompanied the now growing number of forever children stepping into the dark forest, draping their long jala wraps behind them as they climbed slowly toward their own personal religious experiences. The few who did stop to consider the practical side of things and question this hologram sprouting from a mountainside all assumed that this was indeed part of the ceremony, that this was all planned as the culmination of this year's Intella gathering.

Once the camp was nearly empty, Gerrod had little difficulty aiming the synthar and firing it directly at the lone remaining guard while he sat looking around anxiously, knowing that a trap had been set. The poor fellow unfortunately stood just as the beam had been triggered, and the wave converged off target onto his pelvis, severing both legs immediately and eliciting a terror stricken scream before he lost consciousness. Gerrod now panicked; surely the scream would be heard up the hillside all the way to where the Minongins would now be converging. Nevertheless, he had no choice but to continue with the plan and steal up the slope behind them in search of the other two guards.

Until they heard the scream from below, the two forever children who had agreed reluctantly to forego their full Intella experience in the interest of protecting their fellow Minongins had been largely enjoying this little midnight romp, finding this bit of unexpected entertainment amusing even without benefit of the drugs. But when they heard the anguished death cry of their companion, their first suspicions were confirmed.

"Down there, quick! This is just a ruse," said one, turning around.

"Then let's split up. We can't leave the rest of them unprotected."

"No. That's what they're hoping for. Their plan is to split us up. C'mon, both of us together. Fire at whatever moves."

Now Gerrod stopped in his tracks, hearing the deliberate footsteps approaching but unable to see through the thick forest. Afraid to move, he stared intently ahead of him, hoping to pick out any movement from a forest no longer lit by a setting moon. He was lucky this time. In the distance he could barely distinguish two figures, ever so slightly illuminated by the faint firelight as they walked toward him blindly. Waiting patiently, Gerrod held still as long as he could before quickly setting the wave and firing at the closest figure. In the darkness, a purple glow could be seen infusing the guard's midsection before it disintegrated, collapsing his body inward in a quick death. Gerrod quickly retriggered in search of the second of his two intended victims, but the first beam had given his position away, and as he fired his synthar the remaining guard also fired. Both beams missed their targets, but crossed paths midway between them, exploding the two weapons in a flash of fire which ripped apart the hands of the two men holding them.

Screaming with agony, Gerrod took off through the woods, chased by a severely wounded Minongin half his size but running at full speed on pure adrenaline. As he raced between the trees, escaping toward that immensity of wilderness which would increasingly be his ally as he got further and further away, the rebel terrorist tripped twice on downed logs, and before he knew it the guard had caught him, tripping him once again and hitting him repeatedly as he tried to get up. Even with his wounded hand, Gerrod might have easily dispatched the smaller and weaker guard if a trailing group of eight additional forever children had not come upon him just as he was getting the upper hand in his fight with the guard. Pounced on from all directions, the surrounded terrorist now gave up resisting, and as he did so the eight forever children were joined by several others, who stood in a circle around him as if having captured a fox after a long hunt.

Seelin had been hiding in the safety of his spoke of Bay trees as the Minongins began to converge on the apparition, and was soon surrounded in the darkness by forever children feeling their way through the forest high on ZPD. Before any of them had actually reached the image, the hologram had faded, however, and most then switched direction and began sliding slowly back down the hillside. Seelin had been waiting for a solitary straggler he could easily overpower, and, when the screams were heard from below, almost all of the Minongins ran quickly to see what was going on, leaving only a few behind trailing more slowly. Seelin strained to see up the hillside to make sure there were still a few targets which hadn't yet crossed his hiding spot, and held himself achingly still as a threesome passed very close by.

Now he heard a much smaller rustling in the leaves approaching from the clearing. He shifted uncomfortably against the rough bark and tried to gather his courage for this act which felt so unnatural. All the field burnings and transpotter tube blasts had not prepared him for anything like kidnapping a forever child, and he wondered silently if this twisting feeling inside was going to spoil the mission, spoil his return to a more lethal and sophisticated liberation movement. He lifted his foot to make sure it was not asleep and to ready it for the leap forward, but in doing so he scraped it loudly against the tree, and the approaching crackle on the forest floor stopped for a moment, but then continued.

Seelin now suddenly felt the strength to go forward, to carry out the plan, and, instead of waiting for the footsteps to reach their closest approach, he jumped headlong into the shadowy woods and raced at full speed toward the figure he could now see taking off frantically down the hill. In only a few seconds he had overcome the small figure and placed a hand across it's mouth to keep it quiet while he drew a tiny round, sharp object which appeared very much like an old thumbtack and pressed it against a flailing arm. Over the course of thirty seconds the flailing and kicking slowed and then stopped altogether. Now he cradled the limp body in his large arms and tipped the head back gently to see who it was he had so efficiently subdued. It turned out to be a little forever girl who looked no older or less innocent than his own Mistissa.

The forest was quiet around him; apparently no one had noticed the attack, but louder sounds were now coming from down the hillside, large crashes through the undergrowth and occasional screams as a general wave of noise surged from right to left in the distance. He remembered Gerrod's instructions to meet him at the rendezvous spot if they were separated and to not under any circumstances give up a sure capture for the sake of either of their safeties. He sat for a moment to rest and to consider his options. His accomplice had apparently been successful in neutralizing the Minongin's synthars; if not he surely would have seen at least one of them by now. And if that was the case, and Gerrod had lived through it, he would have made his way up the hill toward the rendezvous spot by now. Seelin looked once again at the forever girl he had draped on the leaf carpeted ground beside him, then, leaving her sleeping quietly, lifted himself up and began walking quickly and much too noisily toward a growing rumble of voices which had by now settled onto a single location not too far from the Minongin encampment.

It was not a well thought out rescue plan, but what it lacked in strategy it more than made up for in adrenaline and surprise. When he had found his accomplice surrounded by at least thirty amused and somewhat frightened forever children staring at Gerrod as if he were a monster they never really believed in but now had mistakenly captured, Seelin knew that he would have to act quickly and dramatically. So he raced headlong, screaming and yelling and waving his arms frantically for maximum effect, toward the circle. This by itself was successful at scattering at least half of them who were already nervous enough and just waiting for some reason to hightail it as quick as they could back to camp. When he reached the remaining Minongins who stood fast but nevertheless backed away at his kamikaze approach, Seelin grabbed a forever boy and clasped his forearm around the boy's neck, dragging him along yelling wild threats that he would break the boy's neck in an instant if everyone didn't just back away nicely. In reality, Seelin had no idea how to break a neck, and would never have been able to make good on this threat if the Minongins had called his bluff, but, with two guards dead and all of their synthars disabled, no one was in much of a mood to put up any more resistance. As it was, some of the forever children had already begun to wonder what they would do with this creature they had trapped. So in less than a minute Seelin was able to clear enough of a path for him and Gerrod to escape the circle and make it twenty yards into the forest before he dropped his hostage and the two of them took off running toward home.

They ran as fast and as far as they could before stopping to rest, despite the fact that none of the forever children had given chase, and had made it a good mile into the woods before Gerrod collapsed against a large rock and Seelin gratefully followed suit.

"Why did you come back?" Gerrod panted, gasping for air in huge desperate breaths. "Weren't you able to get one?"

"Almost," replied Seelin. "Chased one down and was getting close, but she climbed a damn tree like a little monkey. Couldn't climb like her, couldn't catch her."

"Shit...I can't believe you didn't have pick of the litter; they should've been all over the place."

"They were. But in groups too large. I screwed up, Gerrod, but I'll make it up next time."

"You're going to have to, my friend. We lost a synthar and got nothing in return. They're not going to be happy about this." He leaned over and put his hands on his knees. "It's going to be up to us to figure out a way to snatch one without a synthar, cause they're not going to give us another one, that's for sure. And we still have our promise to keep, you know."

"I know." Seelin looked back into the forest and paused to listen intently for any Minongins who might be having second thoughts about letting them go without a chase, then added "Don't worry, I'll think of something. We'll make good on this mission one way or another."

8

Fighting his way through a driving winter rainstorm, Kianno of Forshas picked up his frantic pace and squinted into the wind as rain now turned to biting chunks of ice and snow. Visibility was immediately decreased to near zero, but he kept running nonetheless, nimbly hurtling his lithe, eighty pound body around trees seen only at the last minute as the roars of a mountain lion twice his size continued to chase him down from behind. Now a large boulder jumped up at him, and before he could dodge it Kianno stumbled and fell, through the rock and onto a patch of wet grass on the other side. The forever boy pushed himself up off the spongy rubber and looked behind him as a huge lion rose up in the snow and pounced directly upon him, disappearing from sight as soon as the animal tore into his arm.

"Once more," yelled Kianno through the pine trees sagging with newly fallen snow. "Play again, now." But as he stood expectantly in the driving blizzard, nothing but the wind could be heard, so he called again.

"End visuals," he yelled, and immediately the surrounding field unveiled itself as a large room, darkened around the perimeter, with a floor consisting of a soft rubber fully- multidirectional treadmill which instantly responded to pressure applied in any direction. Snow, sprayed and frozen from tightly packed pipes running invisibly through the ceiling, continued to fall, picked up and blown through the room by massive blowers also hidden in all four corners of the chamber.

Kianno looked around him, puzzled at the apparent malfunction. He was a handsome forever boy, with sandy hair and brown eyes shaded with a seriousness slightly out of place above the slight nose and red cheeks frozen in the characterless features of childhood. Although he had changed his first name back to Kianno of his own accord once he'd reached legal age, in appearance he was indistinguishable from the boy who had first entered this great hive thirty long years ago, having completed his first full body skin resurfacing only two years earlier.

"Freeze treader," he commanded, and instantly the floor fixed itself. Kianno then began to walk over to the far side of the room, but before he arrived he was greeted by a girl who had entered the chamber and ran quickly to greet him.

"Kianno, are you crazy? Snow? In only your sara robe?" she asked, now joining him at his side, shivering and hurrying him along toward the exit. She looked at him with striking blue eyes, framed with strawberry blond hair spilling down over her shoulders, which were draped in a light, green silk sara.

"I'm doing a hillside program, of our own nearby mountains," he replied a bit defensively. "In midwinter the rain can turn to snow at the higher altitudes."

"Yea, but they didn't go out in spinza saras either, I bet." She put her arm around him and drew him close for warmth as they approached the exit panels at the far end of the room, then passed between them into the weatherscoper control center. One wall of the center was entirely covered with a huge real time pictorial of the earth, as reconstructed from sensors placed at each of the participating hives. Computer imagery then extrapolated to render a picture of the current global weather patterns, a picture which by necessity was a better indicator of what might possibly be going on rather than an accurate portrayal of the current weather around the globe. Since the last satellite had fallen from the sky almost two hundred years ago, this method was the best available for capturing weather data, strictly for the amusement of forever children like Kianno.

Grateful for the warmth of the control center, Zhrana led her friend to one of several pillowed recliner benches placed in the middle of the room for monitoring the screens. After collapsing into the cushions, Kianno shrugged slightly from Zhrana's arm draped over his shoulder and pointed to the North America plate pictorial.

"Looks like a front moving in from the Gulf of Alaska; we may get an even colder storm in here day after tomorrow." Now he reached for a small laser pointing device lying on an adjacent table, pointed it into the middle of a large comma of clouds situated off the Oregon coast, then pressed a small button at the base of the device. Immediately the point flashed in red and at the same time another screen showing the interior of the chamber itself turned black, then a few seconds later lit up again, this time showing an ocean scene of huge swells driven by sixty mile an hour winds and driving rain.

"Still rain, but it may switch over when it hits land," Kianno commented, then stood as if to investigate the chamber once more, but Zhrana grabbed his hand and pulled him in the other direction.

"C'mon," she implored, "You're not going back in there."

"I just want to see the waves; this one is the biggest of the season..."

"So what? If you want waves, just point to Cape Horn." she replied, successful in her attempts to drag him away from the panels. Her keepers had initiated her a little later than Kianno, so she was a good two inches taller and ten pounds heavier than he was. This was one of the rare occasions when she used it to her advantage. When he reluctantly gave in and accompanied her away from the chamber, she added "Can we do the Bahamas tomorrow?"

"I suppose for a little while. That's so boring, though, and besides I've used up both our slots for this week. We'd have to negotiate."

Outside the weatherscoper the couple entered a long hallway which had once been inlaid with shiny faux marble but which had long since gone out of style and so had been replaced with soft cloth coverings in pastel colors, coverings which themselves were starting to look old and dated. As they walked, Zhrana took hold of Kianno's hand and they swung their arms lightly together.

"We should hurry. You'll need to change out of that spinza before the readings."

"We don't need to go to the readings tonight; they'll do just fine without us," he answered in a sigh. "Besides, I've got to study. I was thinking of going by the quarantine area and seeing if any unusual cases have shown up."

"Are you really still thinking of entering in infectious diseases?" she asked, squeezing his hand a bit tighter.

"It's the most important field right now."

"And the most dangerous," she said, with a touch of respect hiding in her voice. No one entered in infectious diseases; it was a practice usually reserved for the elders who took it up only when they could already see the first signs of terminal disease creeping toward them. "Will they let you?"

"Of course. Why shouldn't they?" he answered in a bothered tone. "You're not going to start after me like Jaslo, are you?"

"No, Kia. I think it's amazing that you're even considering it. But you could still start in death-prevention, then later on..."

"Later on, later on. I've already spent twenty-five years in medical school. You'd think they'd let me actually treat a patient by now."

"You've only got another five years of final studies Then in your residency you'll get your chance."

They had entered the slider by now and stood while the vehicle picked up speed. Within the past couple of years, acceleration tampering waves had been installed in all horizontal sliders, and Kianno was still getting used to the idea of standing and walking casually without any thought about breaking his fall as the slider accelerated and decelerated across the hive. The tampering waves locked onto each passenger independently and allowed only minimal movement during times of acceleration. It was a peculiar sensation; regardless of whether you were standing still, sitting, or walking about, the tamper would let you sway slightly but then catch you before any additional movement in the accelerated direction was possible. As the acceleration decreased, the wave would then gradually restore full freedom of movement again.

When the two of them had reached GGG2354, Kianno went quickly to his own room to change, while Zhrana went ahead to the reading which had already begun. The Saturday poetry reading was the biggest event of the week for the family and the culmination of the week's work for most of the family members, who worked on these poems full time for twenty hours a week. But Kianno had other things on his mind right now, and instead of joining the rest in the Unit Room, he remained behind in his room and opened up the visuals. Searching the medical references, he pointed to "Psychiatric Disturbances and their Treatment", and waited while a figure of an elder forever child seated calmly in a chair appeared in the visuals spot of his room. The elder was reading a thick journal when Kianno interrupted him.

"Excuse me," began the forever boy tentatively, "I have some questions about an illness I may have."

"Yes?" The elder looked up from his journal but did not yet lay it down. "You've come to the right address for that. What illness do you suppose you might have?"

"Ennui," he replied.

"Well, that's a very serious condition. What makes you think you suffer from ennui? After all, it's perfectly normal to experience a little transient boredom from time to time."

"No this is more than that. Even things I used to find interesting I find boring now." Kianno walked through the holograph to his food cabinet and reached for a phial of sea water juice.

"For instance?"

"Well, I'm missing the readings right now, as we speak."

Now the elder put down his journal and turned to look at Kianno. "What other symptoms have you noticed?"

"I'm tired of my medical studies. Even though I'm only in the twenty-fifth year, I'm ready to graduate and I'm bored with the exams and learning parties. Only ten years ago I couldn't wait for each one."

"Hmmm," the elder answered. He took off his glasses and rubbed his forehead. "Has your sleep been affected? Have you been sleeping your full twelve to fifteen hours every night?"

"Yes, closer to fifteen."

"And what about you midday sleep? Has that been affected?"

"I've been taking a longer and longer midday sleep. The only thing that continues to excite me these days is the weatherscoper. Do you think I'm sick, doctor?"

"Yes. You have most of the major symptoms of major ennui syndrome. It's surprising you waited this long to get help. How come you haven't referenced me before this?"

"I don't know. I suppose I figured there's nothing much that can be done, anyway."

"A lot of people think that. But ennui is a very treatable disease. I'll arrange it so that your next regulator infusions be of the Regulator Ex type. You should notice an effect two to three weeks after the switch. Please consult me again in about a month to confirm the effectiveness of this treatment. Are there any other questions you would like to ask?"

"No," answered Kianno, not entirely satisfied. "That's all, thank you." As the projection faded, he got up from his chair and started toward the door. Missing an entire reading would put him in hot water with most of the family members, and might even be a punishable offense depending upon what excuse he might be able to come up with. Before he reached the door, however, he stopped short and turned to face the visual spot once again. Even though he had referenced this same information many times before, he brought up the addresses from time to time anyway, since the database was continually refreshed.

"History reference, year 2315," said a pleasant looking red headed forever girl. "What specific information can I retrieve for you?"

"The earthquake of July, San Jose area. Major death zones, please."

"Primary death zone within civilized society was in Cambria Hive, southeast quadrants of levels 0-19. Collapse due to antiquated inferior construction resulted in over 10,000 citizen deaths. Other major structural failures included north edge of Great Hive, structural failure of rows 235 and 236: 6,500 citizen deaths. Also..."

"Please recount all death incidents in Lexington and Old Los Gatos areas."

"Only very few citizen deaths due to low population. Fourteen deaths from mine cave in, Umunhum Sand mine; twelve deaths in transpotter tube separation, Lexington area..."

Kianno stood now and walked back and forth nervously through the room. This was new, had not been included in previous searches he had conducted.

"Please detail names of dead for transpotter accident," he instructed the holo-gram.

"Unavailable. I'm sorry but the information has not been released."

"Ages, then."

"Ages of all victims were nine to eleven."

"Were all bodies retrieved?" he asked, growing ever more excited but strangely afraid at the same time.

"No bodies were recovered. None were retrievable following subsequent collapse of spotter car in aftershock."

"And how soon after the initial quake did the aftershock occur?"

"It is unknown which aftershock may have caused collapse. Major aftershocks occurred at 23, 34, and 57 hours post-quake."

Kianno stood still while pondering this latest information. Twelve nine to eleven year olds; that had to be the accident that had claimed Seelin of Forshas. For years he had been searching, knowing his predecessor was dead, but mor-bidly curious as to the circumstances, trying to reconstruct the events of that hazy time. Now finally some hard information to go on.

"When did this data of the transpotter incident become available?" he asked.

"Information lock-out expired three days ago and was not renewed," came the reply.

Now Kianno waited, thought deeply to himself, then presented the next question slowly and in a soft voice. "Please relate non-citizen death incidents, Lexington area." Perhaps if this information had also been locked out...

"Large death incident due to collapse of surveillance wall. No details avail-able." It was the same answer he had received for the last twenty years. If anything had been locked out then it was still locked out. Kianno switched off the visuals and walked slowly out the door, thinking he might still catch enough of the Readings to avoid having to come up with a lengthy explanation.

He entered the Unit Room from one of the balcony access doors, hoping to avoid attention, but he had come in between readings, and upon hearing the access panels slide open, all eyes turned up to follow him as he took a seat overlooking the affair. Apparently the reading before had been particularly thought provoking, and so the group was spending some time meditating before proceeding to the next poem. When the eyes had all turned away again, Kianno scanned the audience, hoping that the readings were nearly completed.

"Our next script is by Sofia. Sofia, will you please come forward?" announced the moderator in a small, shy voice, but there was no immediate response so he repeated the call. "Sofia, would you please like to read now?" Several members of the gathering looked about them in search for the missing Sofia and a few started small conversations. After a few minutes, the moderator spotted Kianno and addressed him.

"Kianno, perhaps you might know where Sofia might be?"

"No, I'm afraid your guess is as good as my own," Kianno lied, secretly concerned now that she had not made it back in time and would undoubtedly be questioned as to her whereabouts.

"Then we will proceed with the next poem. Safrili, you have a script for us, I believe?"

Now a beautiful forever girl with brown hair woven with bright red cloth and bundled atop her head approached the center of the room. She stood still for a moment, allowing the room to prepare itself, then began.

tree flowing,
speed of slider off to the east,
gather near,
gather far.

Zina in her full robes,
slide cloth over cloth,
gather near,
gather far...

Kianno sat back into the silky cushions and waited patiently as the room pondered this first of her seven scripts, anxious now whether Sofia had run into any trouble and what she would tell the family watcher once she returned.

***

"Atascin has confirmed there has been an increase in unlawful kidnappings of outsiders, both children and adults," announced a small, chubby forever child with quite a serious expression, to a small group of Naturalists assembled covertly in his room deep within Cambria hive. The group consisted of only six members of the executive committee, and the meeting had been called to discuss information leaked to them from the Naturalists' highest placed sympathizer: His Eminence Public Senator Atascin.

"Has he been able to confirm rumors of new experiments using them as subjects?"

"No. I specifically asked him that and he wouldn't comment, even to myself. I think it's safe to say that something along those lines is going on, but he can't risk a leak, even to us."

"I have my own reasons to believe these rumors that brain transplantation methods are finally being perfected," added Sofia. She stood now and fixed her dark eyes on her associates. Her features, also unchanged in the past thirty years, were strikingly and coincidentally similar to Kianno's, a fact which had always seemed to her to cast a certain divine sanction over their unspoken arrangement. The same darkly serious eyes, sandy brown hair (although she wore hers braided with red cloth in the latest fashion), and narrow nose which disappeared into just a hint of a bridge between the eyes. Her dark brows, however, turned slightly downward on the inside from too many frowns, and the corners of her mouth as well betrayed an expression more often of concern than of levity. Now her face gravitated naturally into that look of apprehension as she continued addressing the group.

"This latest medical technique poses the biggest threat ever to the outsiders and their quest for their freedom." She spoke softly but intently. "We can be sure the state will never legalize the use of a citizen's body for transplant purposes. Just the fact that the procedure is being considered at all suggests that they have outsiders in mind."

"That's impossible," objected another member. "Even the conservatives would never go to that extreme."

"I wouldn't be so sure," added Atascin's aide. "The Senator has told me that if ever we needed to cash in any favors or try to mount an all out public opinion campaign, now is the time. He's obviously concerned about upcoming propositions."

"Which are?" questioned Sofia.

"Full repeal of the rights act of 2310. Basically reverting all outsiders' status to criminal with no rights whatsoever."

"Surely that can't have any support at all except among the conservatives," exclaimed Sofia, alarmed that this was even being considered.

"It wouldn't, unless it was the price to pay for a new body when terminal disease is coming near."

"We need to get support, to draw the old coalition together again," Sofia argued, already thinking ahead to plans for canvassing the lower levels where most of their support lay.

"It's not such a good time for that, either, with news of the Minongin episode racing around the hives," contributed another forever girl who had been silent so far.

"That was an anomaly; the work of an extreme terrorist group."

"But as long as they continue their activities, it's going to be uphill trying to convince the State that they're worthy of greater freedoms. It's going to be hard enough just keeping the ones they have already."

"All right. Enough for now," concluded Atascin's aide. "Sofia, you said you needed to be getting along. Why don't you leave now and we'll plan the next meeting and inform you via messenger."

"I do need to go." She looked around her as if others had already detected her absence and had come looking for her, "In the meantime, I'll inform the keys at the Great Hive and we'll start putting out feelers among the lower levels to see how strong our support may be after this Minongin episode." She took hold of her sack in one hand, and with the other arm reached out to hug her associates, who returned the gesture tentatively. Although they were in political accordance with each other, socially they still felt uncomfortable with her ancient gestures as well as her talk of "mothers" and "daughters" and such. It was a liability, in their mind, which might brand them all as crazy in the eyes of their targeted constituents. But they tolerated it well enough within the confines of their own covert executive meetings. After she had hurried away toward the spotter sublevel, however, they talked amongst themselves whether perhaps her lifestyle was likely to cost them more votes than her savvy and experience might gain them.

**

Later that evening, Kianno stopped by Sofia's room and found her reclining in a sleeping cot reviewing notes from the meeting on a private channel of her visuals. When Kianno announced his presence, she quickly blanked the image and called for his entrance.

"I was worried when you didn't show for the readings," he began, sitting cross-legged on the floor mat. "What did Rokyo say?"

"Oh, the usual. Don't be concerned with him," she replied, sitting up and welcoming with a smile the sight of an unexpected visit by her only son. "He wants me to be moderator next week to make sure I give the readings their due importance."

"And he suspects nothing?"

Sofia hesitated before answering. Although she knew he was aware of her involvement, she had always kept him innocent of any details for his own protection. "No, I was only visiting with friends and had lost track of the hour, that's all," she finally said, but much too softly to be convincing.

"Mother, I know where you were. And if I know then it's not going to be too hard for Rokyo to find out if he really wants to." He spread his feet out in front of him and leaned back on the palms of his hands, looking up at her. "I know a lot more than you think, and I'm tired of pretending otherwise."

Sofia got up from her cot and began walking toward the exit panels, but caught herself midway and turned around to face Kianno once again. His tone of voice frightened her; it revealed a dangerous frankness which she had thus far been so successful at avoiding. "I know, I know," she started, "I've wanted to tell you everything myself but there are those very close to us who..."

"You mean Jaslo," he interrupted.

"Jaslo has done everything for us. He's been with us every step of the way."

"He's been with us, but he still doesn't know of your involvement. And if he did..."

"You wouldn't!" she uttered, surprised that he would bring such a threat.

"No, of course not. But if you're not more careful he'll find out as well."

"I'm more careful with him than you. I know where your sympathies lie."

"How do you know? How?" he responded in a voice tinged now with anger. "You may have presumed all this time, but how would you know?" Now he as well pushed himself up from the pad and looked across the room into her eyes.

"I'm sorry, but it is dangerous enough with just myself. With both of us..." She returned his gaze for the briefest of moments, then looked away again.

For the first time now he understood why she had been hiding this from him. For nothing more than strategic reasons. That such a purpose and rationale even existed he somehow found immensely comforting after so many years of being blinded to this simple possibility by his own false presumptions. He relaxed and leaned against the fabric covered wall.

"I really never knew you were so interested," she added. "If you are, I'm sure there's some way you can help out."

"I'm not sure...that's what I want," he stammered. "I'm not sure now." A long silence followed, during which the sleeping chimes could be heard sounding through the entire quadrant. A quiet slipped into the room and softened the borders of their conversation.

"Mother," he said it once more, filling her heart with a word she had not heard in years, "I need to know about who I am, about who was here before me."

"No, please.." she tried, sliding slowly to the ground, but he continued nonetheless.

"I've lived for too long not knowing. In the beginning I didn't want to know, I just wanted not to lose what you'd given me, not to lose anything more than

I'd already lost. But that's not enough any more. I need to find out everything. I can't keep living this lie!" Immediately he wanted to take it back, never meant to say it in the first place, but there it was and it had cut deep, as deeply into himself as into the woman who now began to cry at his feet. He crouched down and put his arm around her shoulders, not knowing what to say next, searching for anything which might erase the awful words.

"I'm sorry, you know I didn't mean that," he started, but their obviousness only accentuated the poison they tried to dilute. "I only need to find out more, if not from you than some other way..."

"I wish there was more I could tell you," she said at last, in a surprisingly even tone, "I don't know myself the answers to the questions you have."

"Was it the transpotter accident?"

"Yes," she answered, recalling that horrible day. "He was looking at me, waiting for my help and I couldn't help him." Her tears now broke out uncontrollably and she instinctually buried her face in her arms to hide the noise.

"So he was still alive in the spotter car?" he probed, wanting to stop but knowing it would be even harder later on.

"Yes," she sobbed. "His eyes followed me away. His eyes followed me..." She hid once again in her tent of sadness and he did his best to drape it with the comfort of his touch, knowing that whatever more there was to learn he would need to find out for himself.

9

"C'mon, I'll show you. There's a whole register with old monster visuals; some even show them naked making sex with each other," laughed Zhrana's friend Jil, as the two forever girls entered the privacy of Zhrana's room.

"Where did you find them?"

"Register 45J8RTH. I don't think anyone visits there often because there's no guide or set up, just the visuals themselves. Some of them are really gross!"

Zhrana dialed in the address as the two of them settled back on her bed to watch. Immediately a tall woman dressed in flowing red silks walked through the canyons of a large ancient city, abandoned except for herself. The silks were draped lightly and sparingly over her full body.

"Look!" gasped Jil. "Look how huge she is, and fat all over. It's so gross!"

Zhrana, eyes as well fixed at the sight, but more serious than her friend, didn't reply, but instead watched silently as the woman was approached by a tall man, also beyond the threshold by ten or fifteen years. The woman now stopped and looked slowly at the man's chest and upper body, which were exposed to the waist.

"Sicko," Jill squealed, then laughed nervously once again. She looked to her friend for some agreement, but Zhrana was not laughing. As the man reached out to gently caress the breasts of the woman, through the red silk which slowly fell away, Zhrana watched intently, utterly absorbed and fascinated. The size of the two of them, the fullness and definition carved into their bodies, the slow passion which gathered between them, so unlike the quick amusement of the sexmaking she had known.

"Let's switch. This is really sickening," said Jil, getting up from the bed, but Zhrana refused to relinquish controls, absorbed in the intensity, the overpowering physicality of these monsters' sex, stroking her own thigh absent mindedly as she watched the woman tear at the pants of the man, her full and smooth bottom rising up so large yet soft as a forever girl's, his hairy roughness unlike anything she had ever seen aside from the visuals, his command and mastery of the woman and their sex unlike anything she had imagined.

"Zhrana? Zhrana will you admit me?" The portal call startled her back into the room. Kianno's voice. Quickly she voided the visual and admitted his entrance. Jil scampered about with quite a guilty look on her face and tried in vain to suppress a smirk as Kianno walked quickly into the chamber.

"Zhrana, I'm sorry. I didn't know you had company," he began.

"It's no matter," Jil interjected. "I was leaving anyway." She looked back at her friend with a mischievous glance, but Zhrana was all business by now, seeing her to the exit with an efficient stride.

"How are you, dearest Zhrana," said Kianno, joining hands and kissing her forehead, which she returned with a lingering kiss on the lips which took him by surprise. He walked to a bench recessed into a far corner and sat down, followed by Zhrana who sat close enough to touch thighs.

"I need to talk with you," he measured out in a serious tone, but then paused as she took his hand and placed it on her thigh, then reached her other hand to caress the back of his neck, smoothing the lap of his hair onto his skin.

"Zhrana, what..." He ducked under her caresses.

"Don't you want to play?" She continued rubbing his hand over her thigh, while slipping her other hand down his neck onto his shoulders. But he was in no mood to respond.

"Dearest, not now. I have something to tell you."

"Oh c'mon; a little play won't take so long." Now she stilled her wandering hands and sat up straight. "Kianno, if I could get some of the Q drugs, would you take them with me?"

"You're joking, right? Just because I'm not in the mood?"

"No. I'm not joking. I know where we could get some. It might make things more...interesting, you know what I mean?"

"No. I don't think so, Zhrana. They're illegal; we could be pushed down two entire levels if we're caught." He looked at her incredulously. "Besides, they're dangerous and unnatural."

"They're not so dangerous. I've heard they've been formulated to act quickly then disintegrate entirely within twelve hours, so there's not enough time to cause any permanent effects. I was thinking for our sexmaking..."

"No. I'm really surprised you would even consider such a thing." He got up and paced back in forth, agitated at her suggestion. "Of course, if you feel like you need to try them, I'm sure there are plenty of others who'd be willing."

"Kianno, you know I'm fixed with you right now. I don't want that to stop. It was just an idea, that's all." She hurried to switch topics, knowing he wouldn't necessarily agree even to the idea of being fixed to each other. "What is it you wanted to tell me?"

"Zhrana, I'm going to share something with you but you have to promise not to tell anyone."

"Of course."

Now he sat down again beside her and took her hand. "You know how we've talked about where I came from, and how I assumed Seelin of Forsha's spot in this family?"

"Yes," she replied, growing uncomfortable herself now.

"Well, I can't go on any longer not knowing more about that place I came from. I need to find out what it's like there, whether the real Seelin of Forshas may still be alive, whether my parents may still be alive..."

"But Kianno, you've said many times how foolish it is for Sofia to carry on ideas of parents; why should you care now?"

"Because they're my own. You wouldn't know. No one would know because no one else even knows who their parents are. But they were more than that to me." He choked back the rising sensation in the back of his throat. Despite their years, tears came quickly to forever children. "I need to do what I should have done thirty years ago, and that is to find out for sure."

"Can I help you, then? I know of several search addresses which might be able to tell you something."

"No. I've tried everything available on this side. I need to go over to the outside, undercover in the guise of an outsider child to research this among the only people who might still remember."

Zhrana pondered this for a moment, then responded. "And you thought I was crazy for wanting to take the Q drugs. Kianno, of all the dangerous ideas you've pursued, this is by far the most unnecessary and risky. You can hire anyone on the first two levels to investigate this for you."

"I need to do this myself. Apparently you don't understand."

She didn't reply right away, instead squeezed the hand which she had been holding and brought it to her lips. Then she said "I think I do understand, Kia. I wish you could leave it alone and move forward with your life. But I've noticed this growing in you each year, and until you find some answer..." She didn't finish her sentence because she was again thinking of them together, and where the years may take them. "You'll contact me, though, each day and let me know where you are and that you're safe."

"Of course. I'm counting on you as the only one in the family who will know. Even Sofia cannot know..."

"Yes yes." Zhrana leaned forward excitedly. "Now tell me what your plan is."

***

"Public Senator Atascin, please. I need to see him right away."

The short, chubby, but well dressed forever child guarding the portal to His Eminence's private offices looked curiously at the unfamiliar citizen who had so brashly approached someone of his stature.

"How were you allowed into the quadrant?" asked the aide, Xyloru of Jobash, but did not allow time for a response before proceeding to his next question. "Who are you to be asking me to announce you to his Highest Eminence?"

"My name is Kianno of Forshas, and I come on a matter of great importance." When his name failed to elicit the expected response, he added "I am intimately familiar with the activities of my sibling and former keeper, Sofia of Forshas."

Now Xyloru turned and called into a long hallway behind him. "Cryo, please come and watch the portal for a few minutes. I have some business to attend to." Then he ushered Kianno quickly down the hallway and into a private, sparsely decorated room.

"What is it you want, then. If you are one of her keys, then this is a most inane and senseless act you've taken by coming here!"

"I'm not involved with her, or with your activities," Kianno replied calmly. "And I have no particular reason that your involvement should become known, either." He pulled a small tube from his sara. "May I ingest?"

"Please," the aide responded nervously.

"But I do need a favor, and I was thinking perhaps you might be able to help me."

"We won't be blackmailed, if that's what you're thinking."

Kianno let out a small laugh and squeezed some nutty meat paste into his mouth. "I have nothing of the kind in mind. I only need one very small favor and that will be the end of it." The aide did not respond, so he continued. "I need an outsider pass, with open re-entry privileges, that's all."

Xyloru gave him a quizzical glance. "What would you want such a pass for?"

"That is of no consequence to you. Simply authorize the permit and I'll be on my way. I know you have the authority to do so."

"Perhaps, but there are always people who look into such things. I can't issue it without a reason."

"I've already given you as much reason as you should ever need."

Now Xyloru crossed his arms over his black velvet executive sara and thought for a moment before answering. "I'll authorize the permit, but only in exchange for some information you'll gather for us on the outside."

Kianno licked his fingers before replacing the tip of the food tube. "Go on," he replied, curiously.

"I don't know how much Sofia has told you, but we have plans to question some of the more recent relocations. The petitions will be submitted by others within our ranks, of course, but we need testimony as to the actual conditions and situations from which the children were removed. It's possible, with such direct testimony, that the state will be cautious enough to approve the petitions and reinstate the outsider children. You can help us by gathering this information and then testifying as to what you have seen."

"I see no reason for cooperating to such an extent..."

"In return we can provide one of them to accompany you. Whatever your purpose, if you try to cross over by yourself you'll be rooted out. You must have known this."

Kianno had indeed considered this, but had resigned himself to the heightened risks after the old priest had turned down his plea for assistance. Still, the offer seemed curious. "If you need this information, why not just send the giant by himself? What do you need me for?"

"Surely you can see that the testimony of a giant, a monster outside of polite society, would not mean much to the state, especially one as low as level two."

"All right," Kianno replied. "I'll gather some information as you instruct. But I plan to be in the Lexington, old Los Gatos area, and will not venture all over the district for your purposes."

"That is acceptable; we have three relocations from Lexington which we may petition. Come, let me program you and then I'll fill you in on the details."

The aide then led Kianno to a local station for reprogramming. It was a relatively simple device consisting of a small cuff which was placed around the wrist, along with a control panel several feet removed from the cuff. Xyloru entered the information into the control panel quickly, then asked the forever boy to place his wrist into the cuff. After twisting his arm slightly to align the commander device embedded deeply inside Kianno's wrist with the signal generators in the cuff, the aide pressed one final button to send the authorization into the commander unit.

"I do not have authority to permit an unlimited re-entry," the aide cautioned as they returned to the private room. "I was only able to grant you a ninety day window. I trust that will be sufficient."

"More than sufficient, thank you," came the reply. "I'm not planning to be out there for more than a week at the most."

"Good. Because I won't be in any position to help if you should exceed the window. That would be most unfortunate." Xyloru then waved his arm and pulled up a file on his private visual line to begin the relocation briefings, while Kianno did his best to appear as if he was paying attention.

***

It floated by Mistissa and her playmate like a leaf carried on a breeze, drawing both girls' attention away from their simple game of skip-twig: a small toy spaceship floating gently through the air, hovering before them for a moment, then skipping along just out of their reach as they ran after it. Running from the opposite direction and carrying the controls for the elaborate toy came a small boy dressed in threadbare primitive clothing- shorts and a faded cotton shirt, ripped down the side.

"What is it?" exclaimed Mistissa, after the boy had stopped to catch his breath and the spaceship had floated to a soft landing in the dirt road.

"Isn't it neat? I found it three days ago in the waste site."

"Can you make it go wherever you want?" asked Mistissa's friend.

"Yea. It can go so high in the air you can't even see it. Look!" At this the boy directed the ship in a vertical rise high into the endless blue sky until it disappeared completely from sight. "C'mon, let's run to meet it; I'll make it come down over by that tower!"

He ran off in the direction of an old communications tower, both girls following his quick steps. As they approached the tower, Mistissa's friend pointed skyward at the ship returning to earth. Now the boy stopped and blurted out "Spaceship Zefter returning from planetary voyage to the Cretu galaxy." Then they watched entranced as landing pads extended from the ship and red flames shot from the lower jets to cushion the perfect three-point landing.

"That is so neat," gushed Mistissa's friend, but Mistissa herself was wary at the sudden display.

"How come it still has power if you found it at the waste site?" she asked suspiciously, looking carefully at the boy for any signs he might be somehow different from them.

"I don't know. Just lucky I guess. C'mon, let's land it in front of an adult and see what happens!" He got up again, but the wary girl didn't follow this time.

"You're not a forever boy, are you?" she asked, eyeing him questionably.

"Oh yea, right, like I'm a thousand years old really!" he laughed, then ran off again. After her friend had jumped up and ran after the boy, Mistissa slowly concluded it was OK after all and sped to catch up with the two of them.

Meanwhile, only a hundred yards away, Paula Orillo had been watching the new boy's introduction into their play group very carefully. Forever children too often made the mistake of bringing shiny new toys to play with, but she had been around too long to let this go by without further investigation. Seelin had left her and Jask to care for Mistissa while he was recharging his account, and she was not going to let any threat go unrecognized.

"Mistissa!" she called out. "Mistissa come here a moment, will you?"

"Is that your daughter?" asked a pale balding man of about fifty who had approached Paula from behind.

Startled, she looked up and answered. "No, just in my charge, is all."

"It seems my son has found a couple of new playmates," he continued, taking the liberty of seating himself next to her on the broken concrete steps.

"Oh," she uttered, too surprised to know what to say, yet somehow relieved now to know the boy had a father. After a pause, she found her voice. "My name is Paula Orillo. I don't believe I've seen you before."

"Robbo Hispin, and that is my son, Kianno," he replied. "We've just arrived from the northern district. We've been on the move, trying to stay one step ahead of them."

Paula saw Mistissa look back in response to her call, but she could not repeat it now, so the girls continued their play uninterrupted. She turned to the stranger. "Are you in trouble of some kind?"

"Only trouble that comes from the state and their relocation policies. There have been too many up north and so we've come this way hoping things aren't as closely watched down here."

"Well, I'm afraid things are bad everywhere right now. If I were you, I wouldn't let him out of your sight, and I'd take him deep into the woods with as much food as you can afford. We'd do the same, except..." she stopped herself. He may not be a watcher but he certainly wasn't to be trusted yet.

"I need to find out as much as I can about this area and the relocations, if I decide that we should settle here. Can I come by later to talk with you some more?"

Paula hesitated. Instinct told her to say no, but she felt a moral obligation to help a newcomer. "We live in this building here, in the rooms at the very back. Why don't you come after dark, when Jask will be here as well."

"Thank-you. We'll be going now, to find someplace to rest for tonight. Thank you so much for your help." He stood and squinted against the sunlight. "Kianno! Kianno! We've got to be leaving now!"

"Yes father," the boy yelled back obediently. "I'll be right there, father."

***

Later that evening, when the two of them had buried themselves in the far corner rooms of an abandoned old mansion, Kianno activated the visuals and dialed in his required appointment with Xyloru. The image found the aide preparing his horse and saddle for an evening game of polo in the sportscoper.

"Oh, Kianno. So glad you were able to check in on time. Just getting my saddle ready, you know." He put down the stirrup he'd been adjusting. "Have you any information about the first of our subjects- Nicoli Orilla I believe is her name."

"Yes. We've both been able to speak with her parents and observe their living conditions, as well as talk a little about the circumstances surrounding her removal. Sounds to me like they may have violated a few rights laws during the course of her trial."

"Really? That would be an unexpected bonus, if we could prove that."

"There's no way you're going to prove that, but we can fill you in on the details we've come across. That may help." Kianno then went on to recount the incidents of the day, as well as their lengthy discussions with Paula and Jask. Toward the end of their conversations, the aide wrapped up the briefing with a reconfirmation of the arrangement, just to be sure there was no misunderstanding.

"I'll capture these details in the visuals bank, so as to refresh your memory before your testimony." Xiloru reminded the forever boy.

"What do you mean? This is my testimony," answered Kianno with as convincing a sense of confusion as he could muster.

"No, I mean the testimony before the committee."

"I agreed only to give testimony to you, sir. Speaking before the committee would endanger my position and my future. Surely you never expected me to jeopardize my standing simply to help one of you pet projects."

"That was not our agreement, and you know it full well," the aide replied loudly, clenching the stirrups of his saddle in anger.

"I have provided you with valuable information, and I'll continue these nightly debriefings. You can't accuse me of not having helped your cause." Kianno felt an unwelcome stare from above as his accomplice began to appreciate the situation. "You asked for my help in gathering information and I am providing it," he concluded.

"Such information is useless without your direct testimony!" raged Xyloru, pacing back and forth in a rising agitation. "You'll regret it should you go back on your word."

"And you'll have no basis for taking any action when I return. What will you tell the officials, that I failed to carry out your secret plan to return relocated citizens to the outside? That would be an interesting accusation."

The aide began to answer, but Kianno switched off the visuals before any more might confuse his accomplice into questioning whether the terms of his assignment might be changed somehow. It would be the last time Kianno kept his appointment with Atascin's aide, although he would continue to make private entries into the visuals bank to preserve information he would uncover, both for himself and for the naturalist sympathizers, whom he would have liked to have helped further if only there could have been some more anonymous means of giving testimony.

***

That it should have changed so little in the years when everything else had changed so much seemed inconceivable to Kianno as he approached the old hacienda. The same overrun ancient swimming pool, now filled nearly level with dirt and covered with thick underbrush; the same wrought iron fence surrounding the same pool house, slumping against the pull of time and gravity but retaining the red tiled Spanish character which still stuck in his memory from that fateful day; the same heavy wooden entry door, just as tall and just as imposing as when they had first arrived some thirty years ago, holding itself intact in the thin California air which preserved until eternity the dry and the lifeless. It was as if he had stepped alone into his own memories, stripped only of the very ones who had driven those memories into being in the first place.

As he stood now on the doorstep, by himself for the first time in the two days he had stolen under the assumption of a new persona, the sound of gulls in a background of wind, twenty miles lost from their green ocean, swelled and retreated like fire matches struck brightly before fading into a black night. He strained for any announcement of life from the timeless manor, holding himself still in expectation of voices coming from within, but there were only the sounds of the gulls and the wind sifting through a tangle of poison oak which had overtaken the land and crowded onto the top of the tile roof overhead.

"Hello," he called out, only loud enough to be heard within a range he felt certain to be unoccupied, just to fulfill the decency of a warning. He could not understand why such a reasonably complete structure would go uninhabited, and, despite the lack of any response to his cry, it was with a shaky and reluctant hand that he pushed the huge oak door forward and slowly rotated it back into the dark room. Stepping inside, he found himself tucked into the same blackness he had first felt alongside his parents and their friend so many years ago, a darkness which carefully hid her guests from the brilliance and danger of the day outside.

"Jorge?" he said more quietly, but frightening himself nonetheless with his own voice. "Jorge? Is anyone here?" The edge of the beam of light intruding into the room from the doorway played at the legs of a wooden table and a single chair visible on this side of the darkness. Dirt and animal droppings unevenly coated the floor, and a broken water cup lay next to one of the carved legs, cracked into pieces still sharp enough to reflect the intruding sunlight. From a far corner he could now distinctly hear the tiny sounds of an animal scurrying for shelter, and for a moment Kianno entertained the notion of turning and leaving what lay beyond to the darkness which had claimed it, but then reminded himself that he would never again have a second chance to step into that darkness.

Holding himself steady with a hand upon the table, he probed small steps forward into the unseen, thinking that he remembered a window around the corner, and, with eyes slowly adjusting to the room, noticed for the first time the hint of outlines falling from that direction. As he passed by the table, however, his foot casually bumped the leg of another chair and immediately a loud, harsh clattering attacked the stillness and sent his breath back into his lungs. The forever boy froze with the noise, then quickly began stumbling in a panic toward a blanketed window, knocking over unknown furniture and falling several times, reaching out each time to break his fall with hands which found the old abandoned nests of insects and rodents. Finally, he reached the cover of thick carpet which leaked small trickles of light from the edges where it had been nailed fast to the frame, then grasped the fabric with both hands and ripped frantically. The nails pulled easily from the rotting cloth and the carpet fell in a gush of air, sending clouds of dirt and dust swirling in the sunlight which now bathed the entire room. Stepping his way cautiously back toward the door, coughing and choking in the dust, Kianno almost overlooked the catalyst of the moment's commotion.

Lying at the foot of a fallen wooden chair, hands still clutching a smoking pipe, lay a human skeleton collapsed into a pile of bones thinly held together by friction alone, the muscles and tendons having been entirely eaten away or decomposed. Only the head retained vestiges of dried, recessed flesh and hair, matted and frozen in the parched blackness in which it had been buried. Even still, Kianno could recognize the face of Jorge looking up at him.

Now he took off at full speed, out the door and into the tangled yard guarding the entrance, tearing along as fast as he could move his legs away from the pool house. Not bothering to look up beyond his next few steps, he never noticed the giant standing directly in his path, and ran headlong into the ungiving legs and torso of a man three times his size. He looked up with the expression of a child who has just found a real life ghost in his closet after checking only to reassure himself that there really were no such things.

"Hold on there now, boy. Settle down." The balding man with a full, dark beard looked down at the panicky child. "Looks like you've seen a ghost or something."

Kianno nodded and tried to speak but words wouldn't come yet, so the man continued. "You living back here in this place?"

"No," the boy managed to answer, his mind still racing.

"Where're your parents, anyway?"

"In the fields. I was just...exploring, that's all." Kianno tried to squirm away, but the man held a firm grasp on his upper arm. "There's a dead man in there!" he now exclaimed, trying his best to sound as childishly afraid as possible.

Gerrod seemed unamused. "Yea, so what?" He tried to get a good look at the boy's eyes, but Kianno was careful to look away. "Who's Jorge?" he asked.

"I don't know," the boy lied much too quickly and then immediately regretted it. The man must have heard him call the name only moments earlier. He quickly tried to cover up his blunder. "Jorge's my imaginary friend, that's all."

Gerrod searched the perimeter of the fence for any nearby signs of life as he paused to calculate his best approach. It was quite unusual for a watcher to work without any back up at all. If only he had a scanner he could assure himself of no hidden synthar.

"That's funny," Gerrod said slowly, still not fully decided but plunging forward nonetheless. "I seem to recall a Jorge who lived here quite a few years ago, long before you were born." He paused, then added "I would expect." When the boy refused to give him any sign, he continued. "You know, if you're looking for something I may be able to help you. But you'll have to drop the disguise." He looked at the shorts and ripped t shirt. "I mean, really, we may have old ways but I'd like to think we dress our kids a little smarter than that."

"Everything we say and do is being monitored," Kianno said quickly, eager to drop the pretense as well. "If you try anything you'll be found and killed along with any family you might have."

Without a scanner to tell for sure, Gerrod could not dispute this. "Don't worry. I'm not any danger to you. I might actually be able to help, you know, as long as...there might be a little something in it for me."

"I need information. Did you know Jorge, then?"

"I only have vague memories from when I was a child. He was old even in those days."

"Do the names Geryl and Sylvi Tonnar mean anything to you? Maybe you remember them as well, or maybe you know them now?"

Gerrod pulled at his beard and thought for a moment. "No. Sorry, those names don't ring any bell."

"What about Seelin, Seelin of Forshas?"

This time it was the man who did his best to avert his eyes. Without too much delay, which might also have given him away, he replied as evenly as he could. "No. I'm afraid I haven't heard of anyone by that name either. But I can find these things out. We have history archives, you know, which would most likely contain the information you're looking for. I'm a little surprised you don't already know about them."

"Archives?" Kianno stepped back as Gerrod released his grip. "I need to see these archives. Take me to them right now."

The man looked down and chuckled. "It's not so easy as that. We keep records, but they're scattered about. There's no central library, if that's what you're thinking. People only keep what's meaningful to them." He paused to let the boy ponder this, then added "However, if you tell me what you're after, I can ask around and see what I can come up with. For the right price, of course."

"And what would that be?"

"Five months of sublevel 5 credit, which you can arrange after I provide you with whatever information I find."

The boy shifted his feet impatiently and swatted at a fly on his shoulder. "Only if the news you bring is definitive, and substantiated."

"I can't prove anything, if that's what you want. The past is gone and…"

"I'll know if what you're telling me is the truth," Kianno interrupted, in a hurry to finish up the negotiations. "Find out everything you can about Geryl and Sylvi Tonnar, known to have been living in this area thirty years ago, as well as Seelin of Forshas, a citizen who was involved in a transpotter accident at the time of the great earthquake. I need confirmation that there were no survivors, or information about his whereabouts if he did survive. Meet me back at this spot tomorrow, same time."

"This is too dangerous for me, to risk being seen with you. We need to meet at night. Come to the lower city park tomorrow night. That way my talking with you won't arouse any suspicion."

"I warn you, don't try anything. I'll be watched the entire time, and you have already been scanned. If anything should happen to me, like I said before…"

"Yea, I heard. Be there at eight hours. Wander around a little and wait for me to approach."

Kianno considered the risk. It was unlikely that a random stranger would try anything. Considering that on any given day there were at least three or four watchers in the area, it was hard to feel as if he were putting himself into too much danger. Besides, it was beginning to look like it was either this or return empty handed. "I'll be there," he replied, then turned on the balls of his feet and ran full speed out of the yard and into the comfort and relative safety of a street populated with just enough of a crowd for him to disappear into.

***

"I don't understand, doctor. She's grown almost a full half an inch in the two months since her initiation. There must be something wrong with the regulators you're providing."

"Hmmm. We've had her on Cemathin X3, and I've yet to see a patient who doesn't respond fully to that formulation." The doctor, a red haired forever girl with a high forehead covered with freckles, puzzled over the situation for a moment, then continued. "It is possible, of course, that she could be allergic to the medication, and that the reaction could be affecting the potency of the drug. Are you absolutely sure she's been receiving the full dose daily?"

"Of course. Really, doctor, if I wasn't sure of that I wouldn't be wasting both of our time here."

"Because I've got to tell you, in most of these cases it turns out that the child has been corrupted by glamorous fantasies of life beyond the threshold. Either that, or they suffer from ennui or depression and refuse the regulators out of a pathological desire to leave the family behind and start a new life.

The keeper was clearly indignant at these suggestions. "I do not expect such treatment from doctors at this level," she replied. "If you don't take this case seriously, I will be forced to deliver a complaint."

"As you wish," the doctor now conceded. "I'll switch her to a different brand, but I would consider long term injections if she continues to grow."

"Thank you," the keeper replied curtly. "I'm sure with the proper regulator formula that won't be a problem." Following the doctor's lead, she now got up and exited the small office, then the two of them walked the short distance to a room down the hallway where young Nicoli of Grishams had been nervously awaiting their return.

"Everything's going to be just fine," the keeper immediately assured her child. "The doctor informs me that you may be allergic to the type of regulator you've been taking. So she's agreed to make a switch. There's nothing at all to worry about, sweetest." She looked expectantly at the girl, but received only a solemn stare in response. "Isn't that right, doctor?"

"That could be it, perhaps." The forever girl looked across at her patient, reclining slightly while suspended in the examination beam, and searched for any visible signs of rebelliousness or mental disturbance. "I'll need to administer one dose of the new formula at this time, to assure there aren't any immediate side effects." She placed one small capsule in the beam. "It's nutty flavored, so you may ingest it as you would your previous regulators." Then she grabbed hold of the forever girl and abruptly took her aside. "Your keeper and I need to finish some business. We'll be right back."

Before the forever girl could utter an exclamation of surprise, the doctor had hustled her into an adjacent room with a one way glass through to the examination room. Both girls then quieted and watched curiously while Nicoli pushed the red capsule playfully about the beam. She flicked the capsule casually with her middle finger and watched as it bounced off the edge of the beam and flew back at her. Looking around suspiciously, she then pinched the pill between her fingers and placed it into her mouth, chewing contentedly while floating herself up and down the beam.

Now the keeper smiled and turned to gloat at the puzzled doctor, who could only sigh and dig her hands deeply into her pockets. "Maybe you're right, after all," she said at last. "Make sure she doesn't miss any days, and bring her back in one month, sooner should you notice any growth whatsoever. This is a most critical time. If we can't find an effective formula soon, all may be lost."

"I trust you won't allow that to happen, doctor, for all of our sakes," was the cold reply. Then she walked quickly back into the examination room and watched while the beam slowly dissolved in response to the doctor's instructions, releasing Nicoli from it's magical suspension.

Before leaving the medical chambers, the young girl excused herself to use the bathroom, and when she rejoined her keeper several minutes later, no notice whatsoever was paid to a small red smear well hidden at the lower border of her dark blue sara.

10

They had always hoped and expected to die natural deaths, but when the baby was lost almost a full year ago the two of them realized self sacrifice would be the only way to keep their daughter, Fari, alive for a few more years at least. Now Grissel and his wife Jenette stood before the large crowd gathered to watch them give up their lives, with a fear which overpowered the emotions he so wanted to feel at that moment. He'd always imagined an experience of such sadness, of regret for himself but most of all for Jenette, as well as pride for giving to their daughter all that they had left. But now, standing before the still inattentive crowd which shifted and murmured while waiting for them to get on with it, he could feel nothing but an overwhelming physical sense of fear and horror at what himself and his wife were about to experience.

Only a year ago, it had appeared as if they might have avoided such an increasingly common fate, what with Fari's account secured by the state at a level high enough to feed them all for at least the time until her child was ready for transfer. But a terrible virus had descended on the family, sending them all down for two whole weeks and pulling the life from Fari's only child. Since then, they had struggled to sustain themselves on what little work they could find, resorting in the last months to daring raids of others' food caches and desperate pleas to what friends they had left. In the last three months they had wasted away at an alarming rate; both himself and his wife had dropped more than thirty pounds from frames which never had had a whole lot to spare in the first place. Indeed, they would have never consented to such an undignified death if it hadn't meant the survival of their daughter, and if death had not been staring them in the face anyway.

As a forever child in colorful robes stepped forward to present them both with their survival suits (quite a misnomer it occurred to him), Grissel found his mind wandering through the day's events which had led up to this. First the morning meal, compliments of Life After Death, Inc., a full old fashioned breakfast of true food with real strawberries and apricots along with the eggs which he had tasted for the first time. He had only been able to eat one of the eggs and a few strawberries, his stomach and system were so unprepared for such abundance, and poor Jenette hadn't been able to keep any of it down at all. They had tried to save the remainder for Fari, pleading with the company officials that it was their meal and that they were entitled to allow their daughter her first taste of true food, but the businesslike employees had only whisked the valuable fruit away; clearly it had already been allocated as a perk to some especially productive forever child.

"Remove your clothing please," they were now instructed, as the crowd began to silence somewhat in response to the start of the proceedings. Already disappointed that the clear tank had not been set up, most were still intrigued at the methods which might be used this time. Being unpaying visitors, who were encouraged nonetheless for the excitement and tension they contributed to the mind set of the subject vicarians, they were never told ahead of time what the methods might be.

"Do we need to undress right here?" the graying man inquired, seeing the puzzlement and embarrassment on the face of his wife.

"The official thought for a moment, then responded. "Yes. It is required that the entire proceedings be public."

"Grissel looked at his wife with eyes which told her to bear through it, it will soon be over. Then he stepped across the short distance separating them and began to help her off with her sara, a move which was laughed at by many of the more callous in the crowd, but he continued to help her anyway, both of them staring resolutely down at the wooden planks of the vicario platform.

After recovering from their last meal, both had been led to the administrative re-allocation office, where Fari awaited them.

"Please, I ask you one last time. Don't go through with this," she had begged them. "I would rather have us die together, rather have you with me for another few weeks than live without you for another couple of years." She leaned forward as Grissel quietly placed his wrist in the reprogrammer, and sighed with a panicky exasperation. "One last time. You need to believe me!"

But the two of them only did their best to deny her pleas. In the end maybe she was right, Grissel thought as he finished unsashing his wife's long drapes and looked at the back and shoulders he had come to know so well. Perhaps they really were doing this for themselves; such torture it would be to have to watch their daughter die slowly of starvation. Maybe they really were doing this out of their own selfishness, as their daughter had accused.

When they had removed all their clothes and stood naked before a crowd growing impatient and excited with curiosity, another Life After Death official approached them. He wore the white head banner of a doctor, and he carried with him an injection gun. It contained ZPSD, a stimulating agent which enhanced all sensation. It was critical that both of them experience the following events with the utmost sensitivity, and the ZPSD assured this. Silently, for it was difficult to offer much reassurance at this point, the doctor beckoned them to sit, one after the other, in a chair which had been positioned just for this purpose. Each in turn then received their injections, feeling nothing but the mildest sting as the powerful but slow acting drug entered their bloodstreams. They would be over five thousand feet high before the effects would fully take hold.

Fari, still crying and desolate, had accompanied her parents from the reprogramming room to the implant center, the only surgical room outside the hives, set up at great cost to LAD Inc. expressly for the purpose of preparing vicarian subjects for the productions, which in the past few years had become more and more popular and were now staged several times a week. Despite the detailed explanation of the procedure he had been given, Grissel had still opted for complete anesthesia, even though any complications leading to death prior to the show would void the agreement and leave Fari penniless. He couldn't bring himself to witness the implantation of twelve tiny wave sensor/transmitters into strategically located points in his brain. The devices had been designed to detect brain wave patterns as he experienced the ultimate adventure of death itself, and, in real time, send his very thoughts, feelings, emotions, and sensations, back to hundreds of well paying viewers scattered through the topmost levels of the local hives. Thousands more would pay a lesser fee for the recorded experience. Each viewer, then, had his or her own custom designed vicario-helmet, which received the transmissions and redirected them perfectly to recreate the exact wave patterns within the viewer's own brain, superimposing these sensations upon existing electrical patterns. Of course, implanting the transmitters directly in the brain, which was necessary only for the subject, caused the slow burning of surrounding tissues, resulting in certain death within fifteen minutes from the time they were activated.

Yes, they had explained the details quite clearly, although in truth Grissel wished they hadn't told them a thing. The only element of today's activity they did not reveal was the death mode. It was essential to the goal of maximizing their surprise and terror that this not be unveiled beforehand, although Grissel had heard stories of the most popular modes, and had even wandered in curiously to view one such display several months ago. Drowning in the clear tank was one of the most popular for the outsider crowd, however the paying customers were not quite as happy with the mode. "Short but very intense" had been the conclusion of most reviewers, and after several such drownings in a row, LAD Inc. pushed up it's ongoing efforts of searching for another unique, lengthy, interesting, and terror filled mode.

Now, feeling only the smallest quiver and tingling of coolness brushing his skin, a pre-effect of the ZPSD, the old man, who had pushed the envelope at any rate by living to the advanced age of forty-eight, was helped into his survival suit. The suit itself was a one piece full body outfit which would offer as much protection as possible for about ten minutes, or up to about fifty thousand feet above the earth, but also contained the hypercompressed helium/Argon gas which, when activated, would propel the two of them on separate journeys to the edges of space before the extreme elements overcame the suit, and the transmitters burned enough tissue to cause them to mercifully lose consciousness.

Now, as he struggled with the trivial challenge of fitting the awkward suit around his naked body, the overwhelming fear strangely subsided and he looked across to those eyes which had seen his life along with him, the eyes which had greeted him every day for thirty years and had deepened with age into doors to a home as necessary to life as earth itself. And the crowd which had so embarrassed him faded away. And the rewards of their sacrifice faded away. And even their beautiful daughter Fari with the golden hair and the puzzled expression faded slowly into nothingness. Only those eyes he saw, returning his love long after they had disappeared behind the stiffness of the suit which now hid them. Only those eyes, the eyes which had first smiled up at him thirty long years ago when he had seen such a lovely girl peering out her window at the young man walking by. Only those eyes as he ascended slowly at first, then in a rush hurtled breathtakingly toward the sun. Only those eyes as he left his earth behind for the last time.

***

As the crowd began to thin, disappointed that today's show had denied them a look at the final seconds, a small forever boy, still overly disguised, tried to push his way through the towering and overbearing throng. This was a ridiculous plan, he thought, there is no way we're going to be able to find each other in all of this, but he searched frantically nonetheless for the man with the heavy beard he had run into the previous day. Of course, he was unaware at that point that he had been tracked for close to half an hour by no less than four Liberationists, scouting in vain for any accomplices who might be working with the boy. They knew already of the one posing as his father, and had been able to scan him quite easily and without suspicion in a pass-by before the start of the production. The fact that this man had been clean of any synthars or monitoring devices had surprised the group, and had caused them to consider aborting the kidnap; after all, no watcher would dare go into such a situation without some kind of protection. That meant either the devices they were up against had become more sophisticated than their scanners, or the 'father' was really only a decoy and another was hidden nearby as the real protection.

Now that the crowd was breaking up, however, it was time to either take action or abandon the plan altogether. The two primaries in the kidnap, Gerrod and Seelin, eyed the boy from a distance and discussed their options.

"I tell you, he's a fool. We should just nab him and be done with it," Gerrod was saying, but this was greeted only by Seelin's continuing cautious expression.

"Can we follow him for awhile, just to be sure he's not working with anyone else?"

"Yes, but we'll lose the cover here. Right now we can drop him and carry him away like a sack of dirt and no one would see a thing. I say we go on with it, and now."

"No," answered Seelin. "I don't like the feel of this. It doesn't make sense that he should be so totally unprepared."

"He was yesterday, I'm sure of it. There's something different about this one. He's not working like any of the watchers I've ever seen." Gerrod began walking toward the forever boy, but his companion pulled him back abruptly.

"No. Bring him out of this crowd. That way we can tell for sure if anyone else is involved. I'll be waiting at the end of Mazonas Trail; I'll have the others stop any followers, and if he's alone we'll drop him there."

"All right," replied Gerrod, relieved that at least they were going through with it, "Give me ten minutes." And with that he took off at a brisk pace, now having lost sight of the boy but still zeroed in on his location.

Kianno was almost ready to give up and retreat back to the shelter he'd found when a heavy hand fell onto his shoulder.

"Well, my friend, it appears as if you've come after all," began the bearded man, looking down at the boy who now turned his head with a start.

"Of course," he answered, then immediately assumed his disguise once again, acutely aware of being surrounded by outsiders. "Father, the show was good, wasn't it?"

"No, actually it was one of the worst in memory." Gerrod laughed at the games the boy was playing, then began walking toward a small group of buildings at the edge of the clearing. "I have the information you've been looking for," he continued, leading Kianno along. "There is one who knows of Seelin of Forshas, has seen him even."

"So he's alive," exclaimed Kianno, then he hesitated before adding "I don't need to see him directly, if that's what you thought. I only need information, that's all."

"And that is what my friend brings. He can even arrange a meeting, although it sounds like you don't want one after all."

"Perhaps," the forever boy responded, confused at the suddenness of the proposition. "Wait! Where are we going?" he asked now, stopping abruptly.

"Why, to meet my friend, of course. Didn't I explain that already?"

"No." Kianno watched impatiently as the man continued toward the edge of the gathering. "Wait, I said!" But when Gerrod maintained his stride without even the slightest hesitation the boy was forced to run to catch up.

"Why do you need to know about this Seelin of Forshas, and about the Tonnars, anyway?" asked Gerrod when the boy had regained his side.

"That is my business alone." Kianno looked back over his shoulder for the giant as they now left the safety of the crowd behind and started down a wide, rocky trail unevenly lined with oak trees. From the corner of his eye he spotted his only friend on this side of the world, and noticed with relief that the accomplice was following him at a distance. "Does this friend of yours have information about the Tonnars as well?"

"Yes," Gerrod replied a bit too quickly, hearing the falseness in his own voice.

"That's fortunate, then," answered the forever boy. He sensed as well the deception, yet continued on regardless. It was as if he were falling ever faster into a chasm he had been sliding toward for so long that he almost welcomed the opportunity to finish the final drop. The scent of Bay and Pine blew down from the higher ridges; like a powerful drug it brought back the feel of his true boyhood, his days of escaping the watchfulness of his parents and exploring the hidden faces of these mountains. Listening to the birds scatter overhead and the calls of distant cats, he felt strangely alive now like he hadn't since those days so long ago, and drank the fresh air blindly and thirstily. So absorbed in the wild sounds and smells of the darkened wilderness was Kianno that he never even noticed the muffled cry coming from farther back down the trail.

It really was not a fair contest for the poor man charged with watching over the forever child he secretly despised. Surrounded by three men stronger than him, he had no time to react before they had jumped him from the underbrush, kicking and beating him with stones and rods they had brought with them. If he had been given a synthar perhaps he might have had one small chance to get off a beam before he was rendered helpless, but he had been denied the one weapon Xyloru had consented to give them, not trusted to use it for the boy's protection instead of his own.

When he had been beaten nearly speechless, one of the rebels called out for the rest to stop.

"Wait." It was Jask who spoke. "Before he dies he will know by whom and for what reason!" The man panted with the exhaustion of the night and the anger for a lost child. He waited as the rest backed away from the slowly turning and moaning body. "You die so no more of our children will be taken from us. For every one of you we kill, seven of our sons and daughters live." He started to kick one more time at the side of the fallen man, but held back and turned to walk away instead.

"But your children," the man spoke to those who would unknowingly kill the one who had risked his life on their behalf, "Your children, I..."

"Silence him," Jask commanded, hardened with anger. "He can say his peace to the devil!" And with that they set upon him with one last vicious attack which did indeed silence the unknown accomplice. Then they left him lying in the trail to go and see what Gerrod had waiting for them.

***

"He should be here by now," Gerrod said as they reached the meeting spot, trying to fill the long silence which had overtaken them for the last half mile. He stopped and looked around intently, despite the fact that the trail ended and no other directions but the one they had come from were visible in the moonlight.

Kianno, however, was content with the silence, and did not respond, so Gerrod spoke once again. "How would you know of Seelin, anyway?"

The forever boy only turned his back on the man and walked slowly to the forest's edge to peer into the dimly spotted thicket. There was that edge of darkness one more time, drawing him closer.

"Is it his family you're after, then," persisted Gerrod.

The boy waited for a moment, then answered softly. "Is that what you think? That I'm after him or his family? Why can't you believe me when I tell you I only want to find out the truth?"

"Because the only reason your kind have to leave the hives is to take our children. You have a thousand pretenses but only one real objective." The rebel felt free to open up with the stranger a little more, confident now that he had no route of escape. All by himself, with Seelin listening only steps away, it was like taking candy from a baby.

"Enough of this!" Kianno suddenly called out, "Your friend is not here, evidently, and I do not intend to wait all night. If you want your reward, find me at the dead man's mansion tomorrow afternoon. Otherwise I'll look elsewhere." He began walking quickly back down the trail.

If Gerrod had better sensed his opportunities, he would have quickly grabbed onto the forever boy's wrists when they had first arrived at the scene, immediately immobilizing him from recovering any weapon he may have hidden. But Kianno's quick move away to the side of the road had occurred before he had had the opportunity to take advantage of his unsuspected proximity. Now, with the boy retreating further and further away from the spot where Seelin was supposed to grab him, Gerrod had no choice but to give full chase and try to overpower and subdue him. As soon as he began his sprint toward the now running figure speeding across the trail illuminated with only the sparest fragments of moonlight, Seelin emerged immediately to join in the pursuit.

As quick as Kianno was, he still was no match for the two men gaining on him with every step, and as they rounded a bend, Gerrod knew he should nearly have caught up, but instead was suddenly dumbstruck by the absence of any visible movement from up ahead. Pulling up abruptly and searching desperately for any sign of the boy, Gerrod had just started to turn around to call out to his friend when the beam found him and removed his head in a glow of blue light, leaving a voice trailing off into the woods as his body crumbled down onto the rocky path.

In another instant, before Kianno could even comprehend the amazing terror he had created with a single squeeze of the synthar, the full force of Seelin's acceleration slammed into the boy and knocked him sprawling head over heels, his weapon flying unseen into the leaves and branches. He tried to look up, and reached his arms out instinctually to protect himself, but before he could even see the face of his assailant he felt a sharp blow to his head and crossed over at last into the darkness which had been tempting him for so long.

11

It wasn't until the third day of his captivity that Kianno saw the face of his captors, and by that time the pain had accelerated from what had started as a dull ache in a few of his joints into a raging fire spreading from his bones into the muscles of his arms and legs. Until then, he had seen nothing and no one, save the small tubes of manufactured food which had been thrown in from time to time to pay lip service to his growing hunger. It was a hunger which was unknown to him, a hunger which far outstripped anything attributable to his reduced rations, a hunger which added to the pain in his bones to set him writhing through wave after wave of agony until he was weak with the exhaustion of having fought through it for so long.

On the third day, however, the door to his small room opened and a large stranger entered. The stranger looked across at the boy sitting in a far corner, knees brought up and head between his legs, and smiled with the relief he knew he had to offer.

"I've brought you something for the pain," he began, as Kianno eyed him warily from a distance. Now the man approached slowly. "It will alleviate your distress for a little while anyway."

"What are you poisoning me with? The air, the food? Why not just kill me outright?" Kianno replied.

"Oh, be assured that we aren't poisoning you at all. Rather, we're finally letting nature take its course. And, unfortunately, after having been artificially held at bay for so long, nature has a way of wanting to make up for lost time." The man, who now stood directly over the boy, pulled an injection gun from the pack he carried in his other hand. "And you can also be assured that we have no intention of killing you. Quite the opposite, you'll be of no use to us dead, which is why I need to take a blood sample to verify you're not actually close to the danger zone."

Now another powerful wave of pain and nausea swept over the boy, and he gripped his legs with anguish. "Then take your blood, I don't care. But please, can you make me sleep, I only want to sleep." He rocked back and forth and tears came to his eyes.

So much like children they remained, thought Zobert, as he crouched down to aid the pitiful boy. Acting quickly since he knew first weekers were still very unpredictable, he injected him with a precious dose of a pain killer/sedative combination, then held the boy's arm out and carefully drew a vial of dark purple blood. Too intense a withdrawal from the regulators could cause a rebound reaction which involved a rate of growth at the bone ends so rapid that clots could escape the growth sites and lodge in the brain, heart, or lungs, killing the subject instantly. By examining the blood at various intervals in the process, the rebel doctor could determine if small amounts of the regulators would need to be administered to slow the rebound.

"I'm afraid sleep is not something I can guarantee, but this should give you a break for awhile. Enjoy it while you can."

Kianno slumped against the softening wall as the drug swam through his body, loosening it, drifting it just far enough away from him that he could view its sensations as something rather curious and annoying once again. He started to say thank you to the departing man, but stopped himself, barely remembering that it was them who had caused this suffering in the first place. Just before the door closed once again, he heard a voice call out to him. "How does it feel to grow again, Kianno, like the rest of us? How does it feel to finally leave your childhood behind?" But the boy was so dissolved in his relief that the words were not even distinguished until much, much later.

Outside in the hallway, the doctor addressed Seelin, who had been waiting impatiently. He did not like his assigned task of interviewing this forever child, but since he had brought off the successful kidnap, he had been given the 'honor' of coordinating the conversion process as well.

"How's he doing," Seelin asked the doctor.

"I think he's doing about as well as can be expected right now. There were no signs of spontaneous bleeding, and he appears to still be fully conscious."

"Is he ready for questioning?"

"Yes, you should find him coherent enough. I didn't include any truth invoker in my formula, however. Are you sure that's what you want? It's usually included as part of the standard mix."

"No," answered Seelin. "Just something to ease his pain for the time being, that's all. I'll let you know if I need anything else."

The doctor turned to walk away. "You know where to find me," he replied, then disappeared around a corner, leaving Seelin alone with his unwelcome chore. Grasping onto the lever, he pushed down firmly and swung open the door to his prisoner's chamber.

He found the forever child slumped into a far corner of the room, eyes closed, apparently sleeping, but as the man approached cautiously Kianno opened his eyes just enough for Seelin to see he was not fully asleep after all. Having had no direct experience whatsoever with forever children, his first instinct was to attempt to console the child as he would one of Mistissa's friends who had fallen down a hillside.

"Are you feeling any better, now?" Seelin asked, sitting down on the floor next to the boy, but Kianno only shot the man an accusatory glance, so he continued. "If the drugs weren't enough to relieve the pain, let me know. Although they're in short supply right now, we understand how tough the first week is. Believe me, it gets better after this."

"OK then, I'll take some more drugs if you're really offering. Shoot me full of them; give me enough to knock me out for good."

"I'll talk to the doctor, in a while." Seelin tried to remember what the others had told him: start with the fundamentals and probe for any influence he might have inside the hives. He cleared his throat, then began again. "You can make things a lot easier for yourself if you'll let us know who you were sent to watch, and who else is working with you."

Kianno sat up a little and let out a sigh. "That's what the other giant kept talking about, too. You're absolutely sure I'm a watcher, aren't you?"

"Well, what did you tell the other one? You disintegrated him before he had a chance to fill me in on your conversation, in case you don't remember." Seelin spit the words out with bitterness, then waited resolutely for a response.

"What I told him, which is what I'm telling you and which is probably not something you're going to believe anyway, is that I'm not a watcher. I came, along with only one other, in order to find evidence of my past. I was born in Lexington, you see, born as an outsider."

Now Seelin's concentration tightened about this fascinating development. They will tell you everything except that they are watchers, that's what the other rebels had warned him, yet the boy's voice sounded too resigned to be so clever. "Go on," he encouraged the boy, who appeared so sleepy he might slip under at any time.

"I was born Kianno Tonnars, son of Geryl and Sylvi Tonnars. Have you heard the name? Do you know of them?"

"No. I'm sorry, the name means nothing to me. But I've been away. I don't know many around here. Are they still alive, then?"

"That's what I'm trying to find out. I don't believe so. I lost them in the great quake thirty years ago." He stared intently at Seelin. "You look like you might be old enough to remember, if I am any judge of the age of you people..."

"Yes, I remember," answered Seelin, but then stopped himself from elaborating, too interested in the boy's story to begin one of his own.

"They died under the collapse of a huge wall, an ancient dam, which used to run along the south side of this valley. I came back only to find out for sure, to keep me from wondering any longer if they still might be alive, waiting for me somehow..." The pain had already increased to a throbbing in his knees, and the boy shifted uncomfortably in search of a better position.

"How did you become one of...them, then," asked Seelin.

Kianno laughed at the phrasing. "You mean how was I saved from the quick and dirty death of an outsider? I was claimed at a refugee center by a most wonderful old fashioned couple. One minute I was Kianno Tonnars, an orphaned outsider, the next I was Seelin of Forshas, living the good life on Level GGG of the Great Hive of San Jose."

Seelin froze with his own name, the full name he had not mentioned to anyone and had not even heard spoken by another for thirty years. "What was that?" he asked incredulously, suspicious at once of trickery, "What did you say your name was?"

"Seelin of Forshas," the boy repeated, but he had hardly uttered the words when his captor sprang to his feet and pointed a finger down at him.

"What kind of games are you playing. You have already given your name as Kianno. Where did you hear of Seelin of Forshas, anyway?"

Kianno's curiosity was piqued by the startling response of his inquisitor. He suddenly sensed he had something of value and was more reluctant to reveal all the details without first trying for something in return. "You seem particularly interested in my story," he replied slowly. "Bring me one more injection of pain killer and I'll tell you everything."

Seelin tried to concentrate on the best way to deal with this proposition, but his mind was whirling in circles and he could only think of finding out more. "Wait here," he said curtly, as if his prisoner had any choice, then he ran from the room to fetch the doctor.

After Kianno had been given his booster, mixed this time with the truth invoker at Seelin's request, he settled even further into his small corner and answered the questions which once again were posed to him with surprising intensity. The thought did occur to him, as his questioner focused in on the original Seelin of Forshas, that perhaps this man knew of Seelin or might even be Seelin himself. But whatever the forever boy may have thought during the questioning was entirely lost from his memory, so strong was the truth/pain killer/hypnotic combination in which he floated.

For his part, Seelin perspired with nervousness and excitement while waiting for the doctor to lend some scientific validity to the extraordinary words he had just heard. Once he had been given the OK by the doctor, he hurried back to the forever boy's side and continued right where he had left off.

"What is your true name, Seelin or Kianno?" he began.

"My true name now is Kianno of Forshas." the boy responded drowsily.

"Then why did you just now claim to be Seelin of Forshas?"

"That was the name I was given when they found me. That was the name of the one whose place I took. I changed it twenty years ago to my own given name, Kianno."

Seelin heard the words, and knew they must be true, yet still refused to believe them, still thought this must be some kind of elaborate hoax being played at his expense.

"And in what quadrant do you live?" he demanded.

"GGG2354," answered the boy, but Seelin himself could no longer remember the exact number. Yet GGG seemed to reach back at him from the deepest recesses of his memory. GGG and the Unit Room, and Jaslo and Sofia...

"Who is your mother, then?"

"You people have mothers and fathers. That is an obsolete and useless concept nowadays." Kianno paused, closing his eyes, then added "It is funny that you should ask such a question, though, because I alone within my quadrant do have a mother, or one who likes to think of herself as my mother at any rate. Her name is Sofia."

Now swirls of anger appeared scattered through Seelin's disbelief, springing forth like small fountains of color across his still intense curiosity. "Tell me about her, then. Tell me about this Sofia. What is she like?"

Kianno's eyes remained softly closed, and he tried as well to vision her, tried to summon her to his side to comfort him through this confusion. "Such a quiet face, with freckles over her forehead and brown eyes and hair. She is truly a beautiful woman, but with strange beliefs, strange ideas she will not let go of."

Seelin struggled to conjure much more distant memories, but again could not remember enough to know if the boy was tricking him. Yet the words were spoken honestly, and carried the sound of truth. If it wasn't all such an impossible notion. That he had been replaced; that Sofia should have gone in search of another to take his place, as if he were simply a stolen piece of furniture or a lost sara. All these years he had wondered about Sofia, concerned that his absence may have caused such grief. But after his initial attempts to contact the authorities had disappeared into the skeptical and disbelieving ears of whoever he tried to convince, he had given up on attempting any contact, certain of two things: one, that he had no chance of getting a message through at any rate, and two, that in his current state and after so many years, both he and Sofia were probably better off not knowing he was alive. Now he laughed at himself for having been so worried about what his absence might have done to Sofia and the Forshas. It had apparently been quickly filled by another.

Seeing that his prisoner had dozed off completely, he got up and left the boy to his unseen dreams. Hurrying back down the hallway he stopped once more to see his medical associate. Looking up at Seelin's entrance with surprise, the doctor put down the digislides he was observing and turned his chair toward the door.

"Is everything all right?" he asked with a concerned expression. "Has he lost consciousness?"

"Yes, but that's OK. That's not the reason I stopped by."

"So..." the doctor coaxed, eager to continue his studies.

"If we were to reinstate the regulators for this one who calls himself Kianno, what would the effect be?"

The doctor thought for a moment, then answered. "I've never tried such a thing this early in the conversion process. I know it would be impossible to stop his development after two weeks; the regulators would lose their capability. But stopping them this early might work if the goal were to reinstate him to his previous stasis." He looked curiously at Seelin. "Is that something you're seriously considering?"

Seelin hesitated, confused with the suddenness and irrevocability of the decisions forced by the astonishing revelations of his prisoner. Maybe, just maybe, he had the power the save Sofia the second loss of a loved son, to make up in some small way for the grief his own loss might have caused her. Or had there really been so much grief in the first place? Given a second loss, would she again just go out and get another child by whatever means? Everything he knew and remembered about his mother went against his accepting the story he'd just been told, went against the idea that his disappearance had not created a sorrowful absence in her life. Until now, that absence had been the only thing he had left with her, the only part of himself which remained in her world.

"If you're thinking of reinstating, you'd best let me know right away," the doctor repeated, impatient with the long pause.

"I was only asking for my own information," Seelin finally replied. "Of course we have no intention of restoring this subject's artificial childhood. Continue with the sequence as originally planned." Then he turned abruptly and went in search of a distant wood in which to hide and try to make some sense of all this.

***

Even at a pace accelerated at thirty times the natural rate of a boy's progression from childhood through puberty and into physical adulthood, Kianno did not notice many dramatic effects of the regulator withdrawal that first week, save for the intense pain and hunger he endured. Toward the end of the second week, however, he began noticing a distinct tightening in the cuffs of his Sara, and when washing noticed as well the appearance of a small amount of hair growing under his arms and above his genitals, which also seemed larger now and took to arousal much more readily than before. In addition, small red infections began covering his chin and forehead, and his voice started to take on an irregular roughness. These developments sent Kianno into a panic which began to replace pain as the main source of his attention and worry, since he was certain that he was crossing the threshold, and that he was now destined for a quick death in a short forty or fifty years.

Although neither Seelin nor any of the other rebels visited the boy during this traumatic period, they were well aware of the fear and anxiety which the new captive was experiencing, and therefore released their prisoner from the confinement of his room as soon as the vicious pain had subsided at the end of the first week. Three other kidnapped citizens in much later phases of their development and conversion shared a common living quarter, and Kianno entered cautiously and skeptically into their presence, like a cat let loose in a strange house.

The "oldest" of the captives was Romina, a tall blonde who had grown from a stringy child to a beautiful, sensuous woman in only three months. She was surrounded by her entourage of male admirers, two other newer captives like Kianno, only further along, such that they now had grown tall and acquired the broader builds and deeper voices of manhood, even if they still had trouble controlling their newly developed bodies, often tripping over their legs which appeared unrecognizable even to themselves at times.

Seelin, of course, had visual and auditory access to all the communal inter-actions, and was careful to arrange Kianno's visits with either Romina herself, or Romina and no more than one of the others, since the woman was furthest along and also the most successfully converted of the group, and was most likely to favorably influence the conversion process. Fortunately for Kianno, she was also sympathetic and understanding enough to attempt to draw his fears from him, knowing he would be reluctant to bring them up himself.

One evening, three weeks into the newest prisoner's captivity, the two of them sat side by side outside in their enclosed concrete yard, watching birds fly overhead and feeling the warmth of the sun.

"Do you suppose they eat birds, out here?" she began, trying to induce some sort of dialogue with the sullen prisoner. Although she had visited with him twice already, she had not been able to draw him out of his shell, quite unlike the other two who had been brimming with questions.

"Probably," he replied, "They probably eat them live, with their bare hands." He picked up a stone and threw it at the far fence. "I suppose I'm hungry enough to eat one as well. And why not, since I'm becoming one of them I might as well get used to it."

"You're not becoming one of them," she countered quickly. "You're as much yourself as you ever were, perhaps even more so." She looked at his gangly awkwardness as the cheerful noise of a group of children passing by in the street spilled into the yard, capturing both their attentions out of an instinctual response to the voices of their old world. "This is the most difficult time, but you'll see it's not really so bad."

Kianno threw another stone, this time over the top of the fence, and the group of children scattered away. When he didn't respond, Romina continued. "They've told me that they're going to return us to the hive, you know, and I believe them. So if you're worried about never seeing your family again..."

"As if they would see me now. Where do they put freaks like us in the hive, anyway? I've never seen them except when I've accidentally stepped out of the slider on one of the lowest levels."

"That's not true." She gripped his hand to comfort him, crossing a strict boundary she had set with the other two. Somehow he seemed so less aggressive, so much more in need of a reassuring touch. "We'll be given our same families at our same levels, they've promised me that."

Kianno laughed. "And I'm sure they're entirely to be trusted, these snatchers. You almost sound like you're one of them. How do I know you're not, anyway?"

"I guess you don't. I guess it doesn't really matter, anyway," she sighed. "Pretty soon you'll probably be asked the same question." The newly created woman gazed up at the sky, waiting for a new flock of birds, but the sky held only a blue emptiness . She felt the warmth of Kianno's hand, smaller than hers still, and interlocked their fingers together. He then surprised her, surprised himself even, by flattening out the delicate fingers and placing her soft hand on his thigh. She could see now that her touch had been a mistake, could see his arousal lifting the new sara he'd been given.

"I'm sorry," she stammered, lifting herself up off the ground. "I know..." But he looked away, would not return her glance, embarrassed at the urges which now controlled him. She turned reluctantly and walked away, wondering if maybe she had done the right thing in setting boundaries, boundaries between prisoners who had only themselves for consolation.

***

Two days later Seelin once again visited Kianno, bringing with him extra rations of food and new clothes for the rapidly growing youth. The gifts, however, were left behind for later examination, since the real purpose of the visit was to show

the prisoner some of the harsher realities of outsider life, one of the critical steps
in the conversion process.

Kianno, of course, already had had a chance to see enough of the gathering
to have been totally repulsed at the thought of living such a nightmare. But
he had seen it through the eyes of a visitor, and the starvation and disease
had been perceived as little more than reinforcement of his relief at having
escaped this world thirty years ago. Even the idea that his parents might still be
alive hadn't brought home the horror of the impoverished world, since all the
while he had held out little hope of their survival anyway. Even when he did
imagine them alive, his vision willed them into a tidy shelter tucked away cleanly
from the death and misery with which his rational mind would have otherwise
surrounded them. Now, however, he was forced into visualizing this world and
its inhabitants with the eyes of one who knew he was becoming more and more
like them every day, as one who was beginning to wonder whether he might
possibly have lost his ticket home.

As a precaution, Seelin banded his prisoner's wrist and tied it to his own with
a loose rope. Although Kianno had grown significantly in the last three weeks,
he still was no match for the grown man, but the risk that the captive might dart
away and disappear into the streets required some measure of security. For his
part, Kianno welcomed the chance to escape from the drab quarters in which
he had been confined, and needed no coaxing to accompany Seelin on this tour
of the very worst sections of Lexington.

As they walked away from the main district and toward the eastern edge of
the old city, Seelin kept a vigilant eye out for any approaching danger; although
Kianno was now clearly beyond the threshold, he was still close enough that
someone bent on a quick ransom might mistake him for a child who could be
sold to the right people for quite a tidy sum. Others were following just in case,
but he was primarily responsible for the protection of this most promising captive, a responsibility which had been distracting him from his more overriding
objective of establishing some sort of trust between them.

"How is Romina doing these days," Seelin interjected after a particularly long
pause in the sparse conversation he had failed to spark thus far. Kianno did not

respond to this obviously false and utilitarian question, however, so he tried a different, more direct approach.

"I've been able to obtain some definitive information on Sylvi and Geryl Tonnars." He continued looking straight ahead at a row of small shelters and a few young men hanging out on the steps which fronted them. "I'm afraid they were killed in the great earthquake, as you suspected."

Kianno slowed his pace slightly but still did not respond. The news he had been expecting swept over him silently, leaving only a mild sadness and emptiness in its wake. Like Seelin, he had been subconsciously hoping that there was still something of his own left behind in his former world, ugly and menacing as it was. At length, he replied. "What do your people do with them, after..."

"If they are lucky enough to have family or friends left, there's a place in the nearby woods where they'll be buried. But many such deaths are never acknowledged; the remains are cleaned away only when they eventually get in the way." He gestured to the dirt road ahead of them. "The streets are kept free of any bodies; the risk of disease and infection is too great."

Kianno looked around him at the youths watching them carefully, and at a cluster of young women talking under an oak tree which had grown in the middle of the old road. Then he looked over at Seelin with a curious expression. "You must be quite old, older than most of the rest of your people."

"Yes, most of us die soon after our children are grown."

The prisoner stopped and reached down to adjust his shoe, then straightened up and continued. "How can you even go through the motions?" he asked.

"I'm sorry, I don't..."

"How can you even care enough to go through the day when you know you're so close to death?"

Seelin laughed. "Well, I wouldn't exactly say I'm on death's door just yet. I've got a few good years left in me." When his words were met with silence, he added "I plan on living a good forty years more, if I can arrange things well enough."

"But that's impossible. You said yourself that you cannot survive beyond fifty of so, if I am calculating correctly."

"I said that most of us die at that time. Of hunger. Of starvation. Not because it is the end of our natural lives. With the right medical care and enough food, we can live to a hundred years."

The word "we" took Kianno aback. His questions had been out of curiosity, but now he was once again reminded of his sudden mortality. As they advanced toward the far end of the street, Seelin pointed out a cleared area filled with thirty or forty young adults and some children huddled against their mostly sleeping parents. A few sat up in their beds made of dirty old fabrics laid on the bare dirt ground, but most lay practically motionless, buried from the light of day in their cocoons of too-thin blankets and cast out clothing.

"These people are in the latter phases, so they come here where they can be taken care of by those more charitable among us. Most don't even bother coming here, though. Most either die in their shelters or sell their deaths to the network."

Now Seelin stopped at the edge of the clearing and sat down with his prisoner on a newly built wooden bench. The sun was already warming the grasses at their feet, and the uncanny silence which Kianno had noticed since he had first stepped outside the hive pressed down from the high sky.

"It's too bad that you people have not been more successful at building a prosperous society. But then, given the nature of those we sent here in the first place, I suppose nothing much could have been expected. That you should deny food to anyone over fifty is beyond even what I would have expected of you."

Seelin tried to suppress his growing anger, knowing it would be of no use to him in this situation. "On the contrary, it is the state, your state, which will only provide for anyone who may have a child to offer them. Once that possibility no longer exists, they are left to fend for themselves."

"As if fending for themselves is such cruelty," Kianno scoffed. "Why shouldn't you fend for yourselves? You've already demonstrated that you can't fit into a civilized society; that's why you're here in the first place. Now you want special treatment when you're surrounded by such abundant natural resources?" He looked up at the surrounding hillsides. "The true food you could grow here if you set your mind to it could sustain all of you!"

"Yes, you've hit on it," sighed Seelin. "If only all agricultural land, as well as all water rights, did not legally belong to True Food Inc., who bought those rights from the state forty years ago." Seelin stood and pointed to a small patch of land next to the bench. "See this ground? This belongs to no one. It belongs to whoever has enough need and enough strength to muscle anyone else off of it. But the minute I plant a corn seed, or a strawberry cutting, or an avocado tree, it immediately belongs to True Food, and they may kill me without penalty for trespassing. Tell me, how are we supposed to 'fend for ourselves' under those conditions?"

Kianno remained silent. He had not known that it was quite that extreme a situation, but these were criminals after all, misfits who had demonstrated they could not live inside the hives. It was not his fault if they were forced into working for the state. "The corporations pay you enough to survive, if you are willing to work on their land."

"Oh yes, if you are young enough, and strong enough, and lucky enough to find consistent work. Unfortunately that's still just a minority. The rest of us can only live from selling our children, and once they're gone we starve to death."

Again the us word. Kianno had had enough of this preaching. "I'm tired of this You've made your point, if that's what this was all about." He stood abruptly and started off, pulling taught the rope which bound them, until Seelin as well slowly joined him in the retreat. After a few minutes Kianno spoke again.

"What about the other I asked about? What about Seelin? I was told you know of him."

"Yes, what is it you want to know?"

"Does he know about me? Has he been told?" Kianno kicked at a large rock in his path, impatient with pent up energy.

"Yes, we've told him. But he doesn't want to see you now. Perhaps later." Seelin chose his words carefully, eager to quickly put this topic to rest .

After another pause, Kianno added, somewhat cautiously, "While I'm your prisoner, I will be given full protection, will I not?"

Seelin laughed. "Protection? You mean from kidnappers? I suppose we could arrange that." He glanced over and thought he noticed just the smallest hint of a smile pushing the edges of the prisoner's mouth. Despite the warped and callous views of his youthful looking captive, views for which he really could not be fully blamed, Seelin was beginning to like the forever boy who had taken over his own childhood and who was only now relinquishing it painfully through a much accelerated and especially fearful adolescence. He was almost beginning to regret the upcoming period of intermittent intense torture, but the experts had assured him that it was absolutely necessary in order for a successful conversion to take hold.

12

"I see no reason for Dr. Biloff to elaborate further on these fringe experiments of his," Dr. Jaslo of Forshas stood and announced sharply to the small group assembled in the Laboratory's main conferencing chamber. "These experiments were entirely unnecessary in the first place."

A few of the others present shifted uncomfortably and let out small sighs of exasperation, eager for a full run down on Biloff's analysis and tired of Jaslo's moral challenges.

"Dr. Forshas," the speaker responded, "The results are known now, and everyone, I'm sure, is anxious to hear them. We can debate another time as to their implications."

"I agree," added Public Senator Atascin, attending in his ongoing role as the State's monitor. "The direction of these trials don't imply any particular political inclinations. Let us keep politics and science separate, and we are here now to focus on the scientific evidence of all the activities, including those of Dr. Biloff."

Jaslo paused now in the group's anticipation of a heated reply, but instead he answered the Senator in a calm, steady voice. "Your highest eminence, everyone in this room is fully aware that this procedure is much too expensive, in every sense of the word, to ever be wasted on outsiders." He now paced along the length of the table, shifting his gaze from one associate to another. "So why then do we continue any experimentation with transplants of older outsiders into children's bodies?"

Everyone, of course, already knew the answer, but Jaslo answered his own question nonetheless. "Because there are those among us who would use this miraculous new science, this incredible gift of life extension, so that they may forsake the regulated life and enter into the crude, dangerous, hormone-driven existence we long ago rose up from. This new technique is seen by some as a means for allowing previously regulated citizens to experience the immoral pleasures of an uncontrolled physical life, with all of the negative consequences for our society, while still retaining the option to go back for another round, so to speak, once they begin to suffer the ravages of such a lifestyle." As he spoke, others began to murmur dissent, but he pressed on. "That is the only, the only reason for continuing this line of experimentation. Further transplants must be done with regulated and undeveloped subjects only, and..."

But now from the growing dissent came a louder voice from a blonde forever girl seated at the far end of the chamber. "Not everyone, doctor, considers a human being's naturally mature state to be so morally repugnant."

Several heads now turned quickly toward the girl, surprised she would speak an extreme Naturalist view so freely. Seeing the response, and realizing now the risks of such reactionary comments, she now cleared her throat and continued more slowly. "Our jobs are to investigate and determine the boundaries of this new technique, which is the proper role of Dr. Biloff's contributions. The uses of this procedure are not for us to decide at any rate."

Jaslo laughed softly and pressed to take advantage of her ill considered initial statement. "Natural? Did I hear you to say the unregulated condition is some-how more natural?" He let the words hang in the air, and now a few of his associates tried to suppress smiles of their own. "I suppose it's also more natural to run around naked and hang from trees, after all. And, left to nature alone, with no unnatural intervention from medical science, wouldn't most of us die of some virus or another before the age of fifty even? Is that what we really want, a natural..."

"That is enough," Senator Atascin spoke loudly and with authority. He did not share in the smirking among those surrounding him. "This is no place for political debate. We will hear the results with no more irrelevant interruptions." He glared at Jaslo. "Am I understood?"

"I've said my peace. You all know very well where I stand. But let's not pretend that we won't all be responsible for the social effects of our scientific discoveries," answered Dr. Forshas, re-taking his seat and focusing his attention on his colleague at the head of the chamber.

"Thank you." Dr. Biloff stood and read from his notes suspended holographically before him. "From previous testing we have already seen that transplants of those beyond the threshold are associated with only a slightly increased complication and mortality rate than those who are either below the threshold or in a regulated state. I'm not going to review the details of those findings, as Dr. Srinmina has already done an excellent job of that several months ago." Biloff looked over at Jaslo in an attempt to hold him in check with his eyes, but the contrary doctor showed no signs of interrupting, so Biloff continued.

"The purpose of my particular experiments was to explore further into the possibilities involving transplantation of developed outsiders into undeveloped donor bodies. In particular, we attempted to distinguish whether or not gender would be a limiting factor in the successful mating of host to donor. As most of you are aware, the results to date involve only two subjects: "J", who is only two months post-operative, and "B", who is now a full two years post-operative. Both experiments involved the brains of fully mature outsider females into the bodies of immature male donors. The ages of the male donors was eleven and twelve, respectively. We purposefully chose these ages for reasons which will soon become apparent."

Senator Atascin listened intently, fascinated at the sophistication of the scientific technique but somewhat left behind as the doctor spent a great deal of time elaborating on the medical complications and trends seen from the surgeries themselves, as well as detailed comparisons in recovery progress parameters and such. After about ten minutes of this, the doctor recognized Atascin's unfamiliarity with the terminology, and summarized in more general terms.

"So as you can see," Biloff said as he dissipated the multicolored holographic chart. "Gender in and of itself does not appear to be a critical limiting factor to the success of this technique. Such mechanical and tissue related factors such as cranial compatibility, blood type, and tissue type are considerably more significant in matching host to donor. Given a situation where these other more critical factors are matched, gender mismatch should not be a consequential factor in determining the physical and medical outcome of the technique."

The group sat quietly, contemplating the information and taking notes. At length, the blonde forever girl who had challenged Jaslo raised a question. "Dr. Biloff, you say that gender should not be a determinant factor. I find this somewhat surprising. I take it you are referring to the medical consequences only?"

"Yes, that's true. Certainly the psychological consequences must also be taken into account. For us, gender may not seem like such an important attribute, however the same cannot be said for those who have gone beyond the threshold. Certainly among those who have been used to an uncontrolled life, gender might have profound effects upon their ability to continue to fit in and lead productive, contented lives." At the talk of sexual differences among the unregulated, several of the doctors squirmed a little in their chairs and looked around nervously, clearly embarrassed despite their thorough medical knowledge and understanding of mature sexual functioning.

Dr. Biloff paused, then continued. "The real question which we also needed to address in our study was how a brain which has been feminized or masculinized by the presence of hormones within their previous body will react to life where those hormones are replaced by those of the opposite sex. More importantly, the question remains whether or not such individuals will be able to adapt to the roles expected within their new lives."

"This is assuming, again, is it not doctor, that such an individual will purposefully refuse regulators and choose to go beyond the threshold?"

"Yes, that is true, Dr. Jaslo."

"Thank you. Just clarifying." Jaslo looked once more around the room like a father who has found out the children have been naughty.

Dr. Biloff then waved his hand and a new pictorial filled the holographic spot. It showed some boys roughhousing in the sportscoper. He continued his dissertation. "As I mentioned earlier, the donor bodies were chosen at immediate pre-threshold points so that the effect of the masculinizing hormones upon the brain and overall functioning of the previously female subject brains could be examined." He pointed to a shy boy standing back from the rough play of the others. "This is "B", in the new environment in which we placed him only three months post-operative. As you can see, he continued to respond to situations in a more reserved, feminine mode than the rest of his group."

"Was he surrounded with regulated citizens, or outsider children?" asked one doctor, "Certainly if they are children, then the obvious differences in age and maturity would prevent any..."

"We were aware of that constraint. Therefore we did allow B to associate with citizens, so that he could fit in as much as possible. You can see, however, that socially he did not respond like other males, and therefore this initially led to overall dissatisfaction and negative social experiences."

Now the doctor presented another visual, this time of a somewhat older looking B actively engaged in an aggressive K Ball game with other teammates. "This is the same B one year later, after the brain has had a chance to recognize and accept the new hormonal environment. As a result of this particular experiment, we believe humans behave very similarly to animals we have observed in similar situations; that is, that give some time the brain itself becomes masculinized or feminized based upon its new hormonal environment, and as this process occurs, behavior also adapts to the new circumstances. Of course, every individual is different, and we are not psychologists and psychotherapists. But from a medical viewpoint, there should be no reason why the subject cannot fully adapt to his or her new gender and physical age given a year or two of adjustment."

Once more the blond doctor spoke up. "Dr. Biloff, can you say in general whether this subject successfully adapted within his social peer group of citizens?"

The doctor hesitated before replying. "There are numerous factors which I'm sure are involved. Socialization was less than optimal, but as I said we are not psychologists."

"I only ask because there are those who believe that regardless of gender, such socialization may be impossible, since the brain itself may continue to develop beyond the threshold, and therefore interactions with those with…" She hesitated, sensing she was getting herself into trouble again, "…less overgrown brains might be unsuccessful at any rate." The room stirred at her words, and Dr. Jaslo scoffed audibly. But the doctor was undeterred and aimed her next words directly at Jaslo. "Such obstacles would appear even should the subject choose a regulated lifestyle after the operation, isn't that true?"

Jaslo jumped from his chair, unable to restrain himself any longer. "This is utter nonsense, of course, the mystical idea that the outsiders are somehow better than us because of their so called more developed brains. Everyone knows such development is very minimal in terms of overall growth percentage." He now began walking toward the portal. "Besides, even if it were true it's just one more argument for limiting this procedure to regulated hosts and regulated donors. Any other such discussion is blasphemy as far as I'm concerned." He touched the doors and they instantly opened up to the fresher air of the hallway. "Good night, doctors. You may stay to further discuss innumerable strange and perverted possibilities, but I have had quite enough." And with this he stomped loudly out of the room.

***

It had taken her two full days of worry and uncertainty before she came to Sofia's room, and when she finally announced herself it was at the late hour of eight-thirty, a time when she felt certain Sofia would have seen any visitors, particularly Jaslo, away for the evening. But she had not anticipated Jaslo's especially late night at the laboratory, or the unfortunate coincidence of Sofia's romantic impulse of sharing the stimulator tank, and even her bed, with her long time partner. Although, like all forever children, neither one had any real sex drive to speak of, they still enjoyed the stimulator tank, and each others' bodies, appreciating the sensations of sexual excitement more as occasional treats they could easily do without but tasted nonetheless to amuse themselves away from the monotony of daily life. Beyond that, it was another one of Sofia's obsolete beliefs that sharing in this play brought her a muted sense of closeness. In the moments after the play had ended was when she most distinctly felt an absence from the repertoire of her emotions, as if she had gotten close enough to a physical expression of real love that she could see the empty outline in her own ability to experience the intensity and deepness of emotional response that she had read about among the outsiders. It was then that she would lie awake, after Jaslo had retreated to his room, and wonder at the possibilities of becoming a true Naturalist.

No doubt she was hoping to keep Jaslo next to her through this night, but the unusual announcement before they had even begun with the electro-foreplay of the stimulator tank put an abrupt end to her evening plans.

"Sofia, it is I, Zhrana." The words froze Sofia's expression into one of immediate panic. Why had she come with Jaslo here?

Jaslo, of course, also heard the announcement, and smiled at Sofia with an "Oh well, the kids are crying again" shrug. "You two may come in, just give us five minutes to prepare for you." Both of them then quickly dressed and Sofia hurried to greet their visitor personally, while her partner was still pressing his hair in the bathroom.

"Why Zhrana, so good to see you." She was alone, snuffing the small hope that perhaps he had returned. Sofia began to whisper something else, but Jaslo soon approached to within earshot, so she said in a full voice "Have you and Kianno returned, then, from your vacation on the sun level?"

Zhrana silently walked to a chair in the far corner of the room, passing right by the activated stimulator tank as if it wasn't even there, then sat down hard onto a lounge sofa in the corner. "I'm afraid I have some very bad news. I've been living with this for too long now, and it's time both of you knew as well. Kianno and I never went to the sun level. We haven't really been on vacation at all."

"What are you talking about?" Jaslo asked with a bewildered expression, while Sofia wondered only how much Kianno's friend would reveal, already informed of the entire situation through her other sources.

"I've been visiting in another quadrant all this time, while Kianno, he..." She turned away from Jaslo's expectant eyes, unable to face him while saying the words. "He's outside the hive. Outside any hive. He went to search for information about his real family, his old family, and he hasn't returned."

For a moment Jaslo puzzled over her term "real family". It had been so long he had genuinely forgotten for the moment that Kianno had not always been with them. Then a flash of recognition came across his face and he pressed the forever girl for more information, thinking still that he may have heard her incorrectly. "That's impossible. Why would he risk everything to go back there when he must know his parents are long since dead? I'll take this up with the family when he returns." He looked in Zhrana's direction, trying unsuccessfully to draw her gaze. "When will he return?"

"His plan was to stay no more than a few days, but it's been three weeks now and I've lost contact with him two weeks ago. I'm afraid he's run into trouble, snatched perhaps…" She ran her fingers through her hair frenetically as Sofia came over to console her.

"This is unbelievable!" exclaimed Jaslo, now growing angry as the reality of it settled in. "One can't just stroll away from civilization. A permit is required, even then readmission is no sure thing." He paused, then added "I'll begin an investigation immediately. There's no time to waste. If he's out there I'll use everything in my power to bring him back."

"Yes, we must alert the authorities immediately," Sofia said. "There's no time to waste."

"The authorities will do nothing," Jaslo scoffed. "I have my own authorities; I have my own…" He chose his words carefully now. "…resources at my command. I'm confident they'll be much more effective than anything the state will be willing to provide."

They were the words Sofia had been afraid to hear. She had already been working her more subtle connections into the outsider world, and wanted to see Kianno found alive, even if it took more time. But Jaslo would undoubtedly not be satisfied with peaceful but patient techniques, knowing full well what happened to snatched forever children. She glanced at Zhrana with unfairly punishing eyes which confused the poor girl even further.

"I'm sorry." Zhrana now pushed her way past Sofia and toward the portal. "I'm sorry but there's nothing I could have done. You must know that." The metal doors responded instantly to her touch and she hurried away without looking back.

"Wait," Jaslo called after her. "We understand. Wait, I need more information." Cinching up his sara, he took off in pursuit, leaving Sofia alone in the empty hum of the still primed stimulator tank.

***

It wasn't until the second day of attacks, when several zombies were found wandering the broken streets of Lexington, that the city first became aware of a vicious new skull-capping campaign. Outsider liaisons immediately issued protests and submitted what evidence they could against these most recent assaults of interrogations so cruel that the state had taken the extreme position of banning them even against outsiders. Official state spokesmen responded in their routine fashion by denying knowledge of any new activity, and by going on record as denouncing this horrible form of unnecessary violence. But, despite these denials, it was clear to the terrified residents that someone very powerful was conducting a ruthless search, probably with the state's tacit approval. The symptoms of those who lived through the ordeal were unmistakable, and even if they were no longer capable of telling any tales, the clues they carried in their eyes and on their bodies told tales enough.

The first of the victims was Marina, a twenty-eight year old mother who had been late that evening to the water allotment station, and consequently found herself hurrying back through the darkened streets by herself, eager to escape the danger of thugs who might rough her up just for the two gallons of water she carried strapped across her shoulders. As she passed by a distinctive Spanish style mansion along the eastern edge of the city, she was jumped by two small forever children and one adult who efficiently subdued and injected her with a fast acting drug which weakened her and softened any thoughts of resistance. The drug was a truth serum/tranquilizer, the same drug, in fact, used by the rebels when interrogating their captives. The sense of relaxation instilled upon the subject, however, was only the calm before the storm, as Marina was soon to find out.

They led her easily into the courtyard of the old mansion where they had been hiding out, waiting for anyone who appeared to belong to this place. When no one had appeared, the two decided that it was better to start in with a passer by than to let the day go entirely to waste. Inside the yard they had set up the capping apparatus, a relatively small but quite intricate module large enough to require camouflage as the packed trunk of a family moving about like most outsider families. The module was required to be within five feet of the skull-cap during the interrogation, and it was the module which performed the many sophisticated calculations necessary to the effectiveness of the system.

With Marina subdued and drifting unsuspectingly in the drug's lethargy, the two forever-children fitted the cap itself over her head. The fitting process was actually the most difficult and time consuming step, with numerous adjustments resulting from sequential mappings fed from the cap to the module, which in turn provided instructions for additional alignment of the device.

As they neared readiness, one of the interrogators read from the module a series of numbers, which the other verified. When the expert had confirmed the set up was complete, he turned his attentions toward Marina.

"Good evening fellow citizen," he began sarcastically, using the term reserved for residents of the hives. "We're so sorry to disturb you, but we assure you this won't take much of your time and you'll be on your way in no time at all." Marina did not respond but the other forever child laughed audibly behind him. "I want you to clear your mind of any and all thoughts, so I ask you now to just drift along slowly and clear your head of everything," he continued in a soft voice.

The young woman would not ordinarily have been able to clear such thoughts from her mind, especially given the fear of this moment, however the drugs she had been given had been designed and administered specifically for the purpose of inducing a clean palate, so to speak, as well as assuring that all forthcoming responses would indeed be truthful.

After waiting a moment for Marina to do as instructed, the interrogator asked his first question, whose sole purpose was to test the set up. "When did you fall asleep last night," he asked innocently enough.

Marina thought for a moment, then answered "I don't know the time exactly. It was right after the baby had settled down at last, and..."

Midsentence, the interrogator yelled loudly to his associate "Now!" and at that very instant the young woman found herself once again in bed, curled up alongside her already sleeping husband, drowsy with sleep and with the welcome intrusions of bits and pieces of dreams into her receding consciousness, the relaxation of her body mixed with the cool scent of the night air and the familiar smell of Rudy next to her. From above everything, though, a strange voice floated through her head, like the dreamy images which had been passing through. The voice beckoned to her.

"Are you sleeping yet," it asked.

"No, almost." she replied.

"But you are in bed?"

"Yes."

"What do you hear now, from outside? Anything in particular?"

"Yes, a bird calling, outside the window."

"Good. I want you to lift your right hand each time the bird calls, do you understand?"

"Yes," she answered sleepily. Her right hand lifted, then dropped. After another few seconds it lifted once again.

"Very good. Stop now!" the interrogator called sharply to his associate, and suddenly Marina found herself once again sitting before these strangers, with this unusual device covering her head.

"Everything appears to be working properly," the expert informed the other who had been monitoring the module.

In theory, the skull-capping technique was quite simple, however the execution of the theory took enormously sophisticated processing and mapping technology before it had been realized. Basically, the process began with a question aimed at directing memory recall of a specific event or experience. The subject's recall of that experience would then cause an increase in electrical activity from the precise area of the brain which contained that memory. The skull-capper would then detect that electrical activity, pinpoint the precise location, then in turn provide continuous stimulation to that same exact memory location, stimulation so intense that the subject re-experienced fully, with all senses, that same memory. The interrogators were then free to ask questions as the event unfolded. Because the stimulation created a full-re-enactment, the level of detail available to the interrogators was much enhanced from what might ordinarily be available to memory alone. Unfortunately, the damage caused by the stimulation could not be confined to the precise memory location or locations probed, and most subjects ended up with severe damage to many sections of the brain.

Satisfied now that the set-up was correct, the forever child began probing Marina for any knowledge of rebel activity.

"Do you know of the group of outsiders who have been snatching innocent citizens?" he began.

"Yes, I have heard of them."

"Do you know the identities of any of them?"

"No. I've only heard stories, that's all."

One of the interrogators now projected a visual of Kianno before her eyes. "Do you recognize this boy? Have you seen him around here at all?"

Marina studied the face carefully. "No," she replied. "Not one of the kids I usually see running around here."

The interrogation continued for some time, each question failing to elicit even a single clue which might prove valuable to explore with the skull-capper. Finally, the forever boy who had been asking most of the questions kicked at the ground in frustration and turned from the woman.

"This is pointless. She has no memories connected to this case. Let's try someone else."

"Of course," replied the other, approaching closer and surveying their subject. "But don't you want to have a little fun first?"

"Oh if you must, but I'll have no part in this. Just be done with her soon enough. We've wasted our time with this one."

Now the two others walked slowly away toward the other end of the court-yard, apparently uninterested in partaking of such fun, as the first brought the module closer to Marina so that he could ask the questions and control the device at the same time. Once he was ready, he paused, then addressed the woman.

"Can you tell me what was the most painful experience you've ever had?"

Marina needed no time to think that one over. "The birth of my daughter," she answered.

"Can you try to remember, now, the most painful moment of that experience?" he continued, then waited a second more before turning to the module.

...Another wave was coming, this one even more agonizing than the first, following in quick succession with no time to rest in between. And still no sign from Rudy and the others, still no word that the head was coming. Terror gripped her now along with the pain. If it were breach there would be nothing which could be done. She'd heard stories of death taking ten slow hours, of mothers' necks being broken on purpose just to put them out of that slow misery. She yelled and grimaced with the pain, a pain she'd never felt before and wasn't even aware one could experience. Looking at Rudy for some reassurance, some word...

"Think about the pain, concentrate only on the pain..." The words came from Rudy's mouth, but it was not his voice. A stranger's voice and yet she could not help but refocus on the pain, the awful pain, and as she did so it suddenly intensified tenfold, beyond what any human could physically experience under natural circumstances, tearing her apart while her husband looked on with such a concerned face but with that stranger's laugh, that awful stranger's laugh.

They found her the next morning walking by the edge of the fields, humming a forgotten song and staring out at an unrecognizable world.

And throughout the city that night, and over the next two days, memories jumped back into life, ordinary memories for the most part, but, when business was done, extreme memories, memories of the most profound satisfactions, of ecstatic sexual experiences recalled solely for the amusement of the interrogators, of once-in-a-lifetime thrills, but mostly terrible memories, forced revisitations

of pure dread upon those who thought they had long since left those moments
behind.

...She held the drug temptingly in front of his eyes, as if he needed any other
drug but her, but she had brought it nonetheless to him to share with her young,
silky blonde body. As it began to swim through him he felt lifted up, higher
and higher as if the insides of his soul had risen to a spot four inches above
his head, looking down at their nakedness as she took his hand and placed it
on her breast to feel her nipples harden to his touch, her smoothness inviting
him without thought, without knowledge, all absorbed by the drug but the
overriding sensations of their physical desire and the touch of their bodies, the
touch of their sexes, so soft and so smooth inviting him...

"Stop," instructed the forever child, and he was brought back instantly.
"Enough of this. Now I want you to remember pain, concentrate on pain..."

...She had seen a rustling from the corner of her eye, and hesitated before
looking, already aware deep inside that it really was a lion, a desperate lion to
come so far into the city, even at this early hour. For a moment she considered
freezing, tried to remember what she had heard about what to do, but her body
was beyond thinking, and reacted now with a surge of fear and adrenaline that
propelled her at once toward an open door she could see at the far end of the
street. Hurtling her body at full speed across the uneven dirt, hearing now for
the first time the snarling from behind, she nearly tripped on a rock in her path
but the momentum of her terror kept her moving forward, flung her the final
yards with the lion gaining ever closer until she at last reached the open door and
swung it shut as the huge animal pounced on the flimsy wooden frame, mauling
it ruthlessly while she searched for far corners in which to hide...

"Stop, Stop now." The interrogator turned to his associate and called out.
"Hey Gordi, this is a good one. C'mon and I'll replay it for you!"

...Even from fifty yards away he could still make them out through the shim-
mer off the water. Kata sitting pensively on a log of smooth driftwood, shifting
her gaze between her husband slipping in and out of sight between the waves
rolling gently in from the bay, and three year old Mistissa making daring forays

to about ankle depth before screaming with delight and darting back to the delicious warmth of heated sand between her toes.

He called out to her. "Kata, c'mon in. It's not too cold." Now recovered from the initial shock of submersion, he leaned back slightly to feel the sun on his forehead. In all directions the ocean shimmered angles of brilliant light back to an endless blue sky. "C'mon," he repeated, "Mista will be OK."

Even from his distance he could see perfectly her smile and her eyes responding to his challenge, could see them in the spaces where the mind fills in what the eyes cannot fully process. Then his eyes detected what his mind could not have imagined, and what his mind has never since let him forget. A figure sliding down the bluff, rolling toward them from the high end of the beach. A solitary figure but strong and quick.

"Kata!" he yelled, "Kata!" And she must have sensed the fear in his voice because she turned around at his first warning to face the attack, throwing up her hands in desperation and confusion.

"Mistissa," he heard her scream, in a voice strangely detached from the image of his only love running to his only child. "Run, Mistissa!"

Then the furious rush to shore, burying himself in the ocean froth churned up all around him, turbulent with the desperation of his race, fighting against the cruel undertow of seconds lost, that fatal minute she had bought for their daughter, time enough, as it turned out, while he fought violently to reach her, coughing and gasping for air in the chaos of salty foam...

Seelin bolted from his sleep into the foreign warmth of the night, drenched in sweat and out of breath. Around him the sound of crickets filled the night, and the slightest breeze rustled oak leaves along the corridor outside his window. They were out there, he knew, still there, searching him out, waiting for their chance, looking for clues to where he could be found, alone, in the middle of an indifferent sea.

13

"Yes, what can I do for you?" The pleasant but worn smile of Paula Orilla looked down at a small girl who had surprised her with this unusual midday visit.

"I'm looking for Paula and Jask Orilla, and I was told they could be found here," answered the girl firmly and confidently enough to cause Paula to take a step back. This was a forever girl, apparently alone, making no attempt even to disguise herself.

"I, well, I am Paula Orilla," she stammered finally in response, staring down intently at this small girl. Only the self-assured manner and that knowing look from behind the eyes betrayed that this delicate young child had seen as many years as Paula. "What do you want with us?"

Zhrana acted quickly to establish some kind of rapport. The interactions with the other two families had not gone well, and this was her last hope at finding an inroad into the rebels and possibly even to Kianno himself.

"I need to say first off that I know about the relocation of Nicoli, and I know the pain that it must have caused you." When the woman glanced skeptically in her direction, she continued. "As you no doubt have already guessed, I am a citizen. However, I'm not among those who have stolen your daughter. On the contrary, I'm working with a small group of other citizens who are fighting this policy." She tried to meet Paula's eyes, but the woman was looking down the hallway, not yet trusting that others might not be hidden away, awaiting their chance. The corridor remained quiet for a moment in the midday heat, as Zhrana waited for an answer.

"Please come in," Paula replied at last, seeing no movement and realizing now that they had nothing left to lose, nothing left to be stolen. The forever girl was led into a small room with a table and a few cushion seats arranged along one wall. Paula lowered herself tentatively into a seat while Zhrana sat directly on the floor, legs folded beneath her.

"I don't mean to frighten you or to cause you any more grief by my visit," she began. "But I do want you to know that we know exactly where Nicoli is now, and we are working to do whatever we can to return her to you."

"Why did you come here?" Paula replied coldly, not yet convinced of the visitor's good intentions.

"We're preparing an appeal of the relocation for next month, which will be the last opportunity to..." Zhrana's voice trailed off at it's recognition of having trespassed too far into this woman's heartache.

"We've already completed the paperwork for an appeal." Paula shifted in her seat and reached a hand behind her to rearrange one of the cushions.

"That will be denied, of course," answered the girl. Now Paula listened more intently to the visitor, sensing for the first time that perhaps she might be trusted after all.

Zhrana took a deep breath, then continued. "Nicoli is safe and healthy. She's living with a family, not a family exactly as you may think of it, but living with others who are watching out for her well being. You needn't worry on that account, anyway."

"Has anything been...done to her?" Paula asked haltingly, "Does she still remember us in the same way? We've heard stories..."

Zhrana wanted to stand and put her arm over the woman's shoulders to console her, but couldn't help but also feel a certain awkwardness and repulsion at her size. Instead, she remained seated and rubbed an open palm over her own calf as she tried to reassure Paula as best she could.

"The stories you've heard are of forced reprogramming. Until a few years ago this was routine for relocated outsider children. It was a cruel, unnecessary treatment, and due to our efforts it has been suspended. I can't say for sure, since I haven't spoken with your daughter, but I'd be very surprised if they tried such a blatantly illegal act. You can be pretty sure that your daughter is much the same as when she was taken from you."

"Much the same, that is what I'm also afraid of, that she'll be too much the same. She is close to becoming a young woman, and she deserves that right. Will she be given it? Can you tell me that?" Paula's words, spoken with a rising voice, hung in the air for several seconds before they were answered.

"Nothing is irreversible. There are risks, of course, and the process can be painful. But if we can return her to you within the next year or so, then..."

"So why are you here?" Paula interrupted angrily. "You've said yourself that our appeal hasn't got a chance. Why do you come to my home to remind me of her, to remind me of what may be happening to her?"

Zhrana reached inside her loose fitting wrap and pulled out a small photograph of Kianno. So rare now as to be practically obsolete, paper images were used only as keepsakes by outsiders or by citizens when even the relatively small signal device used for the visuals was somehow unavailable. Zhrana had decided that if she was going to gain the trust of the rebels, then her only choice was to leave everything but herself behind, or at least everything but one small, very well hidden contingency plan.

"This is a friend of mine who we believe was snatched by terrorists." The forever girl admonished herself silently for accidentally using such an inflammatory term. "Naturalists may have kidnapped this citizen as part of their campaign to influence political decisions within the hive." She paused intentionally, gauging Paula's response and hoping for a revealing mistake of some kind. Encouraged by the silence, she went on. "What the snatchers may not know is that this citizen was sent here for the express purpose of gathering information about relocated children, including Nicoli, to help us with our appeals." Standing now before the still reclining Paula Orilla, Zhrana handed her the photograph and waited for any sign of recognition. So close to the woman now, the forever child could smell the faint scent of her, a strange animal odor at first repulsive but then darkly enticing and mysterious as well. "His name is Kianno," she added, stepping back.

"I haven't seen him, and you don't seriously think I would help you even if I had, do you?" Her face was weary now, relaxed and settled back into it's natural expression of resignation. Paula looked once more into the eyes of this child visitor, still youthful, still full of hope and promise. Perhaps this girl was indeed sincere. Perhaps it was herself who had forgotten the look of sincerity, could no longer recognize it when finally eyeing it face to face.

"I'll ask around," she replied softly. "Perhaps I can put you in touch with someone who would know about these things." Now she stood, to put an end to this dangerous visit. "But please, please, don't return here again. My daughter is gone, probably for good. But we still have each other, at least there's still that..." She gestured Zhrana to the doorway, but the forever girl stood her ground, unwilling to leave without some hope.

"So where, then, if you can help?" she insisted.

"Walk slowly by the path outside, make yourself visible at sunset tomorrow. If there's anything we can do, we'll approach you. But don't enter this building, ever again. Leave us alone now is all I ask."

Zhrana's arm rose once again to touch this poor woman, but again it could not find its way to a place where it might provide some solace, some comfort. Lost in the confusion of her instincts, it fell once again, limp at her side. She then turned and walked slowly through the doorway.

***

Given no description and not knowing who, if anyone, would be sent to meet her, oddly enough it was Zhrana who recognized him before he had even paid any attention at all to the dusty little girl sitting in the lengthening shadows of the street. As tall a man as she'd ever seen, with a slightly crooked walk as if he'd been injured long enough ago for his body to have nearly compensated for the injury, he turned away at first, his eyes skipping right over the top of her as if she wasn't even there. But she knew it was him. Somehow she knew from the turn of the head, the search of his step, and when he reversed direction and revealed a distant face, she raised herself up from the ground and stood as tall as her four foot eight inch frame would allow, then strode purposefully forward to introduce herself.

As they closed on each other, he at last caught her in his brown eyes, and she met his glance head on to leave no doubt, but then drifted away soon enough, drawing closer to him, drifted to the roughly angled jaw, the narrow nose rising evenly from his dark brows with not even a hint of curvature in it's slope, not even the hint of softness in that face. Only the eyes betrayed the softness of a soul beaten down enough to understand the futility of stubbornness. When they at last stood before each other, it was Zhrana who tilted her head back and spoke first.

"My name is Zhrana," she announced with as much authority as she could muster.

Seelin put one hand on his hip and buried the other in a side pocket of the ragged canvas pants he wore, peering curiously down at this woman child. He suppressed an urge to laugh at the sight of such a cute little girl with a button nose and dishwater blonde hair pulled back into a braidbun atop her head, acting and dressing so grown up, but he succeeded in answering her in an even voice.

"You can call me Joshuen," he said. "C'mon." And with this he walked in the direction of the city center, striding at a moderate pace but quickly enough to cause Zhrana to interject spurts of running into her step in order to keep up. They said nothing while accompanying each other in this fashion, crossing two side streets before arriving at a small but crowded social club known as the Rendezvous.

This was one of several clubs scattered throughout the city, all run by the predominant gang and all serving alcohol as well as other "socially enhancing drugs" such as Miltern and Grinthine. Seelin had chosen it primarily because the noise and bustle would blend them into relative obscurity, and as Zhrana followed him into a small cubby in a far corner, she stared at the sight around her of couples and groups in long and eloquent, sometimes boisterous even, discussions. No visual companions, no holographic friends. She had never seen such a storm of words and passionate interactions generated with no help whatsoever from the visuals. The drugs, she thought, sitting across from her new mystery, it must be the drugs which bring this out.

On the way in, Seelin had picked up two vials of clear liquid and now he took a drink from one of them and set the other on the hard oak directly in front of the forever girl's eyes. Picking it up and wondering which drug she had been given, she was surprised and even a bit disappointed at the taste of plain water.

"You shouldn't be raising the hopes of Paula and Jask about their daughter," Seelin started, "You know as well as I that there's no way she's ever coming back to them. They were just starting to accept that and then you have to come along with talks of appeals and such." He rocked the vial back and forth on the table's surface as he spoke.

"Nothing I said was untrue," she replied. "Believe it or not there are those of us who disagree with the relocation policies and are actively fighting them. Nicoli's case is one we're working on, or were working on until one of our own investigators was kidnapped by one of your so called Liberationist groups."

"So he was working with the Naturalists, is that what you're telling me? If you're referring to the one who sometimes calls himself Kianno and sometimes Seelin, then I think you may be a little confused as to his reasons for entering our world." Seelin elevated his voice as a new group settled into a nearby table, raising the noise level a notch higher with their Grinthine inspired proclamations of deep seated psychological insights. "He never once asked about Nicoli. He was a lot more interested in those connected to his former life."

Zhrana shifted her legs and reached out toward the vial for another swallow. So he knew already. So much he'd revealed in just that one statement. Not only was this Joshuen in with the snatchers, but he knew about Kianno's true mission. Excited now at having accomplished her first objective of establishing contact, she pressed on.

"And so what have you accomplished by his kidnapping, anyway? Have you managed, through terror and brainwashing techniques, to convert one poor soul to your cause while alienating a thousand others inside the hives who might have otherwise been sympathetic enough to support you?"

Seelin remained silent, listening to the same arguments he had made to the council not too long ago. He looked around the room anxiously. Had she really come alone? He had heard that the forever children were not capable of such self sacrifice, that very few of them would ever even consider risking something of their own for another, much less risking their very lives. If nothing else, he had to admire this girl for her courage.

She must have sensed his eyes softening toward her, for she looked away before continuing her lecture. "Listen," she said in a gentler tone which struggled to be heard over the nearby voices, "I don't represent the Naturalists. I know they've been trying to establish an alliance with your groups for a long time now, and violence on both sides keeps getting in the way, but I didn't come for political reasons. I came because Kianno is a friend of mine. And because I know he came here for honorable reasons and doesn't deserve what your putting him through." She watched as he stretched his huge, rough body and leaned back in his chair with a surprising agility and balance she would never have expected.

"I don't think you really want to get into a discussion of what we all deserve," he replied, but not angrily, only as a fact to be pointed out. "What do you want, then? You know we can't just release him to you. Not yet anyway. Even if I..," he began, but retreated immediately and looked across at her. So unusual to be talking this way with such a fine and delicate girl, yet with a mind to keep up with his own.

"Let me see him, then. That's all I ask, to talk with him and reassure him that we'll be there for him when he's released. I assume he will be released like the others."

"Yes, but..." Again he hesitated.

"Look at me," she argued, standing now. "Do you really think I could be of any threat to you or your plans?"

"Anyone who knows of me, or knows of where he is kept is a threat. You could have me killed in an instant, once you escape to the other side."

"And you could have me killed before I leave. I would say you have the distinct advantage."

He couldn't argue, but knew all along that he should never have even shown up for the meeting, should have kept this dangerous interlude from ever occurring in the first place. But now it was too late, and besides, she was right about the alliance, about the need for them to work together.

"There's nothing to be gained by your seeing him. He's changed, you know. Why do you even think he wants to see you at this point?"

"Please," she implored, reaching out instinctually to place her small hands over his, "I've risked everything to see him. You can't deny me now."

At the feel of those large, scarred, bony-strong hands, Zhrana's first reaction was to pull away quickly from what had been accidentally initiated in the first place. But her hands remained in place, resting gently, so small and soft and unmarked atop his which told the story of the years, the story of so much struggle and pain. And with the gentleness of a child's touch, a woman's touch perhaps, and her equally smooth forearms with just the hint of a child's peach fuzz misting her small softness, he as well kept those hands still, for a moment anyway, and in that moment he felt a forbidden stirring rise to the surface, a stirring as frightening as it was alluring.

A moment later he retrieved himself abruptly and stood from his chair. "I've got to be going now," he said quickly. "Come with me and I'll allow you one visit, but only if he's unguarded."

Almost running now, he pushed his way through the crowd, followed closely by a small forever girl, and at greater length by another man who, invisible to Seelin, had been carefully watching the two of them since they had entered the club nearly twenty minutes ago. And as the unlikely pair exited into a welcome coolness carried in by the evening breeze, the observant stranger downed the last of his straight wodka vial and waited for enough distance to clear before stepping out in quiet pursuit.

**

She came to him after nightfall, after the guards had locked up and left the few prisoners alone to tend to their wounds, each one granted the relative luxury of a private room for those nighttime hours when they could count on being untroubled by any of the many painful schemes devised to further their conversion. Although the rooms were indeed private, and surprisingly spacious, the terrorists did require that each of them be lit at night by sulfur lamps enclosed in metal cages to protect the lamps from assault by potentially sleepless captives. The house itself was once the estate of a particularly reclusive Silicon Valley multi-millionaire who demanded such isolation that, in addition to constructing this once fabulous but now run down mansion, he had also been required to build a lengthy access road to connect up to the most remote of the county maintained roads. Now, of course, the roads had deteriorated into overgrown trails, trails which would have long since disappeared altogether had they not been clipped back occasionally by the liberationists to keep them distinguishable among the encroaching thicket of poison oak and blackberry bushes.

She came alone and uninvited as he lay in bed already imagining her as he did so often now, seeing her full breasts, the delicacy of her lips, the freshness of her white body, the smooth skin of her long legs, a smoothness and a smallness which had been quite mundanely his own for so long but now took on a whole new attraction when seen embodied in her, when seen in a woman's body which could be so close to his own, and as he lay in his bed, the dull pain of the day overcome by thoughts of touching her, he was already hard and ready when she surprised him with her visit.

Not that he had been bothersome in communicating his desires to her. On the contrary, unlike the other two, who not only bothered her no end for sexual favors and also engaged her in talk and questions of a sexual nature out of sheer curiosity, Kianno had kept to himself since that day when he had absent mind-edly touched her, and maybe it was in part due to her concern for his unusual shyness and silence (really shame) that she gifted him with this uninvited visit.

In fact, as she approached him silently now he unexpectedly rose from his bed and turned from her, ashamed of the grotesque protrusion showing through even the loose fitting sara he wore, embarrassed at the gross, hairy animal he had become, but she stepped quietly behind him nonetheless and pressed her body against his, caressing his shoulders and following the line of his emerging muscles down along the sides of him, then finding him there and touching him so softly.

Now he turned to look her in the eyes. "I've never..." he stammered, "Like this I mean. What do they do?"

"The same," she replied. "Whatever feels good." She pressed her breasts against his chest and looked up. It was only in the last week that he had grown taller than her, and heavier now as well.

"The same?" he questioned, then "But I've grown too big now."

"Quiet," she said as softly as possible, "Talk with your hands now."

And now he reached around to grab her, to pull her to the ground with a drive still so unfamiliar that he had been afraid to let it out, afraid it was only danger which he contained within him and not realizing that she might also contain this same danger, that she might also feel this same drive for him as well. Now naked beside her, Kianno felt for the first time a grown woman's body, the slope of her stomach, the small but so attentive and willing breasts rising to his touch, the first sensation of her smoothness against his muscles and emerging hair growing quickly over his legs, the open spot between her legs, so unnoticed before in forever girls but so deliciously empty and inviting now, the silky pubic hairs brushing like down against his own so recently grown yet already dark and strong, like his body had grown dark and strong.

He rode her quickly and furiously, overpowered by a flood of rising and irretrievable sensations he had never before experienced in sexmaking, and when he had released himself in an physical crescendo unlike any he had ever felt before, he lay atop her, still supporting himself with his arms but panting for breath as she continued to rock slowly beneath him.

Sensing her continued excitement, he resumed his own small thrusting, but found himself growing limp and unable to press on toward a second climax. Frustrated and confused, he whispered to her.

"I don't understand, I'm ready for more, but..."

"It's different now," she reassured him. "It's all right. It will take some time before..."

She did not need to complete the thought. He already knew it was different now, that there was a whole new language to be learned, so he relaxed his arms and lay side by side, not knowing what to do. Looking down at their two bodies, he was suddenly gripped by a sense of revulsion and disgust as great as had been his physical pleasure only moments before. The animals they had been turned into, he realized, looking down at his own hairy ugliness, and the previous irresistibility of her own fully developed body now filled him with disgust as well. A lifetime of teaching had been temporarily overwhelmed by purely hormonal and physical needs, but now everything he had been taught and experienced for his entire adult life about outsiders who had grown beyond the threshold flooded back to him, and he was immediately more ashamed at his own newly transformed body for having been unable to control it or resist its desires.

"Please," he said quickly to her, shaking with fright and confusion, "You must go now, please." It was the same as if he had watched himself change into a coyote who now bayed at the moon uncontrollably. Not only did he have no power over the horrible changes in his appearance, but it was now fully apparent that he had no control over this body's actions either.

When she had obligingly left, he wrapped himself in the bedding they had given him and closed his eyes tightly against the glare of the sulfur lamp, full of anxiety and dread at the changes which had overtaken him. And this was the state that Seelin and Zhrana found him in when they entered the compound only two hours later.

***

"Kianno. Are you awake, Kianno? It's me, Zhrana." He had come so close to finally escaping into sleep when these words brought him back with a start. He sat upright in a full panic.

"Zhrana!" he exclaimed, peering up at the familiar face he had not seen for a full month, relieved and excited at first, then suddenly realizing what her presence here could mean. "Zhrana, how did you get here?" He scanned the room quickly but it was empty. "Have they somehow managed to capture you as well?" The thought suddenly went through his head that he might now have someone to share his ordeal, a friend who could keep him from having to face the world alone should he ever make it back to the great hive.

"Kianno?" She paused before responding, staring at a face which still contained the seeds of the forever boy she had previously known, but had been transformed and pushed into a deformation of the original structure which was unlike either forever child or man, but rather appeared to be some kind of bizarre combination of the two. Recognizing the awkwardness of her silence, however, she replied at length. "No. It's all right. I haven't been captured. Joshuen has allowed me to visit. He's in the next room."

"Joshuen?" wondered Kianno. "You mean they let you in here just to visit me? That doesn't make sense. Why would they do that?" Irritated now, he looked away from his visitor.

"It doesn't matter. Kianno, are you OK? We've been so worried!"

"No. I'm not OK, as you can plainly see. I can't have you look at me this way. Please, go away, there's nothing you can do for me now." He stood and walked to a window, placing his hands over the sill. "You can tell them that I'm still alive and not in any danger of dying, at least not to my knowledge. But I'm not ready to go back yet."

"What do you mean, not ready?" Zhrana answered in a surprised and worried tone. "Kianno there's something I need to tell you." She walked over to his side, slightly afraid at the size he had become in only a matter of weeks. Looking up at his profile against the darkness of the night outside the barred window, she spoke in a hushed voice.

"Kianno, I've come to bring you back, to get you out of here."

"Ha, that's ridiculous. There's nothing you could..."

"Shh," she interrupted. "I've brought a weapon, a slowstunner. With it we can both escape this place."

"You don't need to escape. Zhrana, don't risk your own life for mine. It's not worth it. You've still got your true self; you've still got everything. Don't risk that for someone who isn't even ready to be freed. I'm serious when I say I'm not ready to face the world like this. I need more time, if ever…"

"Kianno," she said, placing a hand on his back for reassurance, but he shrugged it like a fly. "We know what to expect, and the family has confirmed that you'll still be welcome; you'll still be loved. Sofia especially has been so worried." She tried to get his attention with her eyes, but he remained stoically silent. Failing to elicit any response, she added more firmly. "I'm going to bring you out of here, whether you like it or not. If you don't cooperate, that'll only put me in danger as well."

With these words she pulled up the sleeve of her sara all the way to the shoulder. On the inside of her left arm a small suture about two inches long could be seen. On one side of this scar was a small fold of epidermal tissue which had been bobbed above the remaining skin into a barely noticeable tag dangling outward, appearing like some kind of minor incongruity, perhaps a small birth defect or similar blemish. With her right hand, Zhrana now fingered the tag gently, pausing to gather courage, then grasped it tightly between her thumb and index finger and pulled fiercely.

"Mmmnn" she grunted, trying her best to stifle any sound from the intense pain of ripping flesh. In the last two days the wound had begun to heal, and pulling the tag once again opened the large incision which had been made as a shallow grave for the slowstunner buried under the surface. Now doubled over in pain but still facing away from the door in case Joshuen should reappear, she felt inside her reopened wound and slowly extracted a slim black device about three inches long and one inch wide. It was a fully state-of-the-art stunner weapon, unscannable and undetectable as long as the implantation site was not examined too carefully.

"Zhrana you're bleeding!" Kianno exclaimed, eyes drawn to the fresh wound but still not seeing the weapon she now held tightly in the palm of her right hand. Zhrana was just about to respond when their attentions were interrupted by heavy footsteps and a shuffling noise approaching the doorway. She just had time to tuck the blood stained section of her sara out of view and hide her arms and hands behind her, when a stranger entered the room abruptly, followed closely by Seelin.

"Well isn't this touching," the stranger began, smiling at the two of them backed up against the window, "The little forever girl has come to visit her lost love. Only now he isn't quite the same anymore, is he?" Not waiting for an answer, he continued in a mocking tone. "I hope this doesn't change things between you, I mean, him all grown up and everything." Now the man snapped his fingers and grinned once again. "I know how we can fix this difficult situation. Let's just let the little girl grow up so that you two can still be together again. Of course that's going to take a little time, but fortunately there's plenty of room here at Chez Adolescence for one more visitor."

As he spoke, Seelin looked on with a serious expression which tried unsuccessfully to mask the sympathy he felt for their predicament. Zhrana looked into his eyes and could tell instantly that this had been an accident, that she had not been purposefully lured into this trap.

The stranger turned to Seelin now. "You're more clever than I ever gave you credit for, Seelin."

"Seelin!" Kianno gasped to himself, but in the hush of the tense room his surprise escaped for everyone to hear. He glanced cautiously at Seelin and for the first time the two of them saw each other for who they truly were: caretakers of the roles they had each been torn from so long ago, symbols of what each might have become had their timelines not been so severely disrupted on that fateful day thirty years ago. Before either could utter another word, however, the stranger cut the moment short by addressing Seelin once more.

"I think it best if we separate them for the first couple weeks of her...initiation, don't you think?" he said, stepping toward Zhrana as she trembled inside with anticipation of what could no longer be delayed.

"Stop," she instructed firmly. "Please don't come any closer or I'll be forced to stun you!" She gripped the small device in her hand, then loosened her fist and opened her fingers to make it visible. "I've heard it's not a very pleasant experience."

"What's going on here? You didn't even scan her?" he asked Seelin, not turning around but still staring at the small black weapon aimed directly at him.

"Of course I scanned her," Seelin muttered, taking a step back.

Pausing for a moment to gather his thoughts, the stranger now pulled Seelin aside and whispered furtively. "If it really is a slowstunner, it will take at least five seconds to regenerate for a second shot. If we both rush her, whoever doesn't get hit can certainly take it from her and stun them both. Both of them are still no match for one of us."

"I don't know," Seelin answered. "It was unscannable, and we've never seen that before. And the size of it... How do we know it may not have instant regeneration as well?"

"Well, we don't, do we?" came the response. "But there don't seem to be too many options either."

And before Seelin could answer, the rebel rushed headlong toward the frightened pair, screaming in an attempt to confuse the forever girl into a misfire or a hesitation, but Zhrana stayed calm enough to aim the weapon directly at his solar plexus and fire. Instantly, the attacker froze in position, then toppled over onto the hard floor, as the pose in which he had been frozen was not balanced and his nerves now had lost the ability to react quickly enough to move his legs to regain a balanced position. The slow stunner was a device similar to the weapon which had been used on Jask and Paula during Nicoli's interrogation, in that the victim remained conscious and in full possession of all senses. However, the slow stunner did not freeze entirely all nervous impulses, only slowed down those controlling the voluntary muscles to such an extent that the victim could continue to move his body, only at a much slower rate. So slow, in fact, that it would take the downed rebel a full hour to crawl the ten feet which separated him from Zhrana.

Seelin hesitated for only a moment before following his companion's attack with one of his own, rushing headlong toward Zhrana, while Kianno stood frozen at her side, too shocked to react in any organized fashion. As he ran toward the forever girl, fully expecting to be stunned at any moment, he glanced down at his fellow rebel and saw plainly that his head was faced toward the captives, eyes open and alert.

As it turned out, the newest of slowstunners did indeed have a much reduced regeneration time, however Zhrana still paused much too long after the initial firing to get a shot off before Seelin had come upon her, astonished that this seemingly sympathetic man was suddenly bearing down on her at full speed.

The ensuing collision nearly knocked Zhrana out cold, and sent the slow-stunner clattering across the floor as Zhrana, Seelin, and Kianno scrambled furiously to reach it. Kianno grabbed Seelin around the neck and tried to restrain him enough to allow Zhrana the opportunity to gain the lead in this frantic chase for the device which lay innocuously only twelve feet away. Seelin, however, carried the youth along with no problem whatsoever, then reached back to push Kianno off him while Zhrana fought slowly, still dazed, toward the weapon. When he reached the slowstunner, and just as he was about to grasp it for good, Seelin glanced quickly behind him to see whether or not he was in his companion's direct view, then, in a move visible only to himself and Zhrana, flicked the weapon just beyond his reach and groped slowly but loudly for it while Zhrana regained her senses enough to quickly retrieve the weapon and point it menacingly at him.

His eyes told her to fire, and after only a very slight hesitation she did so, freezing him in a blanket of numbness where he lay for a full twelve hours. By the time both of them were found the next morning, Zhrana and Kianno had made their way to the safety of the quarantine chambers forty feet beneath Cambria Hive.

14

E ven if most of the Forshas family members were unfortunately unable to come to greet Zhrana and Kianno upon their emergence a week later from the isolation chambers, at least the key representatives and closest members had shown up. Foremost among them, and waiting most impatiently of all, was Sofia, who had arrived a full two hours early and was now pacing anxiously as the entire group watched the series of indicator lights proceed through their phases, each one signaling the pair's procession from one decontamination cell to another, until finally the huge portal doors whisked open and the two returning voyagers stepped into the warm embraces of their oldest friends.

"Sofia!" exclaimed Zhrana, gripping her shoulders and leaning over to kiss her forehead, a kiss which Sofia returned delicately.

"Zhrana, how can I ever thank you? I will always be in your debt." Then she turned her attention toward her son, who now towered over her, towered over them all, in fact, to such an extent that it placed him on an entirely different plane from the rest of them. Sofia looked up into his eyes and stepped forth to embrace him, but was met with the awkward question of physical greeting posed by his ungainly size.

"Kianno," she began, wishing she could rise to kiss his forehead and hug him in the way of her father and mother, but when he did not stoop down to allow such an embrace they found themselves in a clumsy hug of her arms reaching around his hips, with Kianno placing one of his large hands on Sofia's back, pressing her to him finally in a reluctant, somewhat embarrassed admission of his inability to greet her in the traditional way.

"Kianno," she said again, full of love and tremendous relief at seeing him again after so much time and so many worries that he might never return. She tried to formulate some words of reassurance, of support, but could not find any amidst the emotion which overwhelmed her, so instead she buried her head once more in his stomach and hugged him as tightly as she could.

Meanwhile, the rest of the entourage took turns stepping forth to welcome Zhrana back: her friend Jil as well as two other especially close friends, Rokyo, head of the family unit, and Jaslo who made his way finally from the back of the group to greet her. In their greetings of Zhrana, nearly all stole quick glances at the newly created giant looming over them who was still held close by his mother, all except for Jaslo, that is, who did not even look in his direction, and immediately returned to the background as soon as he had obligatorily greeted and thanked Zhrana.

Next to speak to Kianno was Rokyo, who made no attempt at an awkward physical display but instead addressed him firmly. "Kianno, I know this is a very troubling time for you, and I know you've been through more than any of us could ever imagine enduring," he said, speaking from a memorized text. "But I wanted you to know that we have discussed this matter as a family, and we have decided that even though we've never had any of..er..your kind in Forshas, we have asked the state to support your continuing as a member of our family. We know this is something you've undoubtedly been thinking about, and so I wanted to let you know right away that we're going to do everything possible to keep you with us." He stepped back and looked at Kianno, who had grown now to a height of six feet and had in the week of isolation begun to fill out and take on a more mature look.

"Thank you," responded Kianno, looking over the tops of their heads. "Thank you for helping me out in the little time I have left."

"Fifty years can be an eternity," volunteered Jil hopefully, trying to brighten the situation. "I know some who do more in fifty years than most do in a lifetime." But no one followed up on her enthusiasm, and the words sounded hollow voiced alone.

"I know," answered Kianno. "I plan to try and make the most of them. And I do appreciate your coming out here to welcome me and all, and especially your allowing me to stay in the family. Right now I'm tired, though. I haven't seen the quadrant for so long..."

"Of course, let us proceed to the slider," Rokyo announced. "I'm sure you can tell us all the fascinating stories later." With this he turned about and led the small group down the corridor toward a rear slider access.

As they walked along, mostly silent now, Jaslo finally brought himself to look at the monstrosity into which his son had been transformed, and came close enough to utter a few words of greeting.

"Welcome to the family," he began, still unable to look into Kianno's eyes, which were unavailable at any rate. "I hope everything will turn out for you." He paused, stumbling a little as he walked along, then added "I'm sorry that you had to pay such a price for..."

"I'm sorry as well," answered Kianno softly. "I'm sorry I had to bring this onto everyone, not just myself."

The two of them now slowed and held back from the main group as they approached the slider entrance, sharing an awkward silence before Jaslo spoke again.

"Did you," he ventured with words delivered reluctantly but necessarily, "find what you were looking for?"

"Yes," Kianno answered smoothly, an answer rehearsed many times with Zhrana in the long hours of quarantine. It was better, they had concluded, that they not know of Seelin. Better for both of them but especially better for Sofia. His response took Jaslo by surprise, however, causing him to stop altogether.

"You mean someone is still alive? Your parents, or..."

"No, not still alive. Long since dead in their world and finally dead in mine. That's all I was looking for, I suppose."

"You should have known; we did everything to be sure before we brought you here. I wish you could have been satisfied with that. Now it will be so difficult and dangerous to make you well again."

"Make me well again?" Kianno puzzled. "What do you mean by that? I can only hope to at least survive the fifty years I have left; you know that."

"Perhaps," replied the elder child in almost an offhand way. "But we shouldn't ever give up hope, should we?" And, before Kianno could follow up on these mysterious words, the slider doors whisked open and they pressed forward with the rest of the group, through the narrow portal and into the close quarters of the slider itself, which brought their short conversation to an end.

***

Before Kianno could even become fully acquainted with his modified living quarters, which had been specially prepared for him in anticipation of his newly acquired handicap, he was interrupted by a stranger's voice announcing itself into his room.

"Kianno of Forshas," it inquired in a businesslike tone, "My name is Batiste and I am here with my associate Crino. We are from the State anti-terrorist tactical unit and we'd like to have a few words with you."

Kianno, grateful that they'd arrived after Zhrana had left, did not hesitate to grant them entrance, and after access had been transmitted the two officials stepped briskly into the room, dressed casually in ordinary saras which gave no hint of their enforcement status.

"We apologize for visiting so soon after your release," began Batiste, a fair skinned forever boy with a tangle of blonde hair, unpressed as was becoming the fashion. He was clearly the driver of the team, and it was primarily himself who conducted the interrogation, with only occasional questions interjected by his associate. "It's just that we've found that more can be remembered if we don't wait too long..."

"It's quite all right, really," replied Kianno. "I've been expecting you."

"If you don't mind us saying so, your particular case gives us certain...opportunities that we're not ordinarily allowed. You see, most often when kidnapped citizens are returned they have already completed the snatchers' brainwashing process, and are, well, let's say less than fully cooperative." The official shifted uncomfortably. He knew this approach was a bit of a gamble, since he couldn't be certain yet of where Kianno's allegiance lay, yet he still felt it was better to proceed with positive assumptions.

"I understand," Kianno answered, eager to leave no doubt. "And let me assure you I want to do absolutely everything I can to help you prevent anyone else from going through what happened to me. Please..." For the first time since his escape, he felt like he could actually contribute something productive, instead of simply doing his best to minimize the burden he now placed on the family.

Batiste drew a deep breath, placed a visual recorder on the table next to him, then began. "I'd like to start with the others who we believe were kidnapped. If you could confirm their status as well as their...leanings, so to speak, that would help us considerably."

So Kianno described in detail all he knew of his fellow prisoners, aware, of course, that their testimony was unlikely to be of much help to the authorities upon their release, which was undoubtedly imminent. The thought did enter his head that it was perhaps of questionable ethics to be revealing information about his fellow captives when it was clear such information was unlikely to quicken their release, but he was determined to demonstrate to the authorities that he had not been brainwashed and could be fully trusted. Such trust was critical, he knew, to his future as a citizen. He also genuinely wanted to do what he could in the war against these snatchings.

After revealing what he could remember about the three left in captivity, the interrogation soon became focused on the kidnappers themselves, as well as their whereabouts.

"How many of them were there?" asked the senior official, anxiously getting into the more critical questions.

"Only three that I came into contact with. There may have been others."

"And can you describe them to me? Please be as detailed as possible."

Kianno hesitated, rubbing his feet together and looking at the floor. Then he brought his eyes up and replied in a strong tone. "I'm afraid I can't help you there. They remained disguised the entire time. I never saw their faces at all." In truth, aside from the doctor, Seelin had been the only one he had seen clearly, and he couldn't bring himself to uncover his identity. Although he still felt anger toward the man who had taken his forever childhood, it was an anger tempered with an unexplainable feeling that perhaps he had deserved it, that he had only been forced to return what he had originally stolen thirty years ago.

"That's odd," questioned the official, rubbing his hand over his forehead. "It isn't entirely consistent with previous reports." He paused, waiting for some kind of explanation, but when none was forthcoming he did his best to appear generous in dismissing the incongruity. "Well, I suppose they may have changed their ways."

"Can you describe, then, the location of where you were held?" interjected the second official, who had thus far been silent.

"Yes," Kianno replied brightly, "I believe from what I saw as we escaped I can pinpoint it fairly precisely, given a map of the area."

At that, Batiste dialed the controls of his visual companion, and after a few minutes was able to project a scaled down topographic visual of the entire Lexington mountain area. Straining to relate the ridges and valleys to his own memories, Kianno struggled for some time before identifying a small canyon hidden in the shadow of Mt. Umunhum.

"I think it was somewhere in this gulch," he concluded, unable to be more precise.

"Wait just one moment," said Batiste. "I believe I can superimpose a structure layer, but it will be approximately fifty years outdated. You said this building was not of recent construction?"

"Yes, very old actually."

"Good."

After searching through indexes of textural image layers, Batiste found what he was looking for and the hologram was suddenly enhanced with an additional level of detail. Alone in the middle of the isolated canyon, the old mansion now stood out distinctly at the confluence of a smaller creek with the main branch.

"That's it, I'm sure of it," exclaimed Kianno, and both officials smiled as Batiste highlighted the structure in red before dissolving the artificial topography.

"Now, and this is most important," The official retook his seat and leaned forward, elbows on knees and hands clenched together into a tight ball. "Did you at any time hear them mention any of their contacts within the hives? Any names or information at all regarding Naturalist sympathizers operating from within?"

Kianno paused, intentionally giving the impression that he was searching his memory, while in actuality he was reconfirming in his own mind a decision which had earlier emerged from the confusion of his ambivalent loyalties. Surely he could say nothing of Sofia, or Zhrana. But there was one who could be given up, one removed from any personal ties but important enough within the organization to effectively strike a blow against internal groups who worked for the interests of those who had taken away his chance at a normal life.

"They didn't mention any names," he replied finally, "But I do have information about a certain individual that you may find very interesting..."

***

No one noticed when the blonde, serious looking forever boy slipped indiscreetly into the meeting room not long after Xyloru of Jorbash had made a much more recognized entrance. Everyone's attention was instead drawn to the front of the chamber, where a member of the radical wing had taken the floor.

"These most recent skull cappings only reinforce what we've been arguing all along, that our political efforts are totally useless. They consider our petitions and appeals while at the same time murdering and skull capping at an increasing rate. Am I the only one who sees them laughing at our so-called peaceful change initiative?"

The small but noisy crowd greeted this declaration with a few cheers but mostly with whistles and boos. One member shouted out above the rest.

"And they can point to the snatchings the same way we point to the cappings. We can't legitimize state terrorism with our own. You know we'll never win a war fought with synthars and rad-scatters!"

"Not as long as they're the only ones who are armed!" the radical shouted back, his words almost swallowed by a rising unease in the room. "It's time to answer their attacks with those of our own. It's time to get the outsiders the weapons they need to escalate the war they're trying to fight with no help from us!"

Now Xyloru stood and raised his hands to the group, imploring the crowd for silence, and the noise did gradually subside as it's most powerful member was recognized.

"I think we can agree," began Xyloru to the stunned silence of his supporters, "that we need to re-establish contact with the activist outsider groups. So that we can work together. Not for war," and with those words the tension eased and the crowd settled, "but toward peace, and a peaceful restoration of outsider rights."

At this, a few radicals hooted with skepticism, but Atascin's closest aide continued. "And we may have an opportunity, perhaps, with the recently freed captive. Sofia..." he called out, searching carefully for his long time friend and, more importantly now, close keeper and family member of Kianno. "Sofia, are you here?"

Surprised at this sudden introduction, Sofia did not answer immediately, but instead waited a moment before acknowledging the speaker. Xyloru's eyes had already found her, though, and he immediately pointed her out.

"Sofia, you've had a chance to talk with this captive. Kianno is his name, I believe?"

"Yes," she answered with uncharacteristic hesitation.

"Is he..." Xyloru began, then searched for a more delicate way of phrasing it. "Do you think he might be persuaded to return to the outside in order to attempt some kind of contact on our behalf?"

"It's very early," Sofia edged, "Too early. He's been through a lot and I don't think he'd be ready to return any time soon. Plus, I doubt he'd have any better idea how and who to contact than we do, based on what we've learned from others who have returned." She waited for the speaker's quick dismissal, but he was disinclined to retreat so easily from his proposal.

"Let's talk about this later, shall we?" he replied at length. "In time, perhaps, if we handle this correctly, we may have a chance to establish the valuable relationship we've been trying for for so long but which keeps slipping through our fingers."

Seated next to Sofia, Zhrana steadfastly held her silence, aware of her own opportunities but too frightened and nowhere near dedicated enough to the cause yet to volunteer her own secrets. Zhrana herself had attended today's meeting more out of curiosity than anything else, and Sofia was not about to chase her away with public questions about how Kianno had been found in the first place.

Meanwhile, sitting patiently only a few yards from the two forever girls, another newcomer observed the proceedings with more than a passing interest, secretly monitoring the entire affair with a visuals recorder hidden deep in the folds of his light brown evening sara.

***

There were fifteen of them, elite members of the state's own zega-squad, equipped with night vision eye implants and Q synthars capable of disintegrating entire walls and structures if necessary. Sweeping in from the woods with cold efficiency, most of them, including their commander, were just a tad disappointed at how easy their mission turned out to be. No return synthar waves, no kamikaze attacks; in fact, no opposition whatsoever as they converged on the old mansion then entered it from five different doorways, finding at first only themselves stalking the empty hallways.

The Liberationists had been correct in their suspicions that Kianno's escape merited desertion of this favorite hideaway, and it was some time before the zega-squad found the only three occupants, tucked away and sleeping soundly in a back room stocked with plenty of food and water to ensure their survival until either they were 'rescued' or enough time had gone by for the outsiders to safely re-claim the building. Actually, the timing of this whole affair worked out quite well for them, aside from the unfortunate loss of the house as a base of operations. Their captives had completed the conversion process, and it was certainly more convenient to have them 'picked up' than to go through the trickier procedure of delivering them as near as possible to a checkpoint, where they would undoubtedly run into a great deal of difficulty convincing the officials of their real identities.

"Commander, we've found three of them hiding in the east wing," a uniformed squad member informed the sleepy looking forever child who had established a small encampment in one of the mansion's great rooms while his team canvassed the house.

"Very good," he replied, not bothering to get up but instead leaning even further back in the lounger he had found. "Prepare them for capping immediately."

"But sir, they claim to be citizens, and even though they're well beyond the threshold they do appear rather young, for outsiders. Plus, we've detected signal implants. I've taken the liberty of sending for a reader."

"Yes, I suppose it would be best to find out, wouldn't it? It will most definitely affect the disposition." The forever boy sat up a bit now and for the first time met his team member's eyes with his own, to emphasize his instructions. "Go ahead and verify their identities," he continued slowly, "and if they're not citizens you may prepare them for capping. If they are citizens, you will also prepare them for capping."

"But sir, if they're..."

"You heard what I said," the commander interrupted. "They're no longer to be trusted, you understand. They undoubtedly have been turned against us, and are as much a danger as the terrorists themselves, perhaps more so. Prepare them as I've instructed. I'll be along shortly to do the honors myself."

The officer looked away from his superior, still not moving, then after only a moment's pause of protest, turned and walked briskly away.

***

"This had better be important," scowled his highest eminence to this stranger who had the audacity to alarm him from such a critical meeting of the Senate

Committee on Outsider Affairs. "On whose authority did you gain access to my call signal?"

"Your eminence," answered the blonde forever boy with utmost courtesy. "I agree that it is most unfortunate that I have had to call you, however I think you will understand..."

"First answer my question. Who are you and on whose authority do you dare pull me from my business?"

"It was my authority," came the reply from a short but exceedingly overweight forever boy, draped in the royal red vestments of Public Senators, who had just entered the room and stood at a distance from the other two.

"Timoty, what's going on?" asked Atascin, but the Senator only gestured to the blonde forever boy with a look which suddenly legitimized this interruption. Atascin turned back to the stranger and listened now.

"My name is Batiste, and I am with the anti-terrorist tactical unit. I know you are a busy man so I'll get right to the point. Your Administrative Operations Chief has been arrested for conspiracy and treason. He is being detained at this time and the state will be pressing for a trial within the week. You know, of course, the penalty for such crimes."

"This is impossible!" exclaimed Atascin, suddenly fighting a swell of fear and anxiety. "There must be some kind of mistake. Xyloru?" Then, in a more threatening tone, "What evidence do you have to back such accusations?"

And there, in the blink of an eye, was the undeniable image of Xyloru addressing the Naturalists, making his impassioned pleas for establishing contact with the terrorists, followed by additional exerpts from the meeting which clearly demonstrated his involvement.

Atascin's first instinct was to try and defend his aide, but he resisted this tendency out of a realization that it was most likely a lost cause to save his associate from such damning and indisputable evidence. All that was left was to distance himself as far as possible from these activities.

"This is impossible. I can't believe what I have just seen," he stammered once the visuals had been dissolved, addressing himself more to his fellow senator who looked on dubiously from the far end of the room. "I've known Xyloru for fifteen years now, and I simply can't believe he's involved in such activities! I believe I owe it to my friend, however, to hear his side of this affair, and to give him the benefit of the doubt that perhaps he was acting to infiltrate these groups instead of participating as one of them. Clearly I can't believe he would advocate violence, and I did not see him do so on what you have just shown me." As soon as the words were out he wished he could take them back; he had ventured too close to defending the sympathizers and would have to be more careful to deflect the suspicion which was naturally directed at himself now.

"I'm sure you'll have a chance to speak with the suspect," answered Batiste coldly. "And you can be assured that the trial will be thorough." He paused and looked toward the overweight Senate floor leader for help.

Now the leader gradually dragged himself toward the other two, speaking as he did so. "Senator Atascin, I have already had a chance to review these findings and indeed to go over them with the Vice-Chairman as well. We believe that, given how close this man was to you and your entire staff, it would be best to suspend your membership on the Committee, at least until this thing can be properly resolved."

"This is preposterous! There are no grounds for…"

"We are not questioning your loyalty, please understand," the leader interrupted. "It's only that the appearance of impropriety may seriously affect your ability to represent your constituents in decisions of outsider affairs. No one is thinking of suspending your status as a Senator or your participation in any other Committees."

Atascin paused before responding, gathering his thoughts carefully. "Your eminence, let me state clearly that I do appreciate your judiciousness in this matter. Of course, I assure you that I had no idea whatsoever of Xyloru's activities, and I would hope that my reputation should be above such trivial suspicions. Nevertheless, I understand that appearances must also be accounted for, and I would suggest as well that removal of myself from the committee at this critical time, with the 563 vote coming up, may also give the appearance of having been politically motivated. I believe this would be most unfortunate. Perhaps if any action were delayed until after…"

"I'm sorry," answered the floor leader. "We can't allow the upcoming vote to be tainted with this."

"Then I will be forced to bring the vote up once more after I'm reinstated. This vote also must not be tainted with politically motivated deception!"

"You may attempt a re-vote, and I wish the best of luck in arranging the necessary support," he replied, turning away from Atascin and walking toward the exit, then called out an afterthought. "You have my word that I would have preferred passing this bill by overcoming your unrestrained opposition." He finished his breath with a soft chuckle, then drew another. "But I won't be too disappointed should our victory be just a little bit tarnished."

Atascin, knowing better than to respond out of sheer anger, stood quietly and watched as the floor leader's flowing red robes disappeared through the portal wings.

***

And that was not even Batiste's last stop of the day, a day which most unit investigators could only dream of but which Kianno had handed him on a silver platter. His next, and final, visit was to the Mustass Kann Research Center for the Diseases of Aging, located deep within the perimeter laid out for the FF Family Medical Clinic. A certain amount of research by Batiste had gone into simply locating the whereabouts of the center, so private were its activities, and when he finally approached a monitor station at the far end of the Orthopedics Hall, he noticed no sign or any other indication that he had actually found the entrance. Cautiously, he addressed the lone forever girl who sat vacantly staring out from her station frame.

"I'm here to see Dr. Jaslo of Forshas," he informed the guard, who for a moment only looked at him with a puzzled expression. Clearly she did not often receive guests at this the only public entrance.

"I'm sorry, but he's not expecting you," she answered, not bothering to check anything in particular. She was well aware that all doctors brought their few guests in with them, and usually through their own entrance.

"I think you'd better call him," answered Batiste firmly. "I have a direct access pass and police authority to speak with him." Uninvited, he placed his wrist in the scan collar adjacent to the station and waited patiently while the guard sat up and took notice of the results on her screen.

"I'm sorry, sir," she coughed. "Please wait just a moment while I call an escort."

Soon thereafter his escort did arrive and the visitor was led through a maze of empty hallways by a somewhat reluctant doctor who was doing his best, Batiste was sure, of avoiding anything of interest whatsoever. Finally he was deposited into a small waiting chamber and paced anxiously before a surprised Jaslo stepped into the room. After an exchange of pleasantries, Batiste got right to the point.

"We have evidence, I'm afraid," he began, "that a close family member of yours, a Sofia of Forshas, has been involved in subversive activities which may possibly involve conspiracy with outsider terrorists."

The doctor released a long sigh and said nothing as the official presented his evidence. The moment was not entirely unexpected, and had been converging upon them slowly, over many years. He had always been aware, of course, of Sofia's leanings, and had even gone along with her early idealistic notions of having a 'son', unwilling to let her unusual ideas interfere with the their love for each other. Through the years, however, she had grown increasingly concerned with the rights of, and so-called injustices against, the outsiders who were the only ones to fully embrace the lifestyle she tried to imitate. For the longest time the two of them had entertained each other with heated debates and political arguments until those arguments could no longer be contained within the boundaries they tried to set, until the animosity from those differences unavoidably seeped into the rest of their day, causing both of them to silently decide to ignore entirely their political differences and activities as the only way of preserving their life together. Yes, he was well aware that she was involved with Naturalist sympathizers, but had chosen to look the other way, knowing that simple expression of support was no crime, and unconvinced at any rate that these groups had any effect whatsoever on outsider laws.

So it wasn't with an entirely honest face that he accepted these accusations with as much surprise and astonishment as he could muster. Then he waited for Batiste to make his move.

"Ordinarily," the official was saying, "we might have already arrested her. Certainly we would have confronted her directly by now." He paused, absently rolling a curl of his hair with his index finger. "But we've decided to handle this case a little differently. First of all, although of course we're certain as to her participation, since her remarks at this meeting were quite limited, the legal status of our case is less clear than we'd prefer. Second, and I trust you'll appreciate our sentiments here, is that we're aware of your relationship with Sofia, and since you're obviously a very influential friend of the State, we wanted to extend this courtesy of informing you first."

Jaslo had been listening from the comfort of one the room's full body support racks, which suspended him in an upright position from countless friction points connected by rods to a t-steel frame. Now he released himself and stepped onto the floor.

"So what, then, do you plan to do with her," he challenged, making no apologies for Batiste's courtesy.

"We don't believe she's a major player. Perhaps if you might be able to keep an eye on her for us..."

"Keep an eye on her? You mean have her trailed?" Jaslo scoffed loudly. "You do know how long we've been together, don't you? You don't think if I asked her..."

"Well, clearly she has been less than honest with you for some time. I must stress, doctor, that the alternative would undoubtedly be arrest, and I believe that would be most unfortunate for her, as well as embarrassing for you."

A chime sounded and the portal wings slid open, admitting an apologetic looking doctor who would have waited for a break in the conversation had he not found himself already in the awkward silence of Jaslo's consideration of Sofia's predicament.

"Excuse me, I'm very sorry to interrupt," the doctor said to Jaslo, "but I'm afraid one of your patients is in some distress."

"Brin?"

"Yes, I'm afraid she's worsening."

"Thank you. I'll be right there." He gestured to the forever boy to leave them, and once the two of them were once again alone, he turned to Batiste and eyed him curiously.

"I'm not sure I understand why you would have me arrange for her to be watched. Surely you have your own people, whose trust would be much more certain than someone so close to her."

"Yes, that's quite true," Batiste replied. "Perhaps you are simply a little too suspicious. As I said, we have decided to let you handle this matter for now, simply out of courtesy to one who has been so supportive in the past, and upon whose support we know we can continue to count on in the future."

"I make no deals or promises. This is your decision."

"Understood, fully." Batiste now started toward the door, satisfied that his business was done. "And besides," he added, "You'll never know for sure to what extent we may be monitoring the situation as well. Only two conditions remain that I need to mention."

"Yes?" Jaslo stopped just short of the portal sensor.

"Of course you'll not tell her anything; we need as much information as we can and her knowing of our infiltration would stop short our investigation. And second, you'll allow your agent to be debriefed by our people at least every week. That's it."

"Acceptable," answered Jaslo, waving his hands to open the portal gates. "I hope you do realize my gratefulness for your handling this matter so delicately. It will not be forgotten. Be assured that I will be contacting you as soon as the arrangements have been made."

The doctor who had interrupted them was patiently waiting outside the room, expecting to escort Jaslo to his patient, but instead he was instructed to accompany Batiste out of the secured area while the researcher hurried off to tend to this latest crisis among his current stable of experimental subjects.

15

"Game of Zinger?"

She had finally found him heading toward the slider, after several unsuccessful attempts at eliciting a response from outside his room earlier in the day.

"I've got things to do. Maybe later." He looked down at her with a still sullen face, feeling much too sorry for himself, she decided.

"Kianno of Forshas turning down a game of Zinger?" she said with mock incredulity. "That's a first. Has your brain been so affected by all this that you can actually refuse me a game in the green court?" She looked up trying to recognize some of the playfulness she could usually draw from him, but Kianno only stared straight ahead and continued walking.

"O.K. Bad joke, I admit it." Now she grabbed onto his hand with both arms and tugged him to a halt. "But really, are you sure you don't want to play?"

This was at least enough to cause him to consider the offer more seriously. It wasn't really that he didn't want to play; he'd like nothing better than a long game of green court zinger just like they used to play. Problem was, it couldn't be that way now. The two of them couldn't just walk into the Sports Hub and claim a court without being noticed and pointed out and asked for explanations.

"I'd like to, you know that. But I'm not ready for...all that yet."

Zhrana reached out to stroke his arm, but Kianno backed away at the touch. He was aware, now, like he had never been aware before, of the sexual possibilities underlying even the simplest physical contact. Zhrana sensed this discomfort and let her hand drop to her side.

"You'll have to go out soon enough, and it'll be a lot easier with me along," she said.

"I know," he answered, looking at her with eyes which wondered how she could have stayed so exactly the same through all of this. "I know full well I should go on as if nothing has happened, unashamed, ready to face the world. But I'm afraid I'm not as strong as my knowledge."

"Are you kidding?" Zhrana challenged, walking briskly away toward the quadrant gate, followed closely by Kianno. "This from the same person who chose to enter in contagious diseases? This from the same person who risked everything to explore the outside and find out his real history?"

"It's easier to take chances when you haven't been burned yet."

Zhrana didn't respond, only kept striding purposefully toward, then through, the quadrant gate, trailing her reluctant friend who followed closely behind despite his best arguments.

The Sports Hub proved less hostile than Kianno had feared, partly due to the fact that they did not run into any acquaintances from other quadrants, and partly due to the advance notice Zhrana had given at the time she had made the reservation. There was, however, some uncertainty as to whether or not the court itself could accommodate someone of Kianno's size.

Zinger was a suspension game, one of the first and simplest of the suspension games. Similar in many respects to handball or racquetball, two players faced each other one on one, swatting a ball (or in this case a laser projected image, or zinger) back and forth. Both players, however, wear melodium lined suits which allow them to be fully suspended between two high power magnets which line two faces of the court. Free to move within a given area, then, each attempts to hit the zinger past his opponent into the opposite goal, using any part of their bodies to either fire or block. Computer analysis instantaneously calculates force and spin imparted to the zinger by any part of the body, typically hands and feet. However, the zinger can not be held or captured, only struck.

When they reached the outfitting station, the outfitter, a small, unusually early-regulated forever girl, did her best to maintain a straight face and a businesslike demeanor while attempting to set up the court for this unlikely pair.

"We don't often get such...large players on this court, on this level," she said, sizing up Kianno after having finished outfitting Zhrana. "The largest suit we have is a triple Z, and that may still be too small. Please remove your Sara and we'll see how it fits."

Reluctantly, Kianno surrendered his clothing and stood naked before the two forever girls. Within the hive, nudity was quite commonplace and was not a source of embarrassment, even between sexes, given the narrow range of differences between most citizens' bodies. Kianno, however, now felt an acute embarrassment as the result of how different from the rest he had become. For their part, Zhrana and the outfitter said nothing as he was suited in the tight fitting outfit, each of them showing no outward sign of their great amusement and even slight fear at their first encounter with a naked, unregulated man. Zhrana could feel Kianno's embarrassment, and attempted to hurry the process along, but did not look away.

Once the two of them had been fully suited and the court had been programmed as best as was possible (there was still some doubt as to whether the magnetrons could properly balance Kianno's great weight), they stepped into the court and waited for activation, which quickly floated the forever girl into position but only gradually lifted an uncertain Kianno and brought him in front of his goal, which had been adjusted for his larger size. Both players ready now, a red light flashed overhead and the aqua-blue zinger materialized in the center of the room and slowly picked up speed toward Kianno, who leaned hard to his left and swiped at it clumsily with his left hand but missed, allowing the zinger to carry softly into his goal.

The score was acknowledged immediately by both the court and by Zhrana. The court did its part by bathing itself in purple light and spinning Kianno head to toe in a playful display, harmless enough for smaller, more agile players, but in this case violent enough to cause Kianno to strain a muscle in his lower back.

"Ha! I'm ahead and I haven't even touched the zinger yet!" exclaimed Zhrana with delight, expecting Kianno, who had always treated these games as light fun and not as competition, to join in the laughter. But he only grunted a little in response and squirmed in an attempt to loosen the suit.

"I think I've hurt my back," he called to her after settling back into position. He was annoyed with himself for allowing a goal right off the bat, but recognized his irritation and covered up quickly.

"Lucky goal. That'll be the last one to get by me today!"

But it wasn't the last to get by him, and when they lifted down onto the floor at the end of their session, Zhrana had outscored him by the greatest margin either had posted over the years they'd played together.

Kianno was still upset even after they had finished spraying and had changed back into their saras, and remained silent to several attempts by Zhrana to divert his attentions with invitations to small talk. As they exited the Sports Hub, Zhrana suggested they forego the slider and walk the great southwest hallway back to the quadrant. After they had cleared the slider axis and found themselves in the relative privacy of the inter-quadrant hallway, she turned her attentions to proposals of a different sort.

"Kianno, you know by now that I've joined Sofia in working toward liberalization of the outsider laws. You saw yourself what we've done to them." She looked up at him, but he continued staring straight ahead.

"That's your business," he replied, still somewhat cold from the anger of his defeat. "I don't need to hear any more about this."

"Yes, you do," she replied forcefully. "Because you're in a position to help us out. You can go over unrecognized and with little to lose, to help us establish some kind of contact with them." When he didn't respond, she added "Surely you understand now, now that..."

"That I'm one of them, is that what you're saying?" he answered angrily. "You think that because I look like them that now I must be on their side, that I'm no longer a citizen?"

"Of course we're all citizens." Zhrana was surprised at this outburst, had not known this kind of anger in Kianno before. "And I'm not expecting your help because you look like them now. But because you've seen the conditions they live under, you of all people should be able to understand why they need their freedom to survive!"

A P-Z Cart rounded a corner and entered the main hallway from one of the diagonal leaders. Zhrana waited until the cart had whisked by them before pursuing the issue further.

"If you can meet with us tomorrow, we already have a plan in place. It won't be very complicated and as long as you're careful..."

"Stop it, will you!" he screamed at her with words which echoed through the red glow of the hallway cast off by the strip lumins. "Stop it already! Don't you think I'm going to have a hard enough time getting my life back in order without something like this? Don't you think I raise enough suspicions wherever I go without adding to them by..." And now he lowered his voice, "...by cooperating with Naturalist sympathizers? What makes you think I agree with your cause anyway?"

"I know you do," she replied softly. "I can tell."

"Well you're wrong. That's all there is to it. And even if I did believe, why would I be foolish enough to risk what life I have left?"

"Because you've been taking chances your entire life, Kianno. As long as I've known you you've been looking for ways to jeopardize your own safety. But I'm beginning to see now that there was never any purpose to those risks, that you were only taking chances for the sake of taking chances. Maybe it's some kind of perverted death wish or something. I don't know. But when it comes to having courage for a purpose, you have no courage and you have no purpose."

There was nothing he could say to answer her, although in the days following he would try over and over again to come up with an argument to prove her wrong. Even if he had found such justification he wouldn't have had much opportunity to share it with her, though, for neither one of them had much immediate interest in a zinger re-match.

***

It was Sofia who came to see Zhrana late one night when the rest of the family was sound asleep and the quadrant was illuminated by only the pale blue shadows cast by the nighttime globes. Zhrana herself had already retired but was not yet asleep when she heard the voice call tentatively outside her room. Rousing herself, curious why Sofia should be calling at this hour, she quickly admitted the visitor and soon the two of them were sitting together on Zhrana's lounger.

"I'm sorry for coming so late, but I wanted to make sure we wouldn't be overheard or interrupted," Sofia began, sitting forward with hands on knees, resisting the slope of the lounger which tried to settle her into a more reclined position.

"I understand," answered Zhrana. "Is this about the meeting, then?" She as well now sat up, anxious with the excitement that Sofia would consider her important enough now to visit for late night conspiratorial visits.

"Yes, in a way. Zhrana, I've been thinking about your recent enthusiasm about what we're trying to do, and, well, I'm concerned that you're getting into this so quickly that you may not fully appreciate the risks." She ran her fingers through her hair and let out a nervous sigh. "I'm worried about you, to tell the truth. We've been friends so long, and now I feel like I may have gotten you involved in something which is more dangerous than you may realize."

Zhrana sat back now, disappointed a little that Sofia appeared less than enthusiastic about her recent participation. "Of course I know what I'm getting into, you explained that fully, and besides, I'm not exactly a child myself, you know. I can take responsibility for my decisions."

"Oh, it's not that at all," Sofia replied. "Please don't misunderstand. We're incredibly grateful for your help, you know that. It's just that you've already done so much for us. I'd hate to see anything happen to you as a result of your continuing on..."

Zhrana now reached over to lightly brush her friend's chestnut brown hair. "Dearest Sofia, please don't feel as if you have anything to pay for what I've done. What I do I do for myself, and that includes my wanting to become more involved. What I saw while I was over there, it..." She didn't finish her sentence, knowing it would start them down a dangerous path, but it was too late, for Sofia picked up on it immediately.

"Zhrana, you've been reluctant to share with us how you did find Kianno. If you were able to establish any contacts at all, you know that's what we need most right now. We have others, not just Kianno, who can go over if we only knew where to go."

"I know," the forever girl answered almost inaudibly, torn between her desire to protect Sofia and the need to further the cause they both felt so strongly about. She looked away for a full minute, her silence intensified within the greater silence of the sleeping quadrant surrounding it, then turned to her friend and spoke.

"Dearest Sofia, forgive me for what I'm about to tell you, but I can't keep it from you any longer. Just promise me that it'll stay between us alone." She looked into Sofia's eyes, which confirmed the promise wordlessly, then continued. "Sofia, your son Seelin is alive."

***

"It's agreed, then. We need a stronger approach. The snatchings have been a complete failure of late. It's time we got serious." Jask spoke in a soft voice to the six members of the coordination team, but it was a voice which had earned respect for its judiciousness, and the words he now spoke represented something of a turning point in the group's tactics. He had never before consented to an escalation of the violence. "It is agreed, isn't it?" he continued, looking Seelin square in the eyes.

"The Retraction Bill is up for vote soon," Seelin replied. "We should wait to see what the outcome is. There's no sense provoking them just when they're looking for a reason to strip us down."

A few scoffs could be heard from the others, but not from Jask, who took his friend's argument quite seriously. "With Atascin removed from the committee, we don't stand a chance, you know that."

"Then let them be the ones who start this. Let's not allow them the satisfaction of saying we forced them into it."

Now an older man with a white beard spoke up. "It's not about who has the moral high ground. If we even start to doubt our own right to freedom then we'll be lost in concessions to so-called morality. This is a war, and we have to fight it with our most powerful weapons."

"Which unfortunately aren't all that powerful right now." The group's leader turned to Jask. "What weapons will we need to carry out your plan?"

Jask looked to Seelin to recognize there was still unfinished business, but when his friend remained silent he answered the question. "I can construct a Quother swell activator with quite small amounts of doped palladium and bio-magnesium."

"Yea, and I can construct a neutrino with just a little anti-matter," laughed the leader, "C'mon, what can you make with what's realistically available?"

Jask thought for a moment before responding. "We can get the bio-magnesium. It's not unrealistic at all." He sat back and challenged the group to prove him wrong.

"Finding and retrieving it from the hive? Are you kidding?"

"Finding it will be the hard part, I admit," Jask answered, scouting the room like a teacher looking for the correct response, "But retrieving it can be done."

"No one's ever gone in and come out alive," protested a younger woman who had been silent thus far.

But the rest knew better, remembered stories they had heard, and slowly the eyes of the room turned to Seelin, who would not acknowledge them yet, still waiting.

"My friend," Jask now spoke for the rest of them, "We need you now. This is why you returned. Not for some simple snatchings or conversions, but because we're entering a new phase of this war and we need you to bring us the weapons. Somehow you sensed this when you walked out of the woods not too long ago. You know you're the only one who's been able to get in there and get out."

This time he didn't keep them waiting for a response. "The vote's in three days," he replied calmly. "If we lose I'll find a way to get in." He closed his eyes briefly, then re-opened them and continued. "What will be the range of the wave?"

"Complete destruction to one full quadrant, with oxygen deprivation to the surrounding five or six."

"And the trigger?"

Jask only shook his head slowly. "Instantaneous. There'd be no way to smuggle the delay mechanism. It's five times the size of the activator itself."

"Then I'll deliver it," Seelin said under his breath, too softly to be heard by anyone but his closest friend. "I'll deliver it."

***

The wind blew furiously that night, a fall wind whipping up before the leaves had fallen, pulling and bending the still green and dangerously full liquid ambers scattered so long ago about the city of Lexington that only very few scholars of the land even knew that they were not native, did not truly belong on these oak covered hills. Their branches scraped against the sky and hurtled contributions to a gathering parade of small debris which tumbled through the dirt paths and came to rest in the corners where doorways stepped into the ancient streets. It was not a simple summertime wind blowing in from the ocean, or even a rarer onshore gale rushing down from the higher slopes, but a larger movement of air, slowly spilling down off of the high pressure dome of summer, lowering it ever so slightly, just enough to allow the first scouts of the winter season to peer over the top and adjust the aim of a jet stream readying itself for the promise of rain.

Awake in the darkness of midnight, Seelin Arears sat looking out at the wind, watching the trees sway and feeling the rattle of the panes shaking with the pressure blasts. The street was empty, save for the few indistinguishable sick who had lost their way and huddled, desperate but unmoving, inside their thin blankets. He gazed patiently out at the empty street for nearly an hour before he rose up wearily and lumbered into the adjacent room to check once more on Mistissa before retiring to his sleeping cot, where he knew he would lie for a full hour or more before finding just enough of a sleep for him to huddle in as thinly as those strewn outside in the streets.

But Mistissa, she slept so beautifully and so soundly, her breaths lifting the covers in an even cadence, her eyes closed by the world and not by herself, unknowing of the dry wind ripping over the rooftop, prying at the eaves. He reached down to brush the sleeping girl's deep brown hair across her forehead, and Mistissa stirred only slightly at his touch, murmuring the mystery of a child's dream before turning her head and laying it once more on the sheet. Her sleep had returned, after that year of terrible nightmares she had found the peacefulness of the night once more. How could he take that away again?

Seelin turned now and pointed his feet back toward his own cot. He glanced one more time back over his shoulder at his sleeping daughter, then walked through the doorway into his room and past its only window. As he pulled the chair away from the window to return it to its place next to the writing table, he uttered a quick but shallow cry and took a step back. Framed behind his own reflection in the glass was the face of a girl looking up at him, her long hair dancing furiously in the wind. It was Zhrana.

16

S he was up early the next morning, staring into the darkness and listening to the sounds of Seelin sleeping on the far side of the room for some time before she stirred from the makeshift cot which had been hastily prepared for her the night before and made her way quietly out the door and into the morning chill. Zhrana glanced at the empty streets, faintly illuminated by a sky lightening slowly in anticipation of the sunrise still a full hour away, then followed the structure around to the back, where a small, unkempt yard afforded her the privacy she sought. Still entranced by the sky and the wind, which had since died down from it's overnight gale, she was like a visitor to another country, another planet even, as she sat silently listening to the birds clattering in the huge madrone which hung over her, excited at her first feel of an early October frost and her first moments shared with these small wild animals who went about their business all around her as if she belonged to their world.

Very few words had been exchanged between them the night before. She had tried to overcome his initial surprise and anger with sincere but vague notions of having come back to help the movement, but she hadn't been able to verbalize any of the ideas she had talked over with Sofia and the rest of them, fumbling forward through explanations aimed more at mitigating Seelin's anger and skepticism than at initiating a well developed plan for working together. For his part, Seelin appeared more concerned with not waking his sleeping daughter than with developing plans for collaboration, and cut short the conversation before any kind of direction could be established. It was enough of a decision on his part simply to allow her to stay the night. Considering the short history

between them, he would have been more than justified in dragging her kicking and screaming to Jask and the others, who would undoubtedly have been
inclined to reward her in some excruciating fashion for her previous heroics in
freeing Kianno. But it was just those heroics which compelled him to give her at
least enough time to state her case. That she would risk everything to save one of
her own was worthy of Seelin's respect, regardless of which side benefited from
that admirable act. That she should return once more, for no apparent reason,
intrigued him enough to trust her in the same home as himself and Mistissa, for
one night anyway. Besides, nothing she had done had contradicted his original
impression that the girl behind those eyes would never intentionally harm them.

As Zhrana sat watching a sparrow come ever closer, following a line of seeds
scattered over the hard dirt, she heard footsteps behind her and turned to see
a small girl of about ten natural years standing next to the building, eyeing her
curiously.

"Hi," Mistissa said tentatively. "Who are you?"

"My name is Zhrana." She got up quickly and reached both hands out instinctively to the girl, who only backed away slightly from this peculiar gesture.
Catching herself, Zhrana brought her hands up to her own hair, covering up
well enough for her to feel confident in continuing. "I'm visiting Seelin, who
lives in one of these rooms here." She paused, waiting for a response from the
still skeptical girl, then added "Do you know Seelin?"

"He's my father," she answered simply, but in a tone which accused Zhrana
of not knowing this most basic fact. "He didn't say anything about a visitor
coming over."

"I came in late last night, you see, while you were still sleeping."

Mistissa now took one more step back and answered uneasily. "What do you
mean you came in late last night? Who are your parents? Are they visiting my
father?" She turned as if to run.

"Wait, it's O.K., really." Zhrana sensed the young girl's fear and immediately
masked her voice in as childish an intonation as she could manage. "My mother
dropped me off last night. I'm supposed to stay here today while they work up
in the mountains. Is that OK?"

"How old are you?"

"Ten. How old are you?"

"I'm going to be ten next month. You talk funny, almost like..."

"C'mon!" interrupted Zhrana, "Race you to the end of the street." And with this she took off at full speed out the yard and down a road still sleeping in the shadows of dawn, breathing the cold air in deep gusts which did indeed make her feel young again, born anew into a world of unknown but strangely familiar sensations. Mistissa, unable to resist the challenge of a race, followed closely behind and caught her halfway to the end of the block, laughing delightedly at her victory as both girls panted for breath.

"I know what we can do," proposed Mistissa as the two were run-walking back toward the house. "My daddy's still sleeping. Let's wake him up, it'll be fun!"

Zhrana was a reluctant but highly amused participant in this game Mistissa usually played with one of her regular friends who stayed the night from time to time. Following closely on Mista's heels, she crept quietly up to the side of Seelin's sleeping platform, which was raised only a few inches above the floor, such that both girls could look down on the deeply slumbering man, grizzled with tangled dark brown hair and a beard much in need of trimming. Mistissa giggled at the sight of her father, and Zhrana laughed a little as well, but kept her eyes focused on the angled face, the lines of struggle radiating from the mouth and eyes, with only hints of softness accenting the corners where those lines met. Looking down at that face she remembered so well, and the still hidden body she could only fill in with her imagination, the forever girl realized she couldn't deny the real motives behind her visit. It was those eyes which brought her back, the same eyes which the two of them now schemed to open with a start.

"We're going to jump his platform," Mistissa whispered. "Do what I do but on this side." Then she crept back to Seelin's other side and placed one foot then the other on his platform, waiting for Zhrana to do the same.

When both girls were in place, Mistissa suddenly yelled at the top of her voice and jumped up and down furiously, gesturing for Zhrana to do the same. Bouncing up and down together, the two of them in very short order had Seelin nearly airborne as he rode the wave of exuberance emanating primarily from a laughing Mista, who didn't notice the moment of genuine fear with which her father awoke. Zhrana saw it though, saw the look of a man who jumped from his sleep with vigilant eyes, ready to counter the surprise attack before realizing that this was just another playful wake up call his daughter had orchestrated. Grasping the blankets with both hands to protect his modesty, he looked with quizzical eyes at his co-conspirator, at first amused by her participation and her childlike pretension, but then his eyes shaded with concern and he turned to Mistissa.

"Mista, you're going to give me a heart attack some day with these tricks," he said, with an unexpected seriousness which disappointed the girl.

"Daddy..."

"And I see you've recruited an accomplice. Are you going to introduce me?" he continued, feeling somewhat trapped by his nakedness underneath the covers.

"Daddy, you know her, don't you?"

Seelin let the question hang just long enough to let the girl second guess herself, then answered.

"As it turns out I do, but I've told you before not to play with unknown children without my permission, haven't I?"

"Yes. I'm sorry. You're such a grouch this morning!"

Seelin now laughed. "O.K., O.K. already. Both of you scoot out of here so I can get dressed. Mista, give our friend something to eat will you, and I'll join you in a minute."

Mista turned and ran immediately toward the door, but Zhrana and Seelin exchanged curious looks before the forever girl as well walked out the door, reflecting on what she had seen. The worry and concern that the father had shown for his daughter in the presence of a strange forever child had not gone unnoticed.

Later, after Mistissa had been encouraged to run off with her friends, Seelin and Zhrana finally had a chance to talk seriously. Showing themselves together in public was much too risky for either one, so they holed up in Mistissa's room, where Zhrana sat cross legged on the hard floor and Seelin reclined in the home's only lounger, a tattered model recovered from the discard lot and restored by his own handiwork.

"There's no point in establishing contact just for the sake of establishing contact. Without any specific purpose, we might as well continue working alone. Besides, if you think you're going to persuade us to tone things down to fit in with your political maneuverings, forget it." Seelin looked out the window and rubbed his chin, freshly shaven for the first time in two weeks.

"You know we'll be that much more effective working together. That way we can coordinate our activities. Otherwise..."

"Otherwise what?" answered Seelin. "Otherwise the violence is going to continue?" He scoffed and looked away. "Well, in case it hasn't occurred to you, the violence isn't going away, and there's nothing either of us can do about that."

Zhrana sat quietly, sensing he was right but still unwilling to abandon the plans they had so carefully prepared, and Seelin took advantage of her silence to drive home his point.

"Have you studied the provisions of the retraction bill?" Not waiting for an answer, he continued. "I suppose you have but let me remind you anyway. Basically it allows for waiver of virtually any and every right of an outsider if justified by the "prudent and reasonable decision" on the part of any citizen. Even the right of appeal can be waived, not by a magistrate or by a citizen enforcer, but by any citizen. There's no reason for allowing this kind of open season on outsiders. It goes beyond even what was allowed before Zavani, and even the extremists would have no reason to go that far unless there was something in the works."

"I know. I've also heard the rumors," Zhrana replied softly.

"Then what is it they're harvesting? Have you found some new chemical that allows you to live to a thousand if only you can extract enough of it from our blood? What's on the current menu for you forever children anyway?"

He had worked himself into an unintentional anger, and took a deep breath to try and restore his equilibrium, then leaned back and stared hard at the wooden ceiling.

"I don't know," Zhrana lied. Sofia had told her but it was too early, too risky to divulge anything yet. She paused, then added "I'm on your side in this, you know."

"I truly hope that's the case, Zhrana." Her head tilted at this first time his voice had spoken her name. "I seem to remember a similar conversation with you only minutes prior to spending twelve hours dragging myself ten feet across a dirty floor."

The forever girl now got up and walked over to the window, hoping to catch a glimpse of the birds who had invited her into their morning. "I don't care, then," she sighed, "I'm obviously not the best candidate for this job, but I was the only one who knew where to go, the only one who knew to recognize you, and the only one who was willing. So if you tell me to go back where I came from I will. If nothing else I wanted to thank you for what you did for us."

"Look," Seelin pushed down hard on the suspend rods of the recliner and searched his mind for a moment, then continued in a softer voice. "I'm not sure why I should believe you, or trust you, but for some reason I do. Please don't ever thank me, though, because there's nothing I ever did to be grateful for, you understand, don't you? I'm afraid the only way you can really help us at this point is by working on our side, not trying to get us to work on yours, no matter how well intentioned your groups are."

"I think I'm beginning to realize that."

"Do you?" Seelin challenged. "I'm not sure you know what's in store for you if you really throw yourself in with us."

Zhrana didn't reply, but in the silence which ensued Seelin reminded himself of the risks she'd already taken, and glanced at Zhrana's profile against the peeling madrone branches outside the window, trying to reconcile that innocent face with the courage he knew she had within her. He lifted himself up slowly from the lounger and walked over to stand next to her, placing his hands firmly on the windowsill and looking skyward through the snarl of branches.

"Have you ever seen a tree of this type?" he asked.

"Yes," she replied. "I've seen them in the scopers. Not really, of course, but almost the same." She reached out to touch a limb curling against the frame. "But I've never felt them before."

"It's called a madrone. Quite common around here. It's constantly peeling the outer layer of it's bark, replacing it with a new layer which in turn immediately begins to peel away again."

"Isn't the bark supposed to protect it?" She watched as he reached out to strip a handful of the flaky surface, crumbling it slowly between his thumb and palm, a palm nearly as large as her entire hand. "It doesn't seem as if it could be very strong."

"Oh the outermost layer isn't, that's for sure," Seelin answered. "But think of how many layers are growing beneath that one. The fact that the topmost skin is so fragile requires the lower layers to grow quickly enough to take its place. It's not so dependent on just the outermost bark that we see."

They stood staring silently out at the tangle of orange branches breaking and spilling the brilliant sunlight into patches of warmth scattered over the crusted dirt. At length, Seelin turned to Zhrana and drew a deep breath as if readying himself to tell her something, but the touch of Zhrana's small hand stroking his forearm released the breath wordlessly, and Seelin looked with surprise and confusion as the small girl's hand and wrist continued to brush the brown hairs of his arm, back and forth. Now she turned to him and placed her other hand on his hip, stroking the roughness of his pants before he could even gather his thoughts.

He reached down now and took hold of her wrists, one in each hand, and gently but firmly held them away from the caresses they had placed on him, watching as they reluctantly returned to her sides, too embarrassed even to rest inside his field of vision.

"It's not right," he uttered, unsure of himself.

"You don't remember, do you?" she asked.

"I know. In my mind I know you're older than I am, but it just isn't right. You're very pretty, you know, but not in a way I could love like that."

"I know," she admitted. "You don't have to explain. I only thought that maybe..."

"Maybe in time I could get used to it, but I don't think so." Seelin paused, then added in a brighter tone. "There are ways you can help us, though, help us tremendously if you're really willing to risk everything."

Then he took her hand as a friend and led her to the writing table, where they sat side by side as Seelin showed her detailed maps of the Great Hive, level DDY.

From time to time, as they sat in the darkened room, Zhrana stole glimpses of the madrone in it's frame of sunlight, and made up her mind what had to be done.

Part Three

Rebirth

17

H e certainly hadn't intended to fall sideways into the threesome of citizens who had been innocently playing a topo-visual game between them as they rode the eastward slider toward the 3700 line. But the still relatively new capture mechanism, designed to hold all riders within a protective zero acceleration zone as the slider entered and exited the terminals, had not been as extensively tested for weights beyond one hundred and ten pounds, and as the room decelerated rapidly toward Kianno's stop, he felt himself give way through the protective wave and fall awkwardly into the unfortunate threesome.

The ensuing collision knocked all four to the ground and sent the three impacted citizens slipping along the polished, false wood floor until the slider came to a full stop, leaving them scrunched against a side bench like small animals who sometimes enter the hive unknowingly and end up trapped in an unyielding corner. One of the three, a forever boy with blonde hair, stared angrily at Kianno as he lifted himself from the floor.

"You have no business on this slider, or on this level for that matter," he said sharply, reaching over now to help his friends up as well.

"The zero acceleration field broke down," Kianno explained.

"It's no wonder," answered the citizen, peering down at his friends and snickering. "I think it's primarily meant for humans. Then he added, more seriously, "What are you doing on this level, anyway? Do you have authority?"

"Of course I have authority," Kianno answered, growing angry in his defense. "I've lived on GGG my entire life, longer than any of you I would guess."

"Yes, right," another of the citizens contributed sarcastically. "In your world I suppose we would be quite young, wouldn't we?" He let out a chuckle and brushed himself off with his hands.

Kianno started to explain, but pulled up short, too tired of justifying his appearance to anyone and everyone who gave him such looks. Perhaps he should have stayed in the quadrant after all, he thought, grateful at least that he had reached his exit point and could now step away from this very uncomfortable situation. The chime sounded lightly and the portals whisked open.

"Get off this level, monster," he heard from behind him as he stepped from the slider and hurried away down the long hallway.

They were much more pleasant at the weatherscoper. Almost too pleasant, it seemed to Seelin, as they greeted him with a smile broader than the desk controllers had ever given him before.

"Ah, Kianno of Forshas, we've been expecting you," the most meticulously dressed attendant beamed up at his guest.

"Spilo? It's me, Kianno. What's with the formality?"

"Nothing, nothing at all," came the response, tinged with a worry which rode on the heels of overconsciousness.

"What's happening today?" Kianno asked as routinely as possible.

"Big hurricane winding up off the coast of the Bahamas; should be some very interesting tropical activity."

"You know I don't go in much for that." Kianno eyed the attendant curiously.

"Ah yes, that's right. You were more of a cold weather aficionado, as I recall. I'm afraid there's not a whole lot going on locally right now. Nothing's hit the mountains yet; too early in the season still."

Now another attendant approached from a back room and took a second look when he saw Kianno standing at the check desk.

"Great hurricane stuff today," he said, again with that huge grin Kianno was beginning to think was meant only for him.

"What about further north, anything in the Cascades?" Kianno ignored the second attendant and directed his questions to Spilo

"Well, let's see what's going on..." After some fumbling beneath the counter, the projection area behind the two attendants flickered and jumped into a western states map, not exceedingly detailed but sufficiently thorough to display major weather patterns, all extrapolated from information fed into the system from hive stations scattered about the more populous areas.

"Looks like some snow around Mt. Baker, if you go up to the higher elevations."

"That sounds good," answered Kianno, eager to get into the scoper itself. This was his first visit since returning and he was looking forward to getting way out into a blizzard, as lost as he could be from the all too interested eyes which now surrounded him.

"Are you set up? Because if not, I'm afraid we may not have your size," Spilo informed him, choosing his words carefully.

"Yes, go ahead and set it up. I'll be ready in ten minutes."

Kianno walked past the desk toward the preparation room, followed closely by the second attendant, who did not let him get far before inquiring as to whether or not he was familiar with the facilities. Kianno assured him that he was, in fact, a regular patron, a statement which drew a skeptical look from the assistant, who backed off a little but still kept an eye on the misplaced visitor as he disappeared into the dressing chamber.

It turned out he had almost everything he needed, but he had neglected to bring along anything warm for his hands. Figuring that even though it was a long shot, they might perhaps have some gloves large enough for him to squeeze into, Kianno left the preparation room and walked back to the front desk again. As he approached through the hallway, however, he slowed as he overheard the two attendants laughing and talking freely with another guest.

"Is this the all-animal weather scoper, then?" the guest asked jokingly.

"Yes, we had two horses in this morning. Wanted a sunny day on the high plains for some reason. Imagine they were in the mood for a good gallop," replied the second attendant.

"Well, glad to know you're an equal opportunity weatherscoper: horses, lions, insects, monsters, as long as they've got level access what does it matter?"

"And don't worry, we clean the scoper after every use, even twice after some of the larger animals!"

The two of them found this particularly amusing, and Kianno waited through their laughter for Spilo to say something in his defense, but when his former friend kept his silence, he decided he'd rather face the scoper with cold hands than interrupt their fun.

Minutes later, Kianno found himself once again inside the scoper, and felt an immediate sense of relief and well being. The landscape had been well prepared, with just a dusting of light snow covering the mixed fir and deciduous trees at this seven thousand foot level. Stepping hard through the snow with breaths reaching deeply for the thin oxygen, he found himself in a long valley surrounded on both sides with high cliffs and scaly rock formations. Threading his way through the pines, Kianno set his sights on a slightly broken down section of the cliffs where it appeared as if he might be able to ascend toward the higher ground at the top of the ledge. He knew this was certainly going to challenge the capability of the scoper, but he was in a mood for adventure, and it had been a long time since he had trekked onto steep ground inside the chamber.

The scoper room itself, in addition to being equipped to accurately simulate just about any weather condition on earth, could also simulate topography to a limited extent. Landscapes were populated primarily with holographic projections of rocks, trees, buildings, etc., and thus most objects had no real substance and could be appreciated from a visual perspective only. However, the floor of the room, in addition to responding instantly to pressure and force applied to it from any direction, was capable of assuming different slopes and even different topographies in response to the specific program in use. Steep uphill slopes, required by individuals pursuing verticality within their programs, presented the most extreme test of the floor's capability. If required, the floor was able to tilt almost fully vertical, and shape itself generally to the programmed topography, even simulating the feel of the surface through textural grids laid into the topmost layer.

It was not the most severe gradient Kianno had attempted. In fact, the crevice leading up between the two cliffs on either side was not nearly as challenging as several he had completed successfully in earlier visits, and as he began to ascend the huge granite boulders, jumping carefully from one to another, he began to feel more in command of his new body than at any time since the snatching. Yes, he was larger and so not quite as nimble as before, but he also had strength which was out of proportion to his extra weight, strength which allowed him to pull himself fiercely from one ledge to another using fully the newfound power of his muscles.

About two thirds of the way up the incline, he reached an exposed section where he would need to balance himself carefully along a small shelf, then grab onto a boulder and hoist himself quickly to another, broader shelf higher up. As he stood looking over his situation, Kianno began to worry for the first time whether or not he had proceeded too far up the slope, whether he was perhaps pushing the scoper floor to its limits. Already he had encountered certain rocks which had been projected by the program instead of simulated by the floor, indicating that he could no longer fully rely on the solidity of the surface he was attempting to climb. If he were to hoist himself up to the narrow shelf and only then found that the hand hold he was counting on was only a projection, he might easily lose his balance and fall.

Pondering his next move, he was startled by the quick movement of the boulder on which he stood, which shifted slightly then slumped downward, sending the climber's feet scurrying across the face to maintain his balance. Accompanying the movement of the rock was a high pitched alarm signal which filled the room with a harsh tone wavering rhythmically in pitch. As the surprised Kianno jumped from the unstable rock onto the steep ground below, the terrain suddenly lost its granitic texture and appearance, unmasked as the soft, rubber-like compound which lay beneath its many disguises. Puzzled, Kianno looked around him to see the program had ended abruptly but the floor had not returned to its normal horizontal position, frozen instead into a warped vertical contortion which had only moments earlier, with just a little window dressing, had been a pretty fair simulation of a mountain crevice.

"Stop!" It was Spilo, running toward him across the flatter, lower sections of the room, followed closely behind by his assistant. "Wait right there! Don't move any more; you might damage it further!"

"What do you mean?" he called back, but obeyed the instructions and stood his ground, even though the steep incline tried to pull him downward. When the two of them reached the bottom of the cliff, they looked up at him like he was the wrong animal accidentally caught in one of their traps. As he watched curiously, the two of them discussed the situation between themselves, occasionally pointing to Kianno but never directing any of the conversation at him.

Finally Spilo gestured angrily with his arm and yelled for Kianno to come down to the flat section. When he arrived both of them greeted him with acrimonious stares.

"What do you think you're doing?" Spilo began, "The floor's not meant to do this kind of thing!"

"I was only following the program," replied Kianno, surprised by the accusatory tone of Spilo's words, "The program should know the floor's limits. It looks to me as if there was some kind of miscalculation or miscommunication between the program and the floor." He folded his arms in front of him and looked past the attendants, eager to get out of there.

"You knew you were pushing the scoper to its limits just by being in here." The assistant now glared up at him. "To start pursuing the program into vertical extremes was nothing short of recklessness. Criminal recklessness."

"That's ridiculous," answered Kianno, a cold sweat now breaking out across his back. He took a step forward and started past his accusers toward the portals, but the assistant grabbed his arm and pulled him back abruptly.

"I'm afraid we can't allow you to leave just yet. Not until there's been an investigation," Spilo said matter of factly, as if Kianno were a stranger he had never met before. "At the very least we'll need to arrange for compensatory repair adjustments. There's been major damage."

"That's crazy!" Kianno shook his arm free from the forever boy's grasp, feeling an anger rise up within him, an anger he hadn't experienced in his previous life, an anger which filled him with terrible impatience and rage.

"No. You're crazy! We should have never allowed you in here. You can be sure we'll never let monsters in again, no matter what their collar says about them," sneered the assistant.

And it was then that Kianno, for the first time since his true childhood thirty years earlier, inflicted an act of physical violence on another human being. It was not a terribly vicious or brutal attack, consisting of a single blow to the assistant's chubby red face with his forearm. And neither was the injury which resulted all that serious, consisting of a swollen lip and a bloody nose which his victim held with both arms, crying as if it had just fallen off. But in a culture where physical assaults were practically unheard of, this single act was enough to shock the world around him into a reconsideration of its safety.

It was also enough to shock the two weatherscoper attendants into a run for their very lives, the bloodied one holding his face as he ran headlong toward the portal, and Spilo scampering away almost as fast, but with just enough courage to cast a quick glance over his shoulder at a solitary Kianno, about to be trapped alone on the scoper floor until the authorities could arrive and sort out his future.

***

"Does that complete the state's evidence, then?" Rokyo looked down from the perch where he stood over the few participants in this case and the larger number of curious observers who milled around behind them, talking quietly amongst themselves about the testimony they had just heard.

The state's defender shrugged his shoulders and smiled. "I believe we've left no doubt as to the events of this case, your most honorable loyalist."

"Yes, I suppose there's not much question..." He turned to Kianno and his speaker. "Do you intend to challenge the testimony given thus far, or claim events happened other than as described?"

Kianno began to answer, but his speaker, a determined but fragile looking forever boy, raised his hand and interrupted the accused. "We do challenge the facts of the case regarding the failure analysis of the weatherscoper. We contend, and have expert testimony to demonstrate, that the accused at no time strayed from the program he was pursuing, and that therefore he should not be held responsible for the damage."

"Very well, then, let's proceed...."

"Your true loyalist," the state's defender now intervened, "The state has also examined carefully the technical elements involved, and while we still do believe a charge of criminal recklessness is warranted, we concede that it's a matter of some technical interpretation. Therefore, we're quite willing to drop that particular charge in the interest of avoiding a protracted discussion, and in light of it's triviality relative to the real charges involved."

"Well, it appears as if this witness has already accomplished your objective. Very well then," Rokyo said to Kianno's speaker, who took this unexpected announcement with an expression of utter confusion and disappointment. He had lined up the most eminent Dr. Philus of Worthing, and had planned to use the foundation of a successful technical counter as the springboard to convince Rokyo that the case was perhaps not so cut and dry as it first appeared. The state's concession instantly threw his defense into disarray.

"You true loaylist. This comes as a bit of a surprise. We respectfully request a delay until tomorrow so that we can better prepare our argument."

At this Rokyo let out a small chuckle. "A delay?" he asked incredulously, "Why, if I'm not mistaken the state has just made your case that much easier! I don't see as to why that merits a delay." He turned serious again and looked straight at Kianno's speaker. "Please proceed with your arguments."

Now the speaker fumbled with his private visual field controls, a newer device that some professionals had begun to use. Requiring a quite extensive surgical procedure on both eyes, it allowed for superimposition of a high resolution, fully controllable field upon one's normal eyesight. The field was linked directly to the visuals transmitter, so all elements currently available on the visuals were accessible, but in a form fully protected from anyone else's view.

Kianno watched his speaker's eyes darting back and forth, occasionally spiking to one side or another in response to the seemingly phantom words and objects. Then, appearing to have regained his composure somewhat, he addressed Rokyo.

"We summon Sofia of Forshas to make a statement relevant to the character of the accused."

At once the state's defender started quickly in Rokyo's direction, speaking as he walked. "Your loyalist, this is absurd. We all know the long, pathologically close relationship between Sofia and the accused. Any statement made by her could not be objective and should not be allowed."

"I agree," replied Rokyo firmly. "Isn't there anyone other than Sofia and Jaslo who is willing to speak for the accused?"

"There is, your loyalist, however she cannot be located just now. If you would grant a postponement of only one day, I'm sure we would be able to find her."

"No delays. I'm sorry. You've had a full two days to prepare for this hearing." He looked around the room and his eyes caught those of Sofia, eyes which pleaded with him to give her son a second chance, but he glanced over the surface of her gaze like a flat stone on water. "Don't you have any statements to present at all?"

"Yes, We do have one by the esteemed healer, Dr. Jaslo of Forshas."

This time the state's defendant only laughed and crossed his arms. "Your truest loyalist..." He looked at Rokyo with the amused look of a child observing his brother being caught red-handed.

"Really," sighed Rokyo with exasperation. "Do you think if I would not allow Sofia to make a statement that I would permit Jaslo?"

"Rokyo," began the speaker, then corrected himself. "Your loyalist, The statement Jaslo will make pertains to his medical expertise only. It is an informed scientific statement, and not a declaration of character support."

"This is absurd. What medical statement would be relevant?" shouted the state's defender angrily, but Rokyo held up his hand for silence.

"Will his statement be confined exclusively to scientific fact?"

"Otherwise I would not waste our time with this, your loyalist," answered the speaker.

"Very well, I will listen to what Jaslo has to say."

Without any further protest by the defender, who was more curious at this point than worried about any danger to his case this surprise statement might present, Jaslo, still standing in the middle of the group of spectators watching from the rear, called out loudly his name.

"I am Jaslo of Forshas," he announced, suddenly drawing the attention of everyone in the room. "You all know my expertise in medical matters. I trust there's no need for me to expound upon them." He paused for a moment, and when no challenges were heard he continued, addressing not only Rokyo but those around him as well. "I know you are all concerned about the inexcusably violent action on the part of Kianno, and I know you are all justifiably concerned about keeping within our quadrant such a large and powerful citizen who, because of hormonal excesses we are all aware of, is uncontrollably more inclined toward such violent acts."

At these words, Kianno looked away in disgust and his speaker turned his head toward Jaslo, giving him a quizzical look. Without even glancing in their direction, however, the distinguished citizen continued his statement.

"However, historical and scientific studies have clearly demonstrated that these uncontrollable acts are most likely to occur within the first few months of the threshold crossover. This is because the brain has not yet adapted to the effects of the chemical overload with which it has suddenly been infused. In time, natural

acclimatization minimizes the chances of future outbursts, and in some such individuals it does not become a significant problem. This, your true loyalist, is not mere speculation but scientific fact."

Immediately upon the completion of his statement, the state's defender waved his arms and spoke to get Rokyo's attention. "I request a counter-statement. Your loyalist, your loyalist, I request a counter-statement," he pleaded.

"In a minute." Rokyo lifted his eyes and peered into the crowd to where Jaslo stood in a small circular clearing left by those who had backed up to watch him give his statement. "How long does this "dangerous" period, during which the brain must adjust to its new environment, last?"

"For those who have been quick-converted, such as Kianno, no longer than six months."

"Thank you. You may make your counter-statement now, Brasholufi."

"Your loaylist, while it may be argued that the risk of violence may possibly decrease over time, it is indisputable that the risk is significantly higher for the unregulated. This has been shown in every study that has ever been performed. It is one of the tenants of our peacefulness as a hive that we are biologically biased toward cooperation and non violence. No scientist, not even Jaslo, can argue otherwise."

"Your loyalist," called out Jaslo despite having already concluded his statement, "I believe I can effect just such a biological preference in Kianno, if the state will only allow me three months."

This surprising and mysterious announcement was met with a wave of discussion among both the crowd and the direct participants in the hearing. While Kianno and his speaker looked at each other for an explanation, the defender tried to make his objections heard over the rising noise. Finally, Rokyo cut all lighting, throwing the entire room into darkness for several seconds, during which silence quickly was restored.

"Will you elaborate on this most astounding proposal, Jaslo of Forshas," he called out into the darkness, then signaled a support authority to re-illuminate the huge chamber.

"No. I'm sorry, but I simply cannot."

Rokyo pondered this for a moment, then replied. "Then I'm afraid I can't consider it in making my decision. Does the accused have any others to speak on his behalf?"

At this, Kianno leaned down to whisper into the ear of his speaker. "Zhrana has to be nearby somewhere. Can't we delay even until the end of the day?"

"We've already requested a postponement. Repeating the request can only anger Rokyo. We're better off leaving it as is." Then, in a louder voice directed toward the front of the room, "No, your truest loyalist, we have spoken for the accused. I only add, if I might, that we request your consideration of the many long years of cooperation and peaceful contribution the accused has made to this family. Let us not banish him as the result of one solitary transgression, regardless of how threatening and violent that single transgression may have been."

As he spoke the last words, interjecting a character statement which, as speaker, he was not allowed to deliver, Rokyo sighed and shifted in his seat with obvious annoyance, but he did not interrupt the shaky forever boy as he brought his statements to a close. The declaration that followed, however, was issued immediately on the heels of the speaker's remarks, indicating quite clearly that Rokyo had already determined Kianno's fate.

"You can be assured, all of you," And with this he lifted his face to the crowd on the far side of the room, which had now quieted in anticipation of his decision. "...that I as well recall Kianno's many years of belonging to this family, and to this level. It was due to his history with us that I took the most remarkably generous step of allowing him return to this quadrant even after he had been unfortunately transformed into a being which, I should have better known at the time, could never completely fit in with the rest of us. But I did give him every opportunity to demonstrate that his handicap and instability would not keep him from resuming a life congruent with the ideals of this family and equal to the dignity of level GGG." He drew a deep breath and smiled, allowing all present to appreciate his compassion, then continued. "But I'm afraid Kianno of Forshas did not, or perhaps could not, fulfill the opportunity which we gave him. Instead, he upset the equilibrium of this family, and indeed this entire level, by his senseless and unprovoked act of violence. I'm afraid I have no choice but to reassign him to Level B."

At this most of the crowd cheered loudly, but there were some gasps which punctuated the general relief and support which spread through the room. Most prominent among them was Sofia's, who did not mean to draw attention to herself but could not restrain her cry at Rokyo's harsh pronouncement. Level B was further down than even the state had anticipated, only one short step removed from the wildlands outside the hive. Jaslo put his arm around the grieving Sofia and did his best to console her, but knew there was little he could offer, at least at this time.

"Quiet please," instructed Rokyo coolly. "Quiet. I know some of you may consider this decision extreme, however I am charged with preserving the peace and integrity of this family, and I will do it by whatever means necessary. All of you are aware of the great principle of the hive by which anyone, including the accused, can ascend to higher levels if they are able to demonstrate that they may fit in with the fundamental tenants of that level. That is all."

Without even a glance at either Kianno, his speaker, or the weeping Sofia, Rokyo turned from the crowd and walked briskly toward the portals, while the authorities took Kianno to gather his belongings. By the end of the day, Kianno would see the last of this quadrant where he had not been born but where he had spent the many years of his forever childhood. And although when he left the family it was with anger and a great deal of sadness for the friends he had lost, later on, looking back on the years he had spent there, he came to feel that all along he had been little more than a visitor to that world, a welcomed visitor without doubt, and with many fond memories of times spent there, but a visitor nonetheless, who had carried inside him through it all the inevitability of his own departure.

18

Hardly anyone at all noticed the forever girl with unusually watchful eyes who slipped into the large group of children and their keepers who had assembled in front of the huge portals marked with an equally large holo-pronouncement which read "Bio-Minerals, Inc. We Make Metals Come Alive!". The instructor was too busy making sure none of the children who were darting every which away actually escaped, and by the time any of the other keepers saw Zhrana they simply assumed that she was just one more citizen from another quadrant who they had yet to meet. A couple of them, however, did take note of the jolts of anguish which periodically surfaced onto her face, despite Zhrana's best efforts to suppress any visible indication of the fiery pain which shot up through her knees and hips. One keeper, in fact, was concerned enough to approach the forever girl cautiously.

"Are you all right?" he asked.

"Oh yes. I'm afraid my arthritis is particularly bad today," she said in a falsely cheery tone. "But I'm used to it and there's no need to be worried. Thank you, though."

"Arthritis..." he muttered slowly, trying to think of something suitably consoling. Juvenile Rheumatoid Arthritis was rare among forever children, but not unheard of, and was especially dreaded for the crippling agony it brought its victims.

"I'm sorry," he finally stammered, backing off from his intention to introduce himself. "I do hope you're feeling better soon."

"Oh thank you very much," she smiled through the pain. "I appreciate the thoughtfulness, but I'm going to be fine."

At least she was hoping she would be fine, although in fact she wasn't anywhere near as sure as she pretended. It had been two weeks now, and her plan of easing into it gradually by reducing to half doses instead of stopping altogether had worked only partially at alleviating the excruciating symptoms. They were worse in the afternoon, always, and judging from the pain of the morning she looked to the afternoon now with increasing fear of facing the unknown all by herself. She had not told even Seelin of her decision, choosing instead to wait until she could prove her commitment rather than simply talk of it, but as the days went by and the pain increased, she was less concerned with appearances and more and more in need of someone to help her into the next day.

Just then a small alarm sounded from the portals and the visual tourmaster flew down from the ceiling in a particularly gaudy entrance, signaling the beginning of the tour. As the group pushed forward through the portals, Zhrana purposefully slowed her steps to allow the rest of the group to pass her in an attempt to fall as far off the pace as possible without being noticed. Entering the highly secure Laboratory without even a scanner search, she had to smile to herself how easy this had turned out to be, at least so far. After hours and hours of brainstorming ideas for secretly breaking into the facility, they had devised an intricate and dangerous plot for sneaking in, a plot involving the elimination of at least three security guards. However, as Zhrana had been watching the Laboratory for the last two days, she noticed no less than four groups of school children entering without any visible security measures. Apparently this was now a popular destination for schooling trips, and Zhrana had immediately thrown out the old plan and worked up this much less dangerous mode of entry. Although smiling at gaining the portals, however, she was still scared to death of what measures might still lie further on, beyond the point where she had already been able to observe the other assemblies.

This particular group was a class of fifteen year olds, only a few years past regulation. Since they had already completed a study in chemical interactions, the tourmaster had been programmed to give them a little more advanced guide than most of the younger kids got. Zhrana, of course, knew well the principles of Bio-Minerology, but listened anyway in an attempt to take her mind off both the constant pain as well as the danger which lay just ahead.

"This is where it all begins," the tourmaster was saying as they came to the first room, a surprisingly small chamber filled with strange machinery and only a few citizens monitoring the process. "This is where the power of the hive is born. In this room, and in the many more such creation cells operated by BioMinerals, Inc., is where the miraculous fusion of specially bioengineered tiny organisms (We call them Zots)" he added with a poorly programmed chuckle, "are fused at the microscopic level to molecules of magnesium, creating bio-magnesium, the first and still the most useful of all bio-minerals."

Zhrana peered anxiously through the clear wall into the room, searching for an entrance, but the crowd of equipment blocked any view of the far side, and no portals could be seen along either visible end of the cell. Straying behind as the tour proceeded to try and get a better look, she was startled by a uniformed forever girl who approached her from behind.

"I can see you're curious," she said. "But I'm afraid an explanation of the process would take quite some time. Perhaps you'd like to join the rest of your class. They must be nearing the more exciting growth test and reactor test cells."

"Oh, yes. Of course," Zhrana replied, turning quickly to deny the company official a good view of her face, then she hurried down the hall to where she could see the tail end of the tour winding its way around a far corner.

When she had caught up with them, acutely aware now of the official guarding the rear, she stopped to listen attentively to the tourmaster while watching with genuine interest as they passed by the next few rooms.

"This is the growth test cell, where we cultivate the first generation while at the same time assuring that the reproduction rate is stable and within acceptable limits." The guide flew through the clear wall into the chamber to direct attention to a large cylinder fed by several tubes entering it at intervals along its length. Inside was a clearly projected recreation of what appeared to be a glowing yellow-green matter, slowly growing from left to right through the tube. "We couldn't show you the real thing, because we've got to protect it behind several layers of t-steel to contain the pressure, but we've simulated here what it would look like if you could see through those layers. The oxygen is fed from the inlets you see here. It's amazing how these little fellas will reproduce in a pure oxygen atmosphere. And this is only a test, remember. Imagine what cells at Hive Power Co. must look like." Again the identical chuckle, which was beginning to get on Zhrana's already frayed nerves.

In a few more minutes they entered the last of the main mock-up rooms, a cylindrical chamber with an inlet fed from the floor and a huge array of energy collection panels lining the ceiling.

"Having already harnessed the living nature of these little beasts, now it's time to harness their mineral nature, as they burn themselves out in a billion fiery deaths a second in a heroic sacrifice to give us the power that runs the hive." The tourmaster bowed his head and took off his hat for a second, then looked brightly up again. "But don't be too sad. After all, they wouldn't have even had their chance at glory if we hadn't made them in the first place!" Now he flew in circles toward a valve high up in the chamber, then continued. "It's hydrogen, folks, hydrogen that does it. So if by any chance you've got any of these beasties coming over to your family huler (which I seriously do not recommend), better keep them away from any hydrogen cause they're bound to blow a little steam, if you know what I mean!"

Time was running very short, Zhrana knew, and with no other options available she decided to do the only thing which at this point might perhaps afford her an opportunity to stay behind within the Lab. Waiting for the company official to once again hurry her along, this time she initiated contact and asked straight away if she could be directed to the nearest release site, as the urgency of her situation required immediate attention. After being shown down a feeder hallway to the site entrance, Zhrana hurried inside to wait the five awful minutes before the official came to investigate the delay.

"Young woman?" the voice called out to her as she struggled to remain silent through the escalating pain which assaulted her in her hiding place within one of the seven release berths lined up in the center of the room, "Young woman, are you all right?"

When Zhrana refused to answer, clutching breathlessly at the synthar buried within the folds of her sara, the official walked slowly down the row of berths, pausing suspiciously before each one, curious but completely unsuspecting of what was about to take place.

Zhrana had never before killed another human being, had in fact long questioned her capacity to do so, and thus her ability to carry out her mission for the Liberationists. Many hours were spent in discussions with Seelin regarding this very issue, and though she remained steadfast in her assurances to him that she was strong enough, inside she had never reconciled herself to such an awful and violent act. Yet in the end it all happened so quickly that she was not even given the chance to think about what she was doing. There was the moment of discovery, the burst of her explosion from the berth, then the quick and eerily bloodless disintegration of the official. The death was quick, as Zhrana had aimed the first wave at the head, but the time it took to recharge for the next three waves required to fully evaporate the body was an eternity. It would last her entire life, as she was later to find out, wave after wave after wave reappearing and disappearing, the body shrinking and waiting, then waiting some more.

When the floor was clean and she once again found herself alone inside the empty room, she crawled back into her tiny berth and waited, for darkness, for the tour to end, for the Laboratory to send its operators back to their quadrants, for her chance to find the test inventory, for a secretly navigated escape, and for the next wave which continued to silently re-charge.

***

"Zhrana, is that you?" ventured a thin, pale forever boy who had spotted her hurrying through the main quadrant at this late hour of eight-thirty.

She stopped and turned toward her old acquaintance reluctantly, slipping off the unusually heavy waistpack and setting it down as unnoticeably as possible. Her plan of sneaking in and out undetected had just been derailed.

"Bayasho, how are you?" she replied as casually as possible, hoping to make this nothing more than a quick exchange of pleasantries. But the furrowed brow and quizzical eyes of Bayasho spread a wave of panic through her trunk and arms. The forever boy slowed as he approached, eyeing Zhrana curiously, and she as well took a step back as he got closer.

"Zhrana, are you feeling all right?" he asked hesitantly but with concern. "You don't look well." Now he noticed that he was peering up at her even though they stood on the same level, and his pale face shaded just a touch paler.

"Yes, I'm fine, thank you. And how are you feeling today?" she answered, trying in vain to deflect his attention.

"I don't know quite how to say this," he continued, "but I'm afraid, well, it seems to me as if you might have grown some." The words were uttered quietly, but with the gravity and horror of a death sentence.

Zhrana searched frantically within her for some excuse, some explanation. She had, of course, been monitoring the effects of her withdrawal, and had been fairly confident that, although she had grown slightly taller, the outwardly visible changes to her appearance had been barely noticeable. But her monitoring had been through a series of daily checks, so she could not have fully appreciated the changes which had taken place over the past two weeks: a somewhat straighter nose, a small lengthening to her facial bone structure which imparted an ever so slight but clearly distinguishable degree of maturity to her previously plump, childish cheeks. She paused, looking away from Bayasho for what seemed an eternity before finally answering him.

"Bayasho, it's true that I haven't been well. May I confide in you to keep a secret?" She lowered her voice and leaned toward the curious forever boy.

"Of course. All in family, as in family," he replied.

"No, even closer than family. Just between you and me. I don't want everyone worrying, you understand."

Bayasho balked at this unusual request, then nodded his head.

"I have a cancer, I'm afraid. A cancer of the thyroid, and it's unfortunately counteracting the effects of the regulators. I really have been growing."

"My God! I'm so sorry. Isn't there anything that can be done?"

"Don't worry. I'll be O.K. They'll be removing it soon." She reached down for her waistpack. "I've got to be going now. It was nice to see you."

"So that's where you've been. They were looking all over for you."

Now she stopped and put the pack down again. "Looking for me?"

"Yes. Kianno, Sofia, all of them. I think they were hoping you would make a statement at Kianno's hearing."

"Hearing? Is he in trouble of some kind?"

"You haven't heard yet? Kianno left yesterday for Level B. He was resettled after attacking two citizens in the weatherscoper."

"That can't be," she whispered hoarsely. "He's been in the family for thirty years. He's as much a Forshas as anyone."

"Not anymore."

Then Zhrana, despite her great hurry, waited patiently while Bayasho filled her in on the surprising events of the past few days. As she listened with growing dejection and remorse, she thought back to her last, unpleasant confrontation with her longtime friend, wondering if perhaps he might not still be sleeping only a few doors down the corridor if only she hadn't been so impatient and severe with him. It would take some time before she would be able to shed her feelings of guilt for Kianno's fate and come to realize that it would only have been a matter of time before GGG found some reason for removing the embarrassment he caused them. Regardless of her own lack of support for her friend, which she would continue to regret, his resettlement was as inevitable as Zhrana's would be, should she continue along the bold, radical path she had chosen.

As Bayasho described the case in surprising detail, Zhrana glimpsed several others rounding a corner and heading in their direction. She immediately turned her face from the group and interrupted his account.

"My friend, I need to leave you now," she said hastily, "You'll remember to keep our conversation between us alone?"

"Of course," he replied, somewhat bewildered at her sudden departure, then watched her rush off, struggling to attach a bulky waistpack as she disappeared down a side hallway.

Sensing there was much too much activity in the quadrant for so late at night, she quickly set about to tackle the task for which she'd risked returning still in possession of the stolen bio-magnesium. Fortunately, Sofia was alone and awake when Zhrana timidly announced herself.

"Zhrana!" her friend exclaimed as she rose from her sleeping pad. After they had greeted each other, unusually enough in Sofia's preferred method, the visitor got right down to business.

"You must contact Xyloru immediately. I need to return to the other side tonight."

"Xyloru has been arrested. There is only Atascin himself who can issue passes, and he's being watched carefully. I doubt he would risk it right now."

"Then you've got to contact him anyway. Sofia, I don't have time to tell you everything that's been going on, but I'm working with the Liberationists now. They've agreed to cooperate, and Seelin and I are teaming up to go beyond what we've been able to accomplish separately." The words flowed forward in a gush of enthusiasm. There was so much she wanted to share with Sofia, but she knew she couldn't risk it, not yet anyway.

"Listen to me, Zhrana." Sofia reached out and grasped her friend's hand in her own, noticing now for the first time the subtle changes as she looked into her eyes to emphasize the advise she was about to give. "You've got to keep the rest of us in on this. It's vitally important that we work together as groups, not as individuals. Do you understand?" She stepped back now, gazing at Zhrana with fear and confusion, afraid of the answer she might get if she were to ask about this sudden growth and change in her friend's appearance.

"Please don't worry. I'll bring you in on everything, but now isn't the time. I promise I'll return within the next week." Seeing the shock in Sofia's eyes, she felt obliged to reassure her. "You can tell I'm going beyond the threshold. It's my own decision is all I can tell you now. I'm doing this because I want to. I know that may be difficult to understand, but it's true and you've got to believe me. This is what I want, Sofia."

"I believe you," answered the forever girl in a faltering voice, choked with emotion. "I myself have wanted to, oh how I've wanted to…" Her voice trailed off into the late night silence, then she cleared her throat and continued more firmly. "You're stronger than I, Zhrana, but please be careful. You don't know what's been going on. So much has happened..."

"Yes. I've heard."

"Please, don't forget your promise," Sofia said, sensing her visitor's imminent departure. "I need to see him. Just once, perhaps, but I need to see him."

"I haven't forgotten." Zhrana paused, then leaned over to kiss her friend on the forehead. "Please contact Atascin tonight. It's my only chance," she called back before leaving.

"I will, but be prepared in case he can't help."

"Thank you my dearest Sofia. I'll return shortly and will let you know everything I can't tell you now." And with these words she disappeared through the portal wings.

As the nervous guest stepped out once again into the hallway, a forever boy hidden deeply into the shadows of a nearby corner watched with heightened attention. After ten days of following Sofia and watching her from every available angle, this was the first suspicious event he had witnessed, and he was tempted to leave his post in order to follow the late night visitor, but knew this would leave him open for possible reproach. So he noted it in his log and sat back for a long, uneventful night watch.

***

Before proceeding to take the vertical slider down to the Depot on the sublevel, Zhrana needed a few minutes to gather her thoughts and prepare herself for the final stretch of this terrifying and dangerous mission she had taken upon herself. She also wanted to retrieve additional items to fill the waistpack, and hoped to find an object into which the heavy, t-steel cylinder of bio-magnesium could be fitted, giving it a better hiding spot than simply being buried at the bottom of her waistpack. Her own room was the only place which afforded her a secure refuge, and so it was with a great deal of relief that she slid unnoticed into her own private, familiar corner of the quadrant. After collapsing on her sleeping mat for several minutes, she rose anxiously and scampered around the chamber in search of camouflage. Unable to find anything useful, she questioned if perhaps the waistpack was really the best way of smuggling the stolen mineral. It seemed too bulky and much too heavy to hide inside her sara, but perhaps if she could devise a sling over her shoulder and somehow conceal the shape within the folds of the flowing robes.

Throwing the waistpack down on the pad, she got up and walked over to the cabinet where all of her saras and robes were kept, riffling through them looking for the largest, most concealing suit. She did find a black morning robe which she had not worn for quite awhile and which might perhaps draw attention if worn crossing over in the middle of the night, but at least it was large enough to fit properly and allow for some extra hiding space. She started quickly to undress, unsashing the sara and pulling it from her shoulders, but before reaching for the robe in order to try it on, she paused, looking down at herself, then slowly removed her undergarments, standing naked in the center of her room.

She could see clearly how her body had begun to cross the threshold, and gazed curiously but excitedly at the small signs of womanhood which had so recently developed. Tiny breast buds clearly swelled around her nipples, which had darkened and spread and now hardened tenderly as she reached down with one hand to feel them, running her fingertips over the so soft, newly born flesh. And along with them, a smoothness and a delicacy to her skin, which seemed to rise from beneath with a softness which now adorned her body, a body on the verge of transformation from an endless childhood into the beauty of youth. Running her hands down from the breast buds along the platform of her still childlike stomach, she found the silky blonde hairs which had begun to sprout over the top of her sex, and brushed them gently with her small hand. Although still apprehensive about the changes which were coming, she looked to them with excitement and enthusiasm, welcoming the freshness of new growth which had for so long been held at bay. Looking down at herself, she wondered if he were here, would he reach out to those small emerging breasts with his large, man's hands? Would she feel the new hint of roundness to her thighs and bottom with his strong man's touch? How much longer until he came to see her no longer as a child but as a woman? And when he did, would she be a woman he could love?

Retrieved abruptly from her dreams by the sight of the cold t-steel cylinder strewn with the other items emptied from her pack onto the sleeping pad, Zhrana at once felt a surge of anxiety fill her at the thought of smuggling the bio-magnesium past the frontier checkpoint. Quickly dressing herself in her most ordinary sara, she re-packed the contraband and surrounded it with as many other oddly appearing but innocent artifacts as she could find. Then she slipped through the portals into the empty hallway, setting off on the final phase of her journey back to the outside.

19

"All right. You've all had the official orientation. Now it's time for me to let you know how things really are." The tall, pudgy man who had introduced himself as Marco addressed about seven or eight recent resettlers who had just arrived from higher levels. Like most of the men and women Kianno had seen since his arrival two days earlier, Marco appeared pale and weak, the result of a lack of any true strip lumins (old style phosphor lamps were used exclusively below level K, and there were precious few of them at that), as well a corresponding lack of any health or exercise opportunities.

Indeed Kianno had received the official introduction to the level yesterday, and it didn't seem as bad as what he had been expecting. The state official who had greeted them assured them that accounts at this level were generally sufficient for adequate food supplies, and living quarters, while not as spacious or as luxurious as what he had become used to, were clean and functional, and far from the squalid conditions he had been warned about before his arrival. It would take some time getting used to life without the visuals, and without any of the entertainment amenities of the upper levels (indeed boredom, not hunger, was the hallmark of poverty on these levels), but it was too early for him to fully appreciate yet the routine of daily life, especially since these first couple of days had been very well orchestrated by the state and by the Krimon quadrant (Quarters were administered by the state, and "families" per sey did not exist below Level K).

Now Marco surveyed the small group of listless newcomers, then continued his remarks. "For most of you, your time here on Level B will be short. More than anything else, this is a brief stopping off point on your way to the outside. You'd all better get used to that as soon as possible."

At these words, Kianno turned his head and scoffed inaudibly, but returned his attention to the speaker, who had noticed his skeptical reaction.

"What we will attempt to do is to make this transition as smooth as possible, and to best prepare you for life outside the hives. But your immediate concern is life on Level B, and for most of you it will be like nothing you've ever before experienced."

Kianno couldn't help but glance at the speaker with a doubtful look when he again reiterated his presumption that they were all on the way out of the hive, and this time Marco did not let it go unchallenged.

"You in the back, what's your name?"

"Kianno of Forshas..., uh, Kianno," he corrected himself, surprised at being singled out.

"Kianno, you look as if you don't believe what I'm telling you. Why's that?"

"No reason," he replied, shifting uncomfortably in the hard chair, "Just I think my situation's a little different, that's all."

"Oh really," mused the speaker. "In what way?"

"I'm not on some kind of downward spiral on my out of civilized society," he answered sarcastically. "I come from GGG, where I was a citizen in good standing for over thirty years. I made a mistake and now I'm paying for it, as I should, but I'll be back up to GGG before long. All that's needed is to demonstrate to the authorities that I can fit in once again. They explained that to us yesterday."

The speaker did not laugh or dismiss this claim out of hand. Instead, he turned to address the others in the group, a few of which had broken smiles at Kianno's statement.

"Sound familiar to anyone?" asked Marco, at which most of the others nodded their agreement. A large woman toward the rear spoke up in a husky voice.

"I was overchair of JJ for more than ten years before my, uh, illness, which caused this." She opened her arms as if inviting everyone to pay attention to her full grown figure. "Wasn't long after that they accused me of conspiracy just for visiting others like ourselves on another level. Said I was a bad influence on the family, but they don't need much of a reason anyway."

Others in the room greeted her account with small verbal affirmations. Then Marco took the floor once again.

"Like it or not, over ninety percent of those resettled here from higher levels have crossed the threshold soon before their resettlement, and almost all of them, all of you, have been good citizens for many, many years. Kianno, your crime is your body, and it's a crime you'll never be able to erase with time or good deeds." He looked around the room, then continued. "And it's a crime, I might add, which will undoubtedly lead to your expulsion from the hive. The sooner you begin preparing for that, the better."

Kianno could not find an immediate answer to this assertion, and looked around him for another to object on his behalf, but they had all long since seen what he so stubbornly refused to accept. Following a small silence, he did raise a question, however.

"I've seen forever children as well on this level. If what you say is true, what are they doing here?"

Marco raised his eyebrows slightly and rubbed his forehead, then responded. "You've all got to be very careful of them. Whatever you're doing at any time, always watch out for the forever children. The fact that they've been placed at this level means they've committed some truly serious crimes up above. They're desperate in a way you don't really need to be. You've all probably noticed that your accounts now are just barely enough to survive with most basic essentials. There's no room for additional amenities like entertainment and such. Which means there's nothing available for the regulators that the forever children are convinced they so desperately need. They'll lie, cheat, steal, do whatever they can to sustain the regulators while still maintaining their accounts, and you'd all be best to avoid them and to watch out for them constantly. Remember," He paused now for emphasis. "The only way for them to climb back up another few levels is to reveal information that the state finds valuable. If the information they reveal implicates you in any way, you'd better hope all they do is expel you.

Remember also that the hearings laws on this level don't allow for the accused to present statements, and the penalties are that much more severe."

Despite his earlier denial that he was spiraling out of control, listening to Marco only reinforced the increasing panic and confusion that had been building ever since the incident in the weatherscoper. He had been holding out hope that this was all a temporary aberration, that soon he would be back with the Forshas, but try as he might he couldn't envision his return except as some kind of return to the past which also restored his forever childhood, and as the meeting progressed he found himself increasingly distracted from the speaker by the anxiety and fear overtaking him.

After the meeting was finished, he tried to run off as quickly as possible, but Marco grabbed his arm and held him back after the others had left.

"What do you want?" Kianno angrily demanded, shaking off the grip which had softened into what was intended to be a reassuring clasp.

"I want your help, Kianno," Marco replied. "They need your help."

"Leave me alone. No one needs my help." He paused, intrigued slightly, then reiterated his assertion as an invitation to denial. "That's absurd that you should need my help."

"No, it's quite true. But you're right that it's not really me who needs your help. It's those on the outside."

"That's even more ridiculous." Kianno started off as if he had somewhere in mind to go, then stopped and turned once again to the stocky man who stood calmly waiting, as if he knew the newcomer was not going anywhere. "How can they need my help?"

"Medicine, my man, medicine. They rely on us smuggling it out to them, you know."

"Oh that's a good one. I suppose that's why you tell everyone they're on the way out, because you recruit them for these illegal missions of yours."

"Not mine, remember. Sick outsiders are the ones asking. I'm just their spokesman."

"Sorry, I've got my own problems," Kianno replied, less angry than confused at this point, but having heard enough to start for the door in earnest this time.

"Have they told you about the changes in your brain yet?" Marco called after him, halting the departure with this intriguing and peculiar question. When enough silence had gone by to assure he'd fully captured Kianno's attention, he continued. "Yes, it's not only your body which has changed and matured, but your mind as well, even though you're so stuck in your old ways that you haven't explored any of the new ways of thinking and relating which are now available to you. Well, I suppose it does take time. But I'm sorry, you were just leaving."

"What new ways of thinking?"

"Well, the hive scientists would never confirm it, of course, but it's well known that threshold growth also occurs within the brain, primarily within the parietal and frontal lobes. You may think you have a less than perfect body at this point, Kianno, but you've gained mental capabilities you never had before. Mental and social capabilities, I might add. It's time you learned how to use them, and what better way than to exercise them as soon as possible. That's why I'm offering you this opportunity." Now Marco himself began to gather up his belongings.

"Tell me more about these changes," asked Kianno.

"Later. After you've thought about my proposition. We survive by an entirely different principle down here, and on the outside as well. It's a principle they simply aren't physically capable of following up above, and it's a principle which will outlast even the most ancient of the forever children. When you're ready to learn more, come by and we'll talk."

Even though he was full of curiosity which had temporarily supplanted the agitation of only a few minutes ago, Kianno held his questions and watched silently as Marco exited the room and disappeared into the dark hallway.

***

"I understand your concern, but you've got to understand we've done everything possible short of the long term injections," concluded the exasperated doctor as she struggled to answer the challenges of the worried keeper who had brought her charge, young Nicoli of Grishams, to the medical center after even the new regulator formula had failed to halt the disturbing inch of new growth which had occurred since their last visit.

"Doctor, you've already said that she hasn't got any illness of any kind."

"As far as we can tell, that's true." The doctor looked up at Nicoli's equally agitated expression and wondered if perhaps this discussion should exclude the girl. "Brida, may I talk with you in private for a moment?"

"Yes, of course. Nicoli, you'll wait for us here, darling?" she said in a much more soothing tone, and when she received a nod of acceptance, the two of them exited the room to continue their discussion in the private office of the doctor.

"I'm afraid there isn't much choice at this point. If we wait any longer she's going to begin crossing. She's already at the point where she'll be somewhat taller than normal even if we're successful with the injections." The doctor spoke calmly, purposefully omitting any information about the possible side effects.

"I've never known any who have used the long term technique," Brida of Grishams answered hesitantly. "I've heard there may be risks involved..."

"Yes. We prefer to use the regulators, of course, however for a very few rare cases we have no choice but to resort to the injections. Please don't worry unnecessarily, however. The possibility of sustenance failure is very small with the newest techniques."

"What are you talking about, sustenance failure?"

"Well, believe it or not the same risk is possible with regulators, although due to the short half life, dosages can be adjusted much more easily. Basically, if the dosing estimates are inaccurate, it's possible that the drug will not only prevent unwanted growth, but also restrain necessary growth needed for normal regeneration of cells which are constantly in need of replacement. Should this occur, wasting disease could set in and, unfortunately, since the effect of each injection lasts for six months, nothing can be done to reverse the process."

At these words, the keeper took a step back and practically fell into the recliner behind her, clearly upset at this unexpected information.

"Isn't there any antidote, anything which can be given to counteract the effects if this...wasting occurs?" puzzled Brida.

"No, I'm afraid not. That's why we don't use the injections unless every other avenue has been explored. Unfortunately, that's the situation we're in now with Nicoli." The doctor now brushed her red hair with her hand, then sat next to the concerned keeper. "I've told you about the possible effects, but please remember that these reactions are very rare. The chances of such a response in this case are very small, please believe me."

Brida sat for a minute, pondering what she'd been told, knowing nonetheless that there was no choice in the matter, no real decision to be made. Then she lifted herself slowly up from the recliner and turned to the doctor.

"All right then, but let me be the one to tell her. She's awfully confused right now and I don't think she needs to know any more than is absolutely necessary." Then the two of them exited the office to rejoin the equally anxious patient.

"Nicoli," Breeda began, placing her hand on the girl's thigh and meeting her deep brown eyes with her own, "Nicoli, the doctor and I have discussed the problem we're having with the regulators, and we've decided that we're going to try something else. Something which will be much easier, actually. The doctor can give you a shot which will last for at least six months, after which she can give you another. That way you won't even need to take them daily, like the rest of us."

"No." Nicoli began crying softly now. "No, not the injections. I'm afraid, Brida, please not the injections."

The keeper placed her arm gently over the weeping girl's shoulders. In their time together she had grown quite fond of Nicoli, and it hurt her to see the young girl so upset.

"But afraid of what, my dearest. You know it's very safe. There's nothing to be afraid of."

"Afraid of never growing up," she answered, unable to tell her keeper of her real fears that she would never again see her mother and father, that entrance into this forever childhood signaled a resignation from her futile attempts to return to her home and her family. She looked over at Brida's affectionate eyes for some reassurance, trying but failing after all this time to see the faces of her parents in her mind's eye. "It's not so bad, is it?" she finally asked of her keeper who had been patiently consoling her through the silence.

"No, my dear. I know it's been difficult for you. But there's a whole new world for you now, and there are people who care about you so deeply in this world, myself included. You'll see that, Nicoli."

The frightened girl now wiped a tear from her eye with the back of her forearm, then reached down for her keepers hand. "All right," she answered in a voice with just a hint of brightness to it. "I'm ready now."

***

He was startled from his morning sleep by a loud clattering which caused him to sit up on his sleeping platform and look around, heart beating wildly and trembling in the confusion of a sudden awakening. For a few seconds he didn't even recognize his own room, so new and still so foreign was it, and as he sat up scanning the bad dream he had awakened into he wondered if perhaps it might all dissolve if he waited long enough. But then the clattering repeated itself, reinforcing the solidity of his predicament, and this time it was accompanied by a loud, high pitched voice.

"Kianno, Kianno are you in there?" It was Jaslo hitting his hands against the mechanical portal, shaking the metal frame in a loud rattling which had shattered the quiet of the room and the ease of Kianno's forgetful sleep. It took him another full minute to even realize what the noise was; there was no mechanism for announcing oneself into these quarters, and since he had not yet had a visitor, he at first could not fathom what such a clamor could be. When he did finally stumble across the floor strewn with placeless belongings collected from thirty odd years, and cranked open the portal, he looked down at the precise and suspicious face of Jaslo peering up at him.

It had been a full two weeks now since he had come into contact with any forever children (at Marco's advise he had purposefully avoided the areas where they were most likely to be found), and the sight now of Jaslo's chubby red cheeks and turned up pug nose struck him with a certain odd sense of childishness. In fact, after having grown so used to the sight of grown men and women like himself, looking back at the immature, childishly neutral face of his long time keeper, he couldn't help but find the sight of the pouty forever boy just a tad humorous, and he suppressed a small smile as he ushered the deadly serious Jaslo into his clutter filled room.

"Jaslo, this is really quite a surprise," Kianno admitted quite truthfully after the two of them had assumed their positions: Jaslo sitting cross legged directly on a cleared spot on the floor and Kianno returning to the still warm sleeping platform. "I thought, maybe..." He stopped his sentence short of completing the thought, which was that he had expected to see Sofia but not Jaslo. "Did you have any trouble finding me?" He filled in, retreating to the safety of pleasantries.

"No. I would have given you notice, but I wasn't aware the visuals were not installed on this level."

"Yes, It's going to take some getting used to."

"Kianno, do you have some time this morning to come with me back to GGG? There's something I'd like very much for you to see."

"Is that possible? I thought..."

"Yes, I've arranged for access as long as you're accompanied by myself."

Kianno thought for a second. Truthfully, he had no desire to return so soon to the sight of his recent humiliation, and answered diplomatically with a question of his own.

"Where would we be going? Back to the Forshas?"

"No," Jaslo replied curtly. "To the medical center. There's something I want to show you, something that I'm sure you'll be very interested in seeing."

This news brought an inward sigh of relief to Kianno. This must be related to his training and to his studies in the medicine of infectious diseases, he thought. Perhaps they had devised some way of allowing his residency to go ahead despite the resettlement, if there was some sort of link established between the program on GGG and whatever medical programs were in effect on Level B.

"What's that?" he couldn't help asking when Jaslo did not elaborate.

"You'll see when we get there. We should be going, though. The pass is for this morning only."

Both were generally silent with each other as they exited the Level B checkpoint and rode the slider up through the social and economic planes so well demarcated into precisely defined levels, until in only a few minutes they stepped out once again into the more secure, familiar world of GGG which Kianno had only so recently left behind. As they approached the medical center, Jaslo slowed the pace but remained quiet about the purpose of this unusual visit, so Kianno broke the silence as soon as the portals came into view.

"I've been looking for a way to resume my studies," he began, "and I wasn't sure if I even could on Level B…"

"Hmmm. I'm afraid I wouldn't know anything about that," his longtime keeper responded in a low mumble, preoccupied himself with thoughts on how best to introduce Kianno to the Lab and to the possibilities which can appear so extraordinary to the uninitiated. "I can see how you would want to continue, though. If you'd like I can look into it for you, but offhand I have no idea what facilities they might have on that level."

Disappointed but still curious, Kianno did not respond, satisfied to wait and let the meaning of this return visit unveil itself. In fact, it did not take long for everything to become perfectly, horrifyingly clear to him over the course of the next hour, during which Jaslo left nothing unrevealed. The technique, the side effects (which by now were practically entirely controllable with the right medication management), the consequences, the opportunities, and even the subjects themselves, which he saved for last, having a very particular reason for introducing Kianno to those children who had been selected from the outside but who had not yet become donors. In fact, so that a fully informed decision could be made, he had made arrangements for all six of them (four boys and two girls) to be put on display, naked and exposed inside a room with a clear wall such that the two of them could review them and Kianno could choose the body he might feel most comfortable occupying for the next two hundred years or so.

At this most shocking and repulsive culmination to a tour during which he had at the same time grown more scientifically fascinated and morally appalled but had throughout kept his objections to himself, Kianno could no longer contain his feelings.

"No, I'm not going to steal any one of those innocent children's lives from them," he exclaimed to Jaslo's bewildered expression. "I can't believe that you would even think I would consider going along with this inhuman experiment of yours!"

Jaslo paused, genuinely confused at the lack of appreciation of this gift of life he was offering, then furrowed his brow and answered. "Their lives are no longer their own, regardless. None of your moral objections will change their futures." When this was met with stony silence, he continued. "I believe it's quite clear, quite rational, that you may as well take one of their lives as your own, given the impossibility of your saving any of them." He gestured with disdain toward the children, who were running back and forth in the room, playing an improvised chase game of some kind.

"It doesn't matter that I can't keep you from pursuing your awful plans. I'll certainly have no part of it!" Kianno turned away from the display room, unable to look at the doomed children, but Jaslo grabbed his arm and faced him once again into the room.

"The blonde boy to the right is strong, and our reports show that he comes from healthy stock. You would be quite happy," and now he waited a second before finishing, "returning to GGG with such a healthy and agreeable body, don't you think?"

"What do you mean?" Kianno challenged angrily.

"I've already arranged it. Rokyo understands medical science enough to realize that the violence you demonstrated before would not be a risk. With the procedure successfully completed, your return to the Forshas is guaranteed."

Now the angry youth twisted free of his mentor's weak grip and stormed down the hallway, followed closely by the still unconvinced doctor.

"I know you may be worried about such a major surgical procedure," he called after the fleeing Kianno. "But there's very little risk, believe me." This claim did not succeed in even slowing the fleeing youth, so an increasingly desperate Jaslo continued his pleas. "This is the only thing that can save your life, don't you understand? Don't you understand that?" But Kianno only raged further ahead, and by the time the forever child had caught up with him, well outside the Laboratory portals, Jaslo had given up on his attempts at convincing the stubborn Kianno to reconsider his precious gift of life.

20

"This was no prank by some low level daredevil. Whoever did this knew what they were doing, and probably has a specific use in mind for the stuff. That much we can be sure of," reiterated the weary police official to his stubborn associate, who still held out hope that the entire matter could be written off as someone's idea of a joke. He adjusted the suspension beam and shook his arms in an effort to relax into the supportive heavy particle stream.

"If you ask me, we've spent too much time on this already. We're never gonna catch her anyway. If you're right about this being some sort of devious plot by outsiders to activate a quother swell inside the hive, then she's long gone by now. You don't actually expect she'd be hanging around here just waiting to get caught, do you?"

His associate snickered at the thought, then scratched the whorl of his bright red hair.

"We know it was one of us, though, and being a forever girl it's possible she might still be maintaining her cover inside the hive. It might very well be part of their plan..."

"Oh c'mon. We've got six other cases we haven't even started on and you want to keep pursuing your conspiracy theories." The associate dialed another file on the visual they both had been viewing, at which the official angrily stepped out of his suspension and re-commanded the visuals back to their previous setting.

"Kyre, the reason why you've never progressed beyond rank three, even though you've solved a good many more cases than I, is that you have no sense of priority. When's the last time you ever heard of any bio-minerals being stolen?"

When his associate failed to respond, he answered his own question. "Two years. That's how long."

"Yea, and that turned out to be a prank, just like this one."

"And hopefully this'll turn out the same way. But I'm not letting it drop till the stuff shows up. Let me see the interviews one more time. Start with the one who talked with her."

Reluctantly, the associate dialed in the same interview they'd already seen several times before, and they watched in silence as the keeper described his brief encounter with the only member of the party who had not been accounted for. As the interview neared its end, the official leaned forward and listened carefully.

"And it was clear, then, that she was in considerable pain?" the examiner was saying.

"Yes, quite obvious. That was why I approached her in the first place. I was worried that she might be having some kind of crisis or something."

"Did you inquire as to the nature of her pain?"

"Yes. She said it was arthritis."

"You're sure about that?"

"Yes, absolutely."

The official now cut the visuals and the interview evaporated once again. He approached his suspension beam, but instead of stepping into it he paced short circles around its perimeter, deep in thought. Finally he turned to his associate.

"And still no positive matches in the medical records of arthritics?"

"Nothing."

"Then we expand the search parameters. What are some other sources of intense pain, but we'd have to assume non-life threatening pain, since she clearly had more than survival on her mind?"

"I'm no doctor," answered his associate, still bothered by the official's preoccupation with this case. "But I would guess they'd have to be pretty rare. Perhaps she had a cancer of some kind and really was dying." This didn't elicit much of a response, so he continued his postulations. "Lupus, Rhymones Disease, I've heard regulator withdrawal can be pretty intense..."

"What was that?" The official stopped his pacing and raised his hand to his forehead.

"Regulator withdrawal. I suppose it's a possibility, like just about everything else."

"Send another alert to all doctors. This time include the same description but reference it to regulator withdrawal or failure as well. If she's out there, and is suffering enough, it's possible she might show up at a center. It's worth a try, anyway."

"Whatever you say," Kyre answered in a dubious tone. "Now can we get to some of these other files?"

***

"Zhrana?"

The voice fell through the room in a flat monotone, unexpecting of any reply. It was the seventh time over the past four days that Sofia had called out to her friend, and with each visit she grew more and more certain that Zhrana had not returned from the outside, if indeed she had ever made it across in the first place. On one occasion two days earlier she thought she had heard a small rustling inside the chamber, but it had never repeated itself, and as she turned away she told herself that this would be the last visit. If indeed Zhrana were hiding from even her closest friend, then there was nothing more Sofia could do but wait and hope.

But as she started away from the stilled portals, she once again heard a low shuffling coming from the other side- small mutinous sounds of betrayal breaking free of their long confinement.

"Zhrana? Is that you? Please Zhrana, I can help," she repeated softly, careful not to draw any attention from a couple strolling down the far end of the hallway. Still no reply, and once again the noise stilled mysteriously. Then quickly, in a gush of stale air escaping from the long sealed chamber, the portals rotated open and Sofia was pulled strongly into the room, eyes wide with surprise at the sudden and shocking presence of her friend.

"Shhh," Zhrana held the smaller Sofia against her to stifle any sound until the portals had safely closed again, then held her out at arm's length before she broke down in tears and the two collapsed into a shuddering embrace.

"I'm so sorry, so sorry I kept you out. I wanted to answer so much, believe me. But you don't know how afraid I've been. Oh Sofia, you don't know what I've done!"

The forever girl did not respond, but instead held her close until the sobs subsided and Zhrana politely led her visitor to the lounger, clearing away empty food tubes scattered about the floor. When they had both regained their composures, Zhrana gazed immodestly at her friend.

"You've grown so beautiful," she said sincerely, but the remark was met with a sigh.

"You're probably the only one in this family who would say so, but thank you anyway." She waited awkwardly for a moment, then chased away her embarrassment with a fresh thought. "Sofia, I'm so hungry. You have to bring me some more food. I thought I'd brought in enough, but you wouldn't believe how much I eat now."

At this the two of them looked at each other and broke into laughter, a laughter which eased the tension and for the first time restored their usual easy going kinship.

"I've been an absolute pig, but I can't help it," she continued. "If I'd have known how much food I would need to cross over, I might have reconsidered the whole idea."

"I'll bring some right away. What about water?"

But before she could respond, the startling voice of Jaslo jumped upon them both and echoed through the hushed room.

"Sofia, Zhrana? May I come in?"

At this alarming interruption, Zhrana rose anxiously and looked around her as if there were somewhere to hide, then both of them scampered aimlessly about the room as their minds raced to find some way out.

"How could he have known? Did he see you," Zhrana whispered frantically.

"No. I'm sure of it. I have no idea how he found out. But listen, we've got to go through this, not around it. It's no crime, your choosing to cross over. You're safe for the time being, anyway."

"Sofia?"

"Yes, Jaslo. You may enter," the forever girl answered over the protesting gestures of her friend, and with those words Jaslo entered the room, accompanied by an inquisitive looking Rokyo who trailed behind.

Although Zhrana sat low to the ground and cowered into as small and inconspicuous a figure as she could, her transformation was nevertheless noticed almost immediately.

"My God!" Rokyo exclaimed at the sight of her, now nearly six inches taller and a full thirty pounds heavier than himself. "Zhrana, what's happened to you?"

"I'm, I'm not feeling well," she stammered, glancing over at her friend for help, at which Sofia stepped forward and pulled the two forever boys aside.

"She's been ill, as you can plainly see," she said in a hushed tone. "I've been administering to her but she's in no condition to receive more guests. Jaslo, I'll see you later and we can talk about how we might help her, but right now I think it might be best if you would leave us alone. She's obviously very upset about what's been happening to her."

"Of course, of course," answered Rokyo, but his associate was not as easily convinced, perhaps sensing from his longtime companion's tone that she was trying to hide something from them.

"This is clearly a very serious illness. Although I myself do not specialize in regulator failure diseases, there is a very good friend of mine, Dr. Tillian of Grenaders, who is perhaps the leading authority in these matters. I would be glad to arrange a visit as early as tonight. I'm sure, at my request, and considering the extreme circumstances, that it would be no problem."

At the sound of this proposal, Zhrana straightened up from her crouch and approached the three of them, who continued to talk about her as if she weren't even there. But before she could dispel this notion of an immediate medical examination, Sofia, who knew there was no way to avoid this inevitability and unaware as well of her friend's true crime, answered abruptly.

"That's very generous of you. Yes, we'd appreciate it if you could contact this doctor and schedule a visit just as soon as possible. This all came very suddenly, and she's been so embarrassed, you understand..."

"Yes, I understand," Jaslo lied, convinced now of the validity of his suspicions. "Of course, by now it's most likely too late. She's gone too far already."

"Then leave me be, will you!" Zhrana demanded angrily, injecting the first taste of hostility into what had been a tense but cordial discussion. "If it's too late then leave me alone!"

A frightening silence ensued, Jaslo and Rokyo too stunned to respond to this sudden outburst, and Sofia unable to quickly soften the antagonistic edge of her friend's declaration. Finally, she turned up her eyebrows at them and formed a puzzled expression as if to say this unusual behavior must somehow be associated with Zhrana's illness.

"I think this whole thing has all of us worried and upset," she said, now giving a cautionary glance to her friend, who had by now realized the foolishness of her response and remained silent. "We're very grateful for your offer. If you can set something up for us as soon as possible, then let us know, we will be waiting here."

"Yes, I agree. I'm sorry. I...I've been confused and embarrassed and I really didn't expect any visitors," Zhrana added, although the two callers remained skeptical at the very least.

"I understand," Rokyo replied. "I think it's best if we were to be leaving now, don't you think?"

"Yes." Jaslo's eyes avoided Sofia's, knowing they might reveal the depth of his suspicions. He turned to join his associate. "I will contact you immediately as soon as I am able to get hold of Dr. Tillian." Then Sofia activated the portals and the two of them finally left the small room, to Zhrana's great relief.

***

The case had sounded quite odd when Jaslo had informed him of it only an hour earlier. He simply did not get emergency calls, any more than a refinishing specialist would get emergency calls; regulator failure was not something you just woke up with. The few cases he did see were generally noticed very early on, when they might be treatable over an extended period of time. But for someone to have gone so far without consulting a doctor, well that was just unheard of, unless of course that someone was crossing purposely.

So he was entirely prepared, as he sat waiting for his patient to arrive, to use his expertise not to stop the poor citizen from crossing, something which, from what he had heard, was pretty much impossible at this point anyway, but rather to ease the withdrawal pain through the use of pain killers and hormonal compressors. After all, it wasn't any of his business if a citizen should choose this accelerated path toward death.

Before long he heard the voice of a forever girl announce itself, and Dr. Tillian rose to meet his patient with some puzzlement, as clearly the voice belonged to one who had not yet crossed over, but his confusion was quickly resolved when he saw the two of them approaching. After a quick exchange of pleasantries, he led the patient, along with her friend who insisted on accompanying them, into the examination room.

"Before we start," the doctor began in a confident, almost instructional tone, "I need to know the reason for your visit. I must admit that I'm a bit baffled by your waiting until now to seek medical help, unless of course you've chosen this for yourself."

"Oh no, I certainly didn't choose for this to happen," Zhrana replied, repeating almost word for word what the two of them had agreed upon on the way over. "At first I didn't really notice the changes, and when I did, when they became so obvious and the pain was so bad, I was too embarrassed. Plus, I'd heard that there was nothing that could be done."

"Well, at this point you're right. But certainly if you'd come to me sooner..."
"I know, I know. If only I hadn't been so embarrassed and afraid," Zhrana answered from the most regretful and sorrowful expression she could form.

"So what is it you want from me, then? We could perhaps investigate the cause of the failure and re-introduce the regulators at this point, although the benefit in terms of life expectancy would be minimal." He looked at the patient carefully, sensing a strange familiarity to the face and to the eyes in particular, searching his memory for where he might have seen those eyes before. Their gazes met briefly before Zhrana pulled hers away, pretending to be impressed with the living artwork which played across the far wall.

"If I may say something, doctor?" Now Sofia interrupted, feeling compelled to help out even though her friend was handling things just as they had discussed. "We want most of all to be sure there's no life-threatening disease which is causing this. We know there's nothing you can do otherwise, but we would like to rule out any major illnesses."

"All right, then. I can do my best to rule out everything other than primary regulator failure. Let's see, from all appearances you have progressed to a natural age of about sixteen or so." Dr. Tillian once again scrutinized Zhrana, examining her face and eyes more than the body which should have been the focus of his attention. "You say at first you didn't even notice the changes?"

"Yes. I wasn't paying much attention, I suppose."

"So there was no pain, early on?"

"No," Zhrana answered hesitantly.

"That's interesting." The doctor now rose and placed the hand held examinator at a measured distance from his patient, then observed the readouts silently, glancing up only occasionally to check the alignment of the device. Finally, he looked up and slipped the tool into a pocket buried in the folds of his medical robe.

"I need to run this data through some programmed scenarios," he said, "Please make yourself comfortable, as this may take a few minutes."

Back in his private quarters, Dr. Tillian commanded his more expensive voice activated visual receiver to once again replay the alert issued three days earlier. At the time he had pretty much ignored it, as these alerts were routinely released whenever the state needed the assistance of professionals in locating an individual who for some reason or another had escaped from the tracking web, and were almost always directed at the lower levels. But this unusual visit had brought the recent notice back to the surface of his memory, and as he reviewed it once again he became more and more concerned: "forever girl, blonde hair, blue eyes, four foot ten, eighty pounds, suffering chronic pain or regulator withdrawal symptoms..." Of course the physical description was off, but if she had withdrawn from the regulators that would be expected. The blond hair and blue eyes matched up. When the recreated pictorial of the suspect was displayed, he froze the visuals and looked hard and long at the eyes. Then he dialed the transmitter channel and waited for an answer.

A few minutes later he walked briskly into the examination room.

"Good news," he proclaimed cheerily. "The results don't show disease of any significance. It looks like it probably really is simple regulator failure."

At this, Zhrana and Sofia sighed a little too audibly with relief, despite their worries which had been heightened by the doctor's unusual departure.

"Thank you so much." Zhrana reached both hands out to Tillian. "We'll be leaving, then. We do appreciate your help at this hour."

"No," the doctor replied much too abruptly, startled by his patient's suddenly proposed departure, then he continued in a softer tone. "I mean, there are still things I can help with. The pain, for example."

"It hasn't been so bad lately, really." Zhrana started toward the door.

"But the next phase will be most difficult. I can give you a long term pain killer which will ease you through it."

"Are you sure?" ventured a calmer Sofia to her friend, who had better sensed what was going on and shrugged the idea with a wary expression.

"Here, let me at least do that much for you," the doctor persisted, pulling an injection gun from his robes. "You'll be glad for it later on, I assure you." He stepped cautiously toward a panicky Zhrana, who at first backed away but then froze in her tracks, knowing now that there was no choice but to flee.

In the next instant she charged straight at the surprised doctor, knocking him over and easily overpowering him with her greater size and strength. With the force of the impact, the injection gun flew from his hand and skidded over the floor toward an equally astonished Sofia, who watched dumbfounded as Zhrana pinned her opponent with her hands and knees.

"The injector!" yelled Zhrana as she struggled to maintain control over the squirming doctor. "Inject him quickly!"

Sofia hesitated, never before faced with the necessity of inflicting harm on another, and as she hesitated Tillian pleaded desperately.

"No, no please!" he cried, and still Sofia stood motionless, unable to bring herself to reach down and grasp the small and surprisingly simple injector gun.

"Hurry," ordered Zhrana firmly. "If it's just painkiller like he says then he's got nothing to worry about."

"No, I beg you. I'll not say a word, I promise," the doctor implored frantically, but his words were not enough to sway a shaky but resolute Sofia, who picked up the device and approached the two of them with deliberate steps.

As she bent down to administer the injection, the doctor heaved with one last effort to free himself, but Zhrana was able to keep his right wrist still enough for her friend to place the target grid firmly against the forever boy's skin and squeeze the handle. Then, in a quick and strangely silent release, the needle plunged deep inside Dr. Tillian's freckled wrist, and the dispenser expelled the full dose which dispersed rapidly into the surrounding muscles, slowly working its way into his bloodstream.

Although certainly unintended, the fortunate effect of this overdose (the pre-measured dosage had been set for Zhrana, and, when given to the much smaller doctor instead, resulted in a severe neural reaction to this usually safe but strong tranquilizer) was to silence forever the only witness who could have implicated Sofia in the attack. Zhrana, already a fugitive and not destined to remain long in the hive at any rate, insisted that her friend deny any knowledge of what happened there, fabricating a scenario in which Zhrana at the last minute chose to go alone to the doctor's, and with a little behind the scenes help from Jaslo there was never any public or state initiated challenge to her story. Only Jaslo, and his hired investigator who was paid quite generously to remain silent, knew the truth of her involvement, and both of them, for the time being anyway, were staying very quiet indeed.

***

It was the true sky, with a depth and a vastness she had never imagined in the years it had invaded her dreams and haunted her mind's eye. The true sky, stretching uninterrupted to all horizons, darkened not to the eternal black that she had envisioned, but rather to a kind of blue, the deepest possible blue, with a cloud of stars smeared across the highest part.

"It's so beautiful," she said to Zhrana, stopping to look around her now that they had left the checkpoint well behind and had climbed into the crystal silence of the fall mountainside.

Zhrana now stopped and lifted her eyes from the dirt trail, reluctantly at first as she was driven toward reaching Lexington as soon as possible, but then she as well was overcome with the wonder of this natural world in which she was slowly starting to feel at home. And as she surveyed the ridge line, jagged with pine trees, and the brown fall dryness of the meadows lower down, faintly illuminated by a waning sliver of moon, she realized that this was now her only home, that she would likely never again return to the warmth and security of the hive which until recently had been the only world she had ever known. A breeze blew up the narrow canyon walls and sent a chill over her skin. It had all happened so quickly and so irretrievably. If only she didn't have to seal the door back to her previous life, to her friends, to her family who had shared all those years with her. If only she could keep the doors to both worlds open, but there was no longer any choice, no longer any path home. She gazed down at the trail winding in and out of the scrub oak which clung in broad patches to the abandoned hillside, and beyond to the valley which bedded the smaller hives of Cambria and Los Gatos, and in the distance the precise rectangular brilliance of the Great Hive, sleeping inside its blanket of lights. Then she turned once again to the darkness up above.

"Will I see him tonight?" Sofia broke the stillness, bringing Zhrana back to her mission, back to her plans and hopes on which her future now rested.

"No, not tonight," she replied, shivering in the chill air. "Are you cold?"

"No. It's different, but I don't mind it." Sofia paused, once again drawn away from herself by the unaccountable familiarity of these nightfallen mountains.

"When, then?" she added at length, breathing the words into a wind which lifted and teased her hair into life.

"Tomorrow. Tonight you stay elsewhere, with friends. Tomorrow, if he's ready..."

Zhrana let the thought escape unfinished into the night, then set her right foot forward onto the rocky trail.

21

It was Mistissa who first heard the tentative mild knocks and scratchings ascending into the quiet of the night, and, after a few minutes of listening curiously from her platform, she rose, sleep still blurring her vision, and padded carelessly across the cold floor toward the front room. When she arrived at the heavy old wooden door, she listened intently, but the strange noises had abated, and for a moment she wondered if perhaps she had been dreaming them, but then she heard once again the soft knocking, this time so close at hand that it startled her from her drowsiness.

"Seelin, Seelin it's me." The words barely crept through the cracks in the warped oak, riding softly on the cold draft which played at her feet.

"Seelin, are you there?" they called again, and Mistissa was tempted to reply, knowing she should run and waken her father but excited at an opportunity to handle this mysterious interruption on her own. She looked over her shoulder toward Seelin's room and tried to distinguish the sound of his snoring, but only the shuffling outside the door, and the usual distant moans of those few tortured hungry and dying who found no relief in sleep, could be heard.

She took a deep breath, shaking now with the cold at her feet and the uncertainty of her bravery, then answered in a voice which broke abruptly from the whisper which ushered it forth .

"Who is it?" she answered, taking a step back from the door.

"Mistissa, is that you?" The voice sounded familiar, but she couldn't place it right away, so she kept her silence and waited for more.

"Mistissa? It's Zhrana. Can you let me in?"

Now the girl relaxed considerably at the name of this friend who had been visiting them on and off but hadn't been seen for over two weeks now, and she reached up to unbolt the clasp and release the door, which tilted slightly on it's hinges, then swung slowly inward at Zhrana's eager push.

When the trusting girl caught her first glimpse of the visitor she quickly pushed back forcefully on the door, not having had time to see the face or eyes, but rather reacting to the presence of this larger figure who clearly could not be Zhrana. But the figure was too quick for her and resisted with greater power, struggling successfully to force the door open and gain entrance into the room. Fleeing from the intruder, Mistissa turned and sped across the front room to the safety of her father.

"Mistissa, it's me!" Zhrana called out, this time loudly enough to wake Seelin, and Mistissa stopped short and turned around. It was the same voice, maybe a little different in a way she couldn't place yet, but it was undoubtedly her friend's voice. Stepping closer to the figure obscuring the still open door, she strained to make out the face in the dim light of the sole sulfur lamp which flickered in the rush of air.

It was a girl, a young woman really, older than Zhrana but with Zhrana's eyes and the fullness of Zhrana's character etched in the face, matured now by five full years.

"Zhrana, is that really you?" she ventured, but before the young woman could answer, the door to Seelin's room swung open and her father burst into the room, rushing quickly to his daughter's side.

"Get out, now!" he commanded instinctively, approaching the intruder with measured steps.

"No, Seelin. It's me," Zhrana pleaded once more, and with those four words Seelin knew instantly it was her, and knew instantly what she had done.

"Mista, it's all right. It's really Zhrana. You needn't worry," he reassured the girl.

"But..."

"I know you don't understand now, and can't understand now. But we'll talk in the morning. Don't be afraid, because you and I both know she's our friend. Now go to sleep and we'll talk all about it in the morning.

The two of them then walked slowly back into her sleeping room, followed by a relieved Zhrana. When the girl had climbed back onto her platform and buried herself into the covers, she whimpered in her best little girl voice. "Story?"

"All right. Just a very short one, though." Seelin sat down on the edge of the platform and cocked his head to one side, searching for the shortest one he could find.

"I know one," added Zhrana from behind, and after a moment's hesitation by Seelin, he scooted over to allow her room.

"Daddy.." Mista protested but much too weakly, welcoming any story at this late hour, and Zhrana, hearing this in her tone, started right in.

"Once upon a time," she began, "in a far off gathering nestled at the top of a huge mountain, lived a beautiful princess named Listissa." At this the girl giggled and squirmed under the bedcovers, but Zhrana continued on. "Now one day, Listissa was spending time in her room, having been sent there because she had been very naughty."

"What did she do?" squealed Mista.

"Uh...She had told a lie."

"What lie," the girl persisted, and now Seelin interrupted, all too familiar with his daughter's tactics of drawing out the story as long as possible.

"Mista, you're to listen to the story," he said solemnly.

"So the princess, bored with her room, climbed out her window and down into the forest, where she explored deeply into the woods." Zhrana paused, expecting another question, but the young girl only looked up with curious eyes, so she continued. "After a while, she came across a trail she'd never before seen, and so she followed it deep into a hidden grove of tall, red trees. Suddenly, as she reached out to touch one of the mysterious trees, the earth gave way under her and she fell through a hole in the ground into the bottom of a secret cave."

"Did she get hurt?" asked Mista.

"No. Even though it was a long fall, she wasn't hurt at all because it was a magic cave she'd fallen into."

Mistissa kicked her legs under the covers, then turned on her side, entranced with the story but also starting to grow sleepy once again.

"Well, the princess immediately started exploring the cave, looking for a way out, but before long a huge flood of water started flowing through the cave, and this made her very afraid, since she couldn't swim. So she wished hard for someone to help her, and then, from around a bend in the cave, a lion appeared."

"Oh no!"

"But this was a friendly lion, you see. And the lion told her to climb onto his back and he would swim on top of the water. So she rode the lion as he swam, and was safe from the flood. But after awhile, she started to get cold and to miss her family, so she asked the lion to try and find a way out of the cave. But the lion, although he was a good swimmer, could not find the way out. The princess then wished hard for someone to lead them out of the cave, and when she opened her eyes a beautiful, red and green talking bird appeared and flew toward them."

Zhrana slowed her story, looking down and seeing that Mista's eyes were closed and her breathing had assumed the deep, purposeful draws of sleep, but continued nonetheless, nearing the end of her story. Meanwhile, Seelin looked on beside her with almost as much enchantment as Mistissa had shown a few moments earlier.

"So the magical bird flew off ahead to find the entrance to the cave, then led the princess and the lion to where the underground river flowed out into the forest. But as the princess stepped out of the cave, she found out that her friends could not follow her. Being magical creatures, they could not leave the cave. They were happy, though, that they were not alone and that the princess had wished for each other to keep them company until Listissa could return to the magic cave."

The girl was now sleeping peacefully, and Zhrana reached down to straighten the bedcovers, then stood up and the two of them walked quietly from the room.

In the soft light of the front room, Seelin reached out to touch her long blonde hair, running it tenderly through his fingers.

"You're so beautiful," he said simply but truthfully, for indeed she had grown quite beautiful in those two short weeks. Although still relatively small and slim, she had grown taller and had assumed the softness and mild fullness of a woman, with a roundness now to her thighs, and the curve of her breasts lightly brushed the sara which his hand now fell onto and caressed gently. She was in the flower of youth, her body finally matured beyond the eternal childhood which had separated them physically even as they both had longed for each other since they had first met.

Now she took his hand in her own, and he reached out to bring her close, to feel her warm, youthfully feminine body against his own, and she fell eagerly into his gathering her all around him, feeling for the first time the touch of a man against the softness of a woman. Then he led her quietly, lovingly, into his own room.

***

Damn this cold, he thought as he huddled against the rotting side beams of the building he'd been led to on this freezing night. Actually, the temperature was not freezing, only in the mid forties, but to a forever child who'd spent his entire life within the comfort of environmentally controlled atmospheres, it could just as well be ten below. He blew on his hands and fiddled with the dials on his wrist visual controller, vowing never again to accept an assignment beyond the boundary of the hive. Having found the channel he was looking for, he paused for a moment to listen carefully. It had been a full hour since the last sounds of activity had died away (and what sounds they were, he thought to himself), but he wanted to be absolutely sure the household was asleep before establishing the link. Satisfied he would not be overheard, he commanded the channel, and instantly the visual of a sleeping Jaslo filled the miniaturized stage he had set between himself and the building.

"Jaslo, wake up," he called, and at these words the forever boy sat up sharply, clearly sleeping very lightly in anticipation of the call.

"Yes, what is it? What have you found?" He rubbed his eyes, then leaned back on his hands.

"I've followed them here," the investigator responded, pointing the sender toward the building, then waving it slowly to take in the surrounding landscape as well. "I'm afraid I have some very... well, some very interesting news. News you may not want to hear."

"That's ridiculous," scoffed Jaslo. "Out with it."

"Well, the two of them crossed at the South Central Gate about four hours ago, then proceeded upward at a very rapid rate to the gathering of Lexington."

"Hmm, as I suspected. Continue."

"They made one brief stop at a residence near the northern edge of the gathering, then they..."

"Where exactly? And what exactly did they do at this residence?" Jaslo interrupted.

Now the forever boy hesitated. In truth, he had lost them coming into the gathering, and had only picked up their trail again as they were entering this building, seeing the last of them, Zhrana, as she entered the front door. Although he had never actually seen Sofia with her, he presumed they had both entered, after stopping somewhere along the way, during which time they had disappeared from his sight.

"I'm afraid I was following too far behind to get the details. The stop was very brief," he lied, unwilling to admit to having lost them altogether. "But I do have the precise location here, and I've been able to gather some information from one of the terminals."

"Yes.." encouraged Jaslo, sitting up Indian style now.

"The residence has been recently occupied by a man named Seelin Arears and his daughter. He is suspected of having been involved in terrorist activities some ten years ago, but was believed to have been killed at that time. His resurfacing should be of great interest to the local authorities here."

"So her involvement is even deeper than I suspected," Jaslo mused, wondering how many of these nocturnal visits she may have already made.

"Yes, and I'm afraid there's something else, as well," the investigator added, feigning a delicacy which belied the secret pleasure he took in revealing such scandal. "I'm afraid, well, there's been some quite enthusiastic sexmaking going on inside there tonight." He waited eagerly for his employer's response, but there was only silence from the shocked forever boy, who now leaned forward and laid his head down upon his knees. At length he rose up and answered the startling report.

"This is to remain between us," he repeated the terms of their agreement.

"Of course, as is all I see for you. Do you want me to kill him?"

Jaslo barely heard the question, so strong were the thoughts which ran through his head. How long? How long had she been seeing this Seelin Arears? And how long had their sexmaking been going on? Perhaps indeed that was her fascination with the old way after all. And this Seelin, odd that he should share the same name as their long dead first child. He lay back now on the covers, lost in thought for several minutes before the investigator found the courage to interrupt him.

"Shall I kill him, then?"

"Kill him?" Jaslo opened his eyes and finally awoke to the question at hand. "Hmm. Does he have a woman, then?"

"No. He lives alone with his daughter."

"Then bring her back. She'll be more useful to us as an instrument of persuasion than he could ever be. With her in our possession, he'll belong to us."

The cold forever boy nodded appreciatively, as he greeted all his employer's insights, then he hastened the conversation to a close.

"If you please, sir, it's very cold and I need to find shelter…"

"All right. Very well. I want the daughter delivered tomorrow, and Sofia is not to see you or suspect anything, you understand?"

"Of course," the forever boy replied, then clicked off the visuals. Standing up, he sucked a deep breath of night air into his lungs and felt a stabbing pain shoot through one of his few remaining natural teeth. Then he shrugged his shoulders and took off in search of a warm corner.

22

As soon as she walked through the door he felt as if he'd entered a dream, as if he had suddenly become a ghostlike participant in the ancient memory of a time so distant it had been nearly forgotten. She was so much the same, so much unaffected by the years which had worn into his own body and soul, that he could only observe as if watching a scene from the past replay itself in his mind, as if she were only a trick played on him by his hidden, dreaming self.

Wearing an eager but shaky smile, she approached slowly toward him, bringing the past with her, accompanied by sentinels of the present just to confuse the issue even further and perfect the trick: Zhrana holding her hand as she introduced the visitor and Mistissa tagging along behind with her ever curious eyes.

When they had advanced into his immediate space, Zhrana stepped back and tried to remove herself from the encounter, but Mistissa ran to the foreground to perform the introductions, unaware of the visitor's true identity.

"Papa, this is Sofia. She's a forever girl but Zhrana says it's all right," she began, bold in the presence of one from whom her father had always warned her. "She's a friend of Zhrana's."

"Yes, I know," he replied, looking into the eyes of the forever girl who had once been his mother, "So you've met my daughter, then?"

"Oh yes. She's a beautiful child," Sofia answered, now summoning the courage to meet Seelin's gaze. Such a tall man, she thought, so large and so old, but he had grown handsome beyond the threshold as well. For a moment she looked into his brown eyes, trying to find the boy she had lost so long ago.

"How old is she now?" she added at length.

"Nine." The two of them shifted uncomfortably, and Zhrana took the awkward silence as her cue to leave them alone.

"C'mon Mista," she grabbed onto the girl's hand. "Let's go play a game."

"We can look for the secret cave!" answered Mistissa quickly, then the two of them ran off into the brilliant sunshine spilling through the doorway.

Alone now, Seelin led Sofia to his old recliner, where the two of them sat next to each other and watched the particles of dust pass through the brightness of the sun ray which fell from the window adjacent to the recliner.

"Tell me about her. I want so much to know. What is she like?" Sofia asked, looking down at his strange, rough hands, still unsure if they could really be the hands of her boy Seelin.

"Well, she's a bit of a tomboy right now," he answered. "She loves to play games in the woods, imagination games." He paused, waiting for some response, then continued. "I think she'll be a scientist if given the chance, and who knows, perhaps..."

"And her mother?" Sofia ventured softly.

"She died five years ago, when she was only six."

"Oh I'm so sorry."

"She disappeared from us for awhile after that. I guess we all did. But now she's coming back. I suppose time does that no matter how much the pain." He shifted his hands and it was then that she saw it, dull and smooth with wear but unmistakable: the ring. The ring of her father and his father and his father, for whose finger it had initially been sized, and through those generations it had been kept and passed along but had never again been worn as it was meant to be worn. Now it fit perfectly around Seelin's left middle finger, the nearly indistinguishable gold 'M' seated in it's bed of black jade. He had kept it, protected it through all those years.

"I tried to find you," she now blurted, choking back the tears which had so suddenly risen into her eyes. "I tried so hard to find you. But you were nowhere, not in any of the centers, not in any of the trails and roads we walked those days. We were certain, certain that you had..." She buried her head in her hands, crying fully and freely now, crying for the years she had missed him, for the years she had never forgotten him even as he lay dead inside her memory.

He reached his arm around her and held her close to him, gathering her tears into himself, forgiving as best he could the scars of his boyhood. And with the shudder and immediacy of her emotion Sofia for the first time rose up from the memory she had been wrapped in and etched herself into the reality of the present, bringing the entire scene and moment with her, out of the dream and into this real world, the real world of his own morning.

After she had gained control of herself, she sat up and began again in a serious tone.

"There's something I need to tell you, something which we had been planning on telling you all along when you got older, but..." She sniffled and wiped her eyes with the back of her hand. "Seelin, when Jaslo and I were together, before you were born, Jaslo was involved in reproductive medicine, working on methods of artificial gestation which have since been banned. It was intended as a way of gaining full independence from the outsiders, but the experiments were a failure. However, as part of his involvement, he had access to certain techniques, illegal even then of course, for non-natural mixed clone conception." She looked for any recognition in his eyes, but he continued to stare straight ahead, still unsure of where she was going. "The technique was used long ago when the first forever children wanted a method of parenting, truly parenting, children of their own, but of course could not naturally do so."

Now she stopped, uncertain about how to tell him, uncertain of how he might respond, then continued in a spotty voice, already broken by tears. "Seelin, Jaslo and I were not only your keepers, and not your mother and father in practice alone, but your real mother and father. I am your true mother, as I was the true daughter of my mother. That is the meaning of the ring, the meaning of what we've been trying to keep alive."

The words fell from her lips and hung in the still air of the October morning, absorbed by the tiny particles passing so quickly from the shadows into the brilliance of the sun's illumination. So clear were the boundaries, thought Seelin, so sharp the edges of the light beam which carried the unknowing minutia for that short time, from shadow to shadow.

"C'mon," he said, standing up and reaching his hand to this small girl who was his mother. "Let's go outside. It's too nice a day. I'll show you the gathering and we can talk." It was too early, too sudden her entrance into his life and the announcement she carried with her. He hadn't yet had enough time to know how he felt. Floating untethered from any past for so many years now, the return of his true mother and father, still living their own lives less than thirty miles from this tenuous world he had scratched together for himself and Mistissa, was still too new and too foreign to elicit much more than shock and confusion. It would only be later that the questions and the feelings would begin to rise to the surface, only later when she would no longer be there to answer them, when she would no longer be there to receive and return the affection which was still forming and crystallizing, invisible yet even to himself. So often in his life the words found their way to his voice only after he was alone once again, far removed from those for whom they were intended, far removed from those who he needed to have hear them.

So they walked out together into the weakened but still warm sunlight, and he told her all about what had happened to him from the time they had last laid desperate eyes on each other in that broken transpotter, all about his rescue and searchings and survival through those early years, but sparing her the hunger, the pain, the loneliness. And as he looked down at her walking along beside him, this small girl who still inhabited the world he had left behind so many years ago, he couldn't help but feel as if somehow he had grown beyond her, grown beyond the eternal childhood which would otherwise have held him tight to this very day. He realized, for the shortest moment as he glimpsed the red and orange liquid amber leaves scattered, wet with the melted frost, over the dirt underneath their feet, that he could no longer regret having been abandoned by his childhood.

***

"I know a place where there really are red trees," bragged Mistissa as she ran out ahead across the trail leading into a deep grove of oaks.

"That was just a story. There aren't any red trees anymore, you know. They used to be all around and they were called redwoods," Zhrana added, mindful of an obligation to advance the young girl's learning.

"Oh yes there are. I know a place," came the almost tauntingly confident response.

The trail Mistissa had picked was quite overgrown, and led up the side of a deep canyon to the north of the gathering, at one point crossing the transpotter tube before climbing steeply over a narrow ridge, then diving down once again into the shade of a steep ravine. As they followed it deeper and deeper into the wilderness, an increasingly nervous Zhrana, unused to being so far away from civilization, struggled to keep up, calling for frequent stops and several times challenging Mista's familiarity with the terrain.

"Are you sure you've been this far away from Lexington without your father?" she panted during one such stop atop a small ridge at the end of a particularly difficult ascent.

"Oh sure, all the time," Mistissa exaggerated.

"And you've been to this place before, you know exactly where it is?"

"I've been there lots of times. It's really neat," the girl continued her exaggerations. In fact, she had been to the red trees only once, over a year ago when several of her friends had taken her, and though she never let on, she was already wondering if they might have passed the trail cut off.

At the bottom of the next ravine, an especially deep canyon shaded by huge overhanging oaks, madrones, and eucalyptus, Mistissa suddenly picked up a pace which had been lagging, and bounced forward with greater assurance.

It's down this creek. There's a pool and the red trees are next to them. Live ones, not like the dead ones we saw before."

Indeed, they had passed numerous dead and decomposing redwoods along the way, but despite the girl's assertions, Zhrana remained skeptical, knowing well from her studies that the last of the living groves had died out some fifty years ago.

So when they did round a bend in the path, a nearly indistinguishable trail at this point, and when the huge, stately trees rose up before them, she stopped in her tracks, overcome with the immensity and the majesty of these three solitary redwoods hiding out from the world at the bottom of this secluded ravine. Zhrana stood still for several minutes in awe, gazing up at the spiral of branches streaming upward searching for sunlight, while Mistissa ran around with the exuberance of being right after all, and the triumph of having found them all by herself.

At length, the sounds of Mistissa running through the nearby woods trailed off, and when Zhrana began walking toward and past the giant trees she called out into the woods.

"Mistissa! Mista, where are you?"

Then she realized. The story. Mista was undoubtedly pretending to have fallen into the secret cave. That was, after all, the initial reason for this adventure in the first place. So she waited for a good ten minutes to allow the girl time to have her fun before once again resuming her calls.

When there was still no response, the now frightened Zhrana hurried back along the trail, hoping this was some kind of hide and seek game, but there was only a distant rustling in the woods far up the trail, too far up the trail to be Mistissa. Perhaps an animal, she thought. So once again she called out frantically, at the top of her voice.

"Mistissa! Come out now! Mistissa!"

But there was still no response, only the far off murmuring of the wind through branches so high up they caught the afternoon sunlight from the depths of this dark canyon.

23

Kianno strained to see over the heads of the other mine laborers who were lined up in two ragged rows ahead of him. Somewhere toward the front was Marco, who had taken the more dangerous assignment of neutralizing the scanners, and a nervous Kianno tried as inconspicuously as possible to locate his new friend in the parade of workers stepping forward through the checkpoint in their drab gray uniforms. The front of the line was already routinely approaching the scanning station, and as he sweated under the many hidden layers secreting pounds and pounds of anti-virulents and anti-bacterials, he was suddenly gripped by an escalating sense of panic. What if Marco were unable to knock out the scanners? Should he turn and run, or would they kill him instantly? If he were to continue on, though, they would surely detect the illegal drugs and kill him regardless. He could already see that the first wave had passed through uneventfully, and the plan was for Marco to be in that first wave. Frantically, Kianno slowed his pace and dropped several rows back, stalling for precious time, when finally he heard a loud thump, followed by the angry yelling of guards up ahead.

Directed by the sounds, he now was able to see Marco clearly, singled out from the rest, while the guards waved their arms and pointed to the scanning device, dislodged from it's pedestal and lying heavily on the hard dirt ground. As his accomplice had explained it, it was remarkably easy to disable the device. Not very sophisticated to begin with, it was quite fragile and could be damaged by simply knocking it to the ground, an act which could be achieved through a single well-rehearsed act of clumsiness. No, the act itself was ridiculously easy; it was the consequences of that act which called for courage beyond Kianno's possession. Depending on who was on duty and what mood they might be in, the punishment for such clumsiness could range from simple exclusion from the mining party, to imprisonment, to immediately inflicted injury or death.

He knew that going in; they had specifically planned for such a contingency. So when one of the guards waved his synthar menacingly at Marco, then, in a moment's flash of anger, released the horrible wave into the midsection of his friend, Kianno should not have been surprised, should not have been taken aback into reconsidering the entire plan. But the sudden casualness of the murder stunned him and sent his mind racing ahead, trying to devise any possible way of retreating from this mission for which he had volunteered. If there had been any possible escape at that moment, Kianno would have gratefully taken it, even though he could see clearly now that the guards were still admitting the entire group, unscanned, through the checkpoint. Apparently satisfied with their discovery of several food tubes poorly hidden beneath Marcos' top uniform, they had concluded that this poor monster had simply been intent on bartering with the outsiders, and never suspected his involvement in a conspiracy to smuggle the immensely more valuable and illegal medicine which lined the inside of Kianno's suit.

But there was no escape, or rather, the best chance for escape by now, as he rapidly approached the final gate, was to continue ahead, into the outside world which had held him prisoner only a matter of months ago. Calmly stepping past the irritated guards, mildly upset with their colleague for causing them all a little extra paperwork at the end of the day, he purposefully kept his eyes straight ahead, afraid equally of accidentally revealing his secret to the guards, and of catching any glimpse of the remains of his new friend.

Safely past the checkpoint, falling behind from the rest of the group as they made their way up the long trail to the magnesium quarry was not at all difficult, and once detached from the main group Kianno slipped unnoticed into a thicket of manzanita, where he hid until the rest disappeared from sight. Then he hurried back down the trail, desperately running the directions Marco had given him over and over through his head, knowing that if he did not find his contact he would never be able to smuggle the medicine back into the hive at the end of the day.

Fortunately, the directions were fairly simple, and before long he found himself outside the window of what appeared to be an unoccupied shed in the easternmost fringes of the gathering. Slipping quietly into an overgrown side yard away from the street, he searched around him for any signs of being followed or observed, then approached the window opening, long since stripped of it's glass, but retaining the rusted iron grating which had been so favored by the builders and original inhabitants of the once affluent town of Lexington. After several long minutes of waiting in silence, the sharp sound of his voice startled him as he called uncertainly into the darkness beyond the lattice.

"Jask," he spoke the name given him by Marco, then waited for a reply. "Jask," he repeated slightly louder, but still no answer. He looked around one more time, then started out to the street once again to re-check the location, but as he rounded the building into the side yard a section of the lower siding of the shed suddenly popped out in a cloud of dust and the dirty face of Jask Orillo swung around to grin up at him.

"C'mon in, quickly," he urged, squinting into the shock of daylight.

Kianno, however, did not at first respond, stunned at the recognition of this outsider he had met briefly before during his previous visit masquerading as a child. He took a step back, uncertain whether or not he had been recognized as well, but when Jask continued to stare anxiously at him and wave him toward the building, Kianno concluded that he had grown beyond the recognition of this man, and he quickly climbed down into the dank, stale air imprisoned from the sun's breath.

For a full minute he stood motionless, unable to see a thing, while Jask issued instructions.

"Remove the uniform first, then empty the anti-virulents into this." Kianno felt something press against his stomach, then reached down to grab hold of a large glass jar. "Where's Marco?" the voice continued from the blackness.

"He didn't make it," he answered bluntly. Both men then worked in silence as Kianno regained enough of his vision to help separate the medicine into four different jars. For the rest of their encounter, Jask never said a single word about Marco, but rather set himself about his business in a most serious and methodical manner.

After he had finished with his share, Kianno stood up and stretched his stiff back while watching his newly discovered comrade finish the remainder of the sorting. Then, fully expecting to hurry off and rejoin the mining party as soon as possible, he picked up the outer layer of the uniform and began to climb back into it.

"It would be better not to wear that," Jask informed him calmly.

"I don't understand. I've got to be leaving now."

"Marco said you were a doctor. There's someone I need you to see."

"Now wait a second," Kianno replied, tilting his head and shifting his eyes in an exaggerated look of surprise. "I've gone to school, that's all. I've never actually treated anyone, so..."

"Well there's no one else who even has that much. Here." He reached down for some old rags and threw them at the visitor's feet. They were outsider style pants and uppers, almost as filthy and beaten up as the man who stood across from him. "Put those on, we've got no time for this chit chat."

***

She was lying on a platform which had obviously been constructed through long, painstaking hours of assembling together numerous small bits and pieces of found wood into a polished sleeper which had been placed in the far corner of this surprisingly clean and well-kept home. A woman older than any Kianno had ever seen, with small green eyes and white hair falling across her care-engraved brow, lay unconscious on the platform.

"She's been sleeping all day," said the younger man who had greeted them and shown them nervously into this neat but sour smelling room.

Having followed the others to this point, Kianno stepped forward now and tried to assume the authority that was expected of him. "Has she been running a fever?" he asked.

"Yes, one hundred and one, for three days straight now." The young man grasped one hand in the other and picked at his fingernails, looking around the room as if expecting another's arrival.

"And what else?"

"Yesterday she began bleeding, from her mouth and ears, and eyes. She hasn't eaten since it started four days ago, and her fingers and toes, she said they hurt like crazy, before..."

"Hmmm," Kianno murmured, growing less concerned about his own appearances and more and more interested in this woman's symptomology.

He approached the platform with cautious steps, then sat himself down on the floor next to her, bending over to listen to her heart, examine her fingers, feel her hands. When he was finished with his examination, he turned to the other two who stood watching curiously from behind.

"The anti-virulents, you brought them, didn't you?" he asked Jask.

"Yes. Which one do you need?"

"Two of the smaller red honeycombs," he answered with growing confidence. Then he turned to the young man. "And some water. Will she drink?"

"Yes. She'll swallow water in her sleep. That's the only thing she's had."

He ran off quickly to fetch a cup of water from the drinking table. When he returned, Kianno carefully placed the honeycombs at the back of the old woman's mouth, then allowed the young man to give her the water. After inspecting the woman's mouth once more, Kianno rose up from the floor, satisfied that the medicine had gone down.

"It's Rumses," he announced. "Not the classical presentation, but I'm pretty sure that's what it is. Without the anti-virulents, she'd have no chance, but right now I'd say she has as good a chance to recover as not. Keep her warm and continue to feed her the water, as much as she'll take. And here..." He reached clumsily into the right pocket of the unfamiliar style of pants he was wearing, drawing out seven more of the small red honeycombs. "Give her one of these each morning, and..." Now Kianno hesitated, on the verge of advising a follow up check in two more days before realizing that there may not be any doctor available to see this patient.

"Is there any doctor nearby?" he ventured.

"Yes. She's off visiting a family living in the fringes; that's why we needed you here. But we should be able to get her to come by tomorrow."

"Good. Then I'll be on my way." Kianno took one more glance back at his first patient before departing, and when he did so he noticed that she wasn't doing at all well. Her face and neck appeared swollen and had taken on a bluish tinge. Alarmed, he rushed closer to examine her and found her wheezing noticeably and struggling for breath.

"What is it?" asked Jask, looking over his shoulder as Kianno frantically assessed his patient for any clues as to what had happened. Even as he worked he could see the poor woman's neck swell further, and now red blotches began to appear over the surface of the already blue skin. She was in imminent danger of death if he couldn't re-establish her airway, which had been critically compromised by the swelling.

"She's having an allergic reaction to the medication," he announced shakily. "I need a surgiknife or she may die!"

At his demand, Jask and the young man only looked around with confusion, as if such an instrument might really be at hand, but as soon as he heard his own words Kianno immediately stood up and scanned the room for anything which might be used as a substitute. Walking quickly about the room, he stopped adjacent to a wall where some old steel building layers protruded through the worn wall coverings which had once concealed them. Grabbing onto one of the thin layers, he twisted and bent the end until it finally broke off, then rushed back to the woman's side.

"Go get me a tube from the water bladder," he instructed the young man, trembling with anxiety with what he was about to attempt. He'd never even observed the procedure except on the visuals as part of his training, but he knew that if he didn't do something the lady would die within minutes.

Feeling blindly for the trachea buried so deeply now within the swollen neck, he found the prominence of hard cartilage and rubbed it with his fingers to verify it's location, then he felt for any strong pulse above it to be as sure as he could he wasn't about to plunge directly into an artery. Looking up one last time in desperation, he saw that the young man was already running back with the water tube, so he grasped the metal fragment tightly and plunged it into the woman's neck.

It was much messier than he had seen on the visuals. Although his initial cut was met with the loud gasping of air which was so frightening to the other two but so relieving to himself, maneuvering the makeshift instrument so as to cut a hole large enough for the tube to fit in proved to be a distressingly slow and difficult process. Fortunately, although he had to work by feel alone, as the wound site was obscured with blood, he had not hit an artery and so was able to avoid a complication he was completely unprepared to handle at any rate.

Finally, after several minutes which seemed like hours, he was able to secure the tube and compress the surrounding flesh enough to stem the bleeding. Sweating profusely now, he stood up and asked Jask for one of the other type of anti-virulents they had brought, then together they repeated the process of administering the drug, and waited tensely for a good ten minutes before concluding that there was no allergic reaction to the medication.

As the two of them were walking back through the streets of Lexington, Jask, who had been so silent thus far, began to talk more freely.

"We have only one doctor for this entire area. When you join us out here we'll be so much better off." Kianno did not protest- he had already resigned himself to that fate, but remained silent to the suggestion, unwilling to make any commitments even though the satisfaction which now infused his whole mind and body was greater than anything he could remember.

"I have a daughter, Nicoli," Jask continued, slowing his step as they pressed on against the lowering sun. "She was kidnapped from us and still lives inside the hives."

Kianno looked ahead, still afraid of being recognized, and not at all proud of his having abandoned Nicoli and the others about whom Atascin had previously sent him to gather information.

"Have you been able to appeal the relocation?" he responded.

"Ha. Relocation. You use that word as if it were legitimate. No, they haven't granted us an appeal, and they never will." Now he paused and drew a deep breath before continuing. "That's why Marco had arranged to bring her back for us." It was a lie, of course, but the two desperate parents were not above doing whatever they could to bring their little girl back to them.

"Bring her back?"

"Yes. We've been able to locate her to quadrant FF2759, and Marco was in the process of making arrangements for having her brought back to us."

"But surely if they found you..."

"Yes, they would kill us and take her once again. But we're willing to take that chance. We'll trek to a new gathering; they may not bother to hunt us down. But Kianno, you must help us to complete the plan. With Marco gone, we're counting on you to carry it forward."

"No!" Kianno reacted defensively to this expectation. "Just because I helped Marco bring over some medicine doesn't mean I'm taking his place. His commitments aren't mine. I'm sorry about Nicoli, and I'll ask around to see if anyone knows what his plan may have been, but I certainly don't know how to go about getting up to FF and sneaking her down the hive and across the checkpoint."

"I understand," Jask replied in a monotone. "I don't really expect you'll be able to help us. You're wrong about one thing, though."

"What's that?" Kianno pressed after waiting too long for Jask to volunteer the information.

"You're wrong about not taking Marco's place. You do take his place, whether you want to or not. I also take his place. He's given that to us and we couldn't refuse it if we tried. So now we only have to decide what to do with it." He stopped and turned his eyes toward Kianno, who met them briefly in the dusty sunlight, then they hurried forward once again. Both knew there was less than an hour before the mining party would be stumbling wearily down the mountainside and into the station checkpoint.

***

In his chamber later that night Kianno was recovering from the excitement of the day when he was startled by a loud clattering from the portal. Immediately fearful it might have something to do with his recent illegal activities, he remained quiet, knowing it was impossible to open the portals from outside. Soon after the initial rattling, however, he heard a familiar voice announce itself.

"Kianno, it's me, Jaslo."

Even though he was sure of the voice, he hesitated nonetheless, and instead of rushing to crank open the portals, he replied through the metal.

"What is it?"

"Kianno, it's me. Let me in. I need to talk to you."

Still doubtful about this unusual visit, especially after the shocking and cold nature of their last meeting, Kianno nonetheless felt he had no choice but to admit his longtime keeper; after all, despite their differences, he had given him many years of care and attention, and Kianno could not deny he felt some degree of affection and obligation toward him. So he grasped onto the handle and rotated firmly, twisting open the aging wings.

As soon as he had done so he regretted it, confronted with the sight of Jaslo accompanied by two others who stood stonily at each side. Sensing trouble, he attempted to step out of his chamber into the common area, but Jaslo greeted him in the old manner and led his entourage confidently into the room.

After a quick exchange of nervous small talk, centered primarily around Sofia's well being, Jaslo got right to the point.

"Have you had time now to reconsider my offer? I'm afraid I won't be in a position to extend it much longer."

Kianno was incredulous. "I have no intention of taking part in such a murderous scheme," he stammered. "If that's the purpose of your visit then we have very little to talk about."

"Kianno, this is your life we're talking about. Perhaps you can't understand this now, what with your mind so clouded by hormones and poisonous biochemicals, but what I'm offering you is life itself. The same life that was robbed from you against your will. You have every right to that."

"What you can't seem to understand," Kianno threw the words back bitterly, "is that there's a life for me here now. A life you have no idea of and are in no position to judge."

" I hope you'll forgive me, then," came the almost inaudible reply. "I wouldn't do this if I wasn't sure you'd forgive me one day."

"What are you talking about?" Kianno uttered, but before he could say another word one of the two silent colleagues pulled a slow stunner from his sara and fired point blank at the helpless Kianno, who crumpled limply to the floor.

***

"I'm afraid we have a problem," the assistant informed an exhausted Jaslo, who sat collapsed into his office lounger.

"What could it possibly be now?" answered the doctor in a voice carrying more than a hint of aggravation. All evening long they had been coming to him with procedural and security questions which they could have easily answered themselves with any degree of creativity, he thought, but then sat up and listened attentively nonetheless, eager to monitor the progress despite the late hour.

"The tissue tests are in on subject #5. I'm afraid they're negative as well."

"Then run them again. There's no choice but to use him as the donor. None of the others are cranially compatible, even after proto-filling." Jaslo stood now and paced nervously across the room. "Administer tissue de-stabilizers if necessary. Subject #5 is our only chance."

"We've already run the tests several times. Survival, even with a perfect surgical event, would be less than ten percent using any of the donors in the current stable."

"Damn! Has he been thoroughly prepped?"

"Well, yes, but without a donor..."

"It's up to you to tissue mold #5 until the odds are at least fifty-fifty. Go start working on him and keep me informed of your progress."

The doctor sat back down in his lounger and waited for his assistant to leave him in peace, but the assistant stood his ground, then addressed his superior in a halting voice.

"Sir, we've taken something of a liberty in our efforts."

"Yes, well that would be refreshing. What is it?"

"We've run full tests on the three captives currently being held but whom you have specifically indicated are not within the donor stable."

"Hmmm. You know there are good reasons why they're excluded, but go on."

"One of them, the newest girl to arrive only last week, shows excellent promise as a match. Cranial topology is proto-formable, and tissue sampling was not perfect, but closer than any of the others." The assistant shifted his feet uncomfortably and scratched an itch on his elbow.

"I have other plans for that one," Jaslo replied slowly, thinking the matter through. After a long pause, he continued. "Have you run a potential side effects profile on the match?"

"Yes. Certain incongruities in the mapping of smooth muscle neurons within the donor's system may possibly lead to intermittent loss of control, however, it's nothing we haven't been able to suppress with Trizone in the previous subjects. There are no unusual mental effects expected."

"And the overall health of the donor?"

"Excellent. Somewhat underweight by our standards, but no significant diseases present. Genetic material is class B."

Once again the doctor pondered this information for quite some time before responding. When he did so, it was in a tone not nearly as certain as his previous instructions, but the words were clear and irretrievable.

"Then we'll use the girl. Prep her as quickly as possible and let me know when both are ready. We'll perform the procedure first thing in the morning."

24

When he entered the surgical chamber and examined the two subjects, he found that they had been expertly prepared in accordance with all of the latest techniques which had so recently been perfected. The full brain and first spinal vertebrae of Kianno, now relieved of the body with which it had previously been saddled, rested peacefully in a column of hyper-oxygenated, variably pressure pulsed bio-enrichment solution, which had also been infused with a strong tranquilizer to avoid the dangerous possibility of Kianno regaining consciousness prior to the completion of the procedure. From the base of the brain, barely visible through the yellow fluid, were two narrow tubes which had been clamped to the carotid artery and superior vena cava. The tubes were connected to a heart-lung simulator which pumped synthetic blood through the brain's vascular network to assure continued full oxygenation of those interior sections which the pressurized enrichment solution could not reach.

Only ten yards away lay this brain's new donor body, the neck and head of which were also submerged in the miraculous solution, formulated only fifty years ago, which significantly reduced the trauma to damaged and cut tissue, and, when used during surgery, reduced recovery and healing time to one-third of that required following more primitive surgical techniques. The body itself was supported at the shoulders by a frame which held it in place throughout the procedure. Stretched across the top of the frame was a thin membrane which formed a tight seal around the shoulders, preventing any of the solution from leaking out of the clear tank in which the head and neck rested, and in which the entire operation would take place. Adjacent to the main tank was a smaller vessel which contained the top half of the cranium, removed to allow for initial placement of the host.

Jaslo approached the group of seven serious doctors who had already been at work for several hours, and closely examined the body for himself. Apparently satisfied at the work which had been completed, he turned to the head of the team to confirm his expectations.

"How did the extraction go? Any unusual events?"

"No. A little slower than we'd have had hoped for, but the re-tuning we did last week paid off. She set a new record on this one- only fourteen lost ends."

"Any major?"

"Nothing which won't be compensated in a few days."

Jaslo smiled, pleased with the extra time he'd spent waiting for one more instrument tuning. 'She' was the newest, most sophisticated auto-surgeon in existence, and her creation had cost the project eighty percent of its entire resources over the past ten years. But the pay off had been beyond their hopes: a machine with such micro-precision and resolution that it was capable of locating and clean-severing thousands of microscopic vessels and nerves, then, after the brain had been manually positioned later in the operation, map and fuse them to those of the donor. These thousands of auto-fusions allowed for survival and maintenance of basic functions for the several days which were needed for the enhanced natural regeneration to complete the process. It had been routine to lose fifty or more of these fusions during the extraction process, nerves which had not been clean-severed and so could not be fused properly to the donor. This represented the greatest risk of later complications and side effects, so it was with great relief that Jaslo greeted the news of only fourteen non-critical losses.

"Start the blood transfer," he now announced to the group, then he turned to a small, chubby doctor who had been closely monitoring the donor body. "How much time have we got?"

"Oxygen levels have already begun to drop. If we switch to donor blood at this time, I estimate ninety minutes."

Despite all of the advances over the past hundred years, one barrier which had not been overcome was the time limit for maintaining blood through the heart-lung simulator. Artificial blood was used with the host to buy time, but it was essential that it soon be switched to the blood of the donor, blood which was currently pumped by the simulator, since the donor had obviously lost any capability to sustain critical functions on its own.

"Let's see the support structure topography," he now ordered the doctor, and the two of them walked briskly to the visuals stage nearby, followed by most of the consulting physicians who gathered around. Calling up the visuals, they then walked around the simulation, examining it from all angles, looking for possible weaknesses and unacceptable compromises the computer may have made in planning the structural accommodation modifications.

"Hmm," mused one of the doctors observing from the rear, "Do we really want to shave five full millimeters from cranial sector twenty-seven? Can't we balance that on the other side more efficiently?"

At once Jaslo commanded the visuals to re-simulate the suggestion. Appearing satisfied with the result, he focused his attention now on the most critical spinal support apparatus.

"We still appear to have a two millimeter overlap adjacent to the foramen magnum. Pressure to the cord is within boundaries, but there must be something we can do to reduce it further."

"Why not replace the straight brace with a butterfly, like we did last month?" ventured his chubby associate, and once again Jaslo commanded a re-simulation with a corresponding re-calculation of stress and contingency factors. After pondering these for several minutes, he instructed the computer to fix the adjustment.

"A butterfly's going to be tough to position correctly, but I agree it's called for in this case." He paused, scrutinizing the display carefully once more before asking for any more final comments. When his words were met with silence, he turned on his heel and switched off the visuals.

"All right, then. Let's get started. We have less than ninety minutes now to work with."

***

For three days she floated in and out of time, drowned beneath the heavy tranquilizers which only occasionally allowed helpless glimpses of the surface, briefest hints of consciousness, before the adjusters delivered yet another dose to pull her back down again. She did not dream or remember during this time, so dense was her somnolence, existing in a state entirely void of awareness, imprisoned in the purgatory between death and re-birth.

Finally, in the darkness of the night awaiting the fourth day, Kianno lifted her eyes and looked slowly about the room. A dimmed lumin strip bathed the room in a familiar green, casting long shadows across the mostly empty hospital chamber. Only the hum and occasional clicking of the overhead scanner interrupted the silence which enveloped her. For nearly a minute she sat in utter confusion, forgetting completely the events preceding the operation. Then, in a single instant, it all came flooding back to her and suddenly she remembered what had happened and what must have occurred to her since she last succumbed to a fog of sedatives in what seemed several dreams ago. The knowledge, however, did not startle her, did not precipitate the same anger and defiance which had characterized her pre-operative reaction. Indeed, more than anything else, she was aware of a quiet calm which had descended on her, or rather re-descended on her, for it was a feeling very similar to the stillness which had preceded her kidnapping so many months ago: a calm sadness, as if a fierce but rare blizzard had played itself out and the snow now melted peacefully in a warming breeze. A torrent of indignation and misunderstood righteousness which had swirled through her the last few months had now lifted and evaporated, leaving a flat tranquillity swimming through her arms and legs, a tranquillity only partially attributable to the small amounts of sedatives still coursing through her bloodstream.

Her eyes now adjusting to the faint light, she looked down at her small arms with curiosity, wondering who she had become, the previous anger replaced now with an intense personal and medical inquisitiveness about the miraculous transformation she had undergone. The arms were small and soft and smooth, and the hands equally tiny. She clenched a fist with one of them, testing her new body, then lifted her arm and placed it gently down on the bed sheet, probing for any noticeable incongruities between her mind and this new body. Without even thinking, she reached over and quickly scratched an itch on her wrist so naturally and so fluidly that it was as if she had lived her whole life this way, as if the body had a memory of its own and she was as much controlled by it as it was controlled by her. There was no line between the two, no gap which separated herself from this much younger, child's body. As if in a dream, in which a lifetime of artificial memories can be created in an instant, Kianno did not all feel as if she had only four days ago gained possession of this new self, but instead felt as if she had been one with this body for her entire life.

Turning her head, she noticed for the first time the long hair falling across her neck, tickling her, and when she reached up with her hand she felt silky hair between her fingers. It was then that the thought first entered her head that she might, in fact, now be a girl. Curious, she reached her hands down to feel across her thighs, wiggling her legs with the wonderment that they, as well, were fully her own, then felt gently between them. As with the rest of her, she felt there as she felt everywhere else, with a knowledge remembered from the body itself, as if she had been a girl all her life, so natural and intrinsic was the feeling; already she tried to remember what it felt like physically to be the forever boy, the man, she had been until so recently.

Wanting now to see herself, to see more of her new appearance, she swung her legs around to the side of the platform and placed her feet tentatively on the cold floor, then spoke for the first time, in a child's delicate voice.

"Visuals," she uttered before realizing that she had no sender and that the room had not been equipped to respond to her voice. So she rose shakily and took several unstable steps toward the washroom, then gained confidence as her pace became more assured, trailing the long sara she had been dressed in behind her over the floor.

When she reached the washroom, she first took water from a bladder located in the corner of the small room, then turned to the presentation table and reached over to flick the station on.

A first she did not recognize the eyes looking back at her, only remarked to herself that this was quite a pleasing face, a face she could live with easily enough. But then she remembered, and suddenly the eyes were no longer her own; they stared back at her from the soul of the girl she had played with those many months ago, the friend of Nicoli who had trusted Kianno and given him his first chance at discovering his past. In that instant, this body disowned him, burned into him with those eyes, reminded him, with a look he would never be able to shake, that no matter how healthy and natural he might feel, this body was not his own, this body carried the ghost of another who would never let her forget.

Twisting herself away from the horror of her own gaze, she took too large a step in the direction of the platform and tripped over the sara which had gathered beneath her feet. Reaching out to break her fall, Kianno's arm knocked solidly against the station table, sending a wave of pain flooding through the newly refused neural paths and overloading several mismapped fusions. Lying on the floor, she suddenly lost all control of her right leg, which began shaking in violent spasms. Simultaneous with the spasms, a loud whistling alarm broke the stillness, issuing forth from the overhead scanner which continued to monitor her brain wave patterns.

Within a minute, several attendants and one doctor rushed into the room, quickly finding the frantic Kianno lying on the floor grasping wildly with his arms in a vain attempt to bring his right leg under control.

"Trizone levels must have dropped. Quick, two milliliters spinal insertion!" The doctor fiddled with a small packet, then bent down to Kianno. "And two more of Drethane along with it!"

Kianno felt the hands of the two attendants grasping onto his leg, steadying it as much as possible as the doctor reached behind her long golden hair. In the next moment she felt a sharp sting on the back of her neck, and the now welcomed darkness of the void enveloped her once again.

***

"Well, whatever it is, let's get through it quickly. I've told you countless times how I'm not interested in these experiments of yours. You know that I don't like them. I don't see any reason for you to insist on my coming here." Sofia hit her heels hard against the smooth floor, sending echoing raps across the hallway.

"This has less to do with my experiments than with us," Jaslo replied.

"What could anything in there," she said, gesturing to the lab entrance which had just come into view as they rounded a corner, "have to do with us? You, perhaps, but not us."

Jaslo did not respond to this and they walked along even quicker, a cold fog of secrecy following them along. Neither had yet told the other what they had found out about each other. Sofia was strangely afraid of his response to the notion of their son still being alive and living as an outsider. He had become so anti-Naturalist in recent years that she feared his reaction even to his own son, and so had spent the past week trying to think of the best way to tell him.

As for Jaslo, he had originally been planning on warning his companion about what he had found out, and the threat posed by the authorities if she did not stop her forays beyond the hive, but after the operation he grew reluctant to bring up the topic, worried that his choice of donor might be misinterpreted as revenge for her explorations, sexual and otherwise. He knew there was no way to avoid the revelation, but had put it off until tonight with the expectation that her joy at seeing her son rescued from a short and difficult life would overshadow any anger at the sacrifice of the girl, who Sofia would undoubtedly recognize.

She was sleeping when they entered her room, heavily sedated to avoid any repeat of the dangerous episode of last night. As they approached, Sofia saw only the distant figure of a small girl lying on a medical platform with an attendant at her side. Before they could get any closer, Jaslo pulled her aside and spoke excitedly.

"Sofia, my dear, you know what my experiments have been about. I've made no attempt to hide them from you. Now we've been able to use this new science for our own family, for you, for me, for Kianno."

"What are you talking about?" she asked, the words slowing as they fell from her mouth. A knot of worry suddenly rose in her stomach.

"We've both grieved at what's happened to Kianno. It was a tragedy which seemed insurmountable for us. But with this technique, we've been able to rescue him. We've been able to restore his forever childhood, and bring him back to GGG to live with us once again. Come, what I have to show you is nothing short of a miracle."

With those words he led the dumbfounded Sofia by the hand to the side of the sleeping girl, then quickly dismissed the attendant.

At first, Sofia did not fully digest what had been explained to her, and as she saw the girl she exclaimed "Mistissa, Mistissa what's wrong?" Then, gradually realizing what had happened, she raised her hand to her forehead and stumbled forward, steadying herself by resting a hand on the bed sheets next to the sleeping Kianno.

"My God, what have you done?" she exclaimed with an anger rapidly over-taken by unspeakable sadness.

"This is Kianno, my dear. He'll outlive us now."

"Do you know who this is?" she demanded, trembling with mounting an-guish, still refusing to acknowledge Kianno within the young girl's body.

"Yes, I know about your visits to the outside. I know exactly who this was, and I can forgive you. But you must know what a dangerous position you're in. If you can't..."

"No!" she screamed with an anguish she had felt only once before at the loss of Seelin thirty years earlier. "Don't you realize what you've done?" But he only looked at her with unsettled eyes, so she continued on with the words she could scarcely believe herself. "You've killed her. In your foolish attempts to make us all live forever you've killed our only grandchild! You've killed our only true grandchild!"

And as Jaslo stood silently, still not comprehending the meaning of her words, a bereaved Sofia knelt beside the platform and held the girl's warm hand in her own. "Mistissa," she sobbed, "Mistissa…"

25

In honor of the occasion, frozen strawberries and apricots had been allocated from the Forshas' reserve account, and had been spread in an elegant display set up in the laboratory conference room. Approximately thirty members of the Forshas crowded the room, including Rokyo, who was dressed in the royal blue sara he always wore when administering formal occasions. It was the same sara he wore only a couple of months earlier when he had reluctantly banished Kianno from the family and from the level, and as the distinguished administrator mingled delightfully through the crowd he carried a small green collar in his right hand, a collar only slightly larger than a child's wrist but provided with a touch sensor pad along the top edge.

As he approached Kianno, he smiled broadly and grasped her shoulders. He had been concerned about this meeting, concerned that perhaps she might still bear some grudge against him. However, peering across at this charming girl who bore no resemblance whatsoever to the Kianno he had banished, he found it so much easier to forget the past and to greet her as if nothing had never happened.

"Kianno, I'm so glad to see you once again." He took a deep breath, then added "And we're all so happy for your good fortune. How are you feeling, anyway, after such an ordeal?"

"Oh I'm feeling quite well," she replied, returning his smile and showing no hint of any smoldering animosity. "Thanks so much for asking. I have to say I'm feeling much more myself now, much more like before this whole troubling episode began. And I do appreciate your willingness to allow me another chance."

"Of course, of course. I think we all knew it wasn't really you who attacked that poor assistant in the weatherscoper. We all know it was the effect of...well, you know what I'm trying to say."

"Oh yes," Kianno helped him out, then she gestured to the collar gripped tightly in Rokyo's right hand. "Is that for the ceremony?"

"Yes. It shouldn't take but a minute, but Jaslo and Sofia wanted this little get-together to mark the occasion." Now he clasped his hands behind him, temporarily hiding the collar. "How much longer until you'll be able to return home?"

"They say another week or so. It's already been ten days, and I feel like I'm ready to go home right now, but apparently there's a medication which needs to be administered here at the hospital for a little while longer."

Now another forever boy joined the two of them, and Rokyo took the opportunity to excuse himself. The forever boy was a former acquaintance of Kianno's who she hadn't seen in quite some time, but who had come to the gathering more out of curiosity than anything else.

"Kianno, is that really you?" he exclaimed with an amused tone she was growing tired of by now.

"Yes. Hello Kalo. Long time no see," she replied in a bored monotone.

"Wow! I can't believe they turned you into a girl. Does it feel different, huh?"

"Not too much. Have you seen Zhrana?"

"No. Nobody's seen her for months. You haven't heard? We think she's either gone to live as an outsider or is hiding on another level somewhere." Again the forever boy examined Kianno with disbelieving eyes. "Have you tried sexmaking as a forever girl yet?"

"Shut up Kalo," she replied, growing annoyed. "Why don't you try some of the strawberries. I heard they're going fast."

"Really? I'll be back; I want to find out some more," he answered, disappearing into the crowd once again.

In another few minutes Rokyo called out to get everyone's attention, and soon the group quieted down and gathered around the administrator and Kianno, who he had summoned to his side.

"Kianno, before admitting you formally and officially as a full member of the Forshas family, I must ask whether you fully embrace the ideals of the family, and whether you renounce your previous actions for which you were expelled." The words were pronounced in the grandiose style Rokyo had perfected through the years.

"To all of the Forshas I say yes, I embrace your ideals, and I sincerely apologize for the act of violence which I previously committed. I pledge to make myself worthy of belonging once again to this esteemed family."

Rokyo then drew forth the collar, placed it on the table directly in front of the girl, then entered his code as Kianno watched carefully.

"You wrist, please," he instructed, and she held out her wrist, which Rokyo grasped and placed firmly into the collar. As he programmed the device to send the clearance into the cell buried just beneath the surface of the girl's skin, he announced regally "I now admit you to this family, and grant you permanent GGG level access, as well as full hive visitation access. Congratulations."

At this, the room burst into cheers, and Kianno nodded her head to acknowledge the welcome back.

Later that evening, as Rokyo was unpacking the belongings he had brought with him to the ceremony, he looked up from his pack in disbelief.

"The access band, it's not here!" he exclaimed anxiously to a visitor who had come to spend the night.

"Don't worry about it," the visitor answered. "It's your turn in the stimulator."

"You don't understand. It can't be lost!"

"And it isn't, Roky dear, you just left it at the laboratory, that's all. I bet they're holding it for you as we speak, and tomorrow you can pick it up."

He hesitated, quite concerned but at the same time tired with the events of the day and looking forward to some well-deserved pleasuring.

"You're probably right," he admitted, slipping the soft gray sara off of his shoulders. "I'll be there in a minute."

***

"Mistissa!" the sleepy girl practically yelled with surprise, bolting upright from a shallow sleep at the sight of her old friend.

"Ssshhh!" implored Kianno, placing her hand gently over the girl's mouth and looking at her with wide, frightened eyes. "Yes, it's me, but be quiet. I've come to take you back to your parents."

Nicoli stared back, frozen in disbelief. After all this time she had only just recently begun to accept her fate, and now Mistissa of all people should appear at her side, as if her friend had jumped from one of her many dreams of the two of them playing and running through the woods, mistakenly landing here, in this world, on the other side of the cruel line which separated Nicoli from her memories of home.

"Oh Mista," she now gushed, unable to control herself, and an obliging and touched Kianno played along as best she could, holding the poor girl and stroking her hair softly.

Suddenly, Nicoli lifted her head and cast a worrisome glance. "But what if we get caught?" she uttered, confused by a mix of rekindled hope of seeing her parents once again alongside the very real fear of retribution for attempting any escape.

"We're not going to get caught, I promise you," answered Kianno with more confidence than Mistissa would have shown. Then she looked deeply into Nicoli's eyes, affirming those words with an equally assured expression.

"How did you get here?" Nicoli now practically squealed in conspiratorial delight, but Kianno would entertain no such playfulness.

"I'll tell you later. Quick, get dressed. We've got no time to lose."

"No time to lose?" whispered the girl as she got up and quickly scampered across the room to gather her clothes, "No time to lose?" Now she repeated the words in a teasing voice, clearly making fun of her friend's grown up expression. "I've got no time to lose, but you've got time to lose. If you lose my time, be sure to let me know..."

"Sshh!" implored Kianno, realizing now that he would have to be more careful with his language. "C'mover here. I want to show you something really neat."

"What is it?" Nicoli wondered aloud at the sight of the green metallic collar, throwing sparkles of light about the room.

"It's a fun game. Put your hand in it, like this." Kianno took Nicoli's hand and wrist and carefully placed it into the collar. "Now hold it there. I'm gonna enter in a secret code. Then we'll be secret spies together."

Nicoli watched enthralled with this game and with the miracle which had entered her room from out of nowhere, and as Kianno entered the code into the access band Nicoli couldn't help but grasp her playmate's hand with her own and hold it tightly, filled with a surge of excitement and thankfulness for this gift of a lost friend returned from the darkness of the night.

They had very little trouble avoiding anyone on their way through the hallways of Level FF, and were also lucky enough to have caught an empty slider to ride down to the sublevel; at this late hour of ten o'clock nearly the entire hive had retired to their sleeping platforms.

When they stepped into the sublevel, however, they were greeted with the loud clamoring and raucous shouts of several mining teams waiting to board the last of the transpotters south. Looking nervously in all directions, the two girls searched for any other forever children who might be riding the transpotter, but the only children anywhere in sight were the station officials, who gave them questioning looks but reluctantly accepted their accounts for passage to the Los Gatos Gate. Only the final boarding attendant, concerned at seeing the two of them without any apparent weapons or outsider bodyguards, stepped over to their cart before take-off to inquire about their intentions.

"Are you sure you want this flight?" he asked politely, leaning over to check their straps.

"Oh yes, thanks so much for asking, but we're fine." answered Kianno.

"You do have some protection, just in case?" the attendant persisted, seeing from the rest of the passengers that the girls' presence had not gone unnoticed.

"Yes." Kianno gestured to the side of her sara as if something were concealed there, "We're quite prepared."

After they had been left alone and the cart began it's shuddering acceleration through the station, Nicoli again pantomimed Kianno's words. "We're *quite*

ready, oh yes, *quite* so I would say." But this time Kianno only laughed along
with her, all be it a nervous laugh at best.

In the transpotter, they were quickly joined by four of the miners, who
sat down beside them and attempted some false conversation aimed only at
discerning the extent to which they might be armed, as well as the extent to
which they might actually be receptive to their sexual insinuations. After all,
they thought to themselves self-servingly, why else would two forever girls board
a transpotter in the middle of the night, alone with a poorly supervised mining
team?

"You mind if we join you?" asked a thin, dirty man dressed in a miner's
uniform decked out with night beams attached to the suit. He sat much too
close to Kianno, and the other three snickered as he addressed the two of them
in a voice drenched in mock-politeness.

"Please, we'd rather be alone, if you don't mind," Kianno answered, growing
more and more aware of the danger at hand.

"Are you miners, then?" the man continued sarcastically. "Maybe out to
refresh your accounts a little?" As he spoke, another, larger man seated himself
next to Nicoli.

"No," Kianno answered firmly. "And we'll have nothing to do with you. I'm
sure you must know that we're being scanned as we speak, and should you
attempt any act of aggression it will only be a matter of time before you're
captured and executed."

"Hmmm," the thin man sat back a little and pondered her words, then replied
"I don't see any sender. Why don't you show us the sender, then?"

"Why would I be so foolish as to do that?" she answered in a faltering voice,
as a growing wave of fear spread through her.

Now the man reached out suddenly and grasped her wrist in his huge hand,
squeezing it painfully, and saying, in a tone which finally matched his thoughts
"I don't think you have any sender. I think you two girls made a big mistake
and got on the wrong spotter, didn't you?" When neither of them replied, he
continued. "Well, the good news is that if you do everything we ask, we just
might let you live."

Kianno pulled back violently from the grip, but she was no match for the strength of this man who was more than twice her size. At her resistance, he struck out in anger and rapped her hand against the hard surface of the spotter wall behind them.

Kianno felt it growing this time, like a sneeze. It had been a full week since the last one, and even though she knew she was in danger by removing herself from the Trizone a few days early, she had been counting on having healed beyond the risk of any further attacks. Clearly, she realized, feeling the trembling rise up from her right leg once again, she had been mistaken.

"What the hell?" exclaimed the man who only seconds earlier nudged his huge thigh up against the helpless Nicoli, as his companion now released his grip on Kianno, watching with surprised amusement as the girl fell to the floor and began to convulse out of control.

"Mistissa!" yelled Nicoli, looking down at her friend, whose face had turned ashen in just a few short seconds, and whose eyes had rolled up into her head, exposing only the frightening whites trying desperately to see the light beyond.

It lasted only ninety seconds, and when it was over Kianno gradually regained consciousness as Nicoli continued to talk to her in a voice which approached slowly from the shadows and led her back into awareness.

Responding to the commotion, two other miners now entered the car and immediately sized up the situation: two forever girls, apparently injured on the floor, surrounded by four miners.

"What are you guys doing?" one of them demanded angrily. "Are you trying to get us all killed?"

"Stay out of this," answered the thin man, not very forcefully or convincingly. "This is our business."

"Like hell it is." Now the man turned to the others who were standing around, still confused by the girl's convulsive attack. "You all ready to face the guards once they find out about this? Well I'm sure as hell not. You heard what happened to Zedra team last month, random synthar firing. So if that's what you guys are after, you're gonna have to fight us first."

Now the others started mumbling amongst themselves, then slowly shuffled away from the scene as the two newcomers stood by and waited until the room had cleared, then sat opposite Kianno and Nicoli to watch over them and prevent any more incidents until the two girls gratefully departed the spotter at the Los Gatos Gate, leaving the mining team behind in a transpotter picking up speed on its way to the coast.

Again they had little trouble getting past the gate after the programming Kianno had done earlier, and when they stepped out into the late November air they felt a strong south wind picking up. Kianno knew, from her many experiences in the weatherscoper, that rain would follow the south wind, so the two of them made their way only as far as a rock overhang at the mouth of Lexington canyon before taking refuge and bedding down for the night, huddled close to each other for much needed warmth as the wind whistled through the rocks of the canyon wall.

***

Morning. Gray light slowly washed from a thinning sky, shedding itself in huge wet drops which struck the yellow rock and ran in tiny rivulets down the sheer face, cascading over the entrance to their shelter with a sound of remembrance, a sound of belonging, a sound of running water.

Kianno opened her eyes and softly lifted the arm of a still slumbering Nicoli, ducking away as gently as she could from her embrace. The girl murmured, but her eyes remained closed, and Kianno turned from her to the sky of morning.

She looked out at the waves of rain carried on huge gusts of wind which shook the oak trees clinging precariously to the far side of the canyon. On the slopes spread out above the rocky cliffs, grasses yellow with the sun of an endless summer bent to welcome the rain, gathering the precious water and tucking it safely into their thirsty soilbed. In the coolness of the air floated the unmistakable scent of an early season rain, a scent she remembered from her boyhood so long ago, a scent which had been waiting quietly within her all this time for recovery, for release. Far below she could hear the rush of the creek through the panels which had been placed over the water to protect it from illegal access by outsiders. But the sound could not be protected. The excitement and unexplainable sense of redemption imparted to the land, and to herself as well, by a late November storm could not be locked away, could not be kept from her any longer. This was where she belonged, she could not deny it. This was the one constant which had remained through all of the changes she had endured, the one voice which had never stopped calling to her since those long ago days as a boy tramping through forests and sliding down leaf-blanketed hillsides.

Now Kianno stepped carefully over the sand and pebble strewn ground and placed her hand on her friend's shoulder, shaking her lightly.

"C'mon Nicoli, wake up now."

Still asleep, Nicoli stretched one arm out and shifted her head on the small pack they had brought with them, unwilling to be brought forth from her slumber.

"C'mon Nicoli," Kianno repeated. "We're almost home."

***

She waited outside, shivering behind a Bay tree, while Nicoli stood in the doorway of her home and waited for her parents to usher her back into the warmth of their love. Nicoli did not understand why Mista would not want to accompany her, but she agreed finally to part ways and meet later on, once they had each been reunited with their families.

It was Paula who opened the door, and Kianno could see clearly the shocked look of joy and disbelief as she hugged the girl and held her tightly, rocking from side to side in their tearful embrace. Then the two of them disappeared into the room, Nicoli casting a still curious eye back in Kianno's direction before the door closed behind them.

Shaking with cold now in her wet sara, she had just turned to leave and head off into an uncertain future when the door swung open once again and Jask came running toward her.

"Mistissa!" he exclaimed, panting for breath and reaching out to hug her as if she were his own child. "Mistissa it's a miracle. Nicoli told us what you did. We can't believe it, that you were able to escape!" He hugged her again, this time feeling her shivers through the embrace. "Come inside to warm up and get some dry clothes on before we go to see Seelin."

"No, I'll be O.K.," she tried to protest. She had planned on leaving for another gathering as quickly as possible, to avoid any encounter with Seelin, but Jask would have no part of letting this little girl head out into the rain by herself.

"After you warm up. You must be starving. Come along..." And with this he led her over the muddy ground and into the building where an equally overjoyed Paula removed her sopping robe and cleaned her with some water and a friction cloth, then gave her some of Nicoli's clothes to put on.

When they had finished gulping down an entire tube each of beef flavored dinner paste, Kianno noticed that she hadn't seen Jask for quite some time, so she asked Paula where he might be.

"He's gone over to get Seelin and Zhrana. They should be back very soon," she replied.

"Zhrana?" she asked with noticeable bewilderment.

"Yes. You remember Zhrana." Paula paused, the added "Don't you?" The woman came over to Kianno's side and felt her forehead nervously. "Are you sure you're feeling all right? Did they...do anything to you in there?"

"No, I mean I'm fine. Zhrana, of course," she stammered. Yes, she did remember a Zhrana but it couldn't possibly be the same one, could it? Doing her best to stifle any more conversation, she resumed ingesting the sticky paste while pondering the idea of perhaps inventing some sort of story to account for her lapses in memory which would soon become even more apparent.

"I don't remember...everything," she said at length. "I don't..."

But at that instant there was a great commotion from outside and the door burst open, admitting an exhausted Seelin and Zhrana, who had run the entire mile from the other side of the gathering.

"Mista, oh Mista my darling!" He rushed at Kianno, who got up from her chair and took a step back in alarm at the onrushing man, but then remembered herself and realized she had no choice but to play along.

He picked her up and swung her around and around, gripping his lost daughter with an overpowering feeling of relief and happiness such as which he had never known before. All the terrible waiting filled with dread and despair which followed her disappearance now lifted away and levitated his spirit into a dance which played him, like a puppet, in circles about the room. He was positively drunk with joy at the sight of his beloved daughter, and Kianno, seeing the poor man's misled happiness and the love he must have felt for his daughter, could no longer restrain herself and burst out crying uncontrollably, sobbing for the first time since her forever childhood had been stolen from her, crying tears which streamed from the free flowing ducts of a child and fell onto the broad shoulders of Seelin.

"Now now, It's O.K." he tried to console her, but she found herself unable to stop, despite her intellectual knowledge and control of the situation. Again, her body had a mind of it's own, and it forced its own tears into the heart of Kianno, remembering the touch of a father, remembering the love which had been lost and could never be found again. So she cried herself out on his shoulder, mourning the loss of this innocent girl, mourning the father who cried his own unwitting tears of joy.

Only when Kianno had regained her composure did Zhrana approach from the background, where she had remained, intent on not coming between the child and her father. Yes, it was Zhrana, thought Kianno as she looked up at this beautiful woman her old forever child companion had become. Strawberry blonde hair flowed from a high forehead, still spotted with fading freckles, and beneath the freckles those eyes which he would recognize even if she were older by a hundred natural years. But she could never recognize Kianno's true identity, gazing fondly into the eyes of a small girl she had so recently befriended.

"Hi Mista," she said, then bent to hug the girl, and Kianno felt the softness and the fullness of her womanhood enveloping her. She took the girl's hand in her own and squeezed it affectionately. "I'm so glad you're all right. We can play later if you want."

Kianno continued to look with disbelief even as Zhrana stepped away again, unable to ignore how beautiful and attractive she had become. She felt herself growing aware of being aroused instinctually, incapable of breaking from the thoughts which had so occupied her mind during her past life as a man. But this time there was only the knowledge of her attraction, a knowledge unsupported by any force, any urge, any drive needed to mature that knowledge into a physical feeling. So it passed quickly into the realm of mere curiosity. Already the new set of hormones coursing through her bloodstream had begun to affect her brain, her feelings, and her thoughts.

"Come, it's time to go home. You can visit with Nicoli tomorrow. Right now we'd best be getting on before the storm worsens," Seelin announced in his deep voice. Then he placed one of his large hands on Kianno's head affectionately and slowly guided her toward the door.

As the three of them hurried off into the drizzle, Kianno thought to herself how, despite the tragedy which lay hidden from their sight, Zhrana and Seelin had been so fortunate to have found each other. She searched herself for any feelings of jealousy or animosity, but found only satisfaction at the thought of their happiness.

***

"Is she asleep?"

"I think so. She was awfully tired. I hope she can sleep through till morning, after all she's been through."

"Seelin, Paula told me that Nicoli saw her have some kind of attack on their way out. We need to get a doctor over here as soon as possible." Zhrana stood behind him, massaging his shoulders as she spoke.

"I've already sent word, " he replied. "She's having trouble with some of the simplest things. I don't know. Does she seem different to you at all?"

"The poor girl's been through a lot the last couple of weeks. I'm sure it's just the shock of the ordeal."

"I hope so." Seelin ran the side of his hand absently back and forth over the surface of the table. "You know, when I started the numbers game she just looked back at me as if I was crazy. She asked me to repeat myself, like she had no idea what I was talking about."

"Give her some time, Seelin dear." Now she pulled a chair underneath her and joined him at the table, where they sat for several minutes in silence before he spoke again.

"Radall came by today to do the final testing on the activator. He says it's ready to go."

"Oh God, please don't say that," Zhrana uttered in a low voice, the words riding a wave of panic and dread. "Seelin, I can't bear having that thing in this house. I can't bear the thought of it at all, of..."

"Zhrana, you've known all along. I never tried to hide it from you."

"But don't you see how she needs you, how we both need you? Please, you know there are others ..."

"Are there?" He reached under the table to place a comforting hand on Zhrana's thigh. "Are there others who can deliver it?"

"Radall himself has volunteered. He's older, without any family. Seelin it only makes sense..."

"Radall's never in his life seen the inside of a hive. He has no idea how to locate the target. Plus he'd give himself away just trying to get in."

"How do you know that?" Zhrana's voice was now tinged with a rare bitterness and anger. "There are others who can do this. Seelin, please!"

Now he slid his chair closer to hers and put his arm around her, but she looked away from his overture, shaking her head as if to clear the air of the words which still poisoned it.

"Zhrana, you know that I couldn't live with myself, that I couldn't face Mistissa for the rest of my life knowing I had a chance, with one single act, to move us closer to a true fight for our freedom than we've ever seen. You know that if we can pull this off there's no telling how many of those who've given up who might suddenly take this whole movement seriously once again. They'll see that we can fight back, that we have the very real power of striking deep into the hives, where we can plant the same fear which long ago was enough to frighten them into leaving us alone."

Now Zhrana shifted her moist eyes back in his direction, pleading with those eyes for him to stay with them, for now, forever. "But you said there might be someone else who could deliver it. Please, Seelin. Let another be the hero this time. Mistissa and I are your true life. You can't deny that."

"You know you're right, Zhrana. You two are my life now," he answered in all truthfulness, squeezing her fingers in his own, unable to let go, his heart torn with the prospect of what he knew could not be avoided. "There is one other who has asked, and might be coached. I don't know..." His words trailed off weakly, for even as he spoke them he knew the remoteness of the hope he was tossing her, knew exactly what could not be put off any longer.

Just then there was a quick, muffled rap from the direction of Mistissa's room. Looking up with exaggerated alarm, Seelin rose from the table and walked across the floor, followed by an equally concerned Zhrana.

"Did you hear that?" he whispered to her as they both listened carefully outside the heavy oak door, then, hearing nothing, swung it open and approached the sleeping platform in silence.

They found their Mistissa dozing soundly, curled up on her side and breathing heavily under the bed sheet. She clung tightly to a hand sewn lion given her years ago, and her feet stuck out from the edge of the sheet, which Seelin delicately pulled down to cover the sleeping child. Seeing the beauty of this gift which had been miraculously returned to them, Zhrana for the quickest moment forgot the uncertain and terrible future they might face beyond tomorrow, and smiled across at Seelin, who bent forward carefully to place a kiss on the forehead of his precious daughter. Then they stole silently from the room, never noticing the small semicircular play block which continued to rock imperceptibly back and forth on the hard floor only a few feet away from their hushed footsteps.

26

She woke the next morning before the slow November light had emerged from the horizon, lying in bed for long minutes in darkness, able to think only of that terrible device in the basement and how it might be removed forever from their lives. As early as it was, Seelin had already pulled himself from the bed just before her own awakening, unusually early for his exercise meditation, thought Zhrana, and she strained to listen for sounds of him from the yard outside. As her eyes began to adjust to the weak light spotted on the floor by a moon mostly hidden behind the madrone outside the window, her thoughts began finally to release their grip on Seelin and his capture by this awful but necessary act which had so occupied them and the rest of the insurgents for the past two months. More pleasant thoughts of Mistissa's return began slowly to drift through her mind, the young girl sleeping only two rooms away, so close to the gathering room, and to the basement as well, where the activator had been placed.

She sat up now, nagged with the mildest of apprehensions. In another couple of hours she would be up, and they had not yet hidden the activator. Surely it was unlikely that Mista would make her way to the basement after awakening, but the possible nightmare which might ensue if she were to stumble upon it and mistake it for some sort of plaything was enough to drive Zhrana from the warmth of her bed and out the door into the main room.

A cold draft floated through the larger living chamber, seeping in from the many cracks in the old wooden structure. She had helped him decorate the room with cloths and rugs, which had also helped to keep out the cold. But even still, Zhrana was not looking forward to the coming winter, having not yet fully adjusted to the variations in temperature. Strewn over the floor lay the books and toys which the two of them had eagerly brought out for a tired Mistissa yesterday in an attempt to welcome her home and restore some sense of ordinary life. But she had only given lip service to the toys, and now they remained, mostly untouched, a minefield that Zhrana slowly stepped her way through with her bare feet. Reaching the cut section of floorboards which served as the basement entrance, she knelt down and, as quietly as possible, unlatched the clasp and lifted the heavy door upward in a cloud of dust which escaped from the depths below. She then secured the door in its upright position and climbed down the wobbly old ladder.

Now immersed in total darkness, Zhrana fumbled blindly for the magna lamp which was always kept on a table at the bottom of the ladder. Sweeping her hand across the length of the table, however, she found the smooth surface entirely empty, and she stepped forward into the darkness, bewildered at not finding the lamp. It was then that her foot brushed a small object, sending it spinning with a sound which startled the silence of the night with a harsh clattering. She reached down to grope for the object and found with relief that it was only the misplaced lamp. Seelin must have carelessly let it fall from the table when he was down here last night examining the activator, she thought to herself.

Switching on the lamp, her eyes retreated at the sudden brightness, and she shaded them briefly with her free hand, then turned toward the center of the room where the activator had remained fixed for the past few weeks. But her stunned eyes found only the empty positioning frame and the four securement straps dangling loosely in the dusty air.

"Seelin!" she yelled now in a panic which had in an instant entirely overtaken her. "Seelin, Seelin!"

***

Accounts gathered much later by inspectors confirmed that the wave was felt at virtually every level of the Great Hive, although above TT and below OOOO it was only strong enough to rouse a few forever children from their sleep, or cause them to wonder at the rumbling if by chance they were already awake at the time of activation.

The closer levels, however, felt a shock wave approaching the magnitude of the last great earthquake of 2315, sending terrified families scurrying from their sleeping chambers to huddle together in the quadrant halls, waiting nervously for aftershocks, or perhaps the main shock which some of them believed might still be to come.

They were the fortunate ones. Those within a radius of three quadrants of the activation were killed instantly by the initial blast, which opened up huge gashes in the layers of t-steel separating the levels, collapsing four full families from GGF through GGG and onto those equally unfortunate forever children sleeping on GGH. In addition to killing all those in the direct vicinity of the activation, the destruction of boundary integrity which followed the blast allowed infiltration of the rapidly multiplying bio-magnesium organisms into adjacent levels, where they spread across another eighteen total quadrants before dying out, instantaneously robbing all oxygen from the air and suffocating the helpless citizens in their sleep. A few in the perimeter zone struggled breathlessly to their feet, lungs choked with just enough of the living mineral to very slowly suck their lives away as they rushed in vain to escape. In these most cruelly affected quadrants, large numbers of dead forever children were later found pressed against station portals, killed slowly while awaiting vertical sliders which never came.

Beyond the immediate pain and devastation, the effects of the blast were felt years beyond the time it took for the scars of that single wound to heal. For, as Seelin had predicted, this one act of violence was the first shot fired in a war which was to last five full years, a war finally backed with a full heart and the full sacrifice and devotion of the majority of outsiders, not just the small ragged troupe who had finally succeeded in initiating that war. For the first time, both outsiders and citizens took seriously the threat posed by these terrorists, a realization which hive officials reacted to with even harsher treatment and further tightening of the outsider laws, laws which only strengthened the resolve of those they were meant to oppress, and for the first time rallied the outsiders together behind the courage of an heroic act. Stories of the sacrifices made in the successful creation and delivery of this single devastating quother swell would circulate for years and become a legend which many more would carry with them to their deaths in fighting for their freedom.

***

It was in some respects fortunate that Sofia was with Jaslo the night of that fateful blast. Long afterward she would wonder silently to herself why she had decided to stay one more night with her companion of so many years, even after deciding that she had no choice but to leave him. It was, perhaps, that she could not bear to be alone with the worry that had filled them after learning of Kianno's disappearance from the laboratory that morning. Indeed, they had shared a single bed that night, and were clinging together in their sleep when the alarm sounded from the visual notifier.

While Jaslo rushed to answer the call, Sofia could only pray to a God she had abandoned years ago that it was not the news of Kianno that she so dreaded. Pulling up the covers as if to hide from the bearer of this dangerous information which had interrupted their sleep, she listened nonetheless to the conversation between Jaslo and the Laboratory Director.

"Have you heard yet?" the director inquired quickly, gulping air as if he had been running.

"No. What is it?" Jaslo replied.

"The lab, it's destroyed. A quother swell was set off one hour ago. It emanated directly from the interior of the central laboratory. It's completely destroyed."

"No, that can't be! That can't be!" exclaimed Jaslo, frantically pacing back and forth. "The security is impregnable. There's no possible way of smuggling in such a device, is there?"

"My dear Jaslo, I'm afraid you've got to accept what I'm saying. There's nothing left of the laboratory, or any of the occupants. Fortunately, only the current stable of subjects were inside at the time."

"But the Riffer-C," he persisted, referring to the auto surgeon. "That too?"

"I'm afraid so."

"It'll take us a full year to build a new one." Jaslo whipped himself around in anger to face the image of the director once again.

"If it were only so easy. You're forgetting that the repository itself was also disintegrated. The full design will need to be recreated."

"No," Jaslo answered, revealing just the slightest hint of a smile for the first time since hearing the terrible news. "I've kept a silhouette coin of the entire design, safely here within the quadrant."

"That is strictly forbidden," uttered the flickering image, turning his head from side to side.

"I'll be glad to submit to any disciplinary measures you see fit." Now Jaslo smiled even broader, a smile which was returned this time by his colleague.

"Come to my quadrant chamber immediately. We must discuss strategy for keeping the project alive, before those who would see it die take advantage of our misfortune."

"Of course." Jaslo was about to terminate the connection when Sofia called out his name in desperation, then looked at him with pleading eyes which he read immediately.

"Rathon, one more thing."

"Yes?"

"Have they confirmed whether or not Kianno was inside at the time?"

Now the director paused for five horrible seconds, a pause which by itself pierced Sofia's heart with a poison she would feel the rest of her life.

"I'm sorry Jaslo. He must have returned sometime before the explosion. I'm truly sorry."

Jaslo's voice now softened to a strangely quiet tone. "I'll be down shortly," was all he said, clicking off the conversation and walking quickly to Sofia's side to comfort her as best he could.

When he finally departed half an hour later, Sofia buried herself in the bed covers, masking the awful reality of her loss in an unknowing blackness. Then, numbed by grief, she rose slowly and walked across the room to a small antique cabinet made of rosewood. Opening a small drawer near the bottom of the bureau, she rummaged through numerous old keepsakes the two of them had put aside through the years, small remembrances of a life with him that she was so tempted to bring along with her. But she let them be, pulling out instead a round, shiny coin hidden amidst the nearly forgotten momentous. She held it up to the strip lumins overhead, to read the tiny identification marks along the perimeter, just to be sure, then tucked it into an open pocket in the small bag she had already packed for herself the day before. Trembling with the weight of a frightening and sudden emptiness, she stepped through the opening portal wings and disappeared down the empty hallway.

27

"Now I don't want any synthar firing," instructed the commander for the fourth time that morning. "We have specific orders to capture them alive. Skull capping is to be saved for the professionals later on. Is that understood?" He spoke quietly into the dissipater, which in turn whispered his command to each and every one of his Zena Squad members who had converged on this small house on the western edge of Lexington gathering in the chilly, pre-dawn air. Two of the officials, in fact, listened to his words from a tenuous perch set up in a large madrone which practically filled the small yard behind the structure, shivering in the slight breeze and hoping that the signal would be given soon.

"Sir, if they fire..." ventured one rookie tentatively.

"Then you activate your signal and slow stun them if possible," answered the commander with obvious exasperation. "But they're not to be harmed, not by us anyway." He paused and set the switch before addressing specifically the spotters up above. "Any nearby movement or activity?"

"No. Sir, I think everything is set..."

"I'll say when we're ready to go," the commander interrupted, but then, recognizing the truth in the comment, he switched off the dissipater and clicked on a mini-visual transmission. "How are things over there?" he inquired.

"Almost set." His counterpart at the second site, clear on the other side of the gathering, was rushing about behind a thick set of trees, arranging his squad members for the imminent attack. "Hang on," he advised, then leaned over to talk quietly to his lieutenant who was pointing to several members at the other end of a wide field, attempting to better position them. "Are you absolutely sure this is the place?" he asked.

"No doubt about it. All sources confirm this is the Orillo home. If she was stolen, or escaped somehow, this is where she'd be."

"Because if we screw this up, it'll only tip them off," the commander persisted, but the confident look he received in return satisfied him that all was set.

Now he turned once again to the mini-visual display. "Ready when you are," he announced.

The image of his associate two miles away flickered slightly as he scanned his squad one last time. Then the words rapped out sharply with a crackle of static. "Commence the operation, now!"

***

They stopped after two full days of fighting their way relentlessly through diffi-cult terrain far to the west of where any of them had previously ventured, across fields of brush, steep canyons, and heavily wooded ravines void of any paths or trails. They stopped with the same mournful silence which had accompanied them since their hasty and frenzied departure less than forty-eight hours ago, lost as much in their own thoughts and grief as they were in this vast wilderness which had engulfed them. They stopped with minds still simultaneously mar-veling and grieving at what such a small girl had done, for they did not know then, nor would they ever know, that it was not the miraculously brave and resourceful Mistissa who had accomplished what only her father had previously been able to do, to infiltrate deep into the heart of the great hive and carry the sign of their resolve, the strength of their determination, on her slight shoulders. The only ones who knew otherwise had their own reasons for forever keeping this a secret from the world.

They stopped on the edge of a small, flat bluff overlooking a creek lined with tall Bay and Alder trees which cast a canopy of shade hiding them from the sky above. Nearby stretched a wide grassy pasture which held forth the promise of cultivation, and along the creek below grew thickets of blackberry, ceyanothus, and the tender creekside plants which would draw deer and other game.

They stopped because Seelin himself saw that this was the place, the place where once again he would try to rebuild his life, as he had rebuilt it with his beautiful lost daughter so many years ago, returning to this hidden wilderness once again with a heart heavy beyond his own understanding. This time he came with Zhrana, and Jask, Paula, and Nicoli, to begin again, cut off from the rest of those they cared for until enough time had gone by, until enough years had grown between them and those who now hunted them down.

And while the rest of them set off on the daunting task of creating a new home, Seelin himself wandered slowly away from the bluff, waiting for the spot to call to him, unwilling to begin anything else until he had finished the carving and setting of her stone. When he was done, much later in the day, he laid it lovingly at the base of a young live oak which reached tenderly for the forest canopy as the arms of his only daughter had reached up so eagerly in the time of her young life. And as he sat next to the stone, polished by the swift creek for centuries before he had carved his own love into it, Zhrana found him and sat beside him, holding his hand in hers. She did not yet know, and would not know for some time to come, that, even as they sat together listening for the lost voice of Mistissa, new life had already begun to grow from the bed of their deepest despair.

At length, the sun slipped behind the horizon and the darkness of an approaching nightfall crept surreptitiously through the trees. Rising slowly, they stood and glanced one more time at the small oak and at the forest all around them. It was time to rejoin the others, they knew. As they turned to leave, the wind rose and rustled branches high above, sending a flurry of leaves spiraling lightly downward. And in the distance, woven into the high hush of the wind as it rose and fell in great breaths, could be heard the small but undeniable sound of running water.

CPSIA information can be obtained
at www.ICGtesting.com
Printed in the USA
BVHW031008130423
662220BV00003B/3